She could feel his strength, like a rock, in front of her. She wanted to lean forward and press her breasts into his chest. She wanted to drag his hard mouth down over her lips and kiss him until her knees gave way. Other shocking images flashed through her mind, and she gasped.

His lean hand came to her cheek and his thumb pressed suddenly, hard over her mouth, bruising the soft tissue. His glittery eyes looked straight into hers. "I know what you are thinking," he whispered roughly. "Shall I put it into words, or is it enough that I know?"

**Don't miss these sizzling historical
romances by DIANA PALMER!**

AMELIA
LACY
NOELLE
TRILBY

NORA

Diana Palmer

FAWCETT COLUMBINE • NEW YORK

A Fawcett Columbine Book
Published by Ballantine Books

Copyright © 1994 by Susan Kyle

All rights reserved under International and Pan-American Copyright Conventions. Published in the United States by Ballantine
Books, a division of Random House, Inc., New York, and simulta-
neously in Canada by Random House of Canada Limited, Toronto.

Library of Congress Catalog Card Number: 95-96114

ISBN: 0-449-91267-1

Cover design by Michele Brinson
Cover art by Pino Daeni

Manufactured in the United States of America
First Trade Paperback Edition: December 1995
10 9 8 7 6 5 4 3 2 1

Chapter One

HER NAME WAS ELEANOR MARLOWE, BUT MOST PEOPLE called her Nora. The nickname was straightforward, without artifice. So was Nora herself, most of the time. Born into the Victorian era, she was raised in Richmond, Virginia, in a manner befitting a lady of quality. But she had a surprisingly adventurous streak for so conventional a young woman. Nora tended to be impulsive and sometimes reckless. Her quicksilver nature had been a constant concern to her parents in the past.

As a young girl, she survived dunkings while sailing on yachts, and a broken arm in a fall from a tree while bird-watching near the family's summer home in Lynchburg, Virginia. In private school she achieved high honors, and later she attended one of the best finishing schools. By the time she reached her twenties, Nora had settled a bit, and with her family's great wealth behind her, she became a socialite of note. She had traveled up and down the eastern seacoast and in the Caribbean as well as Europe. She was cultured and well-mannered and very knowledgeable about other countries. But her lingering infatuation with adventure dealt her a devastating blow in Africa.

She had been on safari in Kenya, traveling with three of her male cousins and their wives, and an overbearing suitor who had invited himself along. Their hunting party also included Theodore Roosevelt, who was now running for vice president under President William McKinley, who was seeking a second term.

Roosevelt had gone hunting with her cousins and the other men, while Nora had stayed with her female cousins in an elegant mansion. She was thrilled when she was allowed to join the hunting party for an overnight stay when the men were camped by a nearby river.

Her particularly persistent Louisiana suitor, Edward Summerville by name, was irritated by Nora's continued aloofness. She had a reputation for being cool, while he was known as a ladies' man. Her indifference seemed to enrage him, and he redoubled his efforts to captivate her. When he failed, he made himself frighteningly offensive when they were left briefly alone on the bank of the river. His unwanted caresses had made her panic. In her struggle to escape him, Nora's blouse had torn, along with the net veil that had protected her delicate skin from the bites of swarming mosquitoes along the river. While she was struggling to cover her exposed flesh, she was repeatedly bitten. One of her indignant cousins knocked Summerville down and threw him out of camp. But before he left, Summerville accused Nora of leading him on, and swore vengeance. She hadn't led him on, and everyone in camp knew it, but his pride was crushed and he wanted to hurt her. However, Summerville's ire was the least of her worries afterward.

Nora had known about the dangerous fevers that could come from mosquito bites, but when three weeks passed and she was still healthy, she had relaxed. It wasn't until she was home again, almost a month after she was bitten, and in the throes of a desperately high fever, that the family physician diagnosed malaria and prescribed quinine crystalline powder to combat it.

The quinine upset her stomach at first, and she was told that it would only protect her from infection while she was actually taking it. There was no cure for her malarial condition, a prognosis that made her sick at heart and furiously angry at Summerville for putting her at risk. Her family doctor in Virginia hadn't told her until she was through the first paroxysms of the attack, and on the road to recovery, that he thought it possible that she might yet contract the fatal "blackwater fever." And, as well, he said, the paroxysmal fever would surely recur unpredictably over a period of years, perhaps for as long as she lived.

Nora's vague dreams of a home and family died. She had never found men very attractive physically, but she had wanted children. Now that seemed impossible. How could she raise a child when she was subject to a recurring fever that might one day prove fatal?

Her dreams of adventure died as well. She had wanted to go down the Amazon River in South America, and to see the pyramids in Egypt. But faced with recurrences of the terrible fever, she was afraid to take the risk. As much as she craved travel and adventure, she valued her health more. So she led a remarkably placid life for the next year and contented herself with recalling her African adventure for her friends, who were impressed by her courage and daring. Inevitably her exploits were exaggerated and she became known

4 Diana Palmer

as an adventuress. At times she enjoyed the reputation it gave her for daring, even if it wasn't quite accurate.

She was lauded as a prime example of the modern woman. She was asked to speak at women's suffrage rallies and afternoon charity teas. She rested on her laurels.

Now she was being invited out West, to a fabled land she'd read about and always dreamed of seeing, a region that was as potentially wild as Africa. Her fever had not recurred for several months. Surely there would be no risks out West, and hopefully she would remain healthy for the duration of her visit. She could see something of the Wild West, and perhaps there would be an opportunity to shoot a buffalo or meet a desperado or a real Indian.

She stood with brimming excitement at the lace curtains of the family parlor in Virginia, looking out at the pretty late summer landscape while she fingered the letter from her aunt Helen with delight. There were four Tremaynes of East Texas: her uncle Chester, her aunt Helen, and her cousins, Colter and Melissa. Colter was on an expedition to the North Pole. Melissa was desperately lonely since her best friend had married and moved away. Aunt Helen wanted Nora to come and spend a few weeks on the ranch in East Texas and help cheer Melly a little.

Nora had once taken the train to California and had seen the rugged country between the Atlantic and Pacific through the window. She had read about ranches and Texans. They both sounded romantic. Dashing cowboys fighting Indians and one another, rescuing women and children, and making all sorts of heroic sacrifices paraded through her mind as she recalled the old Beadle dime novels that she'd been reading of late. She would meet a real cowboy if she went to visit her kinfolks on the ranch. And it would be an adventure, even if it didn't involve lions and hunters. It would be a great adventure and she would have a second chance to test her courage, to prove to herself that she wasn't crippled by the African fever that had kept her confined so long.

"What have you decided, dear?" Cynthia Marlowe asked her daughter as she scanned the latest issue of *Collier's* magazine.

Nora turned, the soft material of her lacy blue dress swirling gracefully around her trim ankles. She touched the fashionable big tulle bow at her throat with fingers that almost shook with excitement. "Aunt Helen is very persuasive," she said. "Yes, I should like to go! I look forward to seeing the majestic knights of the range that my novels describe."

Cynthia was amused. She hadn't seen Nora so enthusiastic about anything since her disastrous trip to Africa. Her daughter's chestnut brown hair in its elegant high coiffure caught the light from the window and took on the sheen of copper. Cynthia's hair had been that color when she was younger, before it went silver. But Nora also had the deep blue eyes of the Marlowes, and the high cheekbones of a French ancestor. She was taller than her mother, but not unusually tall. She had elegance and grace and manners, and a gift for conversation. Cynthia was deeply proud of her.

Nora was peculiarly cool with men, especially after the fright Summerville had given her and the dreadful illness that had plagued her. She would really have thrived on the adventurous life, Cynthia thought sadly, but the African fever had clipped her wings. Now, at

twenty-four, she had settled down to spinsterhood with
resignation.

"Among other things, this visit would at least give
you respite from your father's attempts to bring socially
acceptable young men home for you," Cynthia murmured, thinking out loud. Her husband had, in fact,
made himself painfully obvious of late, and he tended
to be overbearing and a little insensitive.

Nora laughed, without real humor. A man in her life
was the very last complication she needed. "Indeed it
would. I shall have Angelina pack for me."

"And I shall have my social secretary make the necessary reservations at the train station," Cynthia agreed.
"I'm sure that you will find the trip enlightening."

"Of that," her daughter replied with sparkling humor,
"I have no doubt. It has been a long time since I traveled so far alone." Her face went taut with the memory
of Africa. "But after all, Texas is not Africa."

Cynthia stood up. "My dear, it is unlikely that the fever will recur so often. It has been several months since
your last bout. Try not to worry. Remember that Chester
and Helen are family, won't you? They'll take care of
you."

Nora smiled. "Of course they will. It will be a delightful adventure."

Nora was to remember those words when she stood
on the deserted depot platform at Tyler Junction, Texas,
waiting to be met by her aunt and uncle. The train ride
had been comfortable enough, but it was long and she
was very tired. So tired, in fact, that her enthusiasm had
dimmed, just a little. And she had to admit that this
dusty railroad terminal did not live up to her expecta-

tions. There were no gloriously attired Indians, no masked desperadoes, no prancing stallions with gallant and colorful cowboys riding them. In fact, it looked like a small eastern town. She became aware of mild disappointment and vicious heat as the Texas sun beat down on her pretty hat.

She looked around again for her relatives. The train had been late, so perhaps they had gone to get something to eat or drink at the restaurant she could see in the distance. She glanced around her at her elegant leather cases and trunk, wondering how she was going to get them out to the ranch if no one came for her. Late summer was going to be even more uncomfortable in southeastern Texas than in Virginia, she decided. She was dressed in one of her stylish traveling suits. The garb that had felt so comfortable when she left Virginia was suffocating her now.

Aunt Helen had written her about this place. Tyler Junction was small and rural, a southeastern Texas town not too far from Beaumont. Here most of the local gossip was passed around at the post office and the drugstore soda fountain, although the daily *Beaumont Journal* gave all the national news as well as social notes and local-interest stories. There were two of Henry Ford's little black automobiles on the dusty streets, driven by founding-family members, and the rest of society made do with buggies and surreys and buckboards and horses. That ranching was still an important local occupation was not difficult to see. In the distance Nora's eyes spotted several men wearing boots and jeans and those wide-brimmed Stetson hats. But they weren't young, dashing men. Most of them, in fact, seemed stooped and bent and old.

Uncle Chester had told her once when he and Helen visited the family home in Virginia that most of the ranches in Texas these days were owned of corporations, held by big businesses. Even Chester's ranch was owned by a big West Texas conglomerate, and he was paid a salary for managing it. The old days of ranching empire builders like Richard King, who had founded the famous King Ranch in southeast Texas, and the equally famous ranching giant Brant Culhane out in West Texas, were gone forever.

These days the money was in oil and steel. Rockefeller and Carnegie had control of those industries, just as J. P. Morgan and Cornelius Vanderbilt controlled the nation's railroads, and Henry Ford the new transportation rage, the automobile. It was an era of empire builders, but industrial ones, not agricultural ones. The day of the cattleman and the cowboy was almost at an end. Aunt Helen had written that a handful of prospectors were drilling for oil over at Beaumont, because some geologist had said a few years ago that the land around the Gulf was probably sitting on a veritable lake of oil. She found the thought amusing. As if anyone were going to find great patches of oil in this lush green land!

As she considered that, Nora absently watched a striking, tall man in chaps and boots and a dark Stetson walk through the dusty street toward the station. Now, there was a real cowboy! Her heart quickened as she imagined what sort of dashing man he was. What a shame to see men like that go the way of the Indian, driven to extinction at the end of a railroad track! Who would rescue widows and orphans and fight off the red man?

She was so engrossed in romanticizing the rapidly approaching myth that it took a minute to realize that the cowboy was heading straight toward her. Her brows lifted excitedly under the pert veil of her Paris hat, and her heart pounded.

It occurred to her quite suddenly that the man she'd been romanticizing about was actually little more than a paid servant. A cowboy did, after all, tend cattle. And she suddenly discovered that looking at a romantically picturesque and immaculate cowboy in the pages of a book was a good bit different from coming face-to-face with the real article.

The cowboy, so dignified and attractive across the width of the street, was a definite shock when he got closer. This man looked unshaven, even dirty. She restrained a fastidious shudder as her eyes fell to the bloodstains on the worn leather chaps that flared out from his long legs as he walked. Spurs jingled musically with each step he took. His boots were curled at the toes and they were liberally caked with a substance that was emphatically and explicitly *not* mud. If this man tried to save a widow or orphan from an upwind direction, both would probably run from him!

His blue-checked western shirt was wet with sweat and plastered to him in a way that was almost indecent, disclosing broad muscles and thick black hair from the area of his collarbone down. She clenched her purse tightly in both hands to maintain her composure. How odd, that she could feel a skirl of physical attraction to a man so . . . uncivilized and in need of cleaning. Why, lye soap would hardly be adequate for such a job, she thought wickedly. He would have to be boiled in bleach for days. . . .

He glowered at her quickly concealed smile. His hair was jet black, straight and damp above a lean face with a layer of dust and streaks of sweat carved in its austere lines. His eyes were narrow and deep-set under a jutting brow, hidden in the shade of his wide-brimmed hat. He had thick, dark eyebrows and a straight nose. He had high cheekbones. His mouth was wide and chiseled, and his chin had a jut that immediately set her on her guard.

"Miss Marlowe?" he asked in a deep Texas drawl and without the pretense of returning her amused smile.

She looked around at the deserted platform with a long sigh. "Indeed, sir, if I am not she, then we must both prepare for a surprise."

He stood staring at her as if he couldn't quite get her measure. She decided to help him. "It is very warm," she added. "I should like to go out to the ranch as soon as possible. I am not accustomed to heat and . . . ahem . . . odors," she added with an involuntary twitch of her nostrils.

He looked as if he might burst trying not to reply, but he didn't say a word. His look summed her up as an eastern woman with more money than was good for her and a lack of sensitivity. He was amazed that he felt insulted.

But he merely inclined his head, glancing around at her stacks of luggage. "Are you moving in?" he drawled.

Her eyes widened. "These are the bare necessities," she defended. "I must have my own things," she added, being unaccustomed to such questioning by servants.

He sighed loudly. "It's a good thing I brought the buckboard. With the supplies I've already bought, this will sure run over the sides."

She turned her purse over in her slender hands and smothered a smile. "If it does, you could run alongside with the overflow on your head. Bearers do that in Africa on safari," she said pleasantly. "I know because I myself have done it."

"You've run alongside a wagon with baggage on your head?" he asked outrageously.

"Why . . . of course not!" she muttered. "I have been on safari! That was what I said!"

He pursed his lips and stuck his hands on his hips to stare down at her ruffled expression. "On safari? A fragile little tenderfoot like you, in a rig like that?" He eyed her immaculate tailored suit and velvet hat with amusement. "Now I've heard everything." He walked back the way he'd come, to a buckboard hitched to a fine-looking horse across the way from the depot.

She stared after him with conflicting emotions. None of the men she'd known had ever been anything less than polite and protective. This man was unflappable, and he didn't choose his words to pander to her femininity. She was torn between respect and rock-slinging fury. He had a fine conceit for such a filthy man.

He hadn't removed his hat or even tipped it in a gesture of respect. Nora was accustomed to men who did both, and kissed her hand in greeting in the European fashion.

She was too censorious, she told herself. This was the West, and the poor man probably had never had the advantage of being taught social graces. She would have to think of him as she did the native bearers she'd spoken of, kind but uneducated folk whose lot it was to serve for their meager fare. She tried to picture him in a loincloth and had to smother another laugh.

She waited patiently until her benefactor drove up in the heavily loaded wagon and tied the horse pulling it to a hitching post before he began to load her bags in with long-suffering patience.

She hesitated at the side, thinking whimsically that she must be grateful that he didn't suggest that she ride in the back with her luggage. She looked to him to help her up to the wide driver's seat. It shouldn't have surprised her that he was already seated, with the reins held impatiently in his lean hands.

"You were in a hurry, I believe?" he asked patiently, and he pushed back his hat and fixed her with a look from the most unsettling eyes she'd ever seen. They were unexpectedly light in that dark face, a gray that was almost silver in color. They were as piercing as a knife blade, and just as unfathomable.

"How fortunate that I have athletic abilities," she said with smiling hauteur before she stepped up onto the hub of the wheel and daintily swung herself into the seat. Sadly, she overshot the seat and ended up in a tidy heap across the cowboy's chaps. The smell was dizzying, although the feel of his hard, muscular thighs against her breasts made her heart run wild.

Before she had time to be very shocked by the intimacy of the contact, he hefted her up with steely hands and put her firmly on the seat. "None of that, now," he said with a stern look. "I know all about you wild city women, and I am not the sort of man to be toyed with, I'll have you know."

She was embarrassed enough at her clumsiness, without being labeled a hussy. She pushed back her disheveled hat with a hand that, appallingly, smelled of the cowboy's boots. Her hand must have brushed the cuffs of his jeans.

"Oh, for heaven's sake!" she burst out, digging furiously for a handkerchief, with which she tried to wipe away the vile smell. "I shall smell like a barn!"

He gave her a narrow glare and snapped the reins to set the horse in motion. He grinned then, and accentuated his West Texas drawl for her benefit. He might as well, he decided, live down to her image of him. "What do you expect of a man who works with his hands and his back?" he asked her pleasantly. "It's the best kind of life, I tell you, living out here in the open. A cowboy doesn't have to bathe more than once a month or dress up fancy and practice parlor manners. He's free and independent, just him and his horse under a wide western sky; free to carouse with loose women and get drunk every weekend! How I love the free life!" he said fervently.

All Nora's illusions about cowboys took a fast turn. She was still scrubbing at her hand when they were on the rough road out of town, having decided that her beautiful gray kid leather gloves might have to be thrown away. The smell would never come out.

It had rained earlier in the week, and there were deep ruts in the road that made the ride on the board seat uncomfortable. "You don't talk much, do you?" he probed. "Eastern women are supposed to be real smart, I've heard," he added, doing his rustic rube imitation to the hilt.

Nora, oblivious, didn't realize that she was being taken for a ride in more ways than one. "If I were intelligent," she said indignantly, glaring at him, "I would never have left Virginia!" She scrubbed furiously at another stain, on the hem of her long skirt. "Oh, dear, what will Aunt Helen think?!"

He gave her a slow, wicked grin. "Well, perhaps she'll think that you and I have been spooning on the way home."

Her expression even through the veil would have sent a lesser man off the wagon and running. "Spooning? With you? Sir, I had sooner kiss a . . . a . . . coal miner! No, I take that back, a coal miner would not smell so foul. I should sooner kiss a buzzard!"

He dashed the reins gently against the horse's flank when it slowed under a shady mesquite tree, and he chuckled: "Buzzards are worth their keep out here. They clean up the rotting carcasses so that the world smells sweet for you dainty little socialites."

That was obviously a bit of sarcasm at her expense. She glared at him, but it bounced off.

"You are very forward for a hired man," she said indignantly.

He didn't reply. She had a nasty way of sounding two steps above him socially, as if to remind him that he was a lowly servant, she a lady. He could have laughed out loud at the irony of it.

Having given up on removing the foul stench from her hand, she fanned herself with a colorful cardboard fan obtained from the porter on the train. It was the last week in August and unbearably hot. It must be from the gulf breezes that danced up from the nearby coast, she thought, wondering at the smothering intensity of it. Back East, one would expect furious storms when confronted with this sort of heat. Just the year before, there had been a hurricane on the eastern coast, one that had taken the life of a cousin. She had nightmares about high water that remained with her even now.

She was almost overcome by the smothering humidity. The corset she was wearing under her long skirt and long-sleeved jacket was robbing her of breath.

Not that her companion looked much cooler, she had to admit. His thin shirt was soaked in front, and she was surprised that her eyes were drawn to the vividly outlined hard muscles of his arms and his hair-roughened chest. She had seen men of other races without shirts, but she had never seen any gentleman in a similar condition. This man was no gentleman, though. It was incomprehensible that a common laborer should stir senses that she had always kept impervious to any sort of physical attraction. Why, he made her nervous! And the slender hands holding the wooden handle of the neat fan, with its colorful representation of the Last Supper on one side and an advertisement for a funeral home on the other, were actually trembling.

"You work for my uncle Chester, do you not?" she asked, trying to make conversation.

"Yep."

She waited, but the one word was all the response he gave.

"What do you do?" she added, thinking that he might work in some more skilled job than just punching cattle.

His head turned slowly. Under the shadow of the wide-brimmed hat, his silver eyes glittered like diamonds. "I'm a cowboy, of course. I work cattle. You might have noticed that my boots are full of . . ." He enunciated the slang word that described the caked substance on his boots. He said it with deliberate intent. To add insult to the word, he grinned.

The reply made her face red. She should hit him, but she wouldn't. She wasn't going to do what he obviously expected her to do and rage at his lack of decency and delicacy. She only gave him her most vacant look and then made a slight movement of her shoulders in dismissal and turned her attention to the fall landscape as if nothing had been said at all.

Having traveled through West Texas once, even without stopping, she was aware of the differences in climate and vegetation from one side of Texas to the other. There were no cacti and desert here. The trees were magnolias and dogwoods and pines; the grass was still green despite the lateness of the year, and high where cattle grazed behind long white fences and gray-posted barbed wire fences. The horizon seemed to sit right on the ground in the distance, as there were no hills or mountains at all. The haze of heat could be seen rising from the ponds, or tanks, where cattle drank. There were two rivers that ran parallel to the Tremayne ranch, her aunt had written, which might explain that lush landscape.

"It is very beautiful here," she remarked absently. "So much more beautiful than the other side of the state."

He gave her a sharp glance. "You easterners," he scoffed. "You think a thing has to be green to be pretty."

"Of course it does," she replied simply, staring at his profile. "How can a desert be pretty?"

His head turned and he studied her with narrow eyes. "Well, a hothouse petunia like you might find it hard going, for sure."

She gave him a hard stare. "I am not a hothouse

plant. I have hunted lions and tigers in Africa," she embroidered on her one-day safari, "and—"

"And one night on the Texas desert would be your undoing," he interrupted pleasantly. "A rattler would crawl into your bedroll with you, and that's the last you'd be seen until winter."

She shuddered at just the thought of a rattlesnake. She had read about the vile creatures in Mr. Beadle's novel series.

He saw her reaction, although she belatedly tried to hide it. He threw back his head and roared. "And you hunted lions?" he asked outrageously, laughing harder.

She made a harsh sound under her breath. "You nasty-smelling brute!"

"Well, while we're on the subject of smells," he said, leaning toward her to take a breath and then making a terrible face, "you smell like sunned polecat yourself."

"Only because you refused to help me into the seat and I fell on your foul-smelling . . ." She gestured helplessly toward the wide leather chaps. "Those things!" She pointed at them, flustered.

He leaned a little toward her, his eyes sparkling with humor. "Legs, darlin'," he contributed. "They're called legs."

"Those leather things!" she raged. "And I am not your darling!" she burst out, her poise deserting her as she flew off the seat.

He chuckled. "Oh, you might wish you were, one day. I have some admirable qualities," he added.

"Let me out of this buggy! I'll walk!" she raged.

He shook his head. "Now, now, you'd get sore feet and I'd get fired, and we wouldn't want that, now would we?"

"Yes, we would!"

He grinned at her red face and wide, furious eyes. They were like blue flames, and she had a pretty, soft mouth. He had to force his attention back to the road. "Your uncle couldn't manage without me right now. Now, you sit easy, there, Miss Marlowe, and just let your blood cool. I'm a fine fellow once you get to know me."

"I have no intention of getting to know you!"

"My, my, you do get riled easy, don't you? And here I thought you rich ladies from back East were even-tempered." He flipped the reins, increasing the horse's speed gently.

"The ones who were probably hadn't met you yet!" she exploded.

His head turned, and something twinkled in his silver-gray eyes before he glanced back toward the road with a tiny smile on his hard mouth.

Nora didn't see that smile, although she had the feeling that he was laughing at her under the enormously wide brim of his hat. He'd knocked her legs right out from under her, until she couldn't even find a comeback. It was a new experience for her, and not one she enjoyed. No man had ever made her mad enough to yell like a fishwife. She was ashamed of her outburst. She settled into her seat and ignored him, pointedly, for the rest of the drive.

The ranch house was long and flat, but it was white as sand and had a long, elegant front porch and a white picket fence around Aunt Helen's beautiful mixed flower gardens. Aunt Helen was standing on the porch when the wagon pulled up at the walkway, looking so

much like her mother that Nora felt immediately home-
sick.

"Aunt Helen!" she exclaimed, laughing as she
stepped onto the hub of the wagon wheel and stepped
gingerly down out of the wagon unassisted, before the
man beside her could display more of his bad manners
by showing her aunt how he ignored common courtesy.

She ran to the older woman and was hugged warmly.
"Oh, it is good to see you again!" she enthused, her
face animated and lovely as she pushed back the veil to
reveal her exquisite complexion and bright, deep blue
eyes.

"Mr. Barton, it would have been courteous to have
helped Nora from the wagon," Aunt Helen told the man
who bore her luggage to the porch.

"Yes, ma'am, I meant to, but she lit out of it like a
scalded chicken," he said with outrageous courtesy,
even tipping his hat to Helen, and he smiled charmingly
as he waited for her to open the front door and direct
him to the bedroom Nora would occupy. Beast! Nora
thought. The word was in her eyes as he passed her, and
his silver eyes registered it and twinkled with pure hell-
ish amusement. She jerked her head around angrily.

When he was out of sight, Helen grimaced. "He is
Chester's livestock foreman, and he is very knowledgeable about cattle and business. But he has a rather unusual sense of humor. I'm sorry if he offended you."

"Who is he?" Nora asked reluctantly.

"Callaway Barton," she replied.

"Who are his people, I meant?" Nora persisted.

"We don't know. We know his name, but we know
very little about him. He works during the week and
vanishes on weekends; that was in the contract he

signed with Chester. We don't pry into people's lives out here," she added gently. "He's rather mysterious, but he's not usually rude at all."

"He wasn't rude," Nora lied, brushing at the dust on her cheeks to camouflage their color.

Helen smiled. "You would not have said so even if he was. You have breeding, my dear," she said proudly. "It's very evident that you come from blue bloods."

"So do you," she was reminded. "You and Mother are descended from European royalty. We have royal cousins in England, one of whom I visit twice a year."

"Don't remind Chester." Helen laughed conspiratorially. "He comes from a laboring background, and mine sometimes embarrasses him."

Nora had to bite her tongue to keep back a blunt comment. She couldn't imagine hiding any part of her own life to placate a man's ego. But, then, Aunt Helen had been raised in a different era, by different rules. She had no right to judge or condemn from her modern status.

"Shall we have tea and sandwiches?" Helen asked. "I'll have Debbie bring refreshments to the living room after you've had a few minutes to freshen up." Her nose wrinkled. "I must say, Nora, that is a very . . . odd scent you're wearing."

Nora flushed. "I . . . fell against Mr. Barton getting into the wagon and brushed my hand against some of that . . . vile material on his . . . on those leather things he was wearing," she faltered.

"His chaps," she said.

"Oh. Yes. Chaps."

Helen chuckled. "Well, it is unavoidable that working men get dirty. It will wash off."

"I do hope so," Nora sighed.

The tall cowboy came back down the hall, his burdens unloaded.

Helen smiled at him. "Chester wanted to see you when you got back, Mr. Barton. He and Randy are working down by the old barn, trying to fix the windmill," she added.

"I'll put up the wagon and join him as soon as possible. Good day, ma'am." He tipped his hat courteously at Helen.

He nodded politely at Nora, his eyes twinkling at her expression, and walked on toward the front door, his spurs jingling musically with every long, graceful step.

Helen was watching him. "Most cowboys are clumsy on the ground," she remarked, "probably because they spend so much time on horseback. But Mr. Barton is not clumsy, is he?"

Nora watched, hoping that he'd trip over one of his spurs and knock himself out on the door facing. But he didn't. She reached up and removed the hatpin that secured her wide hat. "Where is Melly?" she asked.

Helen hesitated. "In town, visiting a girlfriend. She will be back this evening."

Nora was very puzzled as she changed her traveling clothes for a simple long skirt and white middy blouse and rewound her long chestnut braid around her head. Melly was only eighteen and she adored her older cousin. They were good friends. Why wasn't Melly here to meet her?

She joined Helen in the parlor, and while they sipped tea and ate homemade lemon cookies, she asked about Melly again.

"She went riding with Meg Smith this afternoon, and

I know she'll be back soon. I might as well tell you the truth. She was in love with the man her best friend married, and she has been inconsolable. She couldn't even refuse to be maid of honor at their wedding."

"Oh, I am so sorry!" Nora exclaimed. How terrible for Melly!"

"We pitied her, but it was fortunate that the man did not return her feelings. He had some admirable qualities, but he is not the sort we want to marry our daughter," Aunt Helen said sadly. "Besides, Melly is sure to find someone more worthy to love. There are several bachelors who attend services with us every Sunday. Perhaps she might be encouraged to join a social group."

"Exactly," Nora said. "I'll do my best to help her over this sad experience."

"I knew you would," came the satisfied reply. "It's so good to have you here!"

Nora smiled affectionately at her aunt. "I am delighted that I came."

Melly returned home barely an hour after Nora arrived, on horseback, wearing a riding skirt and a straight-brimmed Spanish hat. She had dark hair like Nora's, but her hair didn't have the same chestnut highlights as her cousin's, and her eyes were a soft brown instead of blue. Her skin was tanned, as Nora's was not, and she was delicate and very slender, like a little doll. Looking at her, Nora couldn't imagine a man not wanting her for his wife.

"I'm so happy that you've come," Melly said after she'd greeted her cousin with sad warmth. "I've been rather droopy, but you can help me liven things up."

Nora smiled. "I hope that I can. It has been over a year since we visited when you came to Virginia. You must tell me all the news."

Melly grimaced. "Of course. But you must realize that my life is hardly as full and exciting as yours. I will have little to tell."

Nora thought of the times she had spent in bed, shivering with fever. Melly didn't know—none of them knew—how her adventure in Africa had ended.

"Melly, I do wish that you would not make us sound so dull," her mother murmured. "We do have some social life here!"

"We have square dances and housewarmings and spelling bees," came the short reply. "And the abominable Mr. Langhorn and his son."

"When we have gatherings with other ranchers in the cooperative, Melly helps serve," her mother reminded Nora. "Mr. Langhorn is one of the local ranchers, and he has a little boy who is worse than a wild man. Mr. Langhorn does not control him."

"Mr. Langhorn is the one who needs controlling," Melly added with a chuckle.

"That is true," her mother agreed. "He has a . . . reputation . . . and he is divorced," she whispered the word, as if it were not fit to be heard in decent company.

"Surely that should not count against him," Nora began.

"Nora, our family name is very important to us," her aunt said firmly. "I know that in eastern cities, and in Europe, a woman is perhaps allowed more freedoms than out here. But you must remember that this is a small community, and our good name is our most treasured possession. It would not do for Melly to be seen keeping company with a divorced man."

"I see what you mean," Nora said gently, wondering just how confining this small society really was. Coming from a large eastern city, she was hard-pressed to understand small-town life anywhere.

After dinner they sat in a blissful silence, one so profound and serene that the grandfather clock could be heard vividly, tick-*tock*, tick-*tock*, tick-*tock* . . .

The screen door slammed suddenly and heavy boots made emphatic noises on the bare wood floor.

Cal Barton stuck his head around the door, his hat held in one hand. "Excuse me, Mrs. Tremayne, but Chester would like a word with you on the porch."

Nora wondered why his spurs didn't jingle until she looked down. Of course; his spurs were covered with . . . *that.* So was the rest of him, Nora thought, her expression revealing her opinion of it eloquently as she sat elegantly on the sofa in just the correct posture, looking so at home in the opulence that it put Cal's back up at once.

He saw the disapproving, superior look she gave him, and it irritated him out of all proportion. He didn't smile this time. He simply looked through her, with hauteur that would have done a prince proud. He nodded politely when Helen commented that she would be right out, and he left without another glance in Nora's direction.

She was miffed by his sudden aloofness, and spent the rest of the day wondering why the opinion of a hired man should matter to her. After all, she was a Marlowe from Virginia, and that unwashed son of the great West was nothing more than a glorified male milkmaid. The thought sent her into gales of laughter, although certainly she couldn't share the joke with her ranching hosts.

Chapter Two

Nora's uncle was home in time for the evening meal, looking dusty and tired, but as robust and pleasant as ever. He welcomed her with his old enthusiasm. Later, while they sat together at the table, he passed along some worrying news to his family.

"There was some gossip today, about the West Texas combine not being pleased with my handling of the property. A visiting businessman from El Paso said that he knows the Culhanes and they have not gotten the results they expected from me," Chester told the others, grimacing at his wife's expression. "They must remember that I would have lost this ranch myself if they had not bought it—"

"Because of the low prices people were paying for our beef and produce," his wife argued. "There is not enough money in circulation, and people are not buying agricultural products in enough quantity to let us make a profit. The Populists have tried so hard to effect change. And we have, after all, read that William J. Bryan has been nominated by the Populists to run against McKinley. He is a good man and tireless. Perhaps some changes will be made to benefit those of us in agriculture."

"Perhaps so, but that will hardly change our situation, my dear," Chester said heavily.

"Chester, they would not have let you manage the ranch for so long had they not had confidence in you. You are not responsible for low market prices."

"It might not seem that way to a wealthy family." He glanced at his niece placatingly. "Not yours, my dear. The family I'm worried about is from West Texas, and the father and sons head the combine. The Culhanes are a second-generation ranching family; old money. I understand from Simmons that they don't approve of the fact that I haven't adopted any of the machinery available to help plant and harvest crops. I am not, as they say, moving quickly into the twentieth century."

"How absurd," Nora said. "These new machines may be marvelous, of course, but they are also very expensive, aren't they? And with people needing work so badly, why incorporate machinery to take away jobs?"

"You make sense, my dear, but I must do as I am told," he said sadly. "I don't know how they learned so much about the way I run the ranch when no representative has been here to see me. I could lose my position," he said starkly.

"But where would we go if you did?" his wife asked plaintively. "This is our home."

"Mother, don't fret," Melly said gently. "Nothing is happening right now. Don't borrow trouble."

But Helen looked worried. So did Chester. Nora put down her coffee cup and smiled at them.

"If worse comes to worst, I shall ask Mother and Father to help out," she said.

She was unprepared for her uncle's swift anger.

"Thank you, but I do not require charity from my wife's relations back East," he said curtly.

Nora's eyebrows rose. "But, Uncle Chester, I only meant that my parents would offer assistance if you wished them to."

"I can provide for my own family," he said tersely. "I know that you mean well, Eleanor, but this is my problem. I shall handle it."

"Of course," she replied, taken aback by his unexpected antagonism.

"Nora only meant to offer comfort," Helen chided him gently.

He calmed at once. "Yes, of course," he said, and with a sheepish smile. "I do beg your pardon, Nora. It is not a happy time for me. I spoke out of frustration. Forgive me."

"Certainly, I do. I only wish that I could help," she replied sincerely.

He shook his head. "No, I shall find a way to placate the owners. I must. Even if it means seeking new methods of securing a profit," he added under his breath.

Nora noticed then what she hadn't before: the lines of worry in his broad face. He wasn't being completely truthful with his wife and daughter, she was certain of it. How terrible it would be if he should lose control of the ranch his grandfather had founded. It must be unpleasant for him to have a combine dictating his managerial decisions here; almost as unpleasant as it would have been for him to lose the ranch to the combine in the first place. She must learn what she could and then see if there was some way that she could help, so that he and his family did not lose their home and only source of income.

After that, conversation turned to the Farmers Congress in Colorado Springs, Colorado, and to the Boer War in South Africa, where a Boer general named De Wet was growing more famous by the day with his courageous attacks on the superior forces of the British.

The next few days passed peacefully. The men were away from the ranch most of the day and, it seemed, half the night, bringing in the bulls. Within a couple of weeks, they would be starting the annual fall roundup. Nora's opinion of the "knights of the range" underwent a startling transformation as she saw more and more of them from afar around the ranch.

For one thing, there were as many black and Mexican cowboys as there were white ones. But whatever their color, they were mostly dirty and unkempt, because working cattle was hardly a dainty job. They were courteous and very polite to her, but they seemed to be shy. This trait had first surprised and then amused her. She went out of her way to flirt gently with a shy boy everyone called Greely, because it delighted her to watch him stammer and blush. The stale ennui of European men had made her uneasy with them, but this young man made her feel old and venerable. She had no thought of ridicule. It was the novelty of his reaction that touched something vulnerable in her. But she'd flirted with him once in front of Melly, and Melly had been embarrassed.

"You shouldn't do that," she told Nora gently but firmly when Greely went on his way. "The men don't like being made fun of, and Cal Barton won't stand for it. Nor will he hesitate to tell you to stop it if he ever catches you."

"But I meant no insult. I simply adore the way he stammers when I speak to him," she said, smiling. "I find this young man so refreshing, you know. And besides, Mr. Barton has no authority to tell me what to do, even if he did catch me," Nora reminded her.

Melly smiled knowingly. "We'll see about that. He even tells Dad what to do."

Nora took the remark with a grain of salt, but she stopped playing up to poor Greely just the same. It was unfortunate that she should mention him, and why he amused her, later to her aunt when Greely was within earshot. After that, she had no opportunity to see him. His absence from her vicinity was pointed, and he had a somber, crushed look about him that made Nora feel guilty until finally he seemed to disappear altogether.

Nora was invited out to watch the cowboys work, and she accompanied Melly to a small corral near the house where a black cowboy was breaking a new horse to the remuda, the string of horses used by the men during roundup. Melly explained what would happen in the upcoming roundup, all about the long process of counting and branding cattle, and separating the calves from their mothers. Nora, who had known nothing of the reality of it, was appalled.

"They take the little calves from their mothers and burn the brands into the hide?" she exclaimed. "Oh, how horribly cruel!"

Melly hesitated, a little uneasy. "Now, Nora, it's an old practice. Surely in all your travels, you have seen people work on the land?"

Nora settled deeper into her sidesaddle. She couldn't bring herself to ride astride, as Melly did, feeling that it was unladylike. "I have seen farming, of course, back East."

"It's different out here," Melly continued. "We have to be hard or we couldn't survive. And here, in East Texas, it's really a lot better life than on the Great Plains or in the desert country further west."

Nora watched the cowboy ride the sweating, snorting horse and wanted to scream at the poor creature's struggles. Tears came to her eyes.

Cal Barton had spotted the two women and came galloping up on his own mount to join them. "Ladies," he welcomed.

Nora's white face told its own story as she stared at him coldly. "I have never seen such outrageous cruelty," she said at once, dabbing at her eyes with an expensive lace-edged silk handkerchief. "That poor beast is being tormented by that man. Make him stop, at once!"

Cal's eyebrows shot up. "I beg your pardon?"

"Make him stop," she repeated, blind to Melly's gestures. "It is uncivilized to treat a horse so!"

"Uncivi . . . Good God Almighty!" Cal burst out. "How in hell do you think horses get gentle enough to be ridden?"

"Not by being tortured, certainly; not back East!" she informed him.

He was getting heartily sick of her condescending attitude. "We have to do it like this," he said. "It isn't hurting the horse. Jack is only wearing him down. It isn't cruel."

Nora dabbed at her face with the handkerchief. "The dust is sickening," she was saying. "And the heat and the smell . . . !"

"Then why don't you go back to the nice cool ranch house and sip a cold drink?" he suggested with icy calmness.

"A laudable idea," Nora said firmly. "Come, Melly."

Melly exchanged helpless glances with Cal and rode after her cousin.

Nora muttered all the way home about the poor horse. It didn't help that a gang of tired cowboys passed them on the way back. One was mad at his sidekick and using colorful language to express himself. Nora's face went scarlet at what she overheard, and she was almost shaking with outrage when they reached the barn at last.

"Knights of the range, indeed!" she raged on the way to the front door, having left the horses in the charge of a young stable hand. "They stink and curse and they are cruel! It is nothing like my stories, Melly. It is a terrible country!"

"Now, now, give it a chance," Melly said encouragingly. "You've only been here a short while. It gets easier to understand, truly it does."

"I cannot imagine living here," Nora said heavily. "Not in my wildest imaginings. How do you bear it?"

"I love it," the younger woman said simply, and her brown eyes reflected her pleasure in it. "You've lived such a different life, Nora, so sheltered and cushioned. You don't know what it is to have to scratch for a living."

Nora's thin shoulders rose and fell. "I have never had to. My life has been an easy one, until the past year. But I know one thing. I could never live here."

"You don't want to go home already?" Melly asked worriedly.

Nora saw her concern and forced herself to calm

down. "No, of course not. I shall simply have to stay away from the men, that is all. I do miss Greely. He, at least, was a refreshing change from those barbarians out there!"

"Greely hasn't been around lately," Melly agreed. "I wonder why."

Neither knew the answer to the question of Greely's absence. Days passed, and the cowboys began to look a little less like dirty tramps and a little more like men as Nora's first impression began to waver and then fade. Nora became able to recognize faces, even thick with dust and dirt. She recognized voices, as well, especially Mr. Barton's. It was deep and slow, and when he was angry, it got deeper and slower. She marveled at the way he used inflection to control his men, and the way they responded to even the softest words. He projected authority in a way that made her wonder about his past. Perhaps he'd been in the military. He could have been, with that bearing.

He came riding up the next to the last Friday afternoon of August with a bunch of disheveled, hot, and dirty men. He dismounted at the front steps and tossed his reins to the stable hand, so that his horse could be attended to.

Nora, who was on the porch, stepped back when he approached, because he was dirtier than she'd ever seen him, and he had a three day's growth of beard. She thought that if she met him on the road, she'd expect him to have a pistol in either hand and a mask over his nose and mouth.

He noticed her withdrawal with cold fury. Since her remarks out at the corral, he'd been waiting for an opportunity to tell her how much her superior attitude irritated him. She had no right to look down her nose at hardworking men because they didn't smell like roses or live up to her idea of civilized behavior.

"Where's Chester?" he asked curtly.

"Why, he drove my aunt and Melly into town in the buggy," she said. "Is there anything I can do?"

He pursed his lips and studied the lines of the sleek, soft gray dress that clung to her slender figure. "Do you always dress like that?" he asked with cool mockery. "Like you were going to some fancy city restaurant in one of Mr. Ford's fancy automobiles?"

She bristled. "The automobile is more civilized than a horse, I tell you," she said haughtily. "And we have electric streetcars back East as well as automobiles."

"What a snob you are, Miss Marlowe," he said pleasantly. His smile didn't reach his cold silver eyes. Not at all. She felt chilled by them. "One wonders why you came out here at all when you find us and the work we do so distasteful."

She wrapped her arms across her small breasts and felt herself shiver. The heat was uncomfortable. She hoped she wasn't having a chill, because she knew what it presaged. No. She couldn't have an attack here, she just couldn't!

With her dignity intact, she smiled at him. "Why, I came because of the books."

"Books?" he asked, frowning.

"Yes! I've read all about cowboys, you know," she told him seriously. "Mr. Beadle's dime novels portray the cowboy as a knight of the range, a hero in chaps and boots, a nobleman in spurs."

He shifted his stance and glowered at her.

"Oh, and cowboys are the courtliest gentlemen in the world. That is, when they're not robbing banks to feed little starving children," she added, recalling two of her favorite books.

The glower got worse.

"But there was nothing about the odor," she added with quiet honesty. "People hardly expect a knight of the range to smell bad, or be caked in blood and mud and . . . ahem . . . other substances," she pointed out. "I don't expect you get many social invitations, Mr. Barton."

His pale eyes narrowed. "I don't accept many," he corrected, his face set. "I'm particular about the company I keep."

"One supposes that the reverse is also true," she replied, and wrinkled her nose.

His pale eyes flashed. "I don't like your condescending manner, Miss Marlowe," he added with magnificent honesty. His eyes held no warmth whatsoever. "And while we're on the subject, I especially don't like having you flirt with my men to embarrass them."

She colored. "I did not mean . . ."

"I don't care what you meant," he said levelly. "Greely is just a kid, but when you started teasing him, he worshiped you. Then he overheard you discussing him, confessing that you only played up to him to watch him stammer and stumble about. He was shattered." He looked down into her embarrassed face with cool disregard. "No decent woman does that to a man. It is beneath contempt."

She felt the words like a cut on soft skin. Her chin lifted proudly. "You are right," she confessed. She didn't add that she was so accustomed to sophisticated men who liked to flirt and see a woman flustered that it had secretly delighted her to find a man so vulnerable to a woman's attention. But she didn't say that. "Honestly, I did not mean to hurt him."

"Well, you did, just the same," he said curtly. "He quit. He's gone over to Victoria to get work, and he won't be back. He was one of the best men I had. Now I have to replace him, because of you."

"But surely he did not take it so to heart!" she exclaimed, horrified.

"Out here, men take a lot to heart," he said. "Keep away from my cowboys, Miss Marlowe, or I'll have your uncle send you home on the next train."

She gasped. "You cannot dictate to my family!"

He met her eyes levelly, and chills ran through her at the intensity and power of the look. "You'd be surprised what I can do," he said quietly. "Don't tempt me to show you."

"You are only a hired man, after all!" she added haughtily. "Little more than a servant!"

His expression was suddenly dangerous. His hand clenched at his side, and the glitter in his eyes had the same effect on her as a rattlesnake coiling. "While you, madam, are an utter snob, with greenbacks for blood and parlor manners for a heart."

Her face went rosy. Impulsively she reached out to strike him, but his steely fingers caught her wrist before she got anywhere near that strong, lean cheek. He held her without effort until he felt the muscles relax. Under his fingers, he felt the sudden increase of her pulse. When he looked into her eyes, he saw the faint flicker of awareness that she couldn't hide, and her eyes betrayed her surprise and helpless attraction. A slow, cunning smile touched his hard mouth. Why, she was vulnerable! It made his mind spin with dark possibilities.

With a short laugh of triumph, he drew her hand to his broad, damp chest and pressed it into the muscle. He felt her gasp, and knew that she didn't find him distasteful, because he was watching her face.

"Do eastern men stand for being slapped?" he drawled. "You'll find that we're a bit different out here."

"No doubt a man of your sort would find it acceptable to strike me back," she said with bravado. Under her long skirts, her knees were shaking.

He searched her wide, uneasy blue eyes with quiet confidence. Either she knew less of men than he knew of women, or she was a good actress. Chester had said that she was something of an adventuress, a globetrotting modern woman. He wondered just how modern she was, and he had a mind to find out for himself.

"I don't strike women," he said easily. His pale eyes narrowed and he slowly stepped in closer. He wasn't blatant or vulgar, but with that simple action he made her aware of his size and strength and of her own vulnerability. "I have . . . other ways of dealing with hostility from a female."

She was left in no doubt as to his meaning, because he was looking at her mouth as he spoke. Incredibly, she went weak all over and her lips parted helplessly. Since Edward Summerville's hateful advances, she had never liked men close to her. But her traitorous body liked this one, wanted to incite him even closer, wanted to know the touch of his warm strength in an embrace.

Because her thoughts shocked her, she jerked back

against his restraining hand. "Sir, you smell like a barn!" she stammered angrily.

He laughed, because he saw through the anger to the hidden excitement. "Why, isn't that natural? A cowboy spends a good portion of his time with animals. Or didn't your dime novels tell you so?"

She straightened her cuff, still feeling his touch there. She couldn't remember ever being so flustered. "I am learning that my novels are not altogether accurate."

His firm mouth tugged up at the corner. It pleased him that as a ragged cowboy, he could have such a devastating effect on an adventuress who had been on safari and lived a modern life. None of the women of his acquaintance had dared to flout convention. He found this woman exciting beyond measure, and the thought of leading her down the garden path in his disguise was appealing. If nothing else, it would teach her not to jump to conclusions about people. Taking a man at face value, judging him on his appearance alone and by eastern standards of conduct, was hardly worthy of such a traveled aristocrat. But, strangely, she lacked that glossy veneer that he would expect a hardened adventuress to possess. Now, as he stared down at her flushed face, he thought that she seemed not much more than a flustered girl.

"You are very pretty," he remarked gently. In fact, she was, with that wealth of chestnut hair and her fair skin and deep blue eyes.

She cleared her throat. "I must go inside."

He swept off his hat and held it to his heart. "I will count the hours until we meet again," he said on an exaggerated sigh.

She wasn't certain if he was serious or teasing. She

made a funny sound, like a stifled laugh, and moved quickly back into the house. She felt as if she might suffocate.

Cal watched her go with a pleased smile and speculation in his silver eyes. She was going to make an interesting quarry, he thought as he put his hat back on his head and slanted it over his eyes. When he got through with her, she was going to think twice before she looked down her nose at a man again, regardless of how he smelled.

After that, Cal Barton seemed to be everywhere she went. He was blatantly attentive, and he looked at her with such worshipful eyes that Melly began to tease her lightly about his devotion.

She wasn't convinced that he wasn't playing some monumental joke on her. She didn't respond to his displays of interest, which made them all the more obvious. He made a point of speaking to her with warm affection, regardless of whether she was alone or in company at the time. He was making his company felt, and the way he looked at her made her toes tingle. She had never been actively pursued by a man whom she felt attracted to, and she wasn't certain that she could handle this situation. She didn't want to become attached to Mr. Barton. But the more he pursued her, in his gentlemanly, teasing manner, the more unsettled she became.

She worried about Cal Barton so much that she couldn't sleep at night. To make matters worse, the cowboys had come in from the roundup. The noise from the bunkhouse that night was deafening. She knew that alcohol wasn't allowed unless the cowboys went into town. But they went into town on weekends, and when they came back, more often than not, they were audibly inebriated. Nora was used to noise in the city, but it was disturbing when she heard raised male voices close to her open window. These sounded sober, which was reassuring, but they were loud anyway.

"I won't!" a raspy male voice asserted. "I'm damned if I will! He ain't puttin' me to digging postholes, with my rheumatism in such bad shape! I'll quit first!"

"Dan, your rheumatism is awful convenient," came the amused reply. "It only hurts when you have to work. Best not rile Barton. Remember what happened to Curtis."

There was a pause, and Nora felt the new information about Barton sinking in with deadly meaning.

"Guess I do like it here since Barton came," the first man said on a sigh. "He got us better pay and he made the boss replace those damned worn-out horses. Hard to work cattle on a rocking horse."

"Sure it is. And he replaced the cook, too. I don't mind eating in the bunkhouse these days."

"Me, neither." There was a chuckle. "Sort of tickles me, about Curtis. There he was, throwing his gunman reputation around, intimidating the new kids. And he drew that big pistol on Barton and got his brains half knocked out with it for his pains."

"Barton's no sissy with a gun. I expect he's shot some. He was in Cuba with Teddy Roosevelt; one of them Rough Riders."

"Well, that don't mean he knows Teddy personally," the other man chuckled. "Come on. We got things to do before we bunk down. Roundup will start middle of next month, more's the pity. A cowboy's work is never done, is it?"

Murmuring voices and jingling spurs died away into the night. Nora curled deeper into her pillow with a sense of uneasiness. She was not used to rough men, and the only guns she'd seen used were in pursuit of wild game. She knew about war, that men fought in the unsettled regions of the country and sometimes with guns. But even on her previous trips to Texas, it had never occurred to her that she might meet men who had killed other men outside of war.

It was chilling to think of Mr. Barton with a smoking pistol in his hand, and suddenly she remembered one cold look from those silver eyes in that unsmiling, lean face, and realized what a formidable adversary he might be across the barrel of a gun. But he wasn't like that with her now. He was gentle, attentive, and he smiled at her in a way that made her heart race.

She began to look forward to their frequent chance meetings, because that smile made her feel so wonderful. She turned over abruptly, trying to force it from her thoughts. What good did it do to dream when there was no hope for a future? She had nothing to give to Cal Barton. But knowing that didn't stop her heart from racing every time she thought about him.

It was now the second week of her visit, and as she saw more of the enigmatic Mr. Barton, she began to understand the gossip she'd overheard that night outside her window. Watching him send the men about their chores was an education. He never raised his voice, even when he was challenged. His voice became softer in anger, in fact, and his eyes took on a glitter like sharp-edged steel in sunlight. But whenever he saw Nora, his firm mouth tugged into a smile, and he looked oblivious to everything except her.

"Nice day, Miss Marlowe," he commented as he passed her on his way to the stable, his lean fingers holding a pair of stained work gloves. He glanced at her neat lacy little gloves. She was just pulling them off, because she and Melly had only returned from town. "How dainty you are," he mused. "And always so fastidious." His silver eyes wandered down her body in the high-necked middy blouse and flaring dark skirt that reached to her high button-topped shoes. The intensity of his interest was disturbing. It made her knees weak. "You make my breath catch," he added softly.

She was drowning in his deep, soft voice, in the eyes that held hers so hungrily.

"Please, sir, this is not proper," she faltered.

He moved closer step by step, aware that they were in a very public place in the middle of the yard. He stopped just in front of her and smiled slowly, slapping the gloves absently into the palm of one hand. "What is not proper?" he asked gently. "Is a man not allowed to tell a woman how sweet she looks in her lacy finery?"

She swallowed. She had to look up a long way to see his face. It was hard to remember that she was supposed to be a sophisticated, traveled intellectual when her heart was trying to crawl up into her throat.

"Your attentions could be . . . misconstrued," she said.

He lifted an eyebrow. "By someone else? Or by you?" He reached out and traced a loose strand of her hair, making incredible sensations along her nerves. His voice dropped in pitch, softened. "I find you fascinating, Miss Marlowe; an orchid barely in bloom."

Her lips parted. No one had ever said such things to her before. She was enthralled by his deep voice, by the look in his eyes, his presence. The odors of horse and leather and cigar smoke that clung to him were not even noticeable in her state of excitement. Helplessly her blue eyes went from his deep-set eyes to his straight nose and high cheekbones and down to the wide, thin lines of his firm mouth. The lower lip was a little thicker, almost square, as if it had been chiseled out of stone. She felt her pulse quicken as she wondered shamefully how it would feel to kiss him.

He saw that speculative look, and he smiled. "You are very quiet, Miss Marlowe. Have you no scathing comment to make about the condition of my clothes?"

"What?" She sounded, looked, dazed, as her eyes were forced back up to his by the question.

He bent toward her, so that his eyes filled the world, so that under the wide brim of his hat, she could feel his warm breath right on her lips.

"I said," he said softly, "do you not find me offensive at such close range?"

She shook her head in a helpless little gesture. She could feel his strength, like a rock, in front of her. She wanted to lean forward and press her breasts into his chest. She wanted to drag his hard mouth down over her lips and kiss him until her knees gave way. Other, shocking, images flashed through her mind, and she gasped.

His lean hand came to her cheek and his thumb pressed suddenly, hard over her mouth, bruising the soft tissues. His glittery eyes looked straight into hers. "I know what you're thinking," he whispered roughly. "Shall I put it into words, or is it enough that I know?"

She was too far gone to register the words at all. His thumb played with her mouth and she let it, standing hypnotized by his gaze, his closeness. He pushed her lips against her teeth in his fervor, and she looked up into his eyes with desire plain in her own. For an instant, time ceased to exist. . . .

She realized quite suddenly what was happening to her, and it was frightening. With a tiny sound, she jerked away from him and ran into the house without a backward glance, her lips still stinging from the tender abrasion of his thumb.

She swept into the house red-faced, met by her amused aunt.

"Mr. Barton is in pursuit again, I presume?" the older woman murmured dryly.

Nora's eyes were very eloquent, even without her hectic flush. "He is . . . disturbing."

"He is the soul of courtesy with women, but never have I seen him so attentive," her aunt replied softly. "He is a personable young man, and very intelligent, especially about ranch management. Chester could not operate so large a property without his help. He was very somber and businesslike before, but I have to admit that he has changed since you came." She hesitated then, as if it disturbed her to have to speak when she added, "of course, there is no question of him becoming a serious suitor, you understand."

Nora didn't, at first. She frowned slightly.

"He is a fine young man, but so far beneath you socially, Nora," her aunt continued gently. "You must not become involved with a man in such a low social station. Your mother would never forgive me if I did not advise you thus. It is amusing that Mr. Barton finds you irresistible, but he is not suitable in any way as a contender for your hand."

Nora was shocked. She should have realized how her aunt, as much a descendant of European royalty as her own mother, would feel about Cal Barton paying her so much attention. And they were right. A dirty cowboy was hardly a match for a socialite with a wealthy background.

"Oh, I have no interest in Mr. Barton in that respect," she said quickly, laughing to cover her shock. "But I have noticed that the cowboys respect him. Mr. Barton has had to calm his men down every night."

"They are high-strung," her aunt said with a smile. "And surely you've become used to noise in your travels."

"Not really," Nora recalled as she stood by the window and gazed out over the flat horizon. "I was protected from anything really upsetting, even from the smells and sounds of camp life. And I was always among relatives of one sort or another."

"Relatives?" her aunt asked pointedly. "And not suitors?"

Nora sighed, and a slight frown marred her lovely face. "I fear that I am . . . unusual in that respect. I do not encourage the advances of men, although I like them very well as friends."

"But, my dear, you are lovely," she said. "Surely you will want to marry one day, and have children. . . ."

Nora's face closed up. She turned jerkily. "Melly and I have planned to picnic by the river tomorrow." She glanced at her aunt. "I have a . . . fear of rivers, but

Melly says that this one is shallow and not very fear-ful."

"And she is right," Aunt Helen said, curious about the wording of Nora's remark. "It will be pleasant for you both, and as it is near the house, it is quite safe to go there unescorted. The heat and dust are terrible this time of year, but it is cool beside the river. Except for the mosquitoes," she added with a grimace.

Mosquitoes. Nora felt queasy.

"There, now, the mosquitoes are worst in late afternoon," her aunt said soothingly. "Do not worry."

Nora turned and then she knew that her mother had told Aunt Helen everything. It was almost a relief to have someone know the truth. She bit her lower lip. "It frightens me."

Helen touched her shoulder gently. "You had a bad time of it. But you will be fine here. Do go with Melly and enjoy yourself. It will be all right, my dear, truly it will. Why, doctors are often wrong. You must always keep hope. It is God who decides our fate, not the medical profession; not always, at least."

"I should have remembered that. Very well," she said after a minute, and smiled. "I suppose there are worse things than insects," she added solemnly as she walked out of the room.

Chapter Three

MELLY HADN'T MENTIONED THAT THE PICNIC WAS GO-
ing to involve other people. It was a church picnic. And it wasn't going to be on a river near the house;
it was going to be beside a small stream. When Nora
heard that, she relaxed noticeably.

Aunt Helen laughed when Melly reminded her that it
was the church picnic.

"Oh, how could I have forgotten!" Helen said with a
rueful glance at Nora. "My mind is not on the present.
I do beg your pardon, Nora, I misled you. I know that
you shall enjoy this gathering. There are several eligible
and well-to-do young men among the congregation."

"Including Mr. Langhorn," Melly added with a
strange expression on her face. "He and his son, Bruce,
will probably accompany us, since it is Saturday, but
perhaps he will be less . . . antagonistic than usual. And
with luck, Bruce will behave better than he normally
does."

Nora wondered a lot about her cousin's peculiar way
of referring to Mr. Langhorn. She hoped that Melly
would confide in her one day.

After Helen left to talk to the cook, the two women
went outside to sit on the porch. Nora tidied the bow

under her jaunty sailor collar. "Will any of the men from the ranch be going?" she asked hesitantly.

Melly grinned. "Not Mr. Barton, if that's what you meant. He goes to Beaumont this afternoon."

"Oh. Oh, I see." She colored a little and lifted disappointed eyes. "Does he have family there?"

"No one knows. He never speaks of the visits except in a desultory way. He is very mysterious, our Mr. Barton."

"Yes, so I see."

Melly noticed Nora's distraction and touched her arm gently. "Mama is so old-fashioned. Do not let her interfere too much. Mr. Barton is a fine man, Nora. Social status is not everything."

"Alas, Melly," her cousin said heavily, "for me it is. My mother is exactly like yours. None of my family would countenance Mr. Barton as a suitor for me." She gnawed her lower lip. "Oh, why must I be so conventional? I feel like a sheep, following the herd. But it is so hard to break away from the past, to stand up to social absolutes."

"If you love someone, that becomes imperative sometimes," Melly said sadly.

Nora looked at her. "Does it? I cannot imagine a love strong enough to send me into battle with my peers."

Melly didn't reply. There was a very faraway look in her eyes.

Nora brooded on her predicament for the rest of the day, and finally decided that she could say good-bye to Cal if she wanted to. There was nothing so unspeakable about that. She went looking for him late that afternoon when it was nearing sundown. He was in the barn with his saddlebags packed on his horse, a big bay gelding with a spirited look.

"Is that your horse?" Nora asked from the door of the barn, which was deserted momentarily except for Cal.

He glanced at her and smiled. "Yes. I call him King, because he reminds me of a man I know; one who's just as impatient and every bit as unpleasant when he's upset." He didn't add that the nickname originally belonged to his eldest brother.

"He's very . . . tall."

"So am I. I require a tall horse." He finished his tasks with the horse and turned to move toward Nora. For once, he was cleaned up. He was freshly shaven and smelled of cologne and soap. His hair was clean, neatly parted. His clothes were like new, from his long-sleeved shirt to the neat cord trousers he wore with polished black boots. He looked very masculine, and the intensity of his gaze made her nervous. He paused just in front of her, admiring her trim figure behind the china blue bow that hung below the sailor collar of the white blouse. The bow matched her eyes.

"Shall you be gone long?" she asked, trying to sound unconcerned.

"Only over the weekend, perhaps for a day or so beyond, depending on the train schedules," he said noncommittally. "Will you miss me?" he teased.

She grimaced. "Sir, we hardly know each other."

"A situation which can quickly be remedied." He bent suddenly, lifted her clear off the ground in his arms like a baby, and carried her behind the open door of the barn, out of sight.

Her mouth was open to protest this shocking treatment when his lips pressed softly over it, teasing the tender flesh until it admitted him. Behind her head, she felt the muscles cord in his arm as he brought her closer so that he could advance the kiss. Her breasts flattened softly over the hard muscles of his broad chest, and she felt her heart beating against them.

Outside, she heard the wind rise, and the metallic sound of the windmill as its arms began to spin. There was a rumble up in the darkening clouds. But she was locked fast in Cal's arms and floating blissfully in feelings she had never experienced. His mouth was warm and hard and insistent. She had no inclination to fight or protest. He must have known it, because he was gentle, almost tender with her. When he finally lifted his mouth, she was dazed, fascinated. Her wide blue eyes searched his in a silence broken only by the soft movements of the horse nearby.

His silver-gray eyes glittered as they traced her mouth and then met her shocked eyes. "You're very docile for an adventuress," he whispered deeply. "Do you like lying in my arms?"

She hadn't realized that she was. He still had her clear of the floor. Her arms were around his neck, holding on, and she never wanted to move. It was a surprise to discover that it felt natural to let him kiss her.

"You're dazed, aren't you?" he murmured with faint, tender amusement as he studied her face. "You flatter me."

"You must . . . put me down," she faltered.

He shook his head, very slowly. "Not until I've kissed you again." His lips touched hers, teased, tempted. He nibbled on her lower lip and heard her gasp. "You taste of whipping cream," he whispered, nudging at her upper lip with the tip of his tongue.

"You make me hungry, Nora, for things no gentleman should admit to a lady. . . ."

His mouth crushed down over hers, opening it to the most intimate kiss she'd ever experienced in her life. She cried out and pushed at him, frightened not only by the intimacy of it, but by the sensations it made her feel.

He lifted his head, laughing softly as he saw her eyes. "I thought you were sophisticated," he chided.

She colored. "Do put me down!" she murmured, struggling and flustered.

He did, holding her until she righted herself and steadied. She pushed at her disheveled hairdo and moved jerkily away from him. He had never seemed taller, more menacing, than he did then.

For himself, Cal was pleased with her reactions. She wasn't so haughty now, and he liked very much seeing her at a disadvantage. It was going to be fun to bring the so superior Miss Marlowe down to the level of an ordinary woman. She might even enjoy being human for a change.

He touched her nose with the tip of his finger and laughed again as she looked worriedly around them.

"No one saw us," he said gently. "Our secret is safe."

She chewed on her lower lip and tasted him there. Her eyes sought his, full of unvoiced fears.

"What shall I bring you from Beaumont?" he asked.

"I . . . I need nothing."

His eyebrows arched. "It's my experience that women love little presents. Come, isn't there something your heart desires?"

She was afraid. The way he was looking at her made her knees wobbly, and his kisses had kindled something frightening inside her. She made a helpless gesture with her hands.

"No, there is . . . there is nothing I want. I . . . must go inside. Do have a safe trip," she said.

He just looked at her, aware of new feelings, new curiosities, all of which involved the woman before him. "I shall think of you while I'm away," he said, his voice deep and slow. "When I look up at the stars tonight, I shall imagine you looking at them, and thinking of me as well."

She flushed. "You must not!"

"Why?" he asked reasonably, and smiled. "You have no beau. I have no sweetheart. Why should we not be interested in each other?"

"I do not want that," she blurted out.

He cocked an eyebrow. "Because I'm a poor, dirty cowboy?" he chided. "Am I not good enough for a Marlowe of Virginia?"

She grimaced, and he read the truth in her face. No, a poor cowhand would hardly be a suitable match for a wealthy woman from back East. It rankled that she should think that way, that she should be so bound by convention when she was modern and well traveled and outspoken.

She was an adventuress, she said, but she was certainly very conventional in her private life. She gave lip service to the modern ideals, but she did not practice them. She was just one more prisoner of the social conventions of her set. He was oddly disappointed in her. His mother was a frontier woman, a good and decent woman, but one who lived to please her own sense of morality, not flat rules set down by other people. He had thought at first that Nora had spirit and felt the lure of adventure, that she had come West to test her courage and challenge the unknown. But in fact, she was just another bored rich society woman who toyed with men to get her thrills. He mustn't forget poor Greely.

"Please," she said nervously. "I must go."

His face was shuttered, hard. "Go, then," he said curtly. "It would not be seemly for you to be seen with someone beneath your social station."

She glanced at him worriedly, guiltily. But she didn't deny it. That was what damned her in his eyes, what made him determined to show her that feelings were more important than conventions. He would, if it was the last thing he ever did. He would woo and win her as an itinerant cowboy. And when he was through, she would never judge another man by his clothes or his station in life. He would be the sword of vengeance for Greely and all the other men this spoiled young miss had hurt with her thoughtlessness.

He whirled angrily toward his horse, leaving Nora to walk slowly back toward the house with her heart in her throat. She had driven him away, and she should be sorry. But she had nothing to give him. If he thought that it was because of his station and not her own fears about her illness, then perhaps that was as well, too. Perhaps it would spare her any future wooing. The thought, which would have comforted her, was vaguely discouraging.

She had barely made it to the steps when she heard the horse's hooves sound close by, and then quickly move away. She turned in time to see Cal riding out the gate, tall against the darkening sky, looking as violent as the storm itself.

* * *

The church picnic was a surprise. Nora hadn't expected to enjoy it, but she was having a very good time.
The only fly in the ointment was, as Melly had inti-
mated, Mr. Langhorn's son, Bruce. The little boy was a
holy terror, blond and slight and full of mischief. He'd
barely arrived when he put a bullfrog down a girl's back
and spilled lemonade on the preacher's trousers.

His dad just grinned and watched him, apparently ap-
proving his actions. Melly gave the whipcord-lean man
with the dark hair and eyes a cold glare, but he ignored
her. He was apparently taken with an older woman, a
brunette with a plate of cake and a sweet smile.

"There he goes again, playing up to Mrs. Terrell,"
Melly said irritably. "Not that I care, but she's at least
five years older than he is, and she's got three kids of
her own. She's a widow. A rich widow," she added in
a hiss.

As if he heard, Mr. Langhorn looked at her. He lifted
an eyebrow, gave her a lazy, dismissing appraisal, and
picked up a piece of the widow's cake. There was
something almost spiteful about the way he looked right
at Melly while he bit into it.

"Daring me to say something," Melly muttered.
"Look at him! He's a . . . a blackguard, an uncivilized
boor! She deserves him!"

"But the poor widow is kind," Nora argued.

"She is a black widow," came the terse reply. "I despise her!"

Nora was surprised at the poisonous tones from her
sweet cousin Melly. It was so out of character.

"He told me that I was too young to give him what
a man needed from a woman," Melly said shockingly.
She flushed. "Mama would have a fit if she knew he

had spoken to me in such a way. I pretended that it was another man, my best friend's new husband, who had broken my heart, but it wasn't. It was ... him." She sounded miserable. Her eyes followed the tall man with the widow Terrell, and she jerked them back around with a faint groan. "My parents would never have permitted anything to come of my regard for him, because he is divorced! What shall I do? It is killing me to see them together! He says that he shall probably marry her, because Bruce needs a mother so badly." She clenched her hands together. "I love him. But he feels nothing for me, nothing at all. He has never touched me, not even to shake my hand. . . ."

There was a wrenching sigh, and Nora felt so sorry for her cousin that she could have cried.

"I am sorry," she said gently. "Life has its tragedies, doesn't it?" she added absently, thinking of Africa and the terrible changes it had brought to her life.

"Yours has been much different from mine, and certainly it has not been tragic," her cousin argued. "You have wealth and position and you are traveled and sophisticated. You have everything."

"Not everything," Nora said tersely.

"You could have. Mr. Barton is sweet on you," she teased, forgetting her own problems momentarily. "You might marry him."

She couldn't forget the harsh, cold farewell she'd received from Mr. Barton. She tensed indignantly. "Marry a cowboy?!" Nora exclaimed haughtily.

Melly glared at her. "And what, pray tell, is wrong with a hardworking man? Being poor is no sin."

"He has no ambition. He is dirty and disheveled. I find him ... offensive," she lied.

"Then why were you kissing him in the barn before he left?" Melly asked reasonably.

Nora gasped. "What do you mean?!"

"I saw you from my window," she said with a chuckle. "Don't look so shocked, Nora, I knew you were human. He is very attractive, and when he shaves and cleans up, he would be a match for any of your European friends."

Nora shifted uncomfortably. "He is uncivilized."

"You should spend more time out here. If you did, you would realize that clothes and a fine education do not always make a man a gentleman," Melly said quietly. "There are men here in Texas who have no money, but who are courageous and kind and noble, in their way."

"Like the heroes in my dime novels?" Nora chided. "That is all fiction. I have discovered the truth since I have come West, and it is disillusioning."

"It should not be, if you do not expect people to be perfect."

"I certainly do not expect it of Mr. Barton. He . . . accosted me," she muttered.

"He kissed you," Melly corrected, "which is hardly the same thing. Let me tell you, many of our unattached women in church would give much to have the elusive and stoic Mr. Barton kiss them!"

Nora glared at her cousin. "I would prefer that, too. He may kiss any of them he likes, with my blessing. I have no desire to become the sweetheart of a common cowboy."

"Or of any man, it seems," Melly murmured with a speaking glance. "You are very reluctant to discuss marriage and a family, Nora."

Nora wrapped her arms around her body. "I have no desire to marry."

"Why?"

She shifted. "It is something I cannot discuss," she said, shivering with the memory of how ill she had been. How could she subject a man, any man, to a life of illnesses that would never end? How could she have a baby, and take care of it? "I shall never marry," Nora said bitterly.

"With the right man, you might want to."

Nora thought of Cal Barton's hot kisses, and her heart raced. She mustn't remember, she mustn't. She turned in time to see young Bruce Langhorn making a beeline for another young boy perched precariously on a rock, laughing.

"Oh, no!" Melly gasped, and before Nora could open her mouth, her cousin broke into a dead run toward the children.

She hadn't realized what was going on until she saw the Langhorn boy reach out to push the other little boy, immaculately dressed, into the stream face-first.

"You little heathen!" the boy's mother cried, drawing everyone's attention to Bruce. "You shouldn't be allowed in decent company! The child of a divorced man!" she added with pure venom as she pulled her soaked, weeping child out of the water and began to comfort him.

Langhorn heard. He got to his feet and joined his son, who looked torn between tears and embarrassment.

"I tried to stop him," Melly said, her eyes eloquent as they looked up at the tall man.

He didn't look at her, or seem to hear. He put his hand on Bruce's shoulder. "He's as good as your boy,

Mrs. Sanders," he told the flustered mother. "Of course, he does act like a little boy instead of a little statue sometimes."

Mrs. Sanders's red face went redder. "He hardly has a moral example to follow, Mr. Langhorn."

Langhorn just stared at her. "I thought this was a church party, where Christian people got together to have a good time."

The woman froze, and suddenly became aware of people staring at her, and not very approvingly.

"It seems to me," Nora inserted with exquisite poise, "that none of us is so perfect that he can sit in judgment on others. Or is that not what church is supposed to teach us?" she added with a cool smile.

Mrs. Sanders bit almost through her lower lip. "I do beg your pardon, Mr. Langhorn. I was frightened for Timmy. . . ."

Langhorn's eyes spoke for him. He turned Bruce away. "You find some other little kid to play with," he said loudly. "I want you around boys who aren't made of glass."

Timmy wiped his eyes on his sleeve and jerked away from his mother with a furious glare.

Melly smothered a grin and followed Nora back to their picnic area.

It wasn't long before Langhorn and Bruce joined them. Both were grinning, and Melly was more flustered than Nora had ever seen her.

"You're a haughty one," Langhorn told Nora with pursed lips. "I don't know that I like being defended by eastern aristocrats with toffee noses."

Nora liked him at once. She grinned at him. "I don't

know that I want to associate with a heathen," she returned.

His eyebrows went up and he looked at Melly, who colored prettily.

"I can see that my reputation has preceded me," he said heavily. He sat down on their cloth and lounged on his side. His dark eyes smiled at Nora and then slid reluctantly to Melly, who was trying to dish up chicken and rolls. "Am I invited to dinner?" he asked her softly.

Melly's hands shook. "If you like," she stammered. "There's plenty."

It was nothing tangible, but Nora felt herself wondering at the tension between this man and her cousin. She had told Nora that he wasn't interested in her, but he looked at Melly just a little too long for politeness, and she was shaken—more than shaken—by just his presence. He was attracted to her, but obviously he wasn't going to let her get any closer than this.

"Me, too, Melly," Bruce pleaded. He grinned at her. "Were you gonna stop me? I saw you running my way."

"I wasn't quick enough," she muttered. "You're just impossible, Bruce. Really. . . !"

"Timmy pushed me in last time we went on a picnic," Bruce explained. "I was just going to get even, that's all. His mom didn't say a word when it was me dripping wet." He glowered. "I don't like her. She says I'm not good enough to play with Timmy."

"Like hell you aren't," Langhorn said easily. "Pardon my language," he added politely to the ladies. He looked back at his son. "You don't judge people by their kin."

"You shouldn't," Nora corrected. "Unfortunately, people do."

Langhorn studied Melly carefully as he accepted a plate from her unsteady hands and nodded his thanks. "You came to Bruce's rescue like an avenging angel. Thanks."

Melly shrugged. "Mrs. Sanders is . . . a bit overbearing at times. She's overprotective, too. Timmy is going to wish she hadn't been, one day."

He smiled. "Maybe not. Your parents have protected you. It hasn't hurt you."

"Hasn't it?" Melly asked without looking at him. She felt bitter, fiercely bitter, because if her parents hadn't smothered her with concern, she might have had some hope of a life with Langhorn. But that was in the past. He thought her too young, and perhaps she was.

Mrs. Terrell came sidling up a minute after Langhorn finished his chicken, smiling from under her lacy parasol. "I do hate to disturb you, Jacob, but I'm feeling just a bit faint. Would you mind very much driving me home?"

"But we only got here," Bruce wailed. "And I haven't got to play with the other kids. There's a sack race. . . !"

"He can stay with us and we'll drive him to your place on the way home," Melly offered, angry at the widow—who was obviously jealous—and hurt for Bruce. "Oh, do let him stay," she pleaded when he hesitated.

He looked at his son quietly. "You mind her."

"Yes, sir!" Bruce beamed.

Langhorn glanced at Melly with an unreadable expression and bent to pick up his weather-beaten hat. "I'll expect him home before dark," he told Melly.

"You have no business driving around the country in the dark."

"Yes, sir," Melly murmured demurely, peering up at him impishly.

His face froze, as if her teasing had an unwanted effect on him. He whirled on his heel, taking Mrs. Terrell's arm bruisingly to herd her down the path.

"Thanks, Melly!" Bruce said enthusiastically, grabbing for a slice of fresh-baked apple pie. "You're swell! That's twice you saved my life. Honestly, isn't Mrs. Terrell a hoot? She wants Dad to marry her, but he doesn't like her that way. I heard him talking to himself about her."

Melly smiled to herself. It was nice to know something so intimate about Jacob Langhorn, even if it was only that he talked to himself. She glanced at Nora and sighed at the sympathy and caring in those deep blue eyes. She smiled at her cousin and shrugged.

The rest of the picnic was fun. Melly and Nora cheered Bruce in the sack races and watched him beat the others in the egg carry. There were horse races between the men, which Bruce said his dad was sure going to hate having missed, and music as well, because a couple of the men brought their guitars.

If Cal Barton had been around, Nora would have thought the picnic perfect. She wondered what he was doing, on his mysterious weekend absence.

Down near Beaumont, Texas, a grimy Cal Barton was helping his drill foreman put the final touches on their newest rig while his brother Alan looked on. Immaculate in his suit and tie, Alan wasn't about to get himself dirty. Irritably Cal thought that the snooty Miss Marlowe would have found Alan just her cup of tea.

"That should do it. Let's get started," Cal told the other man, climbing down to join his brother on solid ground.

"You hit a dry hole first time," Alan reminded him. "Don't get too optimistic."

"It's my money, son," Cal reminded him with a cool smile. "Aunt Grace's money, actually, but I was her favorite and she had a passion for oil. That's why you and King were left out. She thought I had the touch."

"Maybe you do. I hope you don't run out of money before you hit the big one."

"That geologist said the oil is here," Cal reminded him. "I'd have come three years ago if I'd had the backing, but none of you believed I knew what I was doing. Least of all King. He made his opinion of foolish ventures crystal-clear before I left home."

"King has mellowed just recently, thanks to Amelia," Alan mused. "You really will have to come home long enough to meet her. She's quite a girl."

"She must have a backbone of solid steel to cope with our brother," he said flatly.

"She threw a carafe at him."

Cal's eyes widened. "At King?!"

"He's still laughing about it. She's more than a match for him. One shivers to think what sort of children they'll have. I want to move away to a safe place before the first one comes along."

Cal chuckled. "Well, I'll be. I thought he was going to marry Darcy, and there were times, mind you, when I thought he deserved to marry her."

"Shame on you. I wouldn't wish such a cold fish on King. Amelia is much more his style."

He glanced at Alan curiously. "I had a letter from Mother about her. She thought you were the one with marriage in mind."

Alan looked uncomfortable. "I was, when she seemed gentle and in need of protection. After her father's death, she changed. She was more woman than I could handle." He smiled ruefully. "I'm not like you and King. I want a gentle, sweet girl, not a warring Valkyrie."

"Not me," Cal said, eyeing the rig. "If I marry, I don't want a woman I can browbeat. She'll need to be spirited and adventurous to keep up with the way I want to live. If I strike anything here, I'll move onto the place and never leave it."

"Camp out here, you mean?"

"Something like that. I don't need a city woman with snobbish attitudes."

"That sounds suspiciously like you've met one already."

"Who, me? Go home, Alan. You aren't suited to drilling. You'll just get in the way. I don't know why you came."

"I'm on my way to Galveston for some fishing. It's just the second week in September, and I won't be gang-pressed into roundup by Father until the end of the month at least. I need a break. This was just a stop on the way," he said, grinning. "I have a train to catch."

"When are you coming back?"

"I don't know. Maybe after next weekend. Maybe a little later." He frowned. "I did want to see a man in

Baton Rouge about some ranch business as well. Maybe I'll go on east first, and then double back. I'll cable you."

Cal clapped his brother on the back. "Go carefully, young Alan. We may be oil and water, but we're family. Never forget."

"I won't." Alan smiled. "Good luck."

"Thanks. I'll need it."

Alan climbed onto his hired horse and waved at Cal as he started back toward Beaumont. Cal watched him with a peculiar sensation in his chest, a feeling of loss. He laughed at his own foolishness and turned back to his chores. He had very little time left before he had to get back to Tyler Junction and the Tremayne ranch. He envied Alan that fishing trip. Drilling for oil was an occupation that was expensive, physically exhausting, and not a little dangerous. Just last week, a derrick had toppled on a nearby piece of property, and a prospector had been killed. The dry hole was an occupational hazard as well, and after days of hope for a strike, it was a bitter break. Cal hoped that this next attempt would be more successful. He hated to leave the drilling crew alone, but it couldn't be helped. He was putting all his spare capital into the venture. He needed what he made as foreman at the ranch to supplement his income.

Besides, it gave him the opportunity to keep an eye on the family's massive investment in the Tremayne ranch. He hated spying on Chester, but it couldn't be helped. As much as the combine had paid to take it over, the Tremaynes stood to lose the most. In these unsafe days, it was better to cover a bet than risk the hand. He had to keep Chester solvent, for the family's sake as well as Chester's. If only he could bring the man around to some modern thinking. He'd have to work on that angle when he got back.

Chapter Four

T HE NEXT WEEK, CAL HAD A TELEGRAM FROM ALAN IN Galveston, mentioning the fine weather and asking about progress on the rig. Cal took time enough to wire him back and tell him, tongue in cheek, that he'd hit the biggest strike in Texas history and hoped Alan wouldn't be sorry he missed it.

He wished he could be a fly on the wall when Alan got the message, although his brother knew him very well and wasn't likely to fall for the joke. He went back to work, but his mind wasn't on it. He was thinking about his new venture and worried about the capital he was investing. Perhaps he was trying to build a life on dreams after all. King had said as much when Cal announced his intention to go looking for a big oil strike near the Gulf. But, then, King was practical and a realist. He was content to manage the ranch and oversee the combine with their father. He wasn't a risk taker.

Nora was out walking when he made his way to the bunkhouse late that evening. He looked unusually solemn.

"Hello," she said gently, hesitating when he stopped just in front of her. "Goodness, you look somber. Is something wrong?"

66

He'd deliberately avoided her since his return Monday afternoon. The way he felt about her confused him. He wanted to make her uncomfortable, to hurt her because of her arrogance, her treatment of Greely. But when it came right down to it, he hadn't the heart.

He studied her quietly, aware that for the first time, she wasn't moving back or wrinkling her nose at him. Her blue eyes were shadowed in the dusk light, and they were curious as they searched his strong, lean face.

"It's nothing I can share with you," he said slowly. "A . . . personal matter."

"Oh, I see." She paused. "Life is not always what we would wish, is it, Mr. Barton?" she asked absently.

He scowled at the proper use of his name. "I have kissed you," he reminded her curtly. "How can you still be so formal with me?"

She cleared her throat and folded her hands at her waist. "You embarrass me."

"My name is Callaway," he persisted. "Usually I'm called Cal."

She smiled. "It suits you."

"What is Nora short for?"

"Eleanor," she replied.

"Eleanor." It sounded right on his tongue. He smiled as he studied her in the fading light. "You shouldn't be here. The Tremaynes are very conventional people, and so, I think, are you."

Her blue eyes searched his face. "You are not."

He shrugged. "I have been a rake, and in some ways, I still am. I make my own rules." His eyes narrowed and he spoke involuntarily. "While you are a slave to society's rules, Eleanor."

Her name sounded magical on his lips. She hardly

heard what he was saying. She wanted to touch him, to hold him. He made her think of beginnings, of pale green buds on trees in early spring. These were feelings that she had never before experienced, and she coveted them. But he was a cowboy. She couldn't imagine what her parents would think if she wrote that she had become infatuated with a working man, with a hired hand. They would have a fit. So would her aunt Helen. Just the fact of speaking with him, alone like this, could cost him his job. Why had she not realized it?

"I must go in," she said uneasily. "It would not please my people to find me here with you like this."

His fingers caught hers and soothed them, eased between them. The contact was shocking. He made a rough sound deep in his throat and had to fight the urge to bring her body into his and kiss her until he made her lips sore. It was in his eyes, that terrible need. It had been a long time since he'd had a woman; surely that was the reason he reacted so violently to her!

He let go of her hand abruptly and moved back. "It is late."

"Yes. Good night, Mr. Barton."

He nodded. He turned and walked away, leaving her staring after him.

Aunt Helen was standing on the porch, looking worried when Nora came up the steps.

"Nora, you should not be outside so late," she said gently. "It looks bad."

"I was only getting a breath of air," Nora said, avoiding the older woman's eyes. "It is so warm. . . ."

"I see." Helen smiled. "Indeed it is. My dear, there was the most terrible story in the paper today, about a family of missionaries massacred in China, with their little children. What a terrible world it is becoming!"

"Yes, indeed," Nora replied. "How nice that we are safe here in southern Texas."

That Saturday there was a storm. Cal and the other men were out getting the livestock seen to, while the water rose to unbelievable levels and tore down fences. They were kept busy all day, and when they came in late that afternoon, they looked like mud men.

Cal came up onto the porch, apologizing to Helen and the women for his appearance.

"Chester wanted you to know that he's all right," he said without preamble, wiping a grimy sleeve over his dirty face. "We had to pull cattle out of the mud all afternoon, and we lost a few head in the flood. Chester's gone with two of the other men over to Potter's place, to see if he and his wife are all right. Their house is close to the river."

"Yes, I know," Helen said worriedly. "What an odd storm, to come out of nowhere like this. They have said that in Arizona there have been unusual changes in the weather, causing many people to become ill. Imagine, and it is only the tenth of September!"

Cal looked uneasy. "The weather has been very odd," he agreed. "I'd like to know if things are this bad along the coast." He didn't add that his brother was there and he was concerned.

"We will know soon enough, I suppose," Helen said. "Do go and have your meal, Mr. Barton, you look so tired."

He smiled wanly, glancing at Nora. "None of us have had much rest. Chester will be home soon, I'm certain."

"Thank you for coming to tell us."

He nodded wearily and turned toward the bunkhouse. Nora had to bite her lip not to call after him. If she had the right, she would tuck him up in bed and look after him. Imagine, she told herself, how silly it would sound if she voiced such a longing. She moved back into the house without saying a word.

It wasn't until Monday that the news reached Tyler Junction about the incredible tragedy in Galveston. A hurricane had come ashore in the seaside city about midmorning the previous Saturday, submerging the entire city underwater. Galveston was almost totally destroyed, and early estimates were that thousands of people had been killed.

When Cal heard this, he was on his horse and gone before anyone had a chance to question him. It was assumed that he was going to Galveston to help with rescue efforts. No one knew that he had a brother visiting there or that he was terrified that Alan might be among the dead. He didn't cable home on the way. If no one in El Paso heard about the tragedy for a few days, he might have something to tell his family before they knew of Alan's danger.

He managed to get on a train heading toward Galveston, but when he got to the city, all lines were down and the tracks were destroyed. He had to borrow a horse from a nearby ranch to get into the city. What he saw would give him nightmares for years afterward.

It wasn't until he saw the devastation firsthand that he realized how impossible it would be to find his brother among the dead. Among the smashed, piled-up buildings of the city, there were more pitiful broken and mangled bodies than he'd ever seen in his life, even in the Spanish-American War. He took it for a few hours, trying to do what he could to help, and then he couldn't take it anymore. He couldn't bear the thought of his brother in that tangle of lifelessness. He rode out of town without looking back, sick at heart and soul. A saint would have a hard time reconciling what he'd just seen with any sort of divine love.

Disillusioned, shocked, grief-stricken, he couldn't bring himself to go back to the Tremayne ranch just yet. He rode until he found a depot with a train bound for Baton Rouge, with no clear idea of where he would go after that.

He booked a room in a hotel where his family usually stayed when they traveled here on business and collapsed on the bed. He lay in bed until dawn and went down to breakfast bleary-eyed and exhausted. He wondered if he would ever sleep again.

Memories of his brother and their lives together had tormented him. He and Alan had never been as close as he and King had, but Alan was very special to him, just the same. It had been Alan who'd continued to encourage him about the oil business, even as he teased him about dry holes. The boy had inspired him to do the things he wanted to do, and he was going to miss him terribly. He wondered how he would manage. . . .

Morose, dead-spirited, he didn't hear the door of his room open and barely felt the hard clap of a hand on his shoulder. "Well, what are you doing here, for God's sake? I've just gotten in from a little town back on the bayous, and saw your name on the register. I was visiting the family of a young lady I've taken a shine to. . . . Cal?!"

Cal had Alan in a bear hug, a bruising grip, and his eyes closed on a wave of relief so great that he almost sobbed aloud with it.

"Thank God," he said huskily. "Thank God!"

Alan pulled back, curious as he saw his brother's ravaged face. "Why, whatever is wrong?" he asked.

Cal took a minute to get a grip on himself before he spoke. "Haven't you . . . heard?"

"About what?"

"About Galveston," Cal said heavily. "It's been destroyed. Totally destroyed. Bodies everywhere . . ."

Alan was very still. His face was pasty. "I haven't seen a paper or talked to anyone except Sally for days. When?"

"It hit Saturday, but we didn't get the news until Monday in Tyler Junction. I thought you were there. I went at once." He smoothed back his hair, his eyes terrible. "I almost went mad when I saw what had happened. You can't imagine. I've been through a war, but this was worse. My God, you can't imagine the devastation," he said in a terse tone as the horrible memory of the things he'd seen and heard left him sick inside.

Alan let out a breath. "And to think that I could have been there, right in the middle of it. My God! I decided Friday to leave Galveston and come here, and took a train out that very night. The weather was worse than usual Saturday, and of course, there was some flooding. But I never dreamed of such tragedy! What of Mr. Briggs and his family? I was staying with them. . . . Have they identified any of the dead, Cal?"

"They'll never identify them all," Cal said, turning away. He still couldn't bear to remember the things he'd seen. "I'll have to cable the ranch," Cal said. "They

may hear about the hurricane and they won't learn all of
it. We have to let them know that you're all right."

"You didn't cable them from Galveston?"

Cal's eyes darkened. "The lines are down," he said
evasively. "I'll go over to the Western Union office and
do that right now. I'll be back in a minute." He smiled
warmly at Alan. "I'm glad you're alive."

Alan nodded. "So am I." He smiled, too, because it
was nice to know that his brother cared so much about
him. Like King, Cal didn't show his feelings often, or
easily.

Alan stayed on in Baton Rouge while Cal got on the
next train for Tyler Junction, and slept with pure relief
most of the way there. The stories he heard on the way
about the flood in Galveston made him even sicker,
now that he'd seen it for himself. He hoped that one
day he could forget the sight, even as he thanked God
that he hadn't had a relative there. The horror grew
daily, along with the threat of terrible disease. He might
have offered to help again, with Alan safe, but he had
his own job to do back in Tyler Junction, making sure
that the Tremayne ranch's cattle weren't lost as well.
And there was no shortage of volunteers to help in
Galveston, for the moment.

There were reports of severe flooding all over Texas,
and he prayed that Galveston's tragedy wouldn't be repeated anywhere else. If the rivers that lay on each side
of the Tremayne property ran out of their banks again,
there could be devastation for the combine as well as
Chester and his family. They had to be his first concern,
now that Alan was out of danger. He could do nothing
for the dead. They would have to be left to providence

and their poor, grieving relatives. He could have wept for their families.

Despite his relief at his brother's safety, he arrived back at the Tremayne ranch pale and depressed. He said nothing about what he'd seen, although Chester had heard enough to turn his stomach; things he hadn't dared share with the women.

Cal had enough to do for the first couple of days after his return home, making sure that the Tremayne cattle were safe. He'd cabled Beaumont from Tyler Junction to make sure that his rig was still standing. The lines had been down at first, but he'd made contact with his drill rigger, and everything was all right. That was a relief. He dreaded hearing that the wind had cost him his investment. Perhaps this was an omen that he was on the right track.

His melancholy was noticed, however, and remarked upon. He came to report to Chester a few days later while Nora was sitting on the porch alone.

He hadn't paid much attention to his surroundings since his return. Nora had noticed his preoccupation, and she had a good idea what had caused it.

She rose gracefully from the settee where she'd been perched, and stopped him just as he was about to knock on the front door.

"You're still brooding about Galveston, aren't you?" she asked gently. "There was a terrible hurricane on the East Coast last year. I lost a beloved cousin. And I have seen floods, although not one on such a scale. It is not difficult to imagine the devastation."

He was surprised by her perception. His pale eyes narrowed as he searched her earnest face. "It's something I'll never speak about," he said tautly. "Least of all to a woman."

Her eyebrows rose. "Am I made of glass, sir?"

His gaze went down her body in the slim skirt and white embroidered blouse. "I wonder, considering the blazing path of some of your contemporaries through saloons with axes."

She giggled softly at the reference to the zealous temperance leagues. "Wouldn't I look at home with an ax in my hand?"

He shook his head. "It wouldn't suit you." He frowned at her. "You've been subdued since your arrival. You ride well, and Chester mentioned that you can even handle a fowling piece. Yet I've not seen you indulge your fondness for it."

She could shoot, but not well. She had missed her shot in England and blown out a priceless stained-glass window that dated to the Tudor period. Her host had taken the loss of his prize window with stiff-lipped good grace, but Nora hadn't been invited back. She hadn't handled a gun since then, either. "It's too hot to shoot," she said evasively.

"It has been unseasonably cool lately."

She searched desperately for a reply.

He lifted an eyebrow, waiting for it.

She cleared her throat. "Very well, if you must know, I do not like guns and I find most of them too heavy for my arms," she said proudly. "I miss."

He chuckled softly. "You fraud."

"But I *can* shoot, after a fashion," she said curtly. "It is only that I have difficulty with the weight of a rifle."

"And what of the safari in Africa?" he persisted.

She paled and averted her eyes. "I do not like to speak of Africa. It is a . . . tarnished memory."

He wondered at her wording and the expression on her face. What a puzzle she was becoming.

"There is a Women's Club social at the courthouse on Saturday evening," he recalled. "I have been appropriated for it, by one of the organizers. Would you partner me?"

Her heart stopped and then ran away. Her mind whirled through her wardrobe and she looked up at him with barely subdued excitement. "Partner . . . you?"

"I dance rather well for a cowboy," he told her amusedly. "And I promise to wear my best boots and plenty of cologne. You may trust me to be discreet."

She colored, because her aunt Helen had repeatedly made her aware of the social distance between them. To be seen with a ranch foreman in public would embarrass not only her, but her family.

He saw her conflicting expressions and his face closed up. "Perhaps one of the town girls would be a better choice after all," he said tautly. "One of them would not be so far above me on the social scale."

Before Nora had time to react, he knocked curtly on the door and was admitted. When he left, he didn't even look her way. He was fuming. Back in West Texas, women had vied for his attentions. The best families from back East had invited him to stay, in hopes of making a match between him and one of their daughters. He was as accustomed to wealth and position as Nora herself, but he was in the position of a man at a masquerade. He could not tell her the truth.

And the more he considered it, the angrier he became. It was a good thing that he saw her as she actually was, he told himself. Had she met him under normal circumstances, he might never have known what an appalling snob she really was.

The social evening was hosted by the local Women's Club, of which Aunt Helen was secretary, and the club's colors of green and white were used in the decorations. Nora wore a simple black silk gown trimmed in duchesse lace and diamonds. Melly wore white organdy, and Aunt Helen wore black taffeta, but their jewelry was made of rhinestones. They were elegant, in their way. But none of the women could hold a candle to Nora, who was so fashionable that she drew most of the attention.

Cal Barton escorted a pretty young girl who was a daughter of one of the organizers of the event. He was attentive to the girl, and once, while he danced with his partner, he gave Nora a look that made her feel two inches high. Her dignity and social position were not enough to compensate for the contempt she saw in his pale eyes. He wouldn't know that Aunt Helen had been very firm about Nora's conduct, and felt a working man would not be a suitable escort for such a lady of quality. Even if Nora had been willing to defy convention on her own, she couldn't shame her aunt and uncle or spoil Melly's chances of marrying well. She resigned herself to losing Cal Barton's company, but very reluctantly.

A middle-aged visiting politician asked her for a dance, and she accepted with grace, smiling up at him with all her charm as they circled the floor. He seemed to be fascinated by her, because he monopolized her through three more dances until her befuddled aunt pleaded with her not to allow one man so much familiarity with her. Embarrassed, Nora retired to the party table. It seemed that she could do nothing to please her aunt.

"Is our Mr. Barton mad at you?" Melly asked when they were standing around the hors d'oeuvres table, where a huge candelabra lit the silver coffee service and savories on silver trays.

"It seems to be my lot in life to be the recipient of his ire, when I am not accidentally creating scandals," Nora said resignedly.

"You mustn't mind Mama," Melly said gently, with understanding. "She means well, but it has been hard for her out here. Like your mother, she was a lady of quality, and now she feels her loss of status keenly. It is only that she wants a better life for me than she and Father have to endure. That's why she's so concerned about convention." She touched Nora's arm lightly. "She doesn't know that you have a . . . a feeling for Mr. Barton. And I would not dare tell her. But I am sorry for you."

"It is of no consequence," Nora said stiffly. "I could hardly expect anything to come of it, considering the difference in our positions." She tried not to feel the wounding of the quiet words. But how she wished stuffy social convention to damnation! If only she were an ordinary woman, or Cal Barton a gentleman of wealth. She sighed more wistfully than she knew, and Melly heard her. To divert her cousin, she glanced around and said quickly, "Isn't that Mr. Langhorn?"

Melly's hand shook, almost upsetting her cup of coffee. Nora quickly steadied it. "Careful," she cautioned under her breath, "lest Aunt Helen suspect and say something to you as well."

"Thank you," Melly said sincerely. She laughed unsteadily. "I daresay, we are both in danger from Mama this evening. And from the look of things, you seem to be on Mr. Barton's list of preoccupations."

"That is unlikely now, since I have been forced to snub him," Nora said carelessly, refusing to look as she saw Cal making his way steadily toward them. "I fear that he finds me totally forgettable."

"Really? Would you look at that scowl!" she mused as he came closer.

Nora's own hands were none too steady, but she had poise and composure that young Melly lacked. She looked up at Cal indifferently, feeling the distance in their social stations keenly as she took in his slightly out-of-fashion suit and the scuffs on his black dress boots. She couldn't know that he'd dug them out of the bottom of his trunk deliberately for the occasion, to reinforce his status as a lowly ranch hand.

"You look very nice, Mr. Barton," Melly said with a grin.

"Thank you, Miss Tremayne," he replied politely. "So do you."

Nora tried not to look at him. She sipped her coffee. "Are you having a good time, Mr. Barton?" she asked. "I take it that social functions aren't your usual sort of entertainment."

She could certainly rub it in, he thought irritably. He smiled coolly. "Well, Miss Marlowe, I have to admit that I prefer a hot game of poker to a cold woman."

Her breath caught just slightly, but he wasn't listening. He held out his hand to Melly, smiling at her so charmingly that she didn't even think of Nora as she let him lead her onto the dance floor.

They moved well together, to Nora's fury. She didn't seem to be the only one who was irritated by them, though. Mr. Langhorn was standing with two other men, and the look he was giving Melly, unseen by her, would have scalded milk. He was quite obviously jealous; but apparently he wasn't going to let Melly know. His reasoning escaped Nora, until she realized that his divorced status put him out of Melly's reach as effectively as her wealth put Cal out of her own. She felt an odd kinship with him, an ache for what she could never have.

She sipped her coffee and smiled as the middle-aged politician came to stand by the refreshment table with her.

"Quite a gathering," he remarked. "I sure am happy I got to come. I've been over to Galveston to look at the situation. I don't know what Washington can do to help, but those poor people aren't going to be able to do much without money. There's talk of building a seawall, you know, to prevent this sort of thing from ever happening again."

"That would be a wonderful project," Nora said. "I would be happy to contribute toward it. Surely others would as well."

His face brightened. "Why, I never thought of it that way. Perhaps I might approach wealthy families and businessmen for pledges."

"An excellent idea." She hesitated. "Have they . . . identified all the dead?"

He hesitated, too. He could not speak of such things to a gentlewoman. "I am certain that they have," he reassured her. He couldn't mention that it was not only impossible to identify the thousands of dead bodies, but that it was equally impossible to bury them. They were being cremated where they lay, and armed guards were having to force laborers to sift through the horror to extricate the remainder of the dead from the rubble. Sharks had gathered in the waters around the shore. The worst of it, to him, was that the flood had come after daylight that Saturday morning. People would have seen it coming, that fierce, relentless, merciless wall of water. . . .

"Sir, are you all right?" Nora asked suddenly. "You have gone very pale."

He lifted his coffee to his mouth with a smile, ignoring the scalding nip of it against his tongue. "I was thinking about my return trip to Washington," he lied. "Do tell me about your uncle's ranch, Miss Marlowe. I am fascinated by the cattle industry!"

Melly danced only once with Cal, enjoying his easy company and ready smile. She was, of course, aware of her mother's quiet disapproval, so she made sure that they parted as soon as the waltz was over. She left Cal and found herself face-to-face with an unsmiling Mr. Langhorn.

Her heart leaped as his dark eyes glittered down at her with an unspoken threat. She flushed at their unexpected hostility.

"Playing patty-cake with the foreman, Miss Tremayne?" he chided with a poisonous smile. "Your mother hardly approves, or did you not notice?"

"It was only one dance, and Mr. Barton is a good dancer," she said airily, refusing to be intimidated.

"He's my age," he reminded her. "Far too old for a child like you."

She lifted her eyebrows and looked innocent. "Why, whatever do you mean?"

His lean jaw tautened. "There are boys your own age here," he said angrily. "Why not dally with them instead?"

"You cannot choose my escorts for me," she told him quietly. "I will dance with whom I please, Mr. Langhorn, and you can do your worst." She smiled at him slyly. "It surprises me that you did not bring Mrs. Terrell along for company."

"One of her children is ill," he said.

She didn't dare show her jealousy. "I am sorry," she said formally. "I hope the child will soon be well. Do excuse me. . . !"

She had started to turn away when his lean hand caught her upper arm and held her in place, unobtrusively. Melly looked around quickly, but no one had noticed his possessive hold.

"Mr. Langhorn!" she gasped.

He jerked her closer, and his eyes, at close range, were unnerving. "Do you do it deliberately?" he asked through his teeth. "I have no wish to become entangled, in any way, with you. I have told you so, and I have told you why. If her child were not ill, I would have brought Mrs. Terrell."

"Why are you not with her?" she choked, tugging futilely against his strength.

"Because it was not her wish," he replied. "I have told you before that I intend to marry her. She can help me provide what Bruce needs, a stable and decent home."

"Mrs. Terrell's boys are heathens," she said coldly. "Bruce is not. He is only mischievous. But if you marry that woman, her vile children will make him into a mirror image of themselves—"

"How dare you speak of her sons in such a way!" he grated.

"I do not mean Ben, who is a kind boy. But how can you not know that his two older brothers are forever in trouble with the town constable?" she returned. "They have almost caused two buggy accidents playing shinny on the streets!"

"It is merely a boyish prank, throwing stones at buggy horses," he began.

"When a buggy overturned in the process and a small child was almost killed?" she emphasized, her dark eyes flashing. "You consider that a boyish prank? Why do you not ask Bruce what he thinks of it? He does not like either the widow Terrell or her sons. And if you force such a relationship on him, you may lose him. What if he runs away?!"

"You are very nosy for such a small woman," he said, throwing her arm away. "I will decide what is best for my own son, without any interference from you!"

"Oh, Melly!" her mother called quickly, red-faced at the confrontation, which was being noticed as the two antagonists raised their voices in anger. "Dear, do come and help me serve, please!"

"At once, Mama," she returned, flushing as she moved away from Mr. Langhorn.

Helen was angry and trying not to show it. "I have asked you not to associate with that man," she hissed. "He is scandalous!"

"Yes, Mama," Melly said, subdued. "I was only talking to him about Bruce."

"Bruce?"

"His son. You remember, Nora and I drove him home from the church picnic. He is a very difficult man to speak to, and Bruce's behavior is worsening. I felt that I must speak to him, but he became angry," she added convincingly.

"I see. I do wonder why Mr. Langhorn came here to-night," she added somberly, glancing across the room toward him and frowning. "He never attends social functions, does he? Perhaps he had business to discuss with someone."

"That is possible," Melly said. She followed her mother's gaze and had her eyes momentarily captured by Mr. Langhorn's unsmiling ones. It was like a jolt of lightning. She felt it all through her body and quickly dropped her eyes.

Her mother's attention was diverted by a young man coming toward them. "Well, this is a nice surprise. It's young Mr. Larrabee." She patted Melly's hand encouragingly. "He is very nice. He was asking for you a moment ago."

"Mama, I do wish you would not push me at men!"

Helen was taken aback. "Don't you wish to marry?"

"Yes. But . . . why not encourage Nora to dance with some of these young men? Mr. Barton, perhaps," she added cautiously.

Her mother's face stiffened. "My dear, Nora is an heiress," Helen said softly. "She will be a very wealthy woman one day. A lady of her social position simply does not dance in public with an ordinary cowboy. People would talk."

"Surely out here we are more democratic," Melly began.

"One must not create scandal," Helen said firmly.

"Now, dear, if you could hand me one of those china cups, I will fill it for Mrs. Blake before you are asked to dance by that nice young Larrabee boy making his way toward us."

Melly agreed quietly, thinking that she felt as sorry for Nora as she did for herself. She'd hoped that her mother might relent a little about the unsuitability of Mr. Barton, but her mind was made up. Poor Nora. If she had any contact at all with the handsome foreman, it would have to be done discreetly and in a clandestine fashion. Melly's eyes flashed as she thought about the unfairness of it all. But, then—perhaps she could help!

=== Chapter Five ===

N ORA WASN'T CERTAIN WHETHER TO BE HAPPY OR SAD
that she wasn't able to dance even once with Cal
Barton. His impatience with her made her miserable. If
only he were someone of wealth and station, someone
she had the right to care about, to be seen with. Aunt
Helen had made it quite clear how she felt about division of the social classes. It made Nora sad to admit
that her mother would have felt exactly the same. No
one was going to approve of Nora getting herself involved with a poor cowboy.

Melly was also subdued, after her unsatisfying confrontation with the abominable Mr. Langhorn. She had
known his plans to marry the widow Terrell, of course
she had. But to have him tell her so brutally ... It
didn't bear thinking about. He seemed intent on breaking her poor heart in as many ways as possible. Nora
seemed to sense that hurt, because she reached out a
gloved hand and touched Melly's arm affectionately. It
was a comforting gesture, and it eased the pain a little.

It was a long ride home in the surrey, with Cal taciturn behind the reins, and Chester and the others talking
in low, subdued voices. When they arrived, Chester

helped Helen and Melly down, so Cal had to lift Nora down from the high step.

His big, lean hands contracted gently at her waist as he lowered her slowly to the ground. He didn't release her at once, and her heart began to race as she stared at his firm mouth and remembered unhappily how hungrily it had kissed her own that once.

In the soft moonlight, he looked down pointedly at her mouth for several seconds. His hands caressed her waist gently before they fell and he moved slowly back to take the surrey on to the barn. That look was magic. It took away Nora's pain and all her fears, because she knew then that he felt something just as powerful as she did. She didn't think about all the reasons why it was impossible, not the least of which was her own infirmity, which might recur at any time. All she knew was a thrill of ecstasy that Cal Barton desired her!

Chester lit lamps for the girls before he and Helen called good night and went on down the hall to their bedroom.

"I'll be along in just a minute, Melly," Nora said as she went to the front door. "I dropped one of my gloves."

Melly wasn't fooled. She called back a reply and went to her room with a smothered grin.

Outside, Nora walked briskly down to the barn, where the flickering kerosene lantern gave Cal enough vision to unhitch the sleek buggy horse and bed it down for the night.

He had just finished when he saw Nora standing in the doorway, watching him. His face hardened. He latched the horse's stall and grabbed the lantern from its nail with subdued fury.

"Aren't you out of place, Miss Marlowe?" he asked coldly. "A barn is hardly your setting, is it?"

She nodded toward the lantern. "Could you put that out, please?"

He hesitated, but only for a minute. "Why not?" He humored her, curious.

"And could you put it down, as well?" she persisted.

He shrugged. He set the lantern on the ground and straightened.

"Thank you," she said softly. And she moved forward, right up against him. She went on tiptoe and looped her arms around his neck.

Cal caught her by the waist, breathing in her perfume, and pushed while he still had enough sense to resist her.

"Don't do that!" he said angrily.

But she wouldn't budge. Her arms tightened, in fact. "Why not?" she whispered. It delighted her that he was so quickly responsive. She could see his shirt jerking with the hard beat of his heart, and it thrilled her. She pressed her hands against the shirt, smoothing them over hard, warm muscle through the fabric. She loved the touch of him.

He barely heard her for the thunder of his heart. He stopped pushing as he felt her breath on his mouth, teasing, tempting. The warmth of her body, the scent of her, made him so hungry that he could hardly stand straight. Would it be so terrible to give in to what he was feeling, just this once? He groaned as the need caught him up in its fervor. Her mouth was so soft, so sweet. He had to have it!

"Eleanor," he whispered huskily, bending. "Oh, God, Eleanor. . . !"

Even as he spoke her name, she pushed her lips upward against his firm mouth and made a tiny sound, deep in her throat.

He groaned, lost to everything except the softness of her in his arms. He lifted her against him and riveted her slender body to his in an intimacy she'd never shared with anyone except him. The feel of his powerful body so close to hers made her reckless and she clung even closer, loving the experienced crush of his hard mouth over her soft lips.

His head spun while he kissed her and kissed her in the silence of the barn. He kissed her until he felt her tremble like a leaf, and then his mouth was briefly cruel because of the fever she raised in him. But eventually she stiffened a little and moaned, and he realized that he was bruising her.

He loosened his hold enough to let her feet touch the ground, but her mouth clung to his lips even then.

"Don't stop," she pleaded, her legs shaking as she held to him to keep her balance. Her face hung just under his, yielded and worshiping, her swollen lips parted and faintly red.

"Don't tease," he said unsteadily. "You know how dangerous it is."

"Do I?" she asked dazedly. "But I only want to kiss you," she whispered. "Please, just a little while longer . . ."

"Eleanor, you must stop this!" He dragged her hands down from his neck and stood gasping for breath, fighting the specter of uncontrollable desire.

"Don't you want to kiss me?" she asked, confused.

He ground his teeth together. How could he confess to her that he was dying to have her? That his body ached to bury itself in the warm innocence of hers, that his hands longed for the naked softness of her breasts and her belly and her legs!

"You try me too far," he ground out. Perspiration beaded his broad forehead. He pressed her hands to the front of his shirt and held them there. "Eleanor, go back inside. This is not the hour for us to speak of personal matters. What would your aunt and uncle think if they saw us now, like this?"

She was barely able to think at all. But it occurred to her at once that they would blame him, accuse him of trying to seduce her. He would suffer, not she. No one would believe that she had deliberately tempted him.

She managed to step back from him, her body hungry for the pleasure she had to deny it. "Oh, I am sorry," she said miserably. "I didn't stop to think. You were angry with me, and I wanted you to know that it was Aunt Helen who forbade me to dance with you."

He moved back a step as well, his tall body faintly unsteady as he realized how close to the edge they'd stepped. He'd never been quite so vulnerable before, and he was no novice. She certainly didn't kiss like one, he thought. He was more curious about her experience than ever before.

It was more than possible that she was playing with him, as she'd played with Greely. It might even be a game to her, seeing how far she could push him. After all, he knew that she was well aware of what she presumed was the difference in their social status. If she wasn't just a tease, why was she permitting him these liberties when she knew her aunt and uncle would disapprove? Certainly she couldn't be in love with him. A woman of her background and status wouldn't allow herself to fall in love with someone as unsuitable as she considered him. She was too haughty. No, she had to be teasing, to see if she could make him respond to her advances. She was toying with him, thinking that he was of the same ilk as Greely—a shy, untried rustic.

The thought strengthened his resolve. She needed to be taught a lesson, and he was just the man to do it. She had a sweet mouth. He enjoyed kissing her. But his heart was unassailable. No woman had ever touched it.

"Why did you come out here tonight?" he asked with a lazy drawl, his hands still holding her waist loosely.

"Because I don't like having you angry with me." She looked up sadly. "You must know that I would have enjoyed nothing more than to have danced with you."

She even managed to look repentant, he thought. He saw right through the subterfuge. "But the politician was your social equal, and I was not," he reminded her. "You did not want people to think that you were associating with someone who was socially beneath you. Isn't that the truth of the matter?"

Her blue eyes shimmered with sadness and resignation. It might be kinder to let him think so than to have to admit the truth about her own hopeless infirmity. But she didn't have the heart to do it.

"I cannot put my aunt in such a position," she said quietly. "She is my mother's sister. Both of them came from European royalty. It would ... Forgive me, it would outrage them to know that I allowed myself to become interested in someone who was ... not of our class," she finished miserably. "Oh, can't you see that it is no wish of mine?" she asked, looking up with tears in her eyes. "Can you not feel my heart beat when you hold me, and know that I . . . that I. . . !"

She was drawing him in with those tears, that wobbling voice. But he knew too much about the vagaries of women to be caught like this. He simply played along.

"That you care for me?" he asked softly.

She dropped her eyes to his chest, all but strangled by the mad beat of her heart. "Yes," she said huskily. "That I care for you."

He had to fight to keep from laughing. She was good at dalliance. He wondered how experienced she really was, under her facade.

She glanced up at his set face, trying with her inexperience to read what was there. Her male cousins had hardly prepared her for a contretemps with a man she desired. She wanted to know everything about him. She wanted to be with him all the time. She wanted only him, if it meant the sacrifice of everything she had.

He drew her face up to his and kissed her briefly on the mouth. "You must go inside," he said quietly. "This is not the time for such discussions."

"I do not want you to go," she said. "I want only to be with you."

He steeled himself not to feel those words right through to his heart. He wasn't going to allow her to toy with him. Poor Greely had suffered at her hands, but Cal was no impressionable boy.

She realized at last that he didn't believe a word she was saying. In his eyes was cynicism and some sort of cool amusement.

"Why . . . you do not believe me at all," she said slowly.

"After the way you treated Greely, do you expect me to?" he said. "You looked down your pert nose at me from the moment we met, making so sure I knew that you wouldn't dirty your little hand by touching a common cowboy."

She faltered. "I . . . have lived in such a different world from yours," she tried to explain it. "Even in my travels, I was sheltered from the realities of life. You must allow for my background."

"Why?"

She didn't know how to reply to such a blunt question. Her soft eyes searched his hard face. It was like talking to granite. "I shall try," she said. "Really, I shall. I . . . want to know about your life, about you. I want to understand."

He touched her soft mouth with his fingertip, tracing it lazily until he felt her lips tremble. She was affected by him physically. She couldn't hide that. But whether or not her heart and mind were involved, he didn't know. His eyes narrowed with calculation.

"You have already said that your aunt does not approve of any contact between us," he reminded her.

She caught his hand in both of hers. Forgotten was her illness, her life before now, her wealth and position. She wanted this man as she had never wanted anything before. It would work out. It must!

"I will meet you, in secret," she said fervently. "Whenever, wherever, you say! I will do anything you ask of me."

He went very still. "Anything, Eleanor?" he taunted softly.

She flushed. "Anything . . . within reason."

"And nothing indiscreet?" he persisted. His pale eyes

narrowed. "It is a poor regard which sets such rigid limits."

She gnawed her lower lip. "I cannot be indiscreet," she whispered. "It is not only my own wishes that I must consider. There is my family." Her eyes pleaded with him to understand. "Surely you understand loyalty to your kinfolk? Don't you feel the same responsibility toward yours?"

He did. More than he could admit. But he wanted her completely yielded, so much in love that she would dare anything, risk anything, for him. He refused to consider his reasoning, or his motives. It was suddenly imperative to bend her to his will.

He pulled her close and bent to kiss her with slow, rough hunger. He felt her soft body tremble in his arms and wondered cynically how many other men had experienced her pretended shy passion. An innocent adventuress was a contradiction in terms.

His big hand slid up her side to touch the side of her small breast. She jumped and caught at his wrist frantically, drawing her mouth back in a flurry of embarrassment.

He let his arms fall away and smiled mockingly. "Limits already, Eleanor?"

She clasped her hands together tightly. "No decent woman—" she began.

"Decency has no license here," he said firmly. "A woman who cares deeply for a man thinks less of rigid social conduct and more of giving pleasure."

She moved back a step. She was appalled at his attitude. Surely if he cared for her, he would not ask such a sacrifice. Her whirling mind struggled to focus.

He was losing her. He saw the uncertainty in her face

and moved forward to take her hands in his and lift
them hungrily, palms up, to his mouth. "Forgive me,"
he said smoothly. "I was testing you. I shall not ask any
great sacrifices of you, Eleanor. I want only the pleasure
of your company, the solace of your kisses when I am
lonely. I shall ask no more than you wish to give."

She relaxed with a soft sigh and smiled at him. Her
love grew by leaps and bounds, and she saw rainbows
of happiness ahead.

The sudden brilliance of her eyes, the radiance of her
face, made him feel vaguely guilty. To stay the unwelcome feelings, he drew her gently to him and brushed
his mouth softly over her own.

"You must go inside, my dear," he whispered. "We
must not be discovered like this."

The endearment melted her heart. At that moment
she would have given him anything. Amazing, to find
love in such an unexpected place, and so suddenly. She
looked at him with her whole heart in her eyes.

He smiled. "You are very pretty," he murmured.
"Will you really meet me, against the wishes of your
people?

"Oh, yes," she whispered fervently. "Whenever you
say, Cal."

His name on her lips made his heart leap. That was
unexpected. He chuckled. "What do they say, that love
will find a way?" he teased, liking her blush. "Then so
be it."

Eleanor nodded happily. Love would find a way, he
said, so that must mean that he felt this same incredible
pleasure that she did. She felt as if she glowed.

He held her hand tightly in his and walked with her
around to the front of the house, up to the front steps.

"We must be careful from now on. You must not be seen like this, alone with me," he said gently.

"Yes, I know. But I thought that you were less strapped by convention, Mr. Barton," she replied, teasing.

He looked at her intently in the faint light of the porch. "You will find that I am quite unconventional, in some ways. But your reputation is important to me."

That pleased her. Her eyes twinkled up at him. "You are old-fashioned."

He smiled faintly. "Why do I gain the impression that you are not?"

She shifted from one foot to the other. "I have perhaps given a false impression of my life," she said slowly. "I tend to . . . exaggerate some of my adventures." The sadness in her eyes puzzled him as they sought his. "I have had so little to look forward to," she confessed slowly. "Perhaps I created laurels to rest upon."

"You are young," he protested. "You have marriage to look forward to, children. . . ."

She went very still. Her eyes sought his, and she saw the cynicism there before he could hide it. "Why, you say it as if you think family life is for fools!"

His heavy brows darted inward toward his nose. "Not for fools," he began. "But I have plans that do not allow for marriage."

That was blunt enough. What had she been thinking, anyway, that they would marry and settle together? She could not marry someone like him, and he did not want to marry at all. Just the same, it might happen, she thought stubbornly. She would not relinquish hope now, not just now.

"When you leave for the weekend, I used to wonder if you had a wife and family that you went to visit," she commented.

"I have a family," he confessed, watching her face fall. "Parents and brothers," he amended, and saw the light come back into her face.

"Are you the oldest?" she persisted.

"The middle brother," he corrected.

"And did you grow up in the shadow of the eldest?"

"My younger brother grew up in two shadows, I fear," he mused, remembering Alan's childhood. Alan had never quite measured up to the two fire-eaters who arrived before him, although he had perhaps the kindest heart of the three brothers.

"I have often wished that I were not an only child," she replied. "But it was not to be."

"You have no siblings?" he asked, startled.

"No. My mother has always been delicate."

He studied her with new interest. She changed sometimes before his very eyes. "And are you delicate, Eleanor?" he asked.

Memories of the horrible bouts of fever, for almost a year, echoed in her mind. She shivered. "I must go in," she whispered. She turned quickly and went up the steps, calling a subdued good night over her shoulder. She couldn't admit to him that she was so weak, so impaired physically. Surely fate would not deny her this little spot of happiness in her barren life. If nothing else, she would have the memory of Cal's kisses to sustain her in the empty years ahead!

Cal was nowhere in sight the next morning, and Eleanor wondered if she might have dreamed the night before. Melly didn't question her too closely, but her aunt Helen's eyes had been full of worry, as if she was uncertain about something.

Later that day, while Nora was helping Melly pick up eggs in the henhouse, Melly explained what was disturbing Aunt Helen.

"Nora," she said, as if she were carefully choosing her words, "a telegram has come for you, from your parents. It seems that you have received an invitation to visit relatives in Europe. They say that you may be presented at court, to Queen Victoria herself!"

Nora felt a sudden panic. This invitation could not have come at a worse time. Certainly it would be something quite special to be presented at court to Queen Victoria. But . . .

"Mama is uncertain about whether or not to tell you. You seem to be having such a good time, and you have been very ill," Melly confided. "You are healthy here, and we do enjoy your company so much. We do not wish you to go away so quickly. But it is your choice, of course. I told Mama that I would speak to you, in private."

Nora fingered the folds of her long skirt. How could she leave now, when she and Cal had only just discovered each other? On the other hand, her mother was not going to be best pleased if Nora missed an opportunity to be presented at court.

"You do not wish to go, do you?" Melly asked quietly. "You do not wish to leave Mr. Barton."

Nora's face contorted. "It is hopeless," she whispered.

"Why? He is a good and decent man," Melly said, "regardless of his circumstances. Surely it does not cause you embarrassment that you find Mr. Barton attractive?"

Embarrassment. Embarrassment. Nora didn't want to consider what she was thinking, but she had to. It was the truth. She was embarrassed. Cal Barton was a marvelous ranch foreman. But could she really picture him dressed for the opera or the theater, in white tie and tails? Could she picture him discussing politics with her father's contemporaries, or receiving guests with her in the parlor at her home? Would he know to keep his feet off the furniture, how to act at table, how to behave as a sophisticated gentleman? She was panic-stricken at the very thought of Cal Barton in a parlor. He, with his eternally nasty boots and worn clothes and unshaven face. Her eyes closed on a wave of grief.

"What shall I do?" she asked Melly. "I cannot stay and I do not wish to leave!"

Melly put an affectionate arm around her. "Do nothing for another week or so. Think about it." Her eyes twinkled. "After all, Nora, so much can happen in a week. And I am your ally, you know."

Nora hugged her back. "Your mother would never approve of any connection between Cal and myself. Nor would my parents."

Melly exchanged a complicated glance with her. "They will never know. Will they?"

Nora smiled gratefully. She pursed her lips and studied her cousin. "This . . . compact . . . would not be the prelude to my doing a favor for you in return, of course?"

Melly flushed. "Oh, Mr. Langhorn would never wish to meet me in secret, I am certain."

"As you say, dear, anything can happen."

Melly burst out laughing. "Well, almost anything," she amended. "Shall we think optimistically?"

"Let's," Nora agreed.

Magic, it seemed, was at work on the Tremayne ranch. For Cal Barton did not go away on his usual mysterious long weekend. With Melly's help, he and Nora managed long walks together and even a buggy ride.

"This is wicked," Nora told him amusedly as they jostled down the rutted road in a misting rain. "Melly will get wet waiting for us at the crossroads with the buggy."

"She has both a parasol and a slicker," he reminded Nora. He had rolled a cigarette and was smoking it. He seemed preoccupied, as he often was when they met. He never talked about himself, about his dreams or his family or his home.

"You are very secretive," she commented. "I have told you about our summer home in the Blue Ridge Mountains of Virginia, and my childhood. I have told you about my family. But I know so little about you."

He took a draw from the cigarette. "My past is uninteresting," he said.

She nibbled at her lower lip. "Don't you mean that you have no wish to share personal things with me?"

He chuckled, drawing the horse off the road under the trees and allowing it to graze in the mist. He put on the brake and turned to Nora, pulling her gently into his arms. "On the contrary. I wish to share very personal things with you," he murmured, and his mouth bent to cover hers.

She permitted the shocking entry of his tongue inside

her mouth, the touch of his lean, sure hands on her breasts. The pleasure she felt disturbed her almost as much as the license she permitted him. It was indecent to allow a man such intimacies, but ah, how sweet it was to feel his long fingers tracing around her taut nipples. Even through the fabric, it excited her. He groaned softly when he touched her this way, and she liked the quickening of his breath, the faint tremor of the mouth that kept hers prisoner so hungrily.

But today there was a difference in him. His hands felt for the tiny buttons at her throat and began to slip them out of their loops. She caught at his fingers, protesting.

"Hush," he whispered, teasing her mouth with his as he continued his task. "You love me, don't you?" he asked tenderly, and saw the faint shock in her eyes. She didn't deny it, and his heart raced. "Then there is no shame in permitting me this pleasure."

He made it sound delightfully correct. Even as she felt the dark pleasure wash over her, she might have protested, but instead of his hands on the white flesh he was exposing, she felt his mouth. She stiffened, shocked at the whip of delight he kindled in her untried body. Her hands fluttered at his head and then suddenly caught in his hair and contracted, pulled, pleaded as his lips traced her throat and then her collarbone.

"Cal . . . we . . . mustn't," she choked.

"Oh, but we must," he whispered ardently. His head lifted, just a fraction, so that he could pull away the fine fabric above the whalebone corset she wore and expose the delicate pink-tipped rise of her small breast under her lacy chemise.

It was not the first time for him. There had been

women. But the sight of Nora's firm, pretty little breast kindled something besides passion in him. He looked at it and had a sudden, staggering vision of a tiny mouth suckling there.

The shock was in the pale, glittery eyes that lifted to meet her dazed blue ones.

His thumb and forefinger gently pressed on the hard nub and she gasped, flushing, because she had never imagined that a man might touch her so in broad daylight and look in her eyes as he did it.

"Tell me now," he said quietly. "Is this the first time for you?"

She bit almost through her lower lip. Her wide eyes dropped to her open bodice, to the lean brown fingers on the paleness of her skin. Her breath caught at the intimacy of it.

"Yes, look," he breathed, aroused even more by her reaction. "See how the nipple hardens when I touch it, see how it lifts to beg for my mouth."

That shocked her, and she looked up at him, flushing.

He searched her eyes. "You did not know?" he asked gently. "It is what a man often enjoys most with a woman; the subtle, sweet taste of her breasts in his mouth."

Involuntarily her back arched just a little and her breathing changed.

He knew, without words. Smiling, he held her while his hand moved and his mouth slowly, tenderly, took its place. He began to suckle her, feeling her stiffen and gasp, and then cry out as the waves of sensation rippled through her yielded body. She had no thought of refusing him anything he asked of her.

And he knew it. He felt the violent throb of her heart

under his mouth. There was a small deserted cabin
nearby, just a few steps off the road. A flash of lightning made her jerk in his arms, and he knew then that
it was fated, this interlude. With a small, triumphant
laugh, he climbed out of the buggy and lifted her in his
arms. He refused to think of consequences. He wanted
her and she wanted him; surely nothing else mattered
now! His body was in anguish from the long weeks of
abstinence, and here was Eleanor, in love and wanting
him. Even his thoughts of revenge retreated behind the
fury of his desire for her. He felt it with every step he
took, like a fire in his brain, in his blood.

"Cal," she whispered, dazed.

"Don't be afraid," he murmured against her mouth as
he turned with Nora in his arms and walked toward the
cabin. "It will be our secret. No one will know, ever. I
need you so, Eleanor," he whispered huskily at her soft
mouth. "I only want to lie with you, to hold you in my
arms and feel your mouth under mine. Nothing terrible
will happen. I will do nothing that you do not want."

He felt her relax and had a moment's guilt. She
trusted him, and he knew that he wanted more than
kisses. He could make her want it, too. It was blatant
seduction, but he was powerless to stop himself. He
ached for her, and she loved him; he had accused her of
it, and she had not denied it. Her soft body went right
to his head. Besides, she was a modern woman. Even
though she was more innocent than he'd thought, it
would be no terrible thing for her to know a man. She
would succumb to someone eventually, as women of
her adventurous nature inevitably did. It might as well
be him. He wanted to be her first man. He wanted it beyond anything! He would be gentle with her, as another

man might not be. He rationalized it until it made sense,
until his conscience closed its eyes to the enormity of
what he was contemplating. His body was in control
now, for the first time in his life.

Nora lay trembling gently in his arms. She knew
what he was going to ask of her, and as he carried her
up the steps and into the darkness of the one-room
cabin, she had just enough sanity left to struggle for an
answer.

Chapter Six

THERE WAS A BED IN THE CORNER OF THE ROOM, WITH a ragged quilt covering it. This old cabin was used by the men in the spring, when they rounded up the cows and new calves and had to stay with them to protect against predators on two legs and four legs. Cal carried her to it. His body throbbed with unsatisfied passion as he gently laid her on it and came down beside her.

"Cal, I cannot—" she began.

His mouth covered hers, stilling the words. He knew so well how to stem her fears, how to coax her into permitting him the same liberties she had allowed in the buggy. But now they were even more intimate. Somehow while he was kissing her, he had eased away the fabric from her breasts, and even now, with his mouth suckling her tenderly, his hands were busy with the laces of the corset.

"Oh, you must not," she whispered weakly. Her body sang from the ministrations of his hands and mouth. She was woman, alive for the first time, made of fire and passion, a willing vessel wanting only to be filled and made whole.

He knew that. He savored her like a fine old wine,

treating her to an intoxication of the senses that he knew now she had never known before. She was as inexperienced as he was experienced, but knowing it wasn't enough to stop him. He was at the mercy of his own aching needs, and that was as new to him as Nora's soft cries of surprised pleasure were to her.

She was shy about her nudity, but his warm, slow mouth gentled her, made her responsive again. She was perfectly formed, all soft skin and delicate coloring, and she smelled of roses. Her smooth white thighs were sweet under his mouth and hands. He liked the tiny cries that pulsed from her mouth when he touched her unexpectedly to make sure that she was ready for what must come next.

Her hands delighted in the thick hair that covered his chest. She stroked him convulsively, blind and deaf and dumb to the world around them, to the storm building outside the warm little cabin. She had no thought of the consequences or the future or anything except the heated pleasure Cal was giving her.

When he was as nude as she, the feel of his masculine body against her feminine one was glory itself. She pressed against him lovingly, jerking a little at the evidence of his desire that pressed hard and hot against the delicate skin of her thighs.

Her wide eyes told their own story. He smiled into them through his own excitement. "I am a man," he whispered, rubbing his mouth gently over her lips. "We are constructed to fit together in this fashion. Did you not know?"

"I have never . . . never seen or known . . ." she faltered.

He lifted himself, straddling her rounded hips. "Look at me," he said softly.

Her eyes widened, rounded, as they sketched the masculine contours of his body. "Oh . . . my!" she choked, reddening.

He smiled. "Is it shocking?" He eased down over her, tenderly closing her eyes with kisses as he nudged her legs apart. "You cannot imagine how sweet it will be, the feel of me inside your body," he whispered.

She shivered. Her nails bit into his arms.

"Gently, my darling," he said. He nibbled her lips while he surged gently forward, one lean hand lifting, pulling, so that he pressed at the soft folds that enclosed the mystery of her body. "I would not hurt you for all the world."

She bit her lower lip. "It stings," she breathed, shivering.

"Only for an instant," he murmured, forcing himself to be patient when the feel of her like this was sending the blood careening into his head, through his veins. His body corded like a strung rope. He was barely able to contain himself.

She stiffened again, making it difficult.

His mouth slid down to her breasts and he teased them gently, nibbled and smoothed over them until she began to relax. His hand went between them to coax her body, and all at once she shuddered and cried out and pushed up at him of her own accord.

Her eyes opened wide as he pressed completely into her, and they froze like that, searching each other's eyes in a fever so hot, they seemed to burn together. He groaned harshly, his hips pressing down as he stared at her shocked face.

The movement was sharp, quick, loud in the stillness. Her gasping breaths were echoed in the throat of the man above her. Her lover, she thought while she could. Her lover . . . her lover . . . !

She cried out his name, clung to him, gasped as she matched his movements. But all too soon, his lean body corded and he cried out harshly, his face reddening as he arched backward and convulsed.

She was unsatisfied. She seemed to throb, but there was no relief. She couldn't stop moving, even after he collapsed on her, and she groaned her frustration as the fever only grew worse.

He managed to catch his breath finally, and he rolled sideways, bringing her back to him with a steely hand. "There may be just enough time left," he whispered, covering her mouth with his.

She didn't understand, but it no longer mattered. He moved her, and himself, until he brought a shocked cry of pleasure from her. "There," he whispered roughly. "Yes . . . there."

The rhythm was quick and sharp, as it had been before, but this time, she went up into the stars. Her wild, keening cries were music to his ears. He felt her convulse and crushed her hips into his, holding her there while she jerked like a dying thing in his arms and finally, finally, collapsed in sweat and tears against him.

They rested, and slept a little. And then came the shame.

She dressed in silence, with her back to him. Her body ached from the new exercise it had performed, and there was a soreness that was unfamiliar. There were stains, too, from which she averted her eyes. The hardest part was fastening the corset, which she managed after a fashion. She felt, and certainly looked, disheveled. She didn't know how she was going to explain her long absence to poor Melly, much less her appearance.

Cal took much less time than she did to pull on his clothing. He was smoking a cigarette by the dingy window when she was through.

He felt sickened at his lack of honor. He had seduced an innocent woman, and all because his pride had been stung by her attitude. It seemed a poor excuse now, in the aftermath of such exhausting passion. He had never known such pleasure before. At least he had given her that as well, despite the price he had exacted from her in return. She was no longer virginal, and there was the risk of a child. He had dishonored her and himself.

"Could we leave now . . . please?" she asked in a pale, subdued tone.

He turned, wincing at the expression on her face. Gone was the confident, faintly arrogant young woman who had first come to the Tremayne ranch. This was a shy and insecure girl, whose guilt and shame were clearly written on her downcast face.

He opened the door for her, hesitating when she came even with him.

"I did not mean it to happen," he said quietly. "If you believe nothing else, believe that."

She nodded without lifting her eyes.

"I will stand by you," he added stiffly, "if the need arises."

The need. As if they had not broken rules of conduct, as if they had not sinned and shamed themselves and their families. He was saying that he would sacrifice himself if she had conceived his child, because convention demanded this of an honorable man.

She looked up at him with fury in her eyes. "You would be fortunate indeed if the need arose, would you not, sir? Considering your financial status and my own, I should say that you would feel blessed if I grew large with a child!"

He felt the words to the heels of his boots. She thought he was a gigolo! It would have been laughable if the circumstances had not been so dire. As it was, she only made his guilt worse, and he lashed out at her.

"You have had enough fun at the expense of the men here," he said coldly. "Your treatment of poor Greely made me determined to show you how easy it would be for a man of experience to make a plaything of you. And I have, madam. You were no challenge at all."

She went from scarlet to stone white in seconds, reeling from the accusation. She could not even deny it. She had fallen into his arms without a single protest, but because she loved him. She loved him! And he had no feeling for her, save one of contempt. He had seduced her to avenge his friend Greely. It had been a cold and deliberate act.

"Were I to tell my uncle, he would kill you!" she raged.

"Were you to tell your uncle, he would throw you out the back door," he said coolly. "He and your aunt are convention's slaves. They would sacrifice you without a single thought if it meant risking censure or gossip on your behalf, and you well know it."

She swallowed down her anger, shivering in the aftermath. "I was seduced," she accused huskily.

"So you were, but willingly," he reminded her. He

smiled, but it was no smile at all. "It surprises me, with your sophisticated background, that your first time should be with a poor cowboy. Would it not have been wiser to save yourself for a more worthy suitor?"

She clutched her cloth drawstring purse tightly in her hands, too ashamed to fight anymore. "Take me back," she said in a bare whisper, and walked past him out the door.

He slammed his hand against the door. He hadn't meant to make her more ashamed than she already was, but she enraged him with her superior attitude, with her accusation that he had deliberately seduced her for financial gain. His lack of reason and restraint enraged him even more.

She was in the buggy waiting when he climbed in beside her. She was composed, but so quiet that he was worried.

"You will not do anything rash," he said curtly, his silver eyes blazing at her. "Do you hear me? If you conceive, the child will be mine as well as yours."

Her hands clenched again on her purse. "I would not send my soul to hell by killing myself, sir," she said in a thin voice. "Nor would I condemn a little child to the same fate. Regardless of what you think of me, I am not coldhearted."

He fingered the reins. He couldn't manage to look at her. His chest rose and fell in a long, hard sigh. "We must decide what to do, Eleanor," he said after a minute.

"The decision is mine, not yours," she told him. "I shall go home."

"Home!"

"Home!" she returned firmly, her blue eyes daring

him to argue. "I shall contact you if ... if there is a
need, but I shall not stay here one day longer! It would
turn my stomach to have to look at you again after—"
she swallowed and averted her eyes "—what happened."

His hands contracted on the reins and his mouth com-
pressed. "It would be ungentlemanly to remind you that
you loved what happened," he said through his teeth as
he turned the horse and set the buggy in motion.

She didn't answer him. Her humiliation was complete
enough without that. He had hurt her more than he
would ever know, she vowed. She had been falling in
love while he was only plotting her downfall, exacting
revenge. And even now, he didn't understand that she
hadn't meant Greely any harm.

She wanted to ask him if his revenge had been worth
it, if he felt that his friend was vindicated. But she
hadn't the heart. She was sick at her stomach, her soul,
her mind. How could she have been so stupid? Looking
back, she realized that he had played on her vanity from
the beginning, flattering her, teasing her, when he was
only calculating what would be the swiftest way to her
downfall.

"Stop tormenting yourself," he said tightly as they
approached the crossroads where Melly sat in the buggy
under a tree with the rain slicker wrapped around her.
"Nothing will undo it."

"More's the pity," she said unsteadily.

"For God's sake, don't cry!" he bit off. "If she sees
tears, she will know everything!"

Nora fought the tears, wiping roughly at her eyes.

"Surely you have had encounters with men," he accused, hating the guilt he felt. "I cannot have been the first man to kiss you or touch you as I did."

Her voice wobbled when she replied, "But you were, just the same. I have had no interest in men."

"Because you found none of your social level to ply your wiles on?" he laughed harshly.

She lifted her eyes to his hard, lean face. If there was pain or guilt there, he hid it well. She lowered her gaze. "Because I have never loved," she corrected huskily, and only then realized what she had admitted.

The terrible contortion of his features told her immediately that he knew she loved him. It also betrayed his guilt. He had hidden it well, but no mask could conceal the shock and anguish of knowing that he had captured her heart in his zeal to avenge Greely. He had that to bear, too; that he had not only dishonored her, but that he had broken her heart as well.

His features softened as he looked at her with faint pity. "My dear," he began slowly, hesitantly.

"I am not your dear," she choked. "Indeed, sir, I hate you now as much as it is possible for me to hate anyone! I only pray that there will be no little baby to suffer for our sins, because hell would be preferable to marriage to you!"

While he was absorbing that unpleasant blow, she climbed out of the buggy and ran to Melly and climbed swiftly into the other buggy.

"Heavens, Nora, what happened?!" Melly exclaimed when she saw the condition her cousin was in.

"The storm caught us," Nora said, "and we had to shelter in a cabin. Oh, it was terrible, Melly, the lightning and thunder and the rain as we ran. . . . Cal threw his coat over me, and I am all but disarranged!"

Melly visibly relaxed. "Is that all!" she laughed. "I am ashamed of my first thoughts. We must get home right away! We will tell Mama that we were caught in the storm and sheltered together in the cabin, just in case."

Nora's eyes blurred with tears. "You are so kind, Melly."

"Would you not do the same for me?" she teased.

Nora didn't reply that she wasn't that cruel. She watched the buggy Cal was driving vanish into the rain and they turned and went the other way.

She didn't speak about her need to leave the ranch when they returned, for fear of giving away what had happened. She changed clothes while Melly told the lie they had concocted, and she came back out neat as a pin and smiling through her pain. She looked the same as always, and fortunately the rain had not caused a chill. But inside, she felt dead.

The next morning, after a sleepless night, she approached her aunt in the sitting room.

"I should not mention it, I suppose, but Melly said that I had received an invitation to visit relatives in Europe through my mother," she began.

Helen smiled sheepishly. "Yes, you did. I should have told you before now, but I hesitated to give you an excuse to leave us. Melly has been so much happier since you came."

"I have enjoyed my visit," Nora replied, and smiled back. "But to be presented at court . . . !" She let her deliberate enthusiasm speak for itself.

"I know. I would have been hard-pressed to refuse the chance myself, dear," Helen said gently. She got up and fetched her sister's letter and handed it to Nora. "It is only a few day's delay, you know. I am sorry, but selfishly, I did not want you to go. There. Read it for yourself."

Nora did. It was an invitation to the Randolph estate near London. The only thing that made her uneasy was that Edward Summerville was a friend of the Randolphs, but certainly he would have given up his mad pursuit of her after the thrashing her cousins gave him in Africa. London. The palace. An introduction to Queen Victoria herself and to the Prince of Wales. Perhaps the excitement of it would take her mind off her fall from grace and help her to forget that a man she had loved had betrayed her.

"I must go," she told Helen, turning. "Really, I must. I am sorry."

Helen shook her head. "There is no need to apologize. But I hope that you may want to return to us when you come back, so that we can hear all about it."

"I would be delighted to return," Nora lied. She would never come near the ranch again as long as Cal Barton worked on it. She couldn't stop thinking about what she had done. She had given herself to a common cowboy. Would he brag about his conquest? Her knees went weak at the thought that he might tell other people what had happened.

"You look ill," Helen remarked worriedly. "You are not chilled from the rainstorm?"

"No," Nora said quickly. "I am a little tired, that is all. The storm was very violent, and we were fortunate to chance on the little cabin."

"Indeed you were."

"I must start getting my things together. Perhaps Uncle Chester could drive me in to the depot tomorrow morning?"

"Yes, and you can catch the early train." Helen moved her hands helplessly. "Oh, my dear, I do hate to see you go. It was like having your dear mother with me again, just for a little while."

Impulsively Nora hugged her. "I shall come back again," she promised. Perhaps one day she could, if Cal Barton ever resigned his post. And if there were no terrible consequences to face from her stupidity. It went without saying that her aunt would immediately disown her if she fell pregnant out of wedlock. Scandalous women were discarded by society; even by kin.

Melly helped her pack, looking morose and sad. "I wish you could stay," she said. "How can you go away when you feel the way you do about Cal? Won't you miss him terribly?"

"Why, of course I shall," Nora said, forcing herself to sound carelessly polite. "It has been fun, meeting him in secret. But you know that I could not become serious about such a man, Melly. Honestly, could you see Mr. Barton at the opera in those boots he wears?" she laughed.

The laughter sounded a little frantic. Melly frowned at her. Nora hadn't been the same since yesterday, and her eyes had been red when she came back to the buggy from her ride with Cal.

"He upset you, didn't he?" Melly asked gently.

Nora bit her lower lip, but the tears came just the same. She buried her face in her hands. "It was all for revenge, Melly, all the sweet things he said to me. He told me so. He was getting even for what he thinks I did to Greely. He was . . . taking me down a peg, that was all. He never cared for me. He only wanted to shame me, to hurt me, to make me sorry for making fun of his friend." She sobbed brokenly. "Oh, I hate him," she whispered. "I hate him!"

Melly wrapped her arms around the older woman. "The snake," she muttered. "How could he be so cruel!"

"I never meant to make Greely quit," Nora said. "I only liked his shyness. I was not deliberately cruel!"

"Hush, dear, I know. I know."

"I loved Cal," she confessed in a whisper. "How could he hurt me so?"

"Men are often cruel, sometimes without meaning to be," Melly told her. "Are you certain that he does not love you in return?"

"He said that I was a fool," she wept. "He said that all of it, the flattery and the secret meetings, were only to make me sorry for what I had done."

Melly held her closer. "And this is why you are going home?"

"I must," she said, hiding her fear from her cousin. "There is nothing for me here. In England I will be far away from him. My heart will heal."

Melly wondered, but she didn't reply. Sometimes words only made things worse. She smoothed the chestnut hair and let Nora cry until the tears finally stopped.

Nora's bags were put into the surrey and she said her good-byes to Melly and her aunt Helen while Uncle Chester gave some orders to his men.

Cal Barton came up beside her, hat in hand, mindful

of the curious glance that came his way from Nora's aunt.

"I hope you have a safe trip back to Virginia, Miss Marlowe," he said politely.

"Thank you, Mr. Barton," she said in a thin voice. Her heart beat madly and she had to drag her eyes away from his. She remembered too well her fall from grace at his hands.

"Look at me!"

Her face jerked up, flushed under the glitter of his pale eyes as they sought the ravages of the day before. He said something under his breath, and his hand crushed the brim of his hat.

"Running away will not solve this," he said.

"Neither will staying," she said with the remnants of her pride. "You have nothing to give me."

He looked away, his face hard with control. "My life was planned," he said. "I have dreams of my own to fulfill, and no place for a woman in them. While you," he added, "have no place in your life for a fortune-hunting cowboy. Is that not so?"

She flushed. "I was wrong to accuse you of such a thing," she said miserably. "I know you that well, at least."

His face tightened. "You know me better than you realize," he said. "In every way."

"Do not!" she whispered frantically.

"We went together to paradise," he said roughly. "Can you forget?"

"Do not shame me!"

He hated their audience, even if it was out of earshot. He didn't want her to go. Something must be worked out; surely he could think of some way to keep her here!

"Stay!" he whispered huskily.

She bit her lip. She couldn't look at him, because if she did, she couldn't leave. He didn't want marriage, he only wanted her body. She couldn't give in to the weakness. She loved him, but he felt no such emotion for her.

"I cannot," she said heavily. "I must not." She lifted her eyes to his finally. "There is so much that you do not know about me," she told him plaintively. "I knew that I could never marry or have a child; I had accepted it. I would never have loved . . . if you had not made me!"

He scowled. "What do you mean?"

Her uncle was coming back. There was no more time. It was too late. Too late!

"Good-bye," she said swiftly, and made to climb onto the surrey. Cal helped her. His hand on her arm was like a brand, burning into her heart forever. She sat heavily on the wood seat, hot tears threatening her eyes.

"Ready to go, girl?" Uncle Chester said cheerfully.

"Yes," she said, forcing a smile and waving to her aunt and cousin. "Yes, I'm ready. Good-bye!"

They called their good-byes back, but Cal Barton stood off to one side, his head bare in the sun, watching her leave him. He hadn't loved her, he told himself, he was only guilty because he had compromised her. But that didn't explain the emptiness inside him that grew bigger as the surrey grew smaller in the distance.

══ Chapter Seven ══

NORA SAILED FOR ENGLAND A WEEK AFTER SHE AR-
rived home from Texas. She was pleasant, even
cheerful, but there was a leaden weight in her heart as
she realized how foolish she had been. If there had been
other men in her life, perhaps she would not have fallen
so hopelessly in love with an unsuitable one. And now
she had to wait to know if there would be consequences
from her fall from grace. She had never felt so alone.

The passengers on the ship were friendly enough, but
Nora kept to herself except when meals were served.
She sat at the captain's table and looked elegant and
cool, while inside she tormented herself with memories
of Cal Barton's arms. These polished, elegant gentlemen would never think of allowing themselves to become filthy or smell. They were monied, sophisticated.
But she remembered, so well, the way Cal had looked
with a tiny, lost calf in his arms. There had been a
strange tenderness in his pale eyes that lingered, once,
when he looked at her. She remembered it without
wanting to, because it had been at variance with the betrayal that came later.

Her upbringing had made him like an alien to her. As
a small child, she was not allowed to play with children

who were not in her social set. She had started out to be
a tomboy, much to her parents' dismay, but a strict gov-
erness had taken the spontaneity and impulsiveness
right out of her. She had learned to be ladylike and correct, with exquisite manners. The alternative was a stick
wielded by her father against her legs. Even through her
thick skirts, it was painful. A child must learn discipline, he informed her many times, or it would grow up
to be idle and without morals. She often wished that
there were a gentler way of insuring such traits. She
seemed never to please her father at all, and her poor
legs were constantly bruised in her youth.

Nor had her mother protested these discipline ses-
sions. In such a way she had herself been taught to
mind. Nora secretly thought that if she ever bore a child
of her own, she would never allow it to be treated in
such a manner, regardless of the consequences to herself. Unlike her mother, she would not be cowed by her
husband.

Life was so riddled with rules and codes of behavior.
She wondered how it would be to wear jeans like a man
and ride astride a horse, or to be allowed to socialize
with anyone she pleased. In her childhood she had envied the small poor children who played with mud pies
and rolled, laughing, through tall grass in pursuit of one
another and the ever-present dogs and cats of the poor
sections. Nora had never been allowed a pet. Animals
were nasty, her father informed her. And of course, a
lady never allowed her clothing to be soiled.

She kept to herself until the ship docked in London,
and a carriage took her straight to the Randolph estate
outside the city. It was October now, and the trip over

had been bitterly cold. She wrapped herself warmly in her fur coat, with the bear robe looped over her legs to keep the cold from them. Her hand touched the long, thick, black fur tenderly, and she felt a twinge of pity for the poor creature whose hide it had been in life. All the same, it was pleasant against the chill.

She still had no idea if her body was fertile now. She had never been regular in her monthlies, and she was probably less so now, with the excitement. She missed Cal so much that she felt torn in two.

The Randolph estate was crowned by a seventeenth-century country house that had often hosted royalty. It was cold as sin, but it had an atmosphere of warmth that made Nora feel right at home. Her elderly cousins Lady Edna and Sir Torrance made her welcome from the first. They were minor royalty, for he was a baronet—a title with which he had been presented by Her Majesty Queen Victoria for military service, not an inherited title—but the elderly couple were less stringent about titles and protocol than many others of their stature. They had no children of their own and adored young company, especially Nora. Nora thought it was providential that they had asked her to visit just now, when she so desperately needed pampering. Her mother was kind and sweet, but her father was a businessman who had little time for paternal duties. She had never once dared think about telling her plight to her parents, for fear of being disowned. Her father would never countenance what she had done, or forgive her for it. His opinion of "loose women" was legendary in the family. And while her mother might have been sympathetic, she would never have stood up to the head of the household.

The one kindness in Nora's tumultuous life was that she had not been revisited by the fever.

"I think your doctor is wrong," Edna said firmly while they were sitting in the parlor late at night. "To tell you the fever is fatal! Indeed! I have known two women who contracted it in Africa, and both lived to ripe old ages and had large families."

"Our physician is very knowledgeable," Nora said sadly. "He has never been wrong before."

"And what does a Virginia physician know of tropical diseases?" Edna harrumphed. "The very idea. A colonial doctor."

"Dear, the colonies are now called America," her husband chided gently.

"The colonies," she repeated firmly, "need better physicians. I shall have our own dear physician examine you, my dear."

"No!" Nora sat back and forced herself to appear calm. "I mean, I do not need examination. I feel fine." She could not allow a doctor to examine her, when she had no idea if she was with child. Perhaps a physician might have ways of discovering it even this soon after conception. She knew nothing of medicine.

"As you wish, dear," Edna said gently. "But it is worth thinking about."

"And I shall, I promise you," she vowed.

The glitter of the English court was unlike anything Nora had ever seen. She could still hardly believe that she was to be presented to the queen herself. For days now she had been carefully coached in what to say, how to behave, how to curtsy. There was a rigid protocol that one must follow, and she paid strict attention to her schooling. Her one worry was her sudden tendency to become light-headed. Heaven forbid that she should faint at the monarch's feet!

About Queen Victoria, she had been singularly ignorant, despite her royal cousins. She knew that the monarch had nine children, that she was widowed the year the American Civil War began. She knew that Prince Albert Edward was the oldest of Victoria's children. She knew that Victoria had celebrated her Diamond Jubilee in 1897, and that she was depressed over the Boer War in South Africa and the Boxer Rebellion in China. It was a sad time to come to England, in many ways, and despite the excitement of her day in the palace, a part of Nora was grieving over her betrayal by Cal.

Since the presentation was in the afternoon, Nora wore her best suit, a black silk one with a lacy white blouse and spotless white kid gloves. She wore a pert little hat with a veil, and her mother's diamonds at her throat and wrist. She felt elegant enough in her finery, but her first glimpse of the aged queen set her heart racing and stopped her breath in her throat.

Victoria was eighty-one years old, but she had the unmistakable proud carriage of her position and a mystique befitting a woman who had governed England for over sixty years. She was beloved by her people and respected the world over. Even Parliament deferred to her. But she looked unwell, Nora thought sadly. Poor thing, to have lived so long without the man she loved most in the world. She felt a strange kinship with her, because she was torn apart at the idea of never seeing Cal Barton again.

Her knees shook as she was presented to Victoria, who nodded and smiled pleasantly. She managed the curtsy without falling, although she was less calm than she appeared. A greeting, a quick retreat, and it was over. A moment to last a lifetime, and there were many others on the list who would cherish their few minutes at court forever.

"Well, my dear?" Edna chuckled when they were having tea in a small café a few blocks from Windsor Castle. "How do you feel?"

"Oh, I shall never wash my glove or change my clothes," Nora murmured dryly. "Otherwise, I shall be quite normal."

Edna and her husband laughed delightedly and offered her another tea cake.

The days passed lazily. Nora began to recover somewhat from the journey and the grief that had preceded it. But she made no pretense at wanting adventure. She was quite content to let the servants bring her tea and cakes and magazines, and to sit in the quiet garden without being disturbed. Edna and Torrance were supportive without being intrusive, as if they knew she had been through some sad experience and wanted only to comfort her.

But at night she relived over and over again that afternoon in Cal Barton's arms in the old cabin. She felt his mouth, heard the tortured whip of his breath at her ear, experienced all over again the feverish ecstasy of becoming a woman in every sense of the word. It was a shameful secret. Not only had she sacrificed her virtue, she had committed the cardinal sin of enjoying it. When she went to church, she kept her veil in place and winced at the sermon. She had sinned quite terribly. Perhaps she would go to hell for it. But she had loved

Cal, would always love him. Did that not balance the scales, even a little? And it was not as if she alone were guilty. He had seduced her. She had been innocent, but not he. Surely he had known exactly what he was doing, had, in fact, seduced her deliberately to show her what easy game she was. That was the most shaming part of it; that she had loved, and he had only used her to satisfy a disgusting appetite of the flesh. He had not loved her. And worse, she had not cared. She had only wanted to please him, while he plotted her downfall. She felt unclean.

There was another worry, a secret one. She was late for her monthly; later than ever. And she began to lose her appetite for breakfast. She had always looked forward to the first meal of the day, enjoying her toast and jam and scrambled eggs. But just lately eggs made her sick to her stomach. The terror of pregnancy made her go cold all over with fear. Where would she go? What would she do? Her parents would disown her.

Cal had instructed her to tell him if there were consequences, but she had too much pride. No, there must be some other way. . . . And then she remembered the terrible fever that might recur and became more worried. Could it hurt the baby? She put her hands protectively over her stomach. Already she thought of it as a living, breathing little human being, even though she had no proof of its existence except suspicions. She lay back, shivering with reaction. She had no idea what she would do. She only knew that she must begin making decisions.

A letter came from her mother late the next week, reminding her that she must come home in time for

Thanksgiving. She also remarked that Edward Summerville had come by the house and asked after her. He was on his way to England, and when he tricked her angry mother into telling him where she was, he said that he planned to stop at the Randolph estate and visit her. Her mother was not pleased about this, and neither was her father, but there was little they could do to stop the man. Edward Summerville was the last person in the world whom Nora wanted to see!

As it happened, he arrived that very afternoon, having come over in the same ship with the mail from America. He was greeted warmly by the Randolphs, who made a big fuss over him, while Nora gave him a cold and unpleasant stare.

He flushed as he met her accusing look. He was almost too handsome; blond and blue-eyed, tall and majestic. He even had an impeccable accent. Women loved him. Most women. Nora found him repulsive.

"I hope that you are well, Nora," he said, reaching for her hand.

She withdrew it before he could touch it. "I was healthier before I went to Africa, Edward," she said pointedly.

He let out a long breath. He looked weary. "Yes," he said. "To my shame, I know it. I have had long months to think about my behavior. I regret so much, Nora. I actually came to apologize. Imagine that," he laughed cynically.

She clasped her hands tightly at her waist. "Now that you've done so, I hope not to have to see you again."

He grimaced and shot a glance at the elderly couple sitting by the fireplace, trying not to eavesdrop. "You will break their hearts," he said under his breath. "They sense a romance."

"That would require some imagination," she said pleasantly.

"Ouch!"

"I have no feeling for you, save one of distaste," she said bluntly. "I have been ill most of the year until the summer with fever. I blame you."

"I blame myself," he said fervently. "Your mother told me of your sufferings. I am a cad, Eleanor. But I never knew it, not really, until Kenya." He leaned on the fashionable cane in his right hand, with its big silver wolf's head. "I hope to change your bad memories of me."

"That will take some effort," she said stiffly.

"I realize it. I have been invited to stay," he added, smiling.

"Then I shall leave."

"No." He stood erect. "Please. At least give me the opportunity to make amends, Eleanor. I promise you that I will do nothing to offend you, nothing at all. I want only the pleasure of your company, when you feel inclined."

She hesitated. He didn't look threatening anymore. In fact, he honestly looked repentant. She was lonely. It was probably a stupid thing to do, but after a minute, she nodded reluctantly, and he relaxed. He would keep her mind off Cal, perhaps, if she could forget the horrors she had suffered since Kenya. She was not hardhearted enough to refuse him forgiveness, when he seemed genuinely sorry about his behavior. They said people could change. Time would tell.

* * *

Back in Beaumont, a weary Cal Barton was watching the drill work on the second tract he and his new partner had purchased. Pike was a thin, dark man, a little older than Cal, who'd spent his life looking for a big oil strike. Cal had needed someone to stay at the rig and supervise the men while he worked on the Tremayne ranch and gently guided Chester toward more modern methods of beef production. His heart hadn't been in it since Eleanor left, but he went through the motions. The thing was, he couldn't be in two places at once, and Chester was digging in his heels over that new cultivator.

"She'll be dry," Pike said curtly when they hit water.

"You can't know that. We haven't gone deep enough," Cal argued.

"I know." Pike wiped his face with a dirty sleeve, and his dark eyes met the other man's light ones. "This is familiar territory to me. Water, then nothing. If there was oil, we'd have seen some sign by now."

"Go deeper," Cal snapped. "The geologist I contacted thinks this is an ideal place to drill."

"Geologists don't know everything."

"Neither do water witches," Cal mused, tongue in cheek.

"No? The water witch said we'd hit water here, and we did," Pike reminded him. "Had a divining rod and everything. Willow stick went crazy and jerked him slam into the ground right there where the rig is. I told you we'd hit water."

"We'll hit oil eventually. There have been other strikes in Texas."

"But not here."

"There will be," Cal said flatly.

Pike shrugged his thin shoulders. "We'll keep going down. What happens when you run out of money?"

"We start on your poke." Cal grinned.

Pike gave him a narrow-eyed stare and went back to work.

Cal boarded the next train north to Tyler Junction. He wondered as he rode along how Eleanor was, if she thought about him, if she hated him. Most of all, he worried about her condition. If there was a child, he couldn't leave her to face the disgrace all alone. He had to do something. But what?

He didn't expect her to write him, and she didn't. But she wrote to her people. He waylaid Melly at the back porch a few days later and asked pointedly if she'd heard from Nora.

"Yes," Melly said hesitantly, cool because she knew he'd hurt her cousin. "She's staying in England with some cousins."

He swept off his hat and ran a hand through his thick, sweaty dark hair. His piercing silver eyes met hers. "Is she all right?"

Melly thought he meant the fever, and guessed that she'd told him about her mishap in Africa. "Yes, she's fine," she said. "She has had no relapses."

Cal found the wording odd, but he didn't remark on it. "Is she planning a long stay?"

"She didn't say, but my aunt Cynthia wrote us, very worried because that Edward Summerville man has followed her to England. He wants to marry her, he says." She laughed coldly. "As if Nora would marry a man who . . . who . . . well, who was such a cad as to leave her in the lurch!"

Cal felt the blood drain out of his face. "What do you mean?"

She glowered up at him. "Surely Nora told you about it. He pursued her everywhere. He's very wealthy and he loves her, or says he does. I suppose it's decent of him to finally offer her marriage, but I don't think that justifies the shame he caused her—"

"Melly! Dear, please hurry, the food is getting cold!"

"Coming, Mama!" She threw Cal an apologetic glance and went quickly inside.

Cal stood on the porch with raging emotions tearing at him. Melly had implied that this man Summerville had been intimate with Nora. Had he? He remembered her trembling uncertainty in his arms, her shocked cries of pleasure. But could not that have been faked? She had accepted his body easily enough, and she had gotten pleasure from it. Had he been mistaken about her innocence after all? He assumed that there had been no man, but should a virgin have enjoyed her initiation so much? She had admitted that it stung, just at first, but she could have been lying.

Yes. She must have been lying, he thought furiously. He had whipped his conscience over what he considered his reprehensible behavior, because he had played her for a fool. But it seemed she had played him for a bigger one. She had come west to escape an amorous suitor who had already enjoyed her innocence, and she had found another man. Perhaps she had been trying to find a husband, in case something came of her indiscretion. Was that why she had yielded to him?

But now Summerville had come to heel, which might be another motive for her trip out West. Probably she and her suitor were even now sipping tea in some majestic British country mansion and laughing at his naïveté. Cal could have kicked himself! How could he have been so stupid!

Well, he thought angrily as he slammed his hat on his head and went back to his chores, he knew better now. He knew exactly what she was. And if there was a child, she had no need to come to him with pleas for marriage. He would send her smartly right back to Summerville, the father of any child she might conceive!

The second week of her stay in London passed, with Edward Summerville attentive and kind. Nora didn't completely trust him, even so, and she liked him even less when he began to speak of other women who came and went in his life. He had a cavalier attitude about her gender which Nora found distasteful. It seemed to be her fate to become involved with men whose presence cheapened her.

The queasiness at breakfast had not left her. She had no idea how a woman knew if she had conceived. She had heard her married friends talk, but only in whispers and not specifically about their health concerns. Now Nora wished she had listened more carefully. She wanted to consult a physician, but that would be easier said than done. And it could cause scandal, especially here, where her royal cousins lived. Perhaps, if she went home, she could go to New York or some other large city and visit a physician to whom she was not known. That seemed dishonest, but it was the only way to spare her family a scandal.

She broke the news to her cousins and Summerville

that very night that she was going to book passage on the next ship home.

"Dear, do stay a little longer," Edna pleaded. "We do so enjoy having you with us."

"Indeed we do," Torrance seconded.

"I should love to, really I should," Nora assured them, "but my mother wishes me to be home in time for Thanksgiving. . . ."

"But that is two weeks away," Edna moaned.

"And the ship could be delayed . . . anything could happen," Nora pointed out. "Besides, I will have to help Mother prepare for the family party she always hostesses. Couldn't you go back with me?" she asked.

They shook their heads, because they, too, had engagements to fulfill. But Summerville smiled as he informed Nora that he would accompany her to the States, and hope for an invitation to the Thanksgiving party. Hope would not be enough, Nora knew. Her mother and father did not like Summerville at all, and she still had doubts about him. Somewhere in her mind, she wondered why he had bothered to follow her to London and stay for two weeks. True to his word, he had not annoyed her or attempted to handle her in any way. However, there had been a watchful look about him.

"Something is troubling you, my dear, is it not?" Lady Edna asked her while she was packing that night.

She nodded, pausing in the folding of a gown. "It is Edward. I do not trust him."

Edna sighed. "I must admit, this sudden visit of his is disturbing, when he hardly ever stops to see us." She lifted her eyes to Nora's. "You know that his family has suffered a decline in fortune?"

Nora's eyebrows lifted. "Ah. I begin to see the light."

Edna grimaced. "Forgive me. I am fond of him, but he is not the sort of husband you need. He likes the women too much."

"I know."

"And a woman should not be married just for her fortune," Edna added indignantly. "I had no idea why he was here until I spoke to Lady Winter at the tea party this afternoon. She asked if Summerville was truly in residence here, and I admitted that he was. Then she laughed and said that he had courted most of the eligible women in our circle without success and was contemplating the loss of luxury with despair. Then Lady Sylvia announced that you were visiting, and everyone knew why Summerville was here." She patted Nora's hand sympathetically. "Forgive me. I would not have allowed him to presume on our hospitality if I had any idea of his motives!"

"I know that," Nora said gently. She hugged the older woman affectionately. "Please, think nothing of it. I know Edward very well, unfortunately. It was he who caused me to get the fever, you know. He tore my dress in amorous pursuit, and the mosquitoes got to my skin. John and Claude thrashed him royally, and I had not heard from him for some time. I suppose he thought he might end up a happy widower if he could convince me to marry him," she added bitterly.

"Nora, you will not die of the fever!" Edna said firmly. "Blackwater fever is not that difficult to diagnose, and you would be dead already if you had it. Certainly you would become ill very quickly and have no appetite and no energy."

Nora felt herself go pale. Could she have been

wrong? Could it be the fever, the killing fever, and not pregnancy at all that was causing her condition? She was horrified.

"Now, you must stop worrying," Edna continued, oblivious to her cousin's shocked expression as she began to help find clothes for the maid to fold and put in Nora's cases. "I am certain that the Almighty has not cursed you in such a way. And as for Summerville, why, he is no more than a fly. I have no doubt that your father will settle his hash for him if he has the temerity to follow you home!"

Chapter Eight

THE VOYAGE HOME WAS A DIFFICULT ONE, BECAUSE THE huge cruise ship hit a storm in the Atlantic and pitched and tossed until Nora thought she would bring up her stomach. She remained in her cabin with the ship's physician attending her, and the seasick pills helped somewhat. But she was worried about her true condition, and too afraid to mention it.

The doctor, a kind elderly man, sat down on the bunk beside her and took her hand in his. "Now," he said, when the steward had placed her jug of juice on the table and departed. "Suppose you tell me what is occupying your mind to such a degree, young lady."

She swallowed another wave of nausea and looked up at him with torment in her blue eyes. "I have been . . . indiscreet," she faltered. "I loved him so much. I thought he loved me," she added in a wobbly whisper.

The doctor, who was no stranger to such confessions, patted her hand. "And now you fear that there will be consequences."

She bit her lip. "Yes . . . or . . ." She looked up.

"Or?" he prompted.

"I have had fever, from mosquito bites I received in Kenya on safari," she told him worriedly. "They say

136

that blackwater fever begins with loss of appetite and nausea, which I have."

"How long ago did you contract this fever?"

She told him.

"And how long ago was this . . . ahem . . . indiscretion?"

She told him that, too.

He smiled gently. "My dear young woman, I fear that blackwater fever is going to be the least of your worries. I must get my nurse to assist me while I examine you."

"No, please," she pleaded. "I don't want anyone else to know. My family . . . the disgrace!"

He let out a long sigh. "What sort of a world do we live in, young woman, where being human is such a crime? Very well, I can do the examination alone, if you will permit me?"

She nodded. "Of course."

It was embarrassingly thorough, and when he finished, he was resigned and reluctant to tell her. He lingered over washing his hands in the basin and drying them before he turned.

"I am sorry," he said quietly. "But there is going to be a child."

She sat rigidly on the edge of the bed. Her first impulse was to panic, to jump overboard, to . . . Then she thought of a tiny black head suckling at her breast, and such a wave of love and joy swept through her that tears stung her blue eyes.

"There are ways to manage something like this," he began in a paternal tone. "Adoption can be arranged. I can send you to the proper people. Judging by your manner of dress, you are well-to-do, which will be a help."

"But I do not want to give up my child," she said earnestly.

"A laudable, noble sentiment. But impractical, unless the father will marry you and give the child a name."

She ground her teeth together. Cal would marry her, of course, if she presented him with the fact of a child. But he was poor, and she would have nothing for herself and the child.

Her father would never accept Cal as a son-in-law. Nor would he accept Nora in her condition without a husband. He would disinherit Nora immediately. If she married Cal, they would be forced to live in a shack on her aunt and uncle's ranch, where he worked, and Nora would have to learn to cook and clean and do for herself. It was a nightmare of a possibility. She had become accustomed to wealth and servants. How could she live like a field hand? It might sound romantic to give up her all for love, but it was hardly practical. She would suffer in that sort of environment, and her illness would be an eternal burden on Cal. Cal might hate her for forcing him to marry her. He might not even want the child. She groaned. It seemed that all her doors were closed.

"Think about it," the doctor counseled. "I will tell no one; you may rest assured of that. When we reach New York, I shall give you a way to contact me. You do not have to decide immediately."

She lifted weary eyes. "Thank you," she said sincerely.

He looked concerned. "I have two daughters of my own. This man . . . You still love him?"

She dropped her gaze to the floor. "At the time, I loved him more than life itself," she said hesitantly.

"My dear, if you did not still love him, the child would not be so precious to you," he commented with a smile.

She was shocked. "I could not love a man who betrayed me!"

"Alas, hatred is part of love. Try not to worry too much. And eat properly and get enough rest," he added sternly, closing his medical bag. "You are delicate now."

"The fever . . ."

He turned. "It may recur," he said. "But even if it does, it will not be fatal. You will learn to live with it, as many men did who came back from Panama and Cuba similarly infected. My dear, it is possible to contract malaria even in the southernmost parts of the United States where mosquitoes carry the plasmodia. I have seen more cases of it than I can remember. You will survive, I promise you. Do you take quinine?"

"Oh, yes," she said miserably. "After the first two attacks, I had to, but it makes me uncomfortable. It . . . will not harm the baby?"

He smiled and shook his head. "Of course not. Now, try to get some rest. The seasick potion should help somewhat."

"Thank you, Doctor."

He patted her shoulder. "I wish that I could do more. Good night, Miss Marlowe."

She watched him go with tired eyes. He was kind, and he did at least have hope to offer about the fevers. But what would she do about Cal's child? That was a problem she couldn't solve in the course of one night.

* * *

Edward Summerville watched her very carefully until they docked, and all the way by train to Richmond. He seemed to know about her condition, because he was very solicitous and concerned.

"Are you going to keep it?" he asked bluntly when they were briefly alone on the platform waiting for her father's servant to drive them home.

She went white as she met his knowing eyes.

He smiled cynically. "Did you really think you could keep such a thing secret?" he asked. "The doctor told his nurse. She, after some flattery and a box of fine chocolates, was quite forthcoming." He cocked his head. "Was it the man in Texas? The one I heard you tell Edna about?"

"My child's parentage is my business," she said with bravado. She was outraged at his meddling, at his unscrupulous behavior. He was a scoundrel.

"What will you do if I tell your parents about the child, Nora?" he asked suddenly, with an unpleasant gleam in his eyes. "What if I tell them, in fact, that it is mine?"

"We . . . we have never . . . !"

"We have been together for weeks in England," he reminded her. "And your condition does not show. Yet."

"You could not do such a thing!" she raged.

"My father has squandered my inheritance on drink and gambling," he said icily, his handsome face ugly with anger and greed. "I cannot live a pauper. I will not. You need a husband, and I need a wealthy wife to support me. We will suit admirably. I will be the picture of a loving husband and father, I promise you, and the little brat will never know the truth about his conception."

"I will not!" she said on a gasp.

He turned to see the carriage approaching and bent to pick up his case. He smiled coolly at Nora. "Think of the alternative, Nora. Your father will force you to marry me."

"He will disinherit me!" she corrected.

He cocked an eyebrow. "I hardly think so. After all, I have an old family name, and he knows nothing of our finances. He is a cowardly man about his family name. He will do anything to keep it unsullied, and save his fine reputation. A banker can hardly afford a scandal, my dear."

He was saying no more than she already knew. Her father considered his social position more important than his life. He would do anything to safeguard it, right down to making Nora marry a blackguard like Summerville.

"I will give you until Friday to think it through. If you have not agreed to marry me by then," he added deliberately, "I will make you."

"You will make me do nothing!" she informed him haughtily. But the strain of the trip and her condition had made her weak. She faltered, and he caught her just as she started to crumple.

"Do not fight me," he counseled. "It will do no good. I mean to have you. I meant to have you in Africa, but your cousins prevented me. Now there is no one to turn to, no one to save you. I will have my way, and your fortune. And there is not one thing you can do to prevent it."

Oh, yes, there was, she told herself firmly. She would stop him, somehow. If only she felt better! She was in no condition for a standing fight, but she must manage one, or she would lose control of her own life, and her fortune. What a terrible fate Cal had led her to!

They arrived at her parents' home minutes later, and Edward helped Nora from the carriage and into the house. She was warmly welcomed by her mother, but there was no similar greeting for Edward, who made himself right at home without an invitation.

"Your father will be along directly," Cynthia told Nora, glancing curiously at Edward. "Excuse me, Mr. Summerville, I do not remember inviting you to stay."

He smiled vacantly. "Nora did. Didn't you, my dear?"

Nora glared at him. "No, I did not."

He got to his feet slowly and paused in front of her. "You have until Friday morning," he reminded her. "I'll see you then . . . darling." He bent to brush his lips over her cheek, but she jerked back accusingly, her blue eyes glittery as they met his.

"I shall have the police waiting for you."

"And I shall have a reporter waiting for you," he countered gently.

Nora was white when he closed the door behind him. Cynthia got her to the sofa and helped her to lie down. "Vile man!" she exclaimed, fussing over Nora. "Is it the fever, dear?"

"I feel ill," Nora hedged.

"No doubt, after that long trip." She had the maid fetch a wet cloth and put it gently over her daughter's forehead. "My poor darling. It is so good to have you home. It is lonely with your father away so much at the bank. I fear that it means more to him than I do."

Nora could have assured her that it did. Her parents

lived together but without a spark of warmth between them. Her father dictated and her mother obeyed. It was such a staid, clinical relationship that it had kept Nora from ever wishing to marry, until she met Cal.

She closed her eyes and hoped that Edward would just go away, that he wouldn't carry through with his threat. But she knew that would never happen. He had his eye on her money, and he was certain that he could maneuver her into marriage.

Cynthia assumed that it was the fever making her daughter ill. She sat down nearby and began to speak of commonplace things in her serene tone. All the while, Nora was searching for a way out of her predicament. Just the thought of telling her father what sort of mess she was in made her terror-stricken. And Edward Summerville was going to complicate the situation immeasurably. If only there was something she could do!

But there was, she realized suddenly. It was an unpleasant, unwanted alternative, but it was the only one she had. She moved the wet cloth aside and opened her eyes with a long sigh. It would kill her pride to ask for help. On the other hand, she had very little choice.

She sat up. "Mama, can you send Clarence to the Western Union office for me? I must send a telegram."

"Why, certainly, my dear. To whom . . . ?"

"Please, do not ask me," Nora replied, meeting her mother's eyes. "Trust that I know what I am doing, can you?"

"Nora, is something wrong?" her mother asked. "First that vile man comes back with you, after I had sent him away several weeks ago, and now you arrive looking like death. Please, can you not confide in me?"

"Certainly I can," Nora said comfortingly. "But not just yet. May I have a pencil and paper?"

With a long-suffering sigh, Cynthia fetched them. "My social secretary could take dictation if she were here," she said.

"I can write it myself. And Clarence will need to wait for an answer. It may ... take some time," she added.

"You are very mysterious, darling," Cynthia remarked.

Nora didn't answer her. She was trying to put a novel into a few scant words. When she finished, she counted the words, took a silver dollar from her purse, and sealed the whole in an envelope.

Cynthia was more than curious, but she relented when she noticed the strain in her daughter's face. Something was wrong, badly wrong, and she felt that it had something to do with that Summerville person. He seemed very possessive of Nora, and he was up to something. It must be something unpleasant. He'd said that he was returning to the house on Friday, and Nora seemed to be upset about it. Cynthia would have to ask Nora's father to be at home Friday morning, and he would not like being asked to stay away from work so long. But like herself, he disapproved of Summerville. Cynthia found the man detestable. She hoped Nora knew what she was doing.

Clarence, the yard man, took the message into Richmond and sent it off. It took half the afternoon to get a reply, but he waited patiently until the Western Union man sent for him and gave him a sealed envelope.

When Clarence brought it back, Nora's hands trembled as she ripped open the envelope with a fast-beating heart. She had been afraid that Cal was away, that she would not be able to reach him. Now, at least, she had an answer. She didn't know what his reply would be or what to expect. She couldn't bear to draw it out, either. She could only hope for the best.

The words leapt off the page, terse and without embroidery. "Will arrive midmorning Friday. C.B." That was all. Nothing more. He was coming. She lay back and closed her eyes. It didn't mean that she was safe, but at least she had a chance of escaping Edward Summerville. She had to trust in the Almighty to do the rest.

Cal Barton stepped off the train in Richmond Friday morning, tired and dusty and half out of humor. It had taken everything short of magic to make it here so fast with all the necessary connections between cities. He was tired and sleepy. But he was here. Now he wanted to hear what the hell that terse little message meant. "Need you immediately. Eleanor," it read, and he wouldn't have missed seeing her face for all the world when he admitted that he knew all about her pal, Summerville. No doubt she had fallen pregnant and planned to accuse him of fathering the child. But now he knew about her other beau, and she was going to jump through some hoops. He promised himself she was.

He got a carriage to the Marlowe home, a big brick affair downtown with a big, private yard and a formal garden that was impressive even in the late autumn. It was the sort of house he'd have expected Eleanor Marlowe to live in.

He was raising eyebrows already. He hadn't bothered

to change into his good suit. After all, he didn't need to impress anyone here. He was glad that he was wearing his working gear, right down to the gun belt strapped around his lean hips that he'd been wearing to help the local sheriff hunt for two bank robbers. He'd just signed on as part of a posse when Eleanor's telegram reached him in town. In his jeans and big boots and wide Stetson, his fringed leather jacket and gun belt, he looked like something out of one of Nora's dime novels. The rolled cigarette between his teeth completed the picture as he used the door knocker. The butler who opened the door damned near passed out. Cal grinned at him.

"Howdy," he drawled. "Nora home?"

The butler stared at him as if he couldn't believe his eyes. He stammered. "I—I—I—"

Nora came to the door herself, looking pale and vulnerable, white-faced with fatigue and worry. "That will be all, Albert, thank you," she said gently.

The old silver-haired man nodded politely, fixed Cal with another shocked appraisal, and went back the way he'd come.

Cal stared at her with narrow, cool eyes, a contrast to the churning emotions that looking at her resurrected. She had been ill, that was evident, and the sight of her pale, worn face made him feel both guilty and protective. He forgot his anger when he saw her gesture with a thin hand that trembled.

"Do come in," Nora said nervously. She couldn't keep her eyes off him, but this was hardly the time to throw herself into his arms. "Please forgive me for involving you. I had no choices left."

His eyebrow arched. What a change this was; no comments about his manner of dress, and even an apol-

ogy. She must be desperate indeed. He forbade himself
to look too long at those soft lips as they moved. They
reminded him of the last time they'd been alone together, and the memory was still haunting him every
night. He had missed her more than he thought possible,
despite his anger.

"Nice place," Cal commented as he looked around,
pretending to be stunned by the luxury around him.
"Damn, this is swell! You really are loaded, aren't
you, honey?"

She ignored the banter. She wasn't feeling at all well.
She sank onto the sofa and folded her hands primly in
her lap while Cal prowled around the room, looking at
everything.

Her eyes went to his caked boots, and she only
smiled complacently. He hadn't ever worn the gun belt
before, and she frowned slightly at the worn handle of
the six-shooter it contained.

"They don't have gunfights in Tyler Junction," she
reminded him. "You yourself told me so, once."

He turned, smoking cigarette in hand, a faint smile on
his hard lips as he looked at her with something less
than affection. "We were going out to track down two
bank robbers when the cable came," he replied. "They
killed a woman."

"Oh. How terrible!"

"They'll be lucky if they make it to trial without being lynched," he replied. "Now. What's this deal about
my being needed?" he added.

Those glittery pale eyes made her heart race. He was
looking at her with none of the concern she'd glimpsed
when she opened the door to him. In fact, now he
seemed amused and vaguely contemptuous.

She looked toward the doorway to make sure her mother and father weren't within earshot. It was Friday, and her father hadn't left early as usual, alerted by her mother that trouble was brewing.

"I—I—" she began, trying to form the words.

"Catching, is it?" he drawled. When she frowned uncomprehendingly he added, "The butler had the same problem expressing himself."

She glared at him. "You are not making this easy for me."

"Should I?" he returned. His eyes narrowed. "Where is he?"

"He?"

"Summerville," he replied, smiling when she started. "Did you think that news of his presence in your life would not eventually reach my ears?"

"So you know," she said heavily.

"Yes." His eyes narrowed. "It needs no genius to know that you are with child. Summerville obviously is in pursuit of you, since he followed you to Europe. I sense a connection between the events."

She glared at him. The insult made her angry. "He wishes to marry me," she began.

"Well, I don't want a wife. So what is the need you spoke of when you cabled me? What purpose am I expected to serve in your complicated life if you have a fiancé already?"

Her eyes met his cold gaze. Hope died in her face. He did not care for her at all. He knew what Edward had done to her, and it did not matter to him. She wished fervently that she had never bothered to ask him for help. It was so obvious that he did not wish to marry her. He knew about the baby and he did not want it, either. She could have wept for her foolishness, for her dreams of their reunion. How sad, to love and be rejected so finally, in such a state.

"Oh, there you are, Nora, I—" Her mother stopped dead in the doorway, an older version of her daughter with the same bright blue eyes. She took in the unkempt cowboy filling her living room with shock and then curiosity as she eyed the gun in his holster. "Are you a desperado?" she asked uncertainly.

He nodded, lifting the cigarette to his mouth.

"Have you come to rob us?" her mother persisted.

He looked around with magnificent disdain. "Madam, you have nothing that I want," he said carelessly, and looked right at Nora as he spoke. Her eyes met his bravely in spite of her hurt, and he fought down a twinge of guilt at the pain he saw in her wan face.

Cynthia frowned. "Sir, you speak in riddles."

"A calling at which he is quite adept," Nora said curtly.

He glared at Nora. "Ask your daughter why I am here. It was she who sent for me."

"Mother, this is Cal Barton," Nora said, and she didn't look at him. "He . . . he is Uncle Chester's foreman."

"Oh." Cynthia, conscious of the need for manners even when confronted by a Texas madman, moved forward and extended her hand. "I am pleased to meet you, sir."

"The pleasure is mine, Mrs. Marlowe," he said, and lifted her hand to his lips as if he'd spent his life in a front parlor.

Nora was as shocked as her mother was delighted. She'd never seen Cal in a parlor before, except for her

uncle's. But he wasn't at all intimidated by his surroundings. In fact, he looked right at home.

Cynthia laughed gently. "Do sit down, Mr. Barton,
and let me have some tea brought in. Unless you prefer
coffee?"

"I do, in fact," he replied gallantly, and even removed
his hat.

Cynthia colored prettily at the gesture. "I shall be
right back!" She left, so flustered that she forgot to ask
why Nora had summoned him.

Nora glared at him when her mother was out of earshot. "How gentlemanly," she muttered. "Can you bow,
as well?"

"Only to a lady," he returned with a cold smile.

Her chest rose with indignation, but before she could
find a reply, the door knocker sounded again and Albert
went to answer it.

"More company?" Cal chided, tossing his Stetson
onto the sofa beside her as he hooked a wing chair and
sat down in it, with a pretty candy dish in his lap to
serve as an ashtray.

Nora turned and looked worriedly at the front door as
it opened to admit Edward Summerville. He looked immaculate in his suit and bowler hat. He removed the hat
from his blond hair and moved into the living room after Albert grudgingly announced him.

"Nora, my sweet," he greeted, trying to catch her
hand. She withdrew it out of his reach.

"I am not your sweet," she said coldly. "And I am
not going to marry you."

"Why, yes, you are," he replied, and cast a curious
glance at the cowboy in the wing chair. "Who is this?"

"This is Callaway Barton," Nora introduced. "And

that is enough small talk. Shoot him, please, Mr. Barton."

Both men looked at her blankly.

"You may shoot him in the foot, if you prefer," she continued, talking matter-of-factly to Cal. "Through the heart would suit me better, but I am prepared to be lenient. Now, if you please," she persisted, waving her hand toward Edward.

Edward's blond brows arched wildly. "Nora . . . !"

Cynthia rejoined the group, laughing gaily at something Mary, the maid, had told her. But the smile faded when she saw the tableau before her.

"Why, Mr. . . . Summerville," she stammered, glancing from him to Cal Barton, who was sitting cross-legged in the chair.

"Do close your eyes, Mother," Nora said calmly, "while Mr. Barton shoots Edward for me."

Cynthia's intake of breath was very audible. She sat down heavily in another wing chair. "Nora. My dear . . ."

"I cannot shoot a man for no reason," Cal burst out, dumbfounded.

"I have a reason," Nora said hotly, glaring at Edward. "He has insulted me, humiliated me, endangered my life, and just yesterday he attempted to blackmail me into marriage!"

Edward gaped at her. "You are unwell!"

"I must agree," Cynthia said, dazed. "Nora, would you like to lie down, dear?"

"No, I would not," Nora said shortly. "It is lying down that is the cause of my present predicament," she added with a furious glare at Cal Barton, who ground his teeth together at the innuendo.

"None of this makes sense to me," Cynthia began.

"What is all this racket?" demanded Nora's father, joining the group. He looked even more irritated than usual, especially when he saw Cal. "Who is this cowboy?" he demanded. "And what is this scoundrel doing here, Cynthia?" he added, glaring furiously at Summerville.

"Why don't you ask me, Father?" Nora muttered. "Or do you think I haven't enough brains to answer you?"

"Nora, be quiet!" her father snapped. "Summerville . . . ?"

"I think the crux of the matter is that Nora doesn't want to marry this fancy dude," Cal drawled, gesturing toward Edward with his cigarette as he finally began to understand the situation.

"No?" Edward asked haughtily, feeling brave. "Well, she will. Won't you, Nora?" he added meaningfully, and the threat was in his very posture. Seeing it, Cal had to resist the urge to get up and punch him.

Nora took a deep breath. "No," she said. "I do not wish to marry you, Edward."

"You have spent weeks with me in England," Edward said, making sure the others got the implication. "And," he added smugly, "you are with child."

There was an outcry that could be heard upstairs. God knew what the servants would say, Cynthia was thinking.

Nora's father looked dangerous. He turned on her. "Is this true?" he asked with cold fury. "Answer me!"

Nora sat up very straight, and it didn't show that she was shaking inside. She looked up into her father's eyes with the last of her courage.

"Yes," she said wanly.

Her father's open hand shot out immediately and caught her on the side of the face. The sound of the slap, along with her gasp of pain, echoed around the room.

=== Chapter Nine ===

BEFORE THE SOUND OF THE SLAP DIED, CAL BARTON had erupted out of his chair with smooth grace and Nora's father was lying flat on his back on the floor.

"You son of a—" Cal bit off the rest. He stood over the older man, his big fists closed and waiting at his sides, looking every bit as dangerous as the desperado Cynthia had first mistaken him for. "You touch her again and I'll break your damned neck!" He didn't even raise his voice, but the threat in it was blatant. His posture alone was intimidating. Added to the cold menace of his pale eyes and the authority with which he spoke, even Summerville took a step back.

Marlowe sat up slowly, incredulous, holding his cheek where his muttonchop sideburns stuck out. The man standing over him looked capable of any sort of violence with that low-slung gun belt. But he wasn't threatening to use the gun. He seemed not to be aware of it. Marlowe struggled with a niggling respect for the man, despite his sore jaw. Not that he regretted his action; Nora had deserved that blow, he thought with remaining outrage at her scandalous behavior. The whole family would be disgraced because of her! He would never be able to face his social equals, and lurid tales of her would be told at local clubs. The thought was insupportable!

Nora's eyes brightened as she nursed her sore cheek. At least Cal cared enough not to let her be manhandled. That was something. And it didn't offend her one bit to see her overbearing father sitting on the floor with that flabbergasted look on his face. Imagine, hitting a pregnant woman!

"The child is mine," Edward Summerville announced loudly. "I am willing to marry Nora, to make it legitimate." He moved a little farther away from Cal as he spoke. The man looked vicious.

Cal glanced at Eleanor, and what he saw in her face contradicted all the things he'd thought up until now. She might have been away with Summerville, he might have wanted to have an affair with her. But that briefly noticeable light in her eyes was unmistakable. Despite everything, she loved Cal Barton. And feeling that way, she was hardly likely to climb into another man's arms. He knew it, deep inside himself, regardless of Summerville's claims.

"No," Cal said quietly. He never took his eyes from Nora's. "The child is mine. And Eleanor will marry me, as soon as I can arrange it."

Eleanor's eyes softened as she searched his.

Her father was outraged again. "My child, marry a common cowboy?!" Mr. Marlowe burst out. "Why, I won't have it!"

"What will you have?" Cal asked coldly. "This dandy as a son-in-law?" He jerked his thumb toward Summerville. Summerville bristled, but he wasn't quite brave enough for a comeback. The man was wearing a big pistol, after all, and he was no fool. Summerville had no wish to join Mr. Marlowe on the floor.

"Edward has no income," Nora added. "He told me that his father has gambled away his fortune. He had in mind marrying me to regain it through you, Father," she said brutally. "The child is not his. I would never allow such repulsive hands to touch me!"

Edward colored. He glared at Nora. "You would marry this beggar? A man who dresses like a tramp on the streets, who does not even know to clean his shoes before he enters a decent home?" he taunted. He moved back another step, just in case. The cowboy looked vaguely murderous. "And where will you live, Eleanor, in a tiny shack? You will have to cook and clean; you will have no servants, no money."

Nora's face had gone a shade paler, but she didn't say a word. She just sat stiffly on the edge of the dark blue velvet-covered sofa, staring into space, unmovable. She had thought of those same things, but she really had no options left. Cal did believe her. That was all that mattered just now.

Cal watched her expression closely. The child might be his. She might even love him. But she was still high society, and it was all too obvious that she didn't think he was good enough for her. She wasn't alone. Her parents were looking horrified as well. He smiled coldly. Well, Miss Eleanor Marlowe could marry him and come back to Texas, but not to the wealth of Latigo, the family ranch near El Paso. Oh, no, there would not be that elegant, monied setting for Miss Marlowe of Richmond. She could come and live with him in the foreman's cabin on the Tremayne ranch and learn how to become a human being and stop looking down her nose at people she considered to be her inferiors. If he had to be robbed of his freedom because of their mistake, she would have to give up her life of luxury. It would be an even trade.

He was taken back to his own childhood as he stared at the older man, remembering one brief setback in his wealthy life when his father had very nearly lost everything. The family had been, just briefly, poor. A wealthy family in El Paso, the Tarletons, had been puppy-friendly while the Culhanes were powerful. But that attitude had changed abruptly when they were approached for a loan by a stiff-necked Brant Culhane when his fortunes sagged. Their attitude, though rare for El Paso, had left a deep scar on Cal's young emotions. The youngest Tarleton boy had been friends with King and Cal. But soon after the financial blow suffered by the Culhanes, he told them that he had no desire to play with poor children. He made fun of the boys at school and generally made their lives miserable for the two years it had taken Brant to recoup his losses and regain his wealth.

Even now, remembering the taunts and gibes made Cal bristle. He had taken them to heart even more than King. When the Culhanes were wealthy again as the cattle market improved, the Tarletons found themselves the outsiders at local social gatherings. They were never again invited to Latigo. The youngest Tarleton boy was automatically excluded from any of the boys' parties. But it was little recompense for the humiliation the Culhane boys had suffered at his hands.

While Cal was reminiscing silently, Nora's father got to his feet at last. He glared at Cal, but he walked well around him. "I shall not countenance such a marriage," he said curtly. "If you marry this ruffian, I wash my hands of you forever!"

"Oh, no, my dear, you can't," Cynthia wailed, finding her voice all too late. She had paled and started forward when he struck Nora, but she was much too intimidated by her husband to protest anything he did very strongly. She always had been.

"I can, and I shall," her father said uncompromisingly. He looked at Cal with cold eyes. "I shall not allow my daughter to marry so far beneath her. She will marry a man of our own class and social level."

Cal lifted an eyebrow at Nora. "So that's where you learned it," he murmured. He looked at her father. "It seems to me that it's a little late to be so choosy. In another month or so, her condition is going to be very noticeable indeed. In fact," he mused, noticing the faint thickening of her waistline, "it's beginning to show already." He found it amazing that he should feel a skirl of pride at the sight of her belly.

Nora gasped and covered her waist, while her father's hands clenched at his sides.

Edward surveyed the general area and shrugged. He put on his hat carefully. "Well, I wish you joy," he told Nora with a venomous smile. "When you tire of living like a slave, I might give you a second chance, Eleanor. If you are still . . . able to marry again."

That was a veiled reference to the fever, and Nora paled. Despite the doctor's reassurance, she had no real optimism about the future. She was afraid not only for herself, but for her baby.

"Someday God will pay you back for your part in my suffering, Edward," she said in a whisper. "I promise you. Cruelty finds its own punishment, eventually."

Edward only laughed, until he noticed the movement Cal made. He moved quickly toward the door. "I must be about my business. Good day."

When he was gone, only the four of them remained.

"I have . . . had Mary make coffee," Cynthia began.

Her husband's face was flushed, and the cheek that Cal's fist had found was very red. He turned to his daughter and looked at her with icy contempt. "Get your bags packed and get out of my house, you hussy," he told Nora. "You will never receive another penny of support from me. You can turn to your . . . lover for that. And for whatever else you need. Never come here again. You have disgraced me!"

He left the room, slamming the door behind him.

Cynthia was in tears. "Oh, Nora, how could you do this to us?" she asked miserably. "We tried to raise you to be a good girl, you were brought up in a Christian manner. . . ."

Cal had had enough. Having seen her home life, he understood Nora much better, although Summerville's veiled references still puzzled him, as did Nora's parting remark to the man. He would have to ask her what that was all about, when he had the chance. Right now, getting her out of this hellhole was most imperative. She looked sick.

"Get your things and let's go, Nora," Cal told her gently, helping her up from the sofa. He couldn't remember a time when he'd felt more protective, or possessive, of anyone.

Nora didn't argue. She went past her mother, sick at heart and trembling all over. Fortunately most of her bags were still packed from her trip overseas, and all Albert had to do was take them out onto the street where Cal obtained a carriage. She left behind the things that were unpacked, without regret.

Cynthia walked out with them. "Oh, Nora, how could you!" she wailed. "How could you shame us so, after all your father and I have done for you! How ungrateful you are!"

Nora looked at the older woman as if she had never seen her before. She was being made to feel like a condemned prisoner, without friend or solace in all the world. She lifted her chin proudly.

"You never defended me," she accused. "All my life, anything he chose for punishment met with your approval. Even this," she added, holding her red cheek.

Cynthia wrinkled her handkerchief. "He is my husband," she said miserably. "It is my lot in life to do as he wishes. Besides, Nora, he is right, you know; you have ruined us."

Nora bristled. "And it is your social status, and father's, which matters most to you, is it not?" she asked quietly. "My condition and that of my child does not concern either of you. I am outcast, discarded because I might cause embarrassment. I tell you that no daughter of mine would ever suffer such a fate in a similar condition, not if I were hanged from the nearest oak limb for defending her!"

Cynthia paled and clutched her handkerchief. "Oh, my dear, you do not understand. Your father's business, his wealth—"

"It says in the Bible that it hardly profits a man if he gains the whole world and loses his own soul, doesn't it?" Nora asked. She watched the flush ran over her mother's delicate features before she turned and was

helped into the buggy by Cal, who had never been
prouder of her.

He took the reins in hand with a cold, speaking
glance at her mother. "One day," he said very quietly,
"you will have much cause to regret your actions. And
so will your husband." He nodded politely to her
mother, without speaking, and started the horse moving.
He was thinking ahead, to the time when Nora would
know the truth, and so would her family. They might be
well-to-do, but their finances were a pittance in compar-
ison with the Culhanes'.

"Don't let her see you break down," he said quietly
when her voice broke on a sob. "You've got guts, I'll
give you that." He glanced at her red-eyed face. "And
you'll need them, where you're going."

She didn't reply. She wiped her tears and composed
herself. Even when they were well down the street,
Nora didn't look back. That part of her life was over.
Somehow she would have to learn to live in a world
drastically different from her pampered one.

They were at the train depot before she spoke. On the
way, she had begun to think about Cal and what she
must have cost him by pleading with him to come all
this long way. Besides that, there was the position she'd
placed him in, surely an uncomfortable one. He didn't
want to marry her. He had rescued her, after a fashion,
but she could hardly ask him for anything more. She
would have to learn to take care of herself. Was that not
what being a modern woman was all about? Perhaps
she could be what she had dreamed of being, despite
her condition and her infirmity, if she only had the courage to defy convention and fly in the face of gossip.

"I have been a great expense to you," she said in a drained, ghostly voice. "But I have a little money saved. I can pay for your train ticket at least." She fought tears as she took a steadying breath. "I only needed your help to escape being forced into marriage with Edward. I will be fine. I can go to New York and find some sort of job there."

Cal studied her profile quietly. "The child is mine."

It was a question. Her head inclined, still without turning. "That is true," she said. "But I don't hold you entirely responsible. The fault was mine as well. You don't have to sacrifice your freedom."

He sat back in the carriage and fingered the reins, staring ahead blankly. He hadn't planned to marry and have a family, not for a long time, if ever. This development was interfering with all his dreams. But how could he desert her now? He felt violent anger at the memory of the things her father had said to her, at the way he had hit her. How dare the man treat his only child in such a vile way? It infuriated him.

"If you could help me get my bags on the train . . . ?" she asked.

He turned and looked at her. "The only train you're getting on is mine. We'll be married along the way, so that we won't shame your kinfolk by announcing your condition to a local minister."

She closed her eyes on a wave of shame. She hadn't thought of that aspect of it. She would be rejoining her aunt and uncle, but in a vastly different manner. Instead of a welcome guest, she would be little more than a servant. Her pride stung bitterly at the thought. "It's not necessary," she began, looking for a way out.

"The child should be our primary concern, not our

own welfare," he reminded her bluntly. "It didn't ask to be created."

She flushed, remembering that frenzy of creation that had occurred. "You don't want me."

"I don't want a wife," he said stiffly. "But I'm not so dishonorable that I can leave you to the mercy of strangers. Come."

She followed him to the platform, standing back while he bought tickets. Her eyes lingered on his tall, broad-shouldered form warmly, loving the strength and size and authority of him. He had an air of command about him, something she decided that he had acquired while serving his country during the Spanish–American War of '98. But it was more than that, too. He spoke with such authority, as if he were used to people jumping when he made demands. And he hadn't hesitated to strike her father when he attacked her. Amazing, that he had no fear of a rich man. It delighted her that he was so fearless. She knew him in a physical way, but actually she knew nothing about him.

He turned, tickets in hand, and escorted her to a seat inside the depot on the smooth wooden benches with their curved backs and arms. She ran her hand over the wood while she sat, waiting.

"Would you care for a soda or some tea?" he asked politely.

She smiled impishly and didn't look up. "Actually, I think a neat whiskey would be more in line with the way I feel, except that I have never tasted spirits in my life."

He sat down beside her, the gun thudding as it brushed the seat. He moved it carefully and leaned toward her. "Are you all right, Eleanor?" he asked gently.

Surprised, she lifted her eyes to his, tingling as she met them at closer range than she'd expected. She laughed a little nervously. "Of course. Thank you for coming; for defending me." Her thin shoulders lifted and fell as she rested her hands in her lap. "I would have fought my own battle, had I not been so ill from the return trip."

"You would not have been up to your father's weight, I fear," he said, glowering as he remembered her cheek. He touched it, lightly. "Does it still hurt?"

"It is only sore."

"That was unforgivable," he said tautly, stroking the soft flesh. He watched her lips part, heard her breathing quicken, and he smiled as she tried to hide the reaction he provoked. "Is this a common thing for him to do, Eleanor?" he added.

"No," she said. "He used to use a cane on me, when I was younger, but he was never brutal," she added quickly.

He looked shocked. "A cane?!"

She shifted. "Why, yes. Isn't it the usual thing for a child to be struck for infractions?"

His jaw tautened and his pale eyes narrowed in anger. "Not a girl child," he said roughly. "It is outrageous!"

She smiled. "He has not done it for many years. Now he only swells up in the face and blusters at me, as a rule. He cares, in his own way. So does my mother." She remembered their horror at her condition and their censure, and tears stung her eyes. She turned her face away to hide them.

"You were never allowed to play with dirty children, were you?" he asked suddenly.

"With those of the lower classes? Of course not," she

said at once, and watched the light go out of his face. She grimaced. "I am sorry. That was rude."

He looked away. She had a long way to go, he thought irritably, and it was going to be a difficult road for both of them. "How about that tea?"

"That would be lovely. Is there a tea shop close by?"

"Yes. And something even better," he added, as his sharp eyes spotted a sign hanging over a doorway just down the street. "Come."

They left the bags with the porter, since the train was not due for an hour—at least—and he escorted Nora down the long wooden sidewalk to a small house apart from the row of shops.

"Here?" she faltered, holding back.

He nodded solemnly. "Here. We might as well get it over with," he added under his breath.

That comment hardly alleviated Nora's own misery as Cal led her inside.

It didn't take very long. The justice of the peace listened to Cal's tale of woe about the two of them having to go all the way to Texas under a cloud of scandal since they weren't married and wanted to be. Nora's reputation would be ruined. He mentioned nothing about her condition, but went on and on, until the justice of the peace's little wife was in tears.

"Why, of course, I shall marry you at once!" the small, elderly man said, and his wife patted Nora's shoulder comfortingly. "Step right in here, Mr. Barton, and we shall fill out the necessary papers."

Cal hesitated. He was going to have to do some fancy talking here, for sure. He couldn't marry under an assumed name, but he had no intention of letting Nora know his surname. He and the justice of the peace filled out the papers, but Nora signed before Cal's last name was added. Cal made sure that he had the license, not her, so there was no chance that she might see her true married name.

The ceremony was very brief, just the usual marriage service, and Nora stood beside Cal—who had taken off his gun for the occasion—in a miserable silence while the words were spoken. She had always envisioned a huge society wedding with all the right people attending, and herself gowned by Worth with a spray of white roses in her hand. Here she stood with a single yellow chrysanthemum, which was the only live flower the little woman could procure for her. She was wearing her oldest gray dress, not even a white one, and had not hat or veil because she hadn't time to search for the hat that matched this garment. In fact, the dress was already too tight in the waist; if it hadn't been a little big and belted to fit in the past, she wouldn't even have been able to wear it. She was pregnant, and the man at her side didn't want her. She felt as if she were being sold into slavery, and it was her own fault. She wanted to bawl.

And she did, when the justice of the peace declared them man and wife. She didn't even have a wedding band. Nor had Cal moved one step nearer when the little man invited Cal to kiss her.

Cal looked down at his reluctant bride and saw the tears rolling past her mouth. His teeth clenched. He produced a handkerchief and slowly dried the tears.

"I didn't even have a proper dress, whether or not I deserved it," she whispered miserably, "and no bridesmaids or a bouquet or a minister. . . ."

Cal's face froze. "Well, you have a husband, at

least," he said sharply. "A woman in your condition should be glad of one!"

She gnawed almost through her lower lip and couldn't look up. He was furious. She felt the anger as a tangible thing.

"There, there," the justice of the peace comforted her, "it's a very emotional moment, isn't it?"

Cal said nothing. Her hasty words had made him aware once more of her condescending attitude toward him. Had he not precipitated this crisis by seducing her, he felt certain that she would never have married him. She would have been counting his money and checking the social register before she agreed to consider it.

Summerville was much more her sort. But she found the man repulsive, didn't she? And, too, there was the matter of those veiled remarks she had made about the man. He glanced at her as she stood talking to the minister's little wife, his eyes narrowing on her slender body. She was pretty and elegant, but except for that afternoon in the line cabin, he had thought her oddly cold. She had been a surprise and a delight to him, with her unexpected complexities. He remembered so vividly the way she had comforted him when he returned from the devastation of Galveston. But he also remembered her attitude toward his work and his clothes. She had been taught to be a snob. He wondered if she could be untaught.

His parents would never understand this lightning marriage. They would have to be told, and his mother would be outraged that her son had ruined a decent woman and had to marry her to save her reputation. She would be good for a fifteen-minute tirade when he finally went home. And as he looked at Nora's shattered face, he wondered how she was going to react to the news that she'd married a very wealthy man.

He would have to tell her eventually. But not right away. He couldn't risk letting the cat out of the bag until he finished gently guiding her uncle into more modern methods of cattle production. There were still a few details he had to work out with Chester. Then Miss Eleanor Marlowe—no, Mrs. Eleanor Culhane if she did but know it—was in for a few surprises.

He took her to the small tea shop and ordered sandwiches as well.

"I could not eat a thing," she said wearily.

"But you will, Mrs. Barton," he replied. "I want a healthy son."

She flushed and glared at him. "Have you told God yet?"

He chuckled at her unexpected fire. "Not yet," he admitted. His pale eyes narrowed on her thin face. "You haven't had an easy time of it, have you?" he asked with quiet sympathy. "The trip overseas must have been an ordeal, coming and going. And I gather that Summerville was present all the time?"

She shook her head as she stirred the tea in the china cup with a distinctive Rogers silver spoon. "He found out from my parents that I was in London and followed me there. His family was friendly with my relatives, the Randolphs, who invited him to stay." She lifted her eyes to meet his. "I detest him. Was it Melly who told you about Africa and what happened there?"

He scowled. "No. What about Africa?"

Her hand stilled. "But you said that you knew about Edward."

"I knew that he was in Europe with you," he said flatly.

That put a different complexion on things. She didn't know what to say now. It was easy enough to tell him, but why put that burden on him, along with the others? Why inflict a worse ordeal than he already had to endure by informing him that he had married an invalid? His poor fortunes were worsening, because now he would have to support her. If she became ill, what then? How would he work and care for her? He was a proud man. It would devastate him. She stifled a sob as she realized the misery she had caused everyone by not being strong enough to refuse him in the cabin that day.

"Are you thinking about the wealth you gave up to marry me and regretting your hasty decision?" he asked when he heard the small sound and misinterpreted it. "Summerville might take you yet."

"You are my husband now," she began.

"And divorce is as unwelcome a prospect as unwed motherhood to you and your family, of course," he said curtly.

"Oh, you infuriate me," she retorted with a cold glare. She sipped her tea, enjoying its warmth. "I was looking forward to a grand party at Thanksgiving with my family and friends at our home, and now I shall eat beef in a cabin instead!" she said with deliberate hauteur, striking back at him where she sensed it would hurt most.

"Not beef, my dear," he informed her blandly. "Turkey. Wild turkey. I trust you can cook. I have no culinary skills."

"Cook?!"

The look on her face brought a smile to his. "And

clean," he added. "And wash and iron and the other things that Texas wives do so cheerfully and with such pride."

"My aunt . . . !" she began.

"Your aunt is now your social superior, or hadn't you remembered that you are the wife of her husband's foreman?" he said with deliberate sarcasm. "Imagine that, Mrs. Barton. Far from eating on delicate china, you may well find yourself working in the big house, washing it." He leaned forward. "And as to the turkey, not only shall you have to cook it, my dear. First you shall have to catch it, and kill it, and clean it!"

Chapter Ten

"**O**H, FOR GOD'S SAKE!" CAL MUTTERED AS HE KNELT to support Nora's sagging body in her chair while she struggled back to consciousness.

She could barely breathe for the corset. How she hated the old-fashioned contraption!

"It's this damned thing, isn't it?" he murmured, plucking at the corset under her dress. "It can't be good for the baby, Nora."

He'd used her nickname, and tenderly. If she hadn't been so faint, she might have enjoyed hearing it in his deep, slow voice. She pulled herself up by the edge of the table and leaned her head forward, trying to get blood back into her head. The nausea that came with it was the worst.

"Speaking of things that are not good for the baby, I would number among them telling me that I shall have to kill a turkey!" she said angrily.

"I'll wear a gag," he said irritably. "If the mere mention of preparing food disturbs you, we will probably both starve to death."

He sounded so male that she began to laugh. His temper wasn't frightening like her father's. Sometimes it was even amusing.

"There, you sound more chipper," he said, relaxing a little. He rubbed her hands, bringing circulation to them. "Are you all right?"

She nodded. "It's the heat, I think, as much as anything," she said.

"This nice cool place?" he burst out.

She remembered East Texas and how hot it had been during her visit. But it was November now. Surely . . .

His face told the story. "East Texas has very mild winters," he said gently. "And it doesn't get very cold."

"Well . . . that might not be so bad."

"It's almost time for the train, and you have eaten nothing. I'll have them pack the sandwiches. We can eat them on the way."

She laid a hand on his sleeve. "I can't."

He clasped her fingers gently. "You shall," he said softly, "if I have to feed you every bite myself." She colored prettily and his eyes twinkled. "Oh, you like that idea, do you? Is it romantic, do you think, to have your husband put tiny bits of food into your mouth?"

She colored even more. "Stop!"

He chuckled. "In some ways, you are far younger than you look. Wait here."

She loved him when he was protective and gentle with her. It was such a change from his usual mocking way. Of course, she mustn't allow herself to become dependent on him. And as for the future . . . well, that would have to be taken one day at a time. Her aunt Helen had adapted to a wild, rough life. Perhaps Nora could, too. She still worried about the reception they would get when they arrived.

"Have you cabled them that we're coming?" she asked uneasily, once they were in the private compartment Cal had arranged for them. The train went all the way to St. Louis, so they didn't have to change until then. She worried aloud at the cost, but he had waved away her comment.

"Of course I cabled them," he said. "I work for your uncle, remember?" he added deliberately.

She flushed. "I could hardly forget." She shifted uncomfortably. The sun was setting and she felt sleepy.

"Why not lie down, Nora?" he invited. "I can turn down the berth for you."

She looked at him blankly. It would mean getting undressed, of course, and they would be sleeping in the same room. Would he want . . . Would he expect . . . ? Her wide eyes and flushed cheeks told him what she was thinking.

It irritated him. "You are in a weakened condition and ill," he bit off. "Do you really think that I would consider insisting on my conjugal rights now?!"

She linked her hands together tightly. "Forgive me," she said unsteadily. "I am . . . I am tired and not thinking clearly. Of course you would not."

He moved her gently aside and prepared the berth for her, right down to turning down the sheets. He closed the blinds as well, shutting out the sparse traffic down the hall.

"I'll go to the smoking car while you change into your night things," he volunteered before she asked. "Take off that damned corset, will you?" he added irritably. "It's insane to expect a woman carrying a child to wear such a torturous garment!"

She wasn't used to men making such intimate comments about her apparel. But he was her husband.

"I cannot go without it," she began.

"You certainly can," he retorted. "You can wear a suit coat tomorrow. No one will notice."

She shifted uncomfortably. "It is indecent."

He took her by the shoulders and held her in front of him. She had forgotten how tall and strong he was until he came close. She smelled the faint scent of cologne and wondered at how neat he looked. Even his fingernails were immaculate.

"Indecent, but comfortable," he said. His eyes searched hers quietly. "How do you feel about the baby?"

The question caught her off guard. She was lost in his eyes, in the touch of him. "Joyful," she whispered.

He hadn't expected the answer. His chest rose and fell roughly. "Joyful," he repeated, as if he didn't understand or believe the word. His eyes fell to her slender body and then lifted to her face. He was confused about the emotions she raised in him. He was a stranger to love, although not to women. But this one made him feel warm inside. She gave him peace. They were odd sensations, and he was also aware of a swelling in his lower body, a tightness that presaged needs she could not, in her condition, satisfy. The urge had been conspicuous by its absence since he had last seen her. How odd that he hadn't realized it.

Nora sighed softly, afraid to break the spell. "And you?" she asked. "Are you sorry about the child?"

His broad shoulders moved under his buckskin jacket, disturbing the long fringe and making it sway. "No," he said briefly.

"But . . . not glad?"

He looked troubled. His hands contracted. "I am thirty-two years old, and I have lived rough. I still do.

I hadn't thought of settling down yet, much less of a family. I will . . . adjust. But it needs a little time, Nora."

"I see." Her disappointed eyes fell to his jacket. She liked the soft feel of it under her splayed hands.

His own big hand spread against her cheek and tipped her sad eyes up to his. He didn't like that sadness. He bent slowly and drew his lips over hers with exquisite tenderness. He wanted just to offer comfort. But then he felt her tremble and heard her breath catch. He felt her fingers turn down against his coat. His head lifted and he looked into a face that displayed embarrassment and longing in equal proportions.

She was a puzzle. So haughty until he touched her, and then so responsive that she sent the blood raging through his body.

"The smoking car," she prompted unsteadily.

He frowned slightly. "Does it embarrass you so to want my kisses?" he asked gently. "For I assure you, it delights me to have a wife who cannot hide her pleasure in my touch."

"It . . . does?"

He found her shy smile fascinating. He returned it. His thumb tugged at her lower lip and he bent his head again, fitting her lips exactly to his in a silence that echoed the slap of the metal wheels against the rails at each joining.

His arms slid around her, drawing her gently against the length of his lean, fit body, pulling her up to press her closer. "No, don't close your mouth, Nora," he whispered when she drew her lips together. "Open it, very slowly. . . . Yes, little one, just like that . . ."

She felt his tongue tease her upper lip and then work

its way around to the lower one. All the while she heard his heavy breath, belying the patience he showed her. Her hands slid up to his throat and pressed just at his collarbone, savoring the thickness of chest hair that covered him.

Her hands excited him. "Wait," he whispered. He paused to shed his jacket. Then he lifted one hand away from her waist and moved it between them, watching her curious face while he unfastened his shirt and slowly pulled it out of his belted blue jeans. Her eyes dilated as she stared at him, her breath unsteady, loud in the car.

He felt himself shudder at the fascinated, hungry expression on her face. With a harsh sound, he threw the shirt off and dragged her hands to him, shivering as he guided them over the hot muscles of his bare, hair-roughened chest. Her breathing matched his now, and her hands were unsteady where they touched him. They felt . . . glorious on his skin!

"Nora!" he whispered in torment, as he bent to grind his mouth into hers.

She clung to his mouth, her legs involuntarily pressing to his and not withdrawing even when she felt the surge of his body against her, the hardness that pressed insistently against their child.

His lean hands released hers and went to her slender hips, to pull them in quick, jerky movements against him and then rotate them in so blatant a seductive dance that she moaned under his demanding mouth.

The heat they generated was blinding. She felt his hands on the buttons of her dress and arched back to give him total access. Her misty, dazed, half-closed eyes looked into his as he fought tiny buttons out of button-holes and his body shivered with its need.

He skinned the dress down her arms and found the laces of the corset, cursing it through laughter. He managed finally to get it loosened enough that he could tug it up over her head and toss it onto the berth.

She didn't try to cover herself when he turned back to her. He looked at her small breasts with pleasure that was tinged with curiosity when he recognized the changes that the baby had made in them.

He touched the wide aureole of one and traced a pale blue vein up to her collarbone while she stood trembling at his fingertips.

"They're . . . different," she faltered. "I don't know why. It isn't something I could ask a man, even a doctor."

His thumb slid over the aureole tenderly and he smiled. "Then shall I tell you what they are?" he asked softly. "A cattleman learns quickly about conception and birth, and the changes that occur in your body occur also in that of other creatures. These," he said, tracing the noticeable veins, "bring more blood to your breasts so that they can prepare milk for our baby. And this," he added, tracing the nipple until it hardened and she gasped, "enlarges to fit his mouth so that he can suckle you."

The imagery and the tender deep, smoky sound of his voice made her knees weak. "I never dreamed . . ." she whispered.

He bent and lifted her, and then sat down on the seat with her in his arms. His hand traced her breasts softly, lovingly, while hers pressed deep into the thick hair over his breastbone.

"Your skin is like alabaster," he whispered. "And you smell of roses. I want the feel of you under my body, Nora, and the softness of your legs sliding against mine as I press deep into you."

"Cal!" She pressed her hot face against his chest, embarrassed at the things he said to her so uninhibitedly.

"You are so shy, my wife," he said at her ear, "to be so responsive to me. Come closer. It's been a long, long time since I felt your skin against mine."

He guided her hands around his neck and brought her up against him, holding her eyes while he moved her softly against his rough chest.

"It feels good, doesn't it?" he asked solemnly.

She hesitated to speak, and he smiled at her.

"A lady does not admit to these dark pleasures, is that it?" he teased.

"A decent woman is not supposed to feel pleasure," she said worriedly.

He chuckled. "Oh, Nora, are you really so naive? Do you think that because society dictates stoic indifference to the sensual, it does not exist? Tell me that you have never peeked at the words of Swinburne."

She colored prettily and her face sought his chest.

The sensations he felt wiped the smile away and his lean hands caught her head, stilling it.

She felt him shiver. Why, he liked her face against his chest, she thought, fascinated. Would he like more than this? He was hesitating, as if he might like to ask something of her but hesitated for fear of shocking her.

Her breath trembled in her throat. "Cal?" she whispered. "I . . . I will do anything you like."

His eyes closed on a silent groan. His hands tightened in her hair. "Nora, sweetheart, put your mouth on

me," he whispered. "No, little one. Open it. And . . .
here." He guided her to the counterpart of her own nipple and pressed her face close.

She was shocked, first at the request and then at the
way he reacted, and then at the pleasure it gave her to
make him groan aloud. Under her mouth, she could feel
the small, tight nipple, and beneath that, the dampness
of his skin and the roughness of hair and the deep, dull,
racing pulse of his heartbeat.

She nibbled at his chest lazily, delighting in their intimacy. Why, marriage was exciting, she thought! She
smiled and lifted her head to look into his pale, glittering eyes.

"Do you like making me like this?" he whispered
roughly. "Do you like seeing me at your mercy?"

She nodded, her breath too shaky for speech.

"Do it again, then."

She slid against him to find the other side, and her
hands smoothed over the warm muscle of him while she
tasted the strange maleness of his chest with soft, eager
lips.

When he could bear it no longer, he bent to find her
mouth and he kissed her until her lips were swollen and
her body was lifting rhythmically to the slow tracing of
his hand.

He had her dress around her hips now, and his fingers
were wandering over the faint swell of her waist and
stomach. He lifted his head and looked down, and
smiled with possession at the soft rise.

"You look very smug," she accused breathlessly.

"I gave you my child," he said simply. He met her
eyes with a faint frown. "It disturbs me that I did it so
easily, and so quickly."

"Because there could be a great number of children," she said, understanding.

He nodded. "The alternative is abstinence." He smiled ruefully. "Or other women. And that, I could not contemplate," he added before she could speak. "Nora, I find that I have no desire for other women, since that afternoon we spent together."

He said it as if it bothered him. It lit up her face. "Do not worry so," she said gently. "We must live one day at a time."

His hand pressed gently on her stomach and he looked into her eyes quietly. "I want you. It would be safe, because there is no risk of making you any more pregnant than you are. But I will do nothing against your will."

"It is shameful to admit," she confessed, "but I . . . want you, too."

"Is it dangerous for the baby?" he asked. "I will be very, very gentle with you."

Her arms looped around his neck. "You were, even the first time," she recalled, burying her face in his hot throat. "Oh, love me," she whispered fervently. "Love me, love me . . . !"

He made a rough sound, deep in his throat, and carried her to the berth.

She shivered for a long time afterwards, cradled against his nude body under the single white sheet that covered them. He smoked a cigarette, with an ashtray propped on his chest, and looked worried.

Her hand pressed flat over his breastbone, testing the hard muscle there. "What's wrong?"

"You bled a little."

She nestled closer. "Yes. But it didn't hurt."

"Still, it may be unhealthy for the baby," he said quietly. "I was rough with you, at the last. I didn't mean to be, but my body was too hungry to listen to reason."

She recalled the fierce, rough buffeting of it with pleasure, seeing again his body arched over her, his face clenched and wet with sweat as he cried out and convulsed. The sight of him brought her own pleasure to a peak, and while it was less violent, it was just as satisfying.

He smoothed over her hair. "I like it when you watch me," he said gruffly, and his fingers contracted. "It makes the pleasure almost beyond bearing to feel your eyes."

She pressed her eyes into his throat, because she couldn't look at his face. "I like . . . to watch you," she confessed in a whisper. "It is very intimate."

"We are married," he reminded her.

"Yes, but I have learned things about myself that make me a little ashamed. I whisper things to you that make me blush afterwards."

"And you think that it's unnatural, between lovers?" He sounded amused.

"You're the only lover I have ever had," she reminded him.

He put out his cigarette and set the ashtray on the floor before he rolled over and pried her red face out of hiding. "You are the only lover I want," he returned, studying her face. Her hair was loose and splayed across the white pillow, its chestnut richness barely visible in the darkened cabin when the lights of a city flashed past and highlighted it momentarily.

His leg eased between hers and he moved her, gently,

so that they were lying side by side, perfectly fitted to each other. He put his finger over her lips when she started to speak.

"Slide your leg over mine, so that I can get closer," he whispered.

She obeyed him, loving the roughness of his long leg against hers. He made no move toward greater intimacy, and seconds later, her head was pillowed on his shoulder, with the cover over both of them.

"Cal, we cannot sleep without our nightclothes on!" she exclaimed. "We are naked!"

"Yes. How glorious it feels, Nora," he whispered, running his hands along her silky back. "How exquisite your skin is to touch."

"But someone might come in," she worried.

"I have locked the door, and the blinds are drawn. Sweetheart, there's nothing to worry about, I promise you. Now, go to sleep. It's been a long and trying day, and you're tired. So am I."

She gave up arguing and closed her eyes. It was sweet, she had to admit. So sweet . . .

When the movement of the sunlight through the window blinds pressed at her eyelids, she was disoriented. She opened her eyes to an unfamiliar place and the sound of quiet breathing.

Her head turned and she stared, shocked, at a staggeringly handsome Cal Barton sprawled nude beside her on top of the covers. Her eyes averted and then homed back, caressing the strong lines of his body and lingering on the secret place at the juncture of his powerful legs. His anatomy fascinated her. She hadn't been able to look at him fully their first time, out of embarrassment. Now, when he was asleep, she could indulge her curiosity.

How different his body was from her own, how frightening as she recalled the driving strength of it above her. Now that she knew something of the way two bodies joined, she began to realize what a shattering thing rape must be. Cal was beautifully made, but he seemed terribly large to her naive eyes, and even though he was slow and tender and very careful, she was still a little afraid of him until her body had absorbed that first gentle thrust of possession.

Her hand reached toward him and then, when she realized what she was doing, she jerked it back. A deep, amused laugh echoed from the head of the bed. Her eyes darted toward the pillow and met a pair of laughing gray ones.

"Touch me," he challenged. "Go ahead, chicken, I won't bite."

"I couldn't!" she whispered.

"Why not? I'm only flesh and blood. God knows, I touched you in every way possible last night."

She drew the cover over her breast and hid her embarrassed eyes from him.

"Come here, you coward." He pulled her down on top of him and cradled her body there while he laughingly slid her struggling hand down to the object of her curiosity. "Stop fighting me," he whispered. "You know you want to. Open your hand."

He felt . . . strange. Alien. But after a minute, she began to relax and give in to the coaxing motion of his fingers. She knew nothing about a man's body, but he told her, gently and without embarrassment, explaining it to her in the early morning silence of the compartment.

"Marriage is very complicated," she said finally, when he let her draw her hand back.

"Oh, yes," he agreed. "But very pleasurable, too." He stretched hugely and moved her aside so that he could get to his feet. She sat up, watching him with fascination; with possession.

He turned and saw her shy gaze and smiled at her. "You see? I am not so shocking anymore, am I?"

She smiled back. "Only a little."

"You are beautiful," he replied. He took the sheet from her hands and drew her out of bed, to stand in front of him. He studied her with solemn appreciation, from head to toe. "Exquisite," he said softly. "Perfect."

She pressed against him, only to be held away with a choked laugh.

"No, you don't," he said breathlessly, turning away. "You're much too fragile for that, and I haven't much control."

"But can't you just hold me?" she asked, curious.

"Sure. After I get my clothes on and calm down," he replied, reaching for his shorts.

That didn't make a lot of sense at first, so he explained it to her while he dressed. Her hands shook as she got back into her own things. Heavens, marriage was going to be complex!

When they were dressed, he turned to her, but his eyes were caught by the faint stain on the sheet. Her gaze followed his and she chewed on her lower lip worriedly.

"Perhaps it is natural," she said.

"You must see a doctor," he replied firmly. He held

up his hand. "No one need know how long we have been married, or where. If you aunt asks, you may tell her that we met in secret and were married before you left here."

"But where, and by whom . . . ?" she asked.

"By a visiting justice of the peace from Richmond, of course," he said. He produced the marriage license from his pocket. His thumb covered the strategic spot. "Look at the place name where the marriage took place."

"Tyler Junction!" she burst out. "But, how . . . ?!"

"A very sympathetic man, the justice of the peace, and knowing that we were unlikely to meet again, he was more than happy to bend the law a little to comply with my request."

It was all becoming clear. The kindness and sympathy of the man who had married them and his wife, the brief ceremony, the lack of questions. "Oh, Cal. You told him about the baby!" she said miserably.

Chapter Eleven

CAL FOLDED THE LICENSE AND PUT IT AWAY. "I HAD TO tell the justice of the peace why we were in such a hurry to marry. He wanted us to wait," he confessed.

She let out a long breath. "What if he tells someone?"

"I can assure you that he is a decent man," he replied. "He will not. Nor will his wife." His voice softened at the vulnerable look in her eyes. "I couldn't take you back to your uncle's ranch in disgrace, Nora."

She lifted her eyes. "You did it to protect me."

His mouth quirked. "I seem to do little else lately."

She shifted a little and peered up at him. "When I am completely fit, I could protect you," she offered.

His eyes twinkled. "An excellent suggestion." He bent and kissed her forehead gently. "You will see a doctor," he repeated. "And we will have no more . . . encounters until you have."

Her face fell.

"For a straitlaced lady, you have an unusually expressive face."

"I don't feel very straitlaced after such a night," she confessed.

He smiled, taking her hands in his to raise them to his lips. "All the same, you are," he said.

She smiled. "I am tired," she said gently. "Perhaps some tea and toast would settle my poor stomach."

He put a warm arm around her. "Let's see."

It was raining the day they arrived in Tyler Junction, and a beaming Chester and Helen and Melly were all three there to meet them at the station in the surrey.

"Why, what a welcome!" Nora exclaimed when she'd been hugged and exclaimed over.

"Cal wired us about your secret marriage, and the very happy event to come," Melly burst out gaily. "Oh, Nora, how lucky you are! A husband and a baby . . . and you will be close to us, so that we can visit!"

Nora's gasp was covered by Cal's arm pulling her close. "I knew they would want to know that we reconciled for our baby's sake."

"We want to hear all about it later," Helen said firmly.

"Yes, we do," Chester agreed. "But meanwhile, we've arranged a little celebration party for tomorrow night. That will give you both a day to settle in at the cabin and rest up, and Cal can help me work out some details on these new purchases. I've been waiting for him to get back before I made any decision." He grinned at Cal. "He's very knowledgeable about this sort of mechanical invention."

"Oh, I've worked on places that had combines and tractors," Cal said, without adding that it was the family ranch enterprise where he learned.

"No talk about work, if you please," Helen said firmly, linking her arm through Nora's. "Melly and I made new curtains for the foreman's cabin and had it thoroughly cleaned. We hope you'll like what we've done."

"I'm sure I will," Nora said. She didn't want to admit how terrified she was of living under such primitive conditions, and being less than a member of the family. But Melly and Helen weren't treating her like an outsider, or an inferior. And the baby shocked no one, thanks to Cal's quick thinking.

She wondered at her aunt's kindness and ready acceptance of her marriage. Aunt Helen had been very vocal about her disapproval before. The question she couldn't ask was answered for her on the way to the surrey.

"I'm sure that this hasty marriage broke your poor mother's heart," Helen said sadly. "She had such great hopes for you, Nora, and so did I. But if you feel so strongly about Mr. Barton, we can only hope that your judgment is not faulty."

Nora smiled, but the smile didn't reach her eyes. "Mr. Barton is a kind man," she said, "and intelligent."

"Of course he is," Helen replied, "but he is a working man, Nora. And because of it, you must now learn to do the things that servants have done for you all your life."

It hadn't occurred to her before that her aunt knew what she was talking about. She turned to Helen and saw the remembered pain in her eyes.

"Why . . . you understand," she faltered.

Helen smiled wistfully. "Yes, my dear, all too well. I married against my family's will and found myself disinherited and living in a line cabin with Chester twenty-five years ago. In those days, this was wild country indeed, and there were still Comanche raids."

"This far east?" Nora was aghast.

"Yes, this far east," came the amused reply. "I myself had to shoot a rifle and protect myself when Chester and his men drove cattle to the railhead in Kansas." She pushed back her graying hair. "I know what it is to be gentle born and suddenly cast into a life of deprivation. I love Chester. But if I had it all to do over again . . . I don't know what choice I would make. It is not an easy life. I thought we were doing well when Chester announced last year that a combine was buying us out because we were on the verge of bankruptcy." She shook her head. "And here we are, at our ages, at the mercy of people we don't even know."

"But things will go well for you," Nora assured her. "Uncle Chester is doing a fine job."

"With your Mr. Barton's help, yes," Helen said gently. "Your mother no doubt sees history repeating itself. She tried to talk me out of running away with Chester, but I would not listen. She has always considered that she made a better marriage than I did. Although," she added with just a touch of hauteur, "frankly, Nora, your father had no money until he married your mother, even if he did have a good family name."

Nora remembered her father's cruelty with unpleasantness even now, and her mother's lack of compassion. "They both despise me for marrying Cal," she said, her voice strained. "It was not a pleasant moment when they were told, but Edward Summerville was trying to pressure me into marrying him and restoring his family fortunes. I had to ask Cal to come and tell them the truth about our marriage."

That wasn't quite the truth at all, because they hadn't been married then. But the comment was enough to placate Helen. "That man!" she said angrily. "That terrible man, and after being the cause of your infirmity . . ." She frowned. "Nora, you have told Cal about it?"

Nora grimaced. "No." She met her aunt's accusing eyes. "I cannot! It's enough that he has me and a baby to burden him; how can I tell him, *now,* that he has another burden as well?"

"Oh, my dear," Helen said helplessly.

"I'll be all right," the younger woman said with more confidence than she felt. "I must be," she added. "Besides, you have been in my position and survived it. So shall I."

Helen forced a smile. "Certainly you will."

The ride back to the ranch was tiring. Cal helped Nora into the small cabin that would be their home, and she forced herself to act happy and bright. But she felt less than confident when she saw the ancient wood stove in the separate kitchen. This was her house and she would have to clean it and cook for Cal, wash and iron his clothes. . . .

She turned, pale. "You were not serious," she began, "about my having to kill a turkey?"

He laughed gently. "Oh, Nora," he said, shaking his head. "Of course not!"

He pulled her to him, and in his eyes there was tenderness and something else. "Stop worrying. I know that it's a big change for you. But you'll cope."

"Yes," she agreed. "I will."

"Tomorrow, though," he added firmly, "you see a doctor!"

"All right."

There was little to do the first night, because they were invited up to the main house for the evening meal. Nora was almost tearfully grateful for the small courtesy. She had no idea how to do the simplest things around a house. She would learn, but it wouldn't happen overnight. And her worst fear was having to produce an edible meal.

"You must loan me a cookbook," she whispered to Melly after they had eaten, while the others were talking. "And show me how to light a fire."

. "Cal can light the fire," Melly assured her warmly, "and cooking is not so difficult, truly. It is mostly a matter of practice."

Nora grimaced. "I shall poison him the first day I cook, I know I shall!"

"No, you won't," came the firm reply. She stared at her cousin with amusement and awe. "Imagine, getting married so quickly and secretly before you left to go home. And you didn't even tell me!"

Nora's eyes dropped. "Well, we were very aware of Aunt Helen's disapproval," she evaded.

"She'll come around. After all, she did it, too, you know," she added with a grin.

Nora met her eyes. "And you and the elusive Mr. Langhorn?"

The smile faded. "Mr. Langhorn is still pursuing Mrs. Terrell. I haven't spoken to him since the night of the Women's Club affair, and I do not intend to speak to him ever again, after what he said to me. The man is rude and crude and utterly unpleasant!"

And Melly loved him. She didn't say it. She touched Melly's shoulder comfortingly. "I am sorry," she said.

Melly shrugged. "I shall get over him. I am teaching a crafts class for children. His son attends. Bruce and I enjoy each other's company, but Mrs. Terrell refuses to let her son come to my class. And I think she has said something to Mr. Langhorn, because Bruce mentioned only yesterday that he is uncertain if he will be allowed to attend much longer."

"That would be petty!"

"Mr. Langhorn is petty," Melly said with uncharacteristic venom. "He only allowed Bruce to come the first evening because it left him free to escort the widow Terrell to the theater."

"What sort of class is it, Melly?"

"I teach art; sculpting, mostly. Bruce has wonderful hands," she added reflectively. "He did a bust of his father that was remarkable. He won't allow me to show it to the vile man, however, for fear of being ridiculed. You see, Mr. Langhorn thinks sculpture is a good pastime for a boy, but is no fit occupation for a man," she muttered. "He wants Bruce to be a cattleman. Bruce doesn't like cattle!"

Nora was dumbfounded. She could see stormy times ahead for the child. She wondered briefly if her own child would have artistic abilities, and if Cal would want to suppress them. Men had odd ideas about the correct occupation for their sons. But agriculture was not the booming business it had once been, and harder times loomed ahead. Nora thought that she might prefer her son to go into business. But the child should be free to decide for himself.

She asked Cal about it later, when they were alone in

their cabin. "Would you insist that our child wear your shoes?"

He eyed his dress boots. "Well, if our child is a girl, we might have to shrink them a good bit."

She laughed. "You know what I mean."

He grinned. "If we have a son, I would like him to be involved in my business, whatever it might be," he said simply, without mentioning oil or Latigo. "But a child should not be forced to follow exactly his father's or even his mother's footsteps."

She smiled warmly. "There! You do feel as I do!"

He chuckled. "You are unconventional in a few ways."

"Only a few, I fear," she said with a weary smile. "If I were more unconventional, I could have spared you a marriage that you didn't want."

He put down the clock he was winding and took her by the shoulders. His silver eyes were serious as they met her wistful blue ones. "I want the child," he said bluntly. "Marriage is not the ordeal I always thought it. In fact," he added, running his eyes slowly over her trim figure, "it has definite benefits."

"Such as?" she teased.

He pulled her close and wrapped her up against him. "Such as getting kisses whenever I want them," he murmured against her eager mouth.

He kissed her until it became uncomfortable and reluctantly eased her away with a chuckle. "My only complaint at the moment is that I cannot strip you naked and throw you down on the bed and ravish you."

Her face colored prettily and she sighed. "Oh, I should like that *very* much!" she said honestly.

He burst out laughing. He lifted her and swung her

around before he kissed her tenderly and let her go. "Never lie to me," he said suddenly, the smile fading. "Your honestly is the one virtue I treasure most."

She averted her eyes quickly before he could see that she still kept secrets from him. But it was a kind secret, she said to herself, justifying it. It was a secret for his own sake.

"And you will be equally honest with me, will you not?" she asked gently, lifting her eyes.

She surprised something in his face that she couldn't grasp, and just as quickly it was gone.

"Of course I will," he affirmed. "I have to check on the stock before I turn in. I won't be long."

She looked at the huge iron bedstead, so different from the polished wood four-poster she had occupied at home. She forced a smile. "We will . . . sleep together?"

"As we have done since we married," he agreed. He lifted an eyebrow. "Do you object?"

She smiled. "Oh, no. I love sleeping in your arms. But it is difficult for you, isn't it?"

His broad shoulders rose and fell. "It won't be forever," he reminded her. "Only until our small cake is baked and ready for icing," he added, staring warmly at her belly.

"What a very nice way to put it."

"Being with child suits you," he said quietly. "You look fragile and very pretty."

She curtsied pertly.

He made a face at her and went out the door smiling.

Breakfast, to put it mildly, was a complete disaster. Cal did light the stove for her before he went to check on the stock in the barn and corral, something he did at least twice a day because some sick animals were contained there.

While he was gone, Nora whipped out the old cookbook she had been lent and tried desperately to make biscuits. The bacon was not too difficult, except that she burned one side trying to get it cooked enough. She was sweating and her hair was all in her face, which was streaked with flour like the blue-patterned dress she was wearing. It was a dress meant for the front parlor, not the kitchen, and it already showed the strain of the use it was being put to.

She fried the eggs in the bacon grease, but splattered herself with popping grease. While she was concentrating on the painful splotches on her arms, the eggs grew darker and harder. By the time she took them up, they would have bounced if she had dropped them.

It was a meal, of sorts, she consoled herself. Edible. Just. She put it all on the table, with the butter from the small icebox, and the jar of grape jelly that had been a gift from Helen.

Cal's nose wrinkled involuntarily at the burned smell of the cabin when he joined her in the small kitchen. He said grace and they prepared to eat.

"I have made my first biscuits," Nora said proudly.

He lifted one without comment.

"Here is the butter and the jelly," she added, pushing both toward him.

He took his knife and tried to open the biscuit. It proved more difficult than he had imagined. Nora stoically put butter on the outside of hers and tried to bite into it. She laid it on her plate without comment and prepared to eat her egg. But this was impossible. The sight of it covered in grease and staring up at her made her queasy. She ran for the back porch and barely made it in time.

"Now, now," he comforted, handing her his handkerchief, which he had wet from the pitcher on the washstand behind her. "That was my first reaction, too, but the eggs aren't so bad. The bacon was a little crunchy, but you'll get the hang of it."

She pressed the cloth to her mouth and looked up. "You haven't mentioned the biscuits."

He grinned sheepishly. "Well, actually, I'm trying to forget about the biscuits."

She laughed, too, and her fears evaporated when he pulled her close to his side and kissed her unkempt hair.

"You're game, Nora," he said proudly. "God, you're game!"

"I want only to please you." She laid her head against his shoulder and stood content in the circle of his arm. "I shall try very hard to be a good wife, Cal. You must forgive me if I'm less than efficient, but I have a great deal to learn. This is . . . new to me."

He felt a terrible pang of guilt. She was pampered, and pregnant. He shouldn't subject her to this sort of life. She deserved better.

He wanted to take her to Latigo and introduce her to his family. He wanted to take her out of this cabin and into the sort of house she had a right to expect. But he couldn't leave Chester in the lurch. And he couldn't stop prospecting for oil when he'd put almost every cent he had into these last two lots and the rigs to use on them. Too much was riding on it. If he lost his gamble, he'd be living on Latigo charity for the rest of his life, and Nora with him. That would hurt his pride. King would inherit Latigo. Although there would be plenty of money left over to divide when their parents were no longer alive, Cal didn't want the family fortune. He wanted to make his own.

"You're very quiet," she remarked.

He kissed her hair again. "I was thinking about something. I must go away this weekend."

She frowned as she looked up at him. "Where?"

He smiled. "It's my secret, for now." He put his finger over her mouth. "It's business, I assure you, not another woman." He pulled her close. "You're as much woman as I can handle," he whispered at her ear, "and more."

She flushed with pleasure and nuzzled her face against his shirt. "I'll ask Melly to drive me in to the doctor," she promised.

"Good girl." He smiled at her wan, pale face. "Take care."

"I will."

She watched him go, thankful that he was patient and not demanding and sarcastic like her father. It boded well for their future that he did not expect too much of her.

The doctor was kind and she liked him at once. She told him about the fever and the slight bleeding— although she blushed profusely at having to admit how it had occurred—and her fears for her health.

After he examined her, they sat in his office and he wore a solemn expression.

"You must not exert yourself," he said unexpectedly. "There is a weakness which is not uncommon in a woman of your build. It need not cause you any problem if you are careful. As to the fever," he began, and hesitated. He took off his glasses. "There are many theories about how it is provoked. I favor fatigue as a causative agent. You must eat well, get enough rest, and take special care not to become ill from any other cause. Even a simple cold might bring the fever again."

"Could it harm me? Could it threaten my child, I mean?" she asked uneasily.

"It is possible," he said. "I would like you to come back in a month to see me."

"Yes. Yes, I shall."

"If you have any difficulties, please do not hesitate to send for me."

She shook hands with him. "You are very kind."

Don't exert yourself. She heard the words echo in her mind over and over again in the days that followed. But how could she avoid it? There was water to fetch from the well and heavy pans to carry back and forth from the stove. There was bending and stooping as she tried to keep the cabin swept, and even the strain of getting into and out of the buggy. Before the week was over, she was exhausted.

"Nora, can't you manage to find me at least one clean shirt?" Cal grumbled as he slung dirty ones around the bedroom. "For God's sake . . . !"

"Here," she said stiffly, presenting him with her first effort. She and Helen had washed the day before, and Nora had done her best to use the heated flatirons to produce something wearable. But she knew before he unfolded it that he was going to hit the ceiling. He did.

"What . . . !" There were scorch marks all down the sleeves and on the back. It was a chambray shirt. She didn't have the nerve to mention the white one she'd burned a hole through. She winced at his expression.

"I was not employed as a personal maid!" she said with a trembling mouth. "You must make allowances for my background!"

He breathed slowly, trying to hold back his temper. Burned breakfast, burned supper, unswept floors, and now scorched shirts.

His mother was a wonderful cook, their home had always been immaculate, and she did her own washing and ironing as good or better than the Chinese laundry in El Paso. Nora was a complete failure at the simplest chores. She couldn't even seem to remember to fill the pitcher with water so that he could wash his face and hands before meals. Her only virtue to date had been her delightful presence in his bed, but her pregnancy even denied him that consolation. Sleeping beside her and being unable to touch her made him as edgy as a sunburned snake.

"I need a daily woman," she said angrily. She pushed back wisps of unkept hair. She was not at all neat these days, he thought irritably, hardly the picture of a bandbox beauty. Even that would not have rankled so had she been able to cook an edible meal.

"I cannot afford a daily woman on my salary," he lied. "And you spent your savings, I believe, on a new Paris hat at the milliner's in town the day you went to see the doctor?"

She colored. It had been an impulse, the new hat, something to cheer her up, but she was willing to admit that she should never have spent so much on something so unnecessary. "I am sorry," she murmured. "I have always spent what I pleased."

"That is at an end," he said curtly. "From now on, before you spend one red cent, you ask me if we can afford it. Is that understood?"

She glared at him. How was it possible to love and hate one man so much? Her teeth closed sharply. "When I was a lady of means, you would not have *dared* speak to me so!" she burst out.

"Wouldn't I?" His eyes gave her a pointed appraisal. "Whatever you may have been before we married, you are now the wife of a ranch foreman, and I hold the purse strings."

She stood breathing heavily, aware of her aching back and sore feet and hands that showed the ravages of unfamiliar labors. She wished she had the strength to lift the iron skillet on the wood stove above her head. She would have laid his skull open with it.

He must have seen the light of battle in her eyes, because he smiled faintly. But a minute later, he shouldered into the burned shirt with visible resignation and reluctance and went to work.

Thanksgiving came and went. Cal gave in when Helen pleaded for them to join the family for the special meal, for which Nora gave thanks. But it was only a one-day respite. The next day she was back to fighting eggs out of shells that came apart in her hands and trying to cut meat with too many bones. She felt terrible and looked it, and her fragile health was beginning to deteriorate under the double strain of her troubled marriage and the physical labor she was not used to performing.

The beginnings of a cold caught her unawares, but she managed to get out of bed and make breakfast for Cal. It was a wasted effort. He gave her latest disaster one cold glare and stormed over to the bunkhouse to eat with his men, muttering all the way out the door about being stupid enough to marry a woman who couldn't boil water. She cleared the food away without looking at it too closely. Her own appetite had faded to nothing, and she wasn't eating properly or resting properly or feeling particularly well. She stopped trying to cook at all, settling for bread and vegetables and bits of meat that a sympathetic and worried Melly sneaked into the cabin.

If Cal noticed, he never said a word. In fact, he would have been hard-pressed to notice. He had started sleeping at the bunkhouse as well as eating there, because, he told everyone, he disturbed Nora, and she needed her rest.

It was a good enough excuse, but she didn't believe a word of it. She thought that he was really just avoiding the arguments that seemed to flare up over nothing these days as Nora's health suffered and her temper reflected her dissatisfaction and discomfort. She hated her mercurial temper, but she couldn't help it. She had a cold and she was afraid that the fever was going to catch her off balance. What would she do when Cal knew the truth, knew how she'd deceived him? He would see her as even more of a burden than she was. He hardly looked at her these days, as if the sight of her hurt his eyes.

In fact, she did hurt his eyes. She didn't know how desperately fragile she looked or how badly her new situation reflected on her. Cal felt guilty, more so by the day. He had moved to the bunkhouse to spare her the cooking and chores that she was unable to perform; and the arguments that did her no good at all.

He had to go to Beaumont and check on Pike's progress this weekend. He thought seriously about taking her on to El Paso afterwards. He was ashamed of the way he'd treated her. Every day he blamed himself more for subjecting her to a life for which she was so obviously not suited. He had thought to teach her how to appreciate the person and not the social station, but he no longer had such ambitions. He had been impatient with her lack of skill in the house, unreasonably so. The strain of being near her and unable to touch her had worsened his temper, and her own was none too good lately. When he came back from Beaumont, he would do what he had to, to spare her any further ordeal. He had caused her enough heartache.

Chapter Twelve

I T DIDN'T SURPRISE NORA THAT CAL WAS ANXIOUS TO GET away Friday afternoon, on his mysterious business about which he told her nothing. She didn't bother him with her minor aches and pains or the cold, much less what the doctor had said. He had become remote and almost unapproachable, and looked as if he had a great deal on his mind. She told herself to remember that at first he had been kind, overlooking her burned vegetables and meat and the disastrous biscuits she had continued to produce until he left to live in the bunkhouse.

He came into the cabin late Friday in a suddenly cold humor, staying just long enough to pack his bag. He made no comment about his neatly folded shirts, at which she had achieved at least some level of proficiency by ironing gunny and flour sacks until she could do it without scorching or burning them, and only then putting the iron to his shirts. In fact, the sight of them made him feel guilty all over again, because he could imagine how much time she'd spent learning to iron so well.

"Thank you," he said stiffly.

She shrugged. Conversation was difficult enough, and

she felt unwell. She stifled a cough but gave in to a sneeze.

"Are you all right?" he asked.

"Dust," she explained, and pulled a handkerchief from her apron pocket to dab at her red nose. "It is only dust."

He looked around him sadly at the thickness of it on the furniture. "Yes."

She glared at him. "I have enough to do without wasting time on the furniture. The dust only comes right back."

"As you say." He wasn't disposed to argue. She looked thinner than ever. "Are you eating?" he asked. "You must try. Are you certain that the doctor said you were all right?"

"He said that I was fine," she lied. "I do nothing really strenuous."

Blissfully unaware of what she had to do around the house, because he was out all day, he only nodded, placated. "Take care of yourself. I should be back Monday afternoon."

Her eyes were on the suitcase. "You packed your gun," she said.

He looked surprised. "I always pack my gun," he said. "We are not as civilized as we like to believe. Men are robbed all the time."

She frowned. "What do you have that a robber would want?" she said without thinking.

His eyes were suddenly cool. "I beg your pardon?"

She flushed. "I mean . . ."

"You still feel that you have married beneath you, don't you?" he asked coolly. "I am a man of no means and not worth robbing, is that it?"

She bit her lip. "Cal, you twist my words," she said, her eyes pleading for understanding. "I am your wife. This is my lot, too, now, to live as ordinary people do. I am trying to adjust. Truly I am."

"But you hate it," he said suddenly. "I have seen your eyes fall when we go to town, as if you are ashamed to have anyone see you with me. You go about doing chores here with the look of a martyred saint, because you were raised to believe that decent women did not work in the home. You are ashamed of your position here and ashamed to have me for a husband."

She ground her teeth together. "Please . . . !"

"Imagine; Miss Marlowe of Richmond, married to a poor working cowboy with dirty boots," he continued, his voice like a whip as he put all his stifled resentments into words. "To cap it all, your aunt stopped me on my way here and asked me if I couldn't afford just a little daily help for you. Because, she said, a *lady* was hardly suited to such tedious physical labor, and you are having to depend on Melly for food that you can *eat*," he added deliberately.

She went red. "But I said nothing to her!" She protested her innocence. "Yes, Melly was kind enough to bring me a few things. . . . You moved out! Why should I cook only for myself?! And I did not ask my aunt for a daily maid!"

He let out an exasperated sigh. "You certainly asked me, and I refused. If you did not ask your aunt to speak to me, perhaps she reads minds," he said irritably. "You profess to love me, Nora, but both of us know that you will never be happy here. You have no household skills whatsoever. You haven't the patience to accomplish anything in the kitchen. You want silk dresses and linen tablecloths, silver and crystal and servants and all the right people to invite to Sunday dinner. You will never be satisfied with what I have to offer you here."

"I will be!" she said angrily.

"Really?" His eyes narrowed on her face. "Then why did you ask your aunt to write your people a letter of apology?" he said finally, voicing the thing that had upset him the most.

She gasped. "I did not!" she said, aghast at being accused of bowing down to her parents, after their cruel treatment of her. Whatever had her aunt been thinking, to tell Cal such a thing? If she thought to make him change his coolness toward Nora with such a prod, it had certainly misfired.

"They are wealthy and you are their only child," he continued with an unpleasant smile. "Well, let me tell you something. If you make it up with them, that's all right, but don't expect to ask them for anything; not for dresses or fripperies or cash. Because as long as you remain my wife, I won't allow you to take one penny from your family!"

She glared at him. Defending the charge was forgotten in the heat of renewed anger. "I'll do what I please! I may be your wife, but you don't own me! I can take care of myself perfectly well, and I was doing so until you seduced me into this . . . this . . . life of abject poverty! At least a man of my own station would not have expected me to cook and clean and work like a scullery maid!" she burst out in a feverish rush. She felt terribly warm. It was probably a little fever with her cold, she thought, but she felt so ill that she hardly knew what she was saying.

He didn't speak. His face closed up and his eyes narrowed. "Honest labor is no disgrace," he said with cold pride. "I work with my hands and feel no dishonor for it, and my mother never complained about having to work in the house or cook and clean for her husband and three sons. In fact, she took pride in it. But if your family name and social position mean so much to you, then make it up with your father and go back to Richmond. God forbid that you should have to live like a scullery maid, Eleanor. Not for all the world would I demean you further."

She couldn't find words. Was he asking her to leave? Throwing her out?

"I have to go," he said tersely. "If you are not here when I return, nothing more need be said between us. Consider me a temporary aberration in your life, if it pleases you. God knows, I never wanted this marriage in the first place," he added cuttingly, and untruthfully. "I only wanted to sleep with you." It was a lie, but it did serve to salvage a little of his wounded pride. He picked up his bag, turning away from her stricken face quickly. Her aunt had made him feel terrible about Nora's lot, and that remark about Nora going begging to her parents to change her poor status made him sick.

Nora felt stiff all over as she stared at him with fever-bright eyes. "You never spoke of your family to me, or of taking me to meet them. . . ."

He lifted cold eyes to hers. "It would never occur to me! Do you think I would take you to my mother, and allow you to shame her for doing her own housework and cooking; let you look down your haughty nose at her? Our marriage was the worst mistake of my life. I have no desire to advertise it to my people!"

She was so taken aback that she couldn't speak. He

was . . . ashamed of her! The blood drained out of her face. He was so ashamed of her that he couldn't bear to introduce her to his family. It was the worst blow of all.

He didn't look at her again. He left her on the porch of the cabin to get into the carriage with the man who was driving him to the station. Nora watched them down the road and wondered without much interest if the man had overheard the argument.

With a cry of distress, she went inside and threw herself across the freshly made bed to sob her heart out. If only she felt a little better, if only her face and throat did not burn so. She turned her face in to the cool pillow and thought how very nice it felt. Later, when she got up, she could worry about the ruin of her marriage and what she could do. She closed her eyes just for a minute and lapsed into a feverish sleep.

Bruce Langhorn was the last student left in Melly's small art class in Tyler Junction that evening. She held the class in the school, with special permission of the school board, and usually the children's parents were right on time to pick them up. But Bruce was still waiting for his father, and it was almost dark. If she didn't take Bruce home to his father now, she would be caught on the road in the dark—a particularly undesirable situation for a lone young woman. Her father would be furious. He might even make her give up the class. Not for all the world would she admit that one of her greatest joys was the glimpse she got of Mr. Langhorn when he came to get Bruce each evening.

She took Bruce out to his father's ranch, watching the darkening sky with worried eyes.

"I don't know where my dad could be," Bruce said worriedly. "He's just never late."

"I know, dear," Melly said with a smile. "It's all right. Really. I don't mind dropping you by your home."

He grimaced. "I hope *she's* not there."

"Mrs. Terrell?"

The expression in her voice tickled him. "She doesn't come alone," he said with a sidelong glance. "She comes with her aunt. It's all proper."

"That's none of my business," she said with pretended calm.

"Sure."

There was a light on in the house when Melly pulled the buggy up at the front porch. It was getting dark and she was worried about the long ride home. Not for all the world would she admit to herself that she was also concerned about the absent Mr. Langhorn, who was, as Bruce said, never late. Could he be ill?

"Hurry inside, now," she said, "and wave if your father is there and everything is all right. I won't get down."

"All right. Thanks for the ride, Miss Tremayne!"

"Of course."

She held the reins tightly, waiting the eternity it took for Bruce to go inside and finally reappear. He ran to the gate. "It's okay, he fell asleep in his chair," Bruce said, chuckling. "They're fixing fences and repairing outbuildings. He worked until he dropped, I reckon."

She relaxed. "Good night, then, dear," she said brightly, sensing movement in the house out of the corner of her eye. Not for worlds did she want to get into a discussion of any sort with his detestable father. She was still wounded from what Mr. Langhorn had said to her at the dance. She flipped the reins at the horse's flank and set him into motion.

The darkness swallowed her up. There was a crescent moon, but it shone very little light on the road. Thank God the road went right by the ranch, and the horse knew the way very well. She should be all right if there were no desperadoes lurking. . . .

The sudden sound of a horse's hooves on the road behind her was loud enough to be heard above the sound of her own horse's measured trot. The horse behind was galloping. It would catch her.

Her heart raced as she thought about a rash of recent assaults on lone women, and she snapped the reins again, harder, pushing the horse faster.

There was a curve in the road ahead and she had to slow down for it, which gave her pursuer time to catch up with the buggy. A pair of long, denim-clad legs in dark boots came into view beside the buggy and she cried out.

As she tried to urge the poor horse into speed again, a lean hand came out and caught its bridle, bringing it to a slow, steady halt.

She knew now who her pursuer was, and it didn't help her heartbeat to decrease. He was bareheaded and angry; she could see it in the economy of movement as he swung his long leg over the saddle and dropped lithely to the ground beside the buggy.

He swept back his thick, straight hair and glared at her, one lean hand resting on the frame of the buggy.

"You know better than to run a horse at that speed!" he grated.

"Naturally your concern would be for the horse and

not my safety alone in the dark, Mr. Langhorn!" she said hotly.

"Why didn't you stop long enough to speak to me?" he asked.

"Because, obviously, I had no wish to speak to you," she told him. "Bruce said that you had fallen asleep in your chair. All I needed to know was that it was safe to leave him before I came away. And it was."

"I had a long day and I was up most of the night with a sick calf," he said.

"Your advanced age must be catching up with you," she said cattily.

"Damn you!"

She caught her breath. "Mr. Langhorn!"

His hand tightened on the buggy, and even in the darkness she could see the glitter of his dark eyes on her. "I have no manners, didn't you know?" he taunted. "I am a divorced man, a disgrace in the eyes of the community. Of course, they neglect to mention that my wife was little more than a harlot, who ignored her own son and sold her body to buy opium. She gave herself to any man who would pay—"

"Please!"

"Is it too sordid for your sweet ears, little Miss Purity?" he drawled. "Don't you want to know all about the man you harbor such a secret passion for? Or did you think I didn't know how you worship me from afar?"

She wanted to dig a hole and crawl in it. He made her feel cheap. Not only was he deliberately insulting, there was a faintly slurred quality about his voice that made her nervous.

"I must go home," she pleaded. "Please move away."

"That isn't what the widow asks me to do," he drawled. "She would do anything I wanted."

"Then do, please, go and permit her to. I wish to go home."

"So do I, but I haven't got a home," he said wearily. "I've got a house that I break my back to keep up, a ranch that takes all my time, a son who gets no attention at all because I don't even have time to be a father. He likes you," he added angrily. "You're all he talks about. Miss Tremayne, his patron saint!"

"Oh, Mr. Langhorn, you must . . . !"

"Come out of there," he muttered, lifting his arms to drag her from the carriage and stand her beside him on the ground.

"The horse will run away," she said quickly.

The horse had, in fact, no breath to run anywhere. He was still breathing heavily and had suddenly discovered some water standing in a track and some tall grass beside it.

Langhorn's steely hands had her face in them, and he was trying to see it through the dimness. "You haunt me," he said unsteadily, "with your big brown eyes and your virginal body and that long, beautiful dark hair that I want to wind around my chest. . . ."

His mouth hit hers with the force of a thunderbolt. She gasped at its impact, shocked, because she had never been kissed in such a way. The shy pecks of boys her own age were suddenly forgotten in the heat and insistence of an adult man's headlong passion.

His arms dragged her against the length of his lean body, making her aware of his steely strength as well as the growing desire that was blatant against her hips.

Frightened, she tried to pull away, but his head was

spinning from the taste and feel of her mouth, and he wouldn't let go.

She felt his hands in her hair, dragging out the pins to let the glorious length of it fall in heavy waves down to her waist. And all the while his demanding mouth never left hers for a second, never let up its fury.

"Stiff," he murmured roughly against her lips while his hands twisted sensuously in her long hair. "Stiff as a board against me, like a piece of wood." He bit her lower lip, making her gasp. "You're no more than a child," he said with disgust, pausing to catch his breath. "You don't know how to kiss, you're afraid of passion, you're of no use whatsoever to a man!"

She swallowed and then swallowed again. Her knees were weak and her mouth trembled, sore where his teeth had bruised the lower lip. She put her fingertips to it. "I want to go home," she choked.

"Sure, why not?" he asked angrily. "You cowering little girl! Now do you see what you were asking for? You can't even pretend that you like it!"

She tried to move away again, but his arms enveloped her once more.

"And now you're going to cry, aren't you?" he taunted.

She rested her forehead against his broad chest, letting the hot tears wash down her cheeks. She didn't make a sound, and her clenched fists stayed right at his shirt collar, not moving.

He felt her tremble. The whiskey he'd consumed had stolen his reason. He hadn't meant to frighten her. A man could only stand so much, and she'd tormented him for months.

His lean hands smoothed her long, silky hair with

rapt appreciation, enjoying the feel of it through his fingers. "Hair like an angel," he remarked quietly. "So soft. Like dark corn silk."

"You are going to marry the widow Terrell," she said gruffly. "You have no right—no right!—to lay hands on me!"

"I know," he said heavily. His lips touched her dark hair, her forehead. "Don't cry."

She wiped at the tears with her fists. It should have been laughable, to stand by the dark, deserted road with the man she loved more than life and beg to be let go. But his opinion of her made his position clear. He hated her silent adoration. He hated her youth and innocence. He wanted nothing from her. So why, she wondered, shaken, would he not release her?

His hands were in her hair again, as if it fascinated him. He wrapped it around his fingers and took it to his lips.

"Mr. Langhorn," she began stiffly.

His lips touched her eyes, closing them. His breath, whiskey-scented, was warm against the chill of the evening. "I have a first name."

"Which I do not intend to use," she said, choking on her pride. He was making her knees go weak again with that sorcerer's touch. The silent tracing of his lips on her face made her feel funny all over, especially when his tongue came out and slid softly over her long eyelashes.

The hands tangling in her hair were moving, sliding down its length. They were over the ruffled bodice of her shirtwaist dress now, the knuckles accidentally brushing the taut rise of her body in a way that made her actually want to lean into them.

There was a swelling in her lower body, an odd ache that seemed to throb harder with every touch of his lips, every brush of his knuckles over her breasts. Their touch on her nipples produced a sudden hardness that she felt.

She should protest. She thought to, when his lips moved down to fit themselves softly to hers. Not quite touching, then touching, then lifting and brushing, then touching again, harder and harder . . .

And while they touched, his hand turned and his thumb and forefinger actually caught her nipple and pressed it between them. She felt fire shooting through her, saw blinding lights behind her closed eyelids. She made a sound—a sort of choked cry—and her lips opened under his.

He whispered something. His hand caught in the thick hair at her nape and pulled her head back just enough to give him total access to her mouth. His tongue worked at her lips and teeth until he teased his way into the sweet, trembling darkness past them. He stabbed into her mouth and she cried out against it; at the same time his lean hand went completely over her breast and swallowed it up.

Afterward, she could never remember who pulled away first. She felt swollen all over, and she could barely speak for the thickness of her tongue. Her whole body felt that way, thick and sluggish and throbbing with some need she didn't understand.

His arms supported her, because she couldn't quite stand up. She clutched at them, leaning her head against the rough thunder of his heart.

He was breathing like a wild thing and his fingers bit

into her upper arm hard enough to hurt. He sucked in air like a man trying to breathe sanity.

"You should not have . . . done that," she managed in a raw whisper.

His cheek nuzzled against her hair. "Shhhh."

"Mr. Langhorn . . ."

He laughed shakily. "Are we not past that? My name is Jacob."

"Jacob," she whispered. Her eyes closed and she shivered with overwrought feelings.

He held her gently, without demands, his hands smoothing up and down her back until she began to calm.

She pulled against him finally and he let go, watching her move away so that an arm's length stretched between them.

He pulled cigarette papers out of his shirt pocket, extracted one, replaced the pack, and tugged out his Bull Durham tobacco pouch. He seemed in no hurry to leave while his horse and her buggy horse grazed in the semi-darkness. He rolled himself a cigarette, produced a match, and lit it.

He let out a long breath of smoke. One lean hand went into his jeans pocket and he stood and just looked at her. Her hair was down around her shoulders, a dark, wavy cloud against the dark pattern of her dress. It was a silky fabric. He remembered its softness when she had permitted him to caress her breast.

The memory made his body tauten. He laughed softly at his own folly. Two neat whiskeys and a wild ride through the darkness, to upset both their lives. Because that was what he had accomplished. Neither of them would ever be able to forget how it felt to kiss each other.

"I am going home now," she said.

"A wise idea. There might be bad men on the road at night."

"Worse than you?" she chided.

He chuckled. "Perhaps. Did I . . . bruise you?" he asked delicately, remembering the fervent caress of his hand on that softness. His eyes fell to her dress to punctuate the question.

She folded her arms across her breasts. "Sir!"

He sighed wistfully. "How did it feel, Melly?" he mused. "You've wanted me for years. How did it feel to have my mouth on yours, to feel my hands on that soft body?"

She turned away toward the buggy with dark, miserable eyes.

He stopped her at the wheel with a lean hand that snaked around her waist and brought her roughly back against his body.

"I'll be along tomorrow," he said at her ear. "Both of us need to have a long talk with your parents."

"About what?" she asked, aghast. Surely he did not mean to tell them what had happened here?!

"About us," he said solemnly. "Do you really think either of us will be able to stop, now that we've had a taste of each other?"

Chapter Thirteen

MELLY TURNED AROUND, HER BIG BROWN EYES SHOCKED and unguarded as they sought his. "What . . . ?"

He touched her mouth with a long forefinger. "I want you, to put it bluntly," he said. "And I'm going to make you want me."

"Jacob!" she cried out.

He chuckled. "Bruce adores you," he said. His voice softened. "So do I."

"But . . . the widow Terrell," she protested blankly.

"A blind, nothing more. I am too old for you, Melly," he said seriously. "Or you are too young for me. But I can't fight it any longer. It took the heart out of me to say what I did to you at the Women's Club dance. I can't hurt you again, even if it is for noble motives. The widow Terrell has been a friend. Only a friend," he emphasized. "There has not been the slightest impropriety."

"You said . . . we will talk to my parents?"

"Yes. Somehow," he sighed, "we must convince them to give me permission to court you."

Her ears didn't register that. Surely she wasn't hearing him properly. She turned around to look at him directly.

"Melly," he said gently, "I want to marry you."

Happiness washed over her in such a wave that she trembled. Her eyes brightened, brimmed over.

He drew her to him hungrily and held her. "What did you think I meant?" he growled at her ear. "Regardless of what some of you seem to think about me, I am not without morals."

"I know that. I'm so happy." She clung closer. "I thought you hated me."

He sighed. "I tried to stop this from happening; to protect you. Melly, you're only eighteen years old. You haven't even lived."

"I never would, if you had married the widow. Without you, I would never have loved again. Never have married or had children."

His arm tightened. "Do you like children? You must, because Bruce thinks you're swell."

"I love children," she replied.

"Then we might have one or two of our own," he mused. "I fancy a little girl with hair like yours."

"Oh, Jacob!" she cried, so close to heaven that she felt as if she could float.

He chuckled and bent to kiss her. "But for the moment, I think we might go our separate ways. I am tired to death and I had a neat whiskey to help me relax; not the most intelligent of combinations for clear thinking."

She looked worried, and he laughed again. "I assure you," he said, "that I am competent to know what I've said. But I need to look it when we confront your parents."

"Tomorrow?" she asked.

He nodded. He looked momentarily worried. "They

do not approve of me, I know. And when their own daughter is involved . . . I hope that it will go well."

"And if it does not?" she asked.

He smiled wistfully. "Your cousin Nora seemed to find her own solution to the disapproval she faced."

"Yes, she and Cal married in secret." Her eyes brightened. "Would we?"

"Only as a last resort," he said. He touched her mouth gently. "So don't worry. All right?"

She smiled and nodded. He put her in the buggy and swung up on his own mount, bareback.

"So that is how you got here so quickly!" she exclaimed, not having noticed before that his horse wasn't saddled.

He chuckled. "I ride quite as well without a saddle, as it happens," he told her. "I will follow you home. Not closely enough to be seen," he added when she looked worried.

It didn't take long at all to get there, and when she reached home, it was to find that no one took any notice of her late arrival. The whole household was in turmoil, and her mother was in tears.

"Why . . . what has happened?" Melly burst out.

"It's Nora," Helen sobbed. "Oh, Melly, she is in the throes of the most terrible attack of fever. And worse, she has lost her baby."

"Oh, no!" Melly exclaimed. "Poor Nora! And Cal . . ."

"Cal has gone for the weekend. We have no idea how to contact him," her mother replied miserably. "He will not return until Monday at the earliest, and she is so ill. So very ill." She said no more, but Melly understood.

They went into the guest bedroom where Nora had been brought when Helen found her raving with sickness earlier in the afternoon. Feverish and drowning in sweat, she was being tended by the solemn, weary doctor. He had been summoned long before supper and had had no time even for a cup of tea.

"Can we get you something, Doctor?" Helen asked gently.

"I would be glad of a cup of coffee and some biscuits," he said gratefully. "She needs more cool water, and her sheets will have to be changed, as well as her gown." He shook his head. "In all my long years, I have never seen a fever quite so bad. Hasn't she been resting, as I warned her to when she came to see me last?"

This was news to Helen and Melly, who exchanged shocked glances.

"I see," the doctor murmured coldly. "She told no one, I gather, not even her errant husband. I warned her that any lifting would be dangerous, that she should not exert herself. Did no one realize that she had the beginnings of a cold, and that it, added with her weakened condition, almost guaranteed a bout of the fever?"

"We didn't know," Helen said sadly. "She has been healthy as far as we knew, but since her marriage, she has kept to herself. We have hardly seen her these past few days, except when Melly carried her things to tempt her appetite. She has been trying to learn to cook. . . ."

"At a most inopportune time, I assure you," the doctor said irritably. They looked so guilty that he relented. "Nothing would have spared the child, I fear. But the fever . . ." He shook his head.

"Will she die?" Melly asked tentatively.

"I cannot say. It is a very bad case."

"What can we do?" Helen asked anxiously.

The doctor looked up at her over his glasses. "Pray."

They did, profusely, for the next two days. Nora was in pain at first and she cried out when they moved her, to sponge her down and help keep the high fever at bay. It exhausted everyone, including Melly, and there was no question of Jacob speaking to her parents. Melly sent word to him about what was happening and went back to her vigil at Nora's side, her own problems temporarily forgotten.

Monday came, and still the fever raged.

A weary Cal Barton climbed off the train and hired a carriage at the livery stable to take him out to the ranch. He and Pike had hit a dry hole, the second since he'd started looking for oil. They had one last tract, in a different location, and Pike was sinking the first part of the shaft today.

Cal had wanted to stay, to wait, to see if this last effort would pay dividends. Everything was riding on it. He had never been a gambling man, and he was gambling everything on one tract of land and his instincts and a geologist's certainty of success. But despite that worry, his argument with Nora played on his mind until it was all he could think about. Somehow they had to reconcile their differences, for the sake of the forthcoming child. If only he knew how.

When he arrived at the ranch and went to their cabin, it was to find it empty. His first thought was that Nora had gone back to Virginia. It was what he had invited her to do, although God knew he hadn't really meant it. He was upset at what Helen had said to him. But he wished he could take back every word he'd said.

His face tight with misery, he walked into the bedroom, expecting to see her cases packed. But there they were. He opened the chifforobe with shaking hands, and her clothes were there. He closed his eyes and thanked God. She must be visiting her aunt and cousin at the big house. And he'd thought she'd deserted him!

With a relieved smile, he went back into the living room and sat down heavily in his rocking chair. He leaned back wearily, wishing the past few weeks undone. If Nora had gone, he would be totally alone. He hadn't realized how much he would miss burned meat and hard biscuits and ruined shirts while he was away, but he had. Now he smiled wistfully at the memory of how hard she'd tried to make a go of the housework. During his absence he'd had plenty of time to consider the difficulty she would have faced, a woman with her monied background trying to live like a field hand. It hadn't been fair of him to put her in this position. He'd decided before he boarded the train for Tyler Junction that he must make amends and forget his stupid ideas of trying to change her. Remembering the painful things he'd said to her, he knew it wasn't going to be easy to make up for them.

But hopefully it wasn't too late. He could take her home to Latigo, and she wouldn't have to suffer this deprivation anymore. The Tremayne ranch was as good as he could make it, and Chester was on the right road. Either he and Pike would strike oil or they wouldn't. If they didn't, Cal told himself, he had a strong back and a good brain. He would swallow his pride and go back to Latigo to work on his own family's ranch. If Nora loved him enough, she would adjust. The rest . . . well, the rest would fall into place somehow. The more he worked at the problem, the simpler it seemed to be to solve.

The light step on the front porch caught his attention. He stood up, smiling, his heart racing as he waited for Nora to open the door and walk in. But the door didn't open. It was knocked on.

He went to answer it and found a worried Melly on the doorstep.

"I thought I heard you drive up," she said. "You'd better come up to the house. While there's still time."

Because of the look in her eyes when she added that last remark, he didn't waste time asking questions. Nora's absence and Melly's pale, worn face told a story he didn't want to hear. He quickened his stride with a heartbeat that threatened to shatter his ribs.

In the guest bedroom, Nora lay bathed in sweat with the doctor still at her side. He hadn't left the ranch since he was first called. He glared at Cal Barton.

"The errant husband, I presume?" he asked icily. "See your handiwork, sir!"

Cal's heart stopped in his chest. Nora looked almost dead. She was the color of the sheet and thin as a rail. Her stomach . . .

The doctor saw his look of horror and where it was placed. "She lost the baby two days ago. Now we're only concerned with saving her life. Didn't you know how dangerous it was to let her lift heavy pails of water and become fatigued in this condition, especially when it was complicated by a cold?"

"She said that you told her she was fine," Cal said. His heart was racing with fear as he looked at Nora, so still and sick. "She sneezed, but she said it was the dust . . . !"

"She caught cold. That was enough, as worn as she was, to bring the fever back. I fear that this bout may well end in her death. I have never seen such a bad case of it."

"Fever?" Cal moved to the side of the bed and looked down at his wife with wide, stunned eyes. His heart froze in his chest. "What fever?" he demanded hoarsely.

"What sort of marriage do you have?" the doctor demanded angrily. "She has had fever for over a year sporadically. Her own physician, although I do not concur with his prognosis, told her that it might one day prove fatal."

That was a blow that hit Cal right where he lived. He took a steadying breath. "She never told me," he managed.

"She never told anyone," Helen said sadly, dabbing at her eyes. "She said that she would never be able to marry, to put that emotional and financial burden of illness on a man, because the fever was incurable. Oh, bother Summerville! If he had not made unwanted advances and torn her clothing, if the mosquitoes had not gotten to her skin in Africa, how different it might have been!"

"Summerville?" Cal leaned against the wall, staring blankly at Helen. "Summerville caused this?"

"Yes," Helen said. Tears sprung anew. "I was so afraid when you brought her back that she would not be strong enough to bear up under being with child and learning a completely new manner of living. This is a hard life for a woman, and she was so fragile. I thought you knew. I should have spoken. I should have said something . . . !"

Her voice broke and she turned away. Cal was just beginning to realize what he'd done to Nora. She was sick with fever and she had never told him. Obviously she hadn't wanted to burden a poor man with an incurable illness that would mean constant medical treatment, even if it didn't prove fatal. How tragically ironic that he had seen her hesitation about working in the cabin as contempt of her surroundings, when she had actually been taking a very slow pace only to protect her health. His eyes closed with pain.

If not for Summerville, he would probably never have known about the baby, ever. She'd never have cabled him and he'd never have been driven to marry her, bring her here instead of to luxurious Latigo. Instead, he'd subjected her to a rugged, rigorous life that hadn't been at all necessary. In his arrogance, he'd meant to teach her a lesson in humility. But he was the one getting the lesson. It had cost him his child already, and might yet cost him his wife.

"Oh, my dear," he said under his breath, shaken to his very soul as he looked down at Nora's tortured body. His eyes lifted to the doctor's. "Will she live? Can nothing else be done? Man, you must save her!"

The doctor had already realized that Cal was not at fault. He relented. Compassion moved him, but its opposite often made a madman of him. He had no patience with people who put their own interests before those of a sick person.

"I've done all I can," the doctor said honestly. "Quinine, baths, bleeding, everything I could think of. If the fever breaks, she has a chance. Otherwise . . ." He spread his hands. "I have treated cases of malarial fever many times, but there is no cure. Further, she is weakened by the loss of her child and the cold, you see."

Cal moved to the bedside and took Nora's thin, hot hand in his. He clasped it firmly, hoping to give her some of his strength. She must live. She must! He said it aloud, torment in the silver eyes that slid over her with equal parts of guilt and hunger. She was part of him. Why hadn't he realized it before, when there was still time to tell her? If she died, her last memory of him would be of his harsh voice telling her that he was too ashamed of her to introduce her to his family, that their marriage had been a mistake. Now he had to bear the brunt of his own cruelty and watch her suffer. He had failed her, in every way.

All that long night, he sat by the bedside, with the doctor across the bed from him. They cooled her with wet cloths, changed the linen, changed her gown, while she shivered and wept and rambled incoherently.

Melly and Helen peeked in frequently, having forgone sleep for so long that they were accustomed to catnaps. Chester went alone to supervise the work on the ranch the next morning, because Cal had no intention of leaving his wife.

The doctor brought him back a cup of coffee soon after daylight.

"When will we know?" he asked the older man.

"I am not God," the doctor replied frankly.

Cal worried his hair while he stared at the slight, wracked figure in the bed. "I tried to be," he said in anguish. "She was so haughty, at first. Laughing at me and my men, teasing me, looking down her pretty nose at me because of the way I dressed, the work I did." He grimaced. "In my arrogance, I thought to pay her back for all those condescending acts; even bringing her here, where she had to do physical labor for the first time in her pampered life." He ran a hand over his pale face. "I never really thought it would harm her. My own mother is robust. Even when she had modern conveniences, she still preferred the old-fashioned way of doing things. She never had servants, except to help with the heavy lifting." His broad shoulders rose and fell helplessly. "I forgot that Nora had never had to perform the slightest task at home. God forgive me, it never even occurred to me that she might put the child at risk with such ordinary chores." He sipped coffee quietly. "She didn't tell me about the fever," he added dully.

The doctor sat back in his chair and looked at his patient. "She is a remarkable woman," he said, his voice very solemn. "She came to see me just a few days ago, and spent ten minutes describing to me the proper way to iron a shirt without scorching it." He chuckled, and Cal actually winced. "She was very proud of the accomplishment. She said nothing about doing any lifting, about any strain or discomfort. It didn't occur to me that she was keeping her fragility a secret from all the people around her."

"I thought I knew her," Cal said heavily. "She's a complex woman. And I haven't been the ideal husband."

"Marriage is a matter of compromises," the doctor advised, smiling faintly. "My wife and I have been married for thirty-six years, and we have never had a serious disagreement."

"You are a fortunate man," Cal said.

The doctor nodded. "My wife is something of a diplomat," he chuckled.

"Mine has an unexpected temper," the younger man mused, looking at her with eyes that showed their wounding. "All the while she was trying to learn to be a frontier wife, she never backed away from a fight. I had no real desire to marry," he confessed, "but once the deed was done, she seemed to . . . fit into my life. I'm lonely without her now."

The admission was full of wonder. The doctor's lips pursed and he looked away from the thoughtful, introspective look on the younger man's lean face. "You might consider telling her so, when she is recovered."

Cal's eyes, unguarded, met the doctor's. "Will she . . . recover?"

"We will know soon."

Soon. The thought sustained him through the afternoon and into the night. Time seemed to run together. He was aware of eating, of comforting voices around him while he held Nora's thin hand and worried himself sick over her condition. She tossed and turned, sweated and cried out, while the fever wracked a body that had never seemed so brittle and delicate.

The doctor went out with the others to eat, leaving Cal briefly alone with Nora in the silent, cool bedroom. He had lit a fire in the fireplace to take some of the nip out of the December air, so that she wouldn't get chilled again.

She hadn't told him about the fever. He should have realized sooner that she was a woman who kept secrets, even when telling them would have been to her advantage. He should have realized it when he learned about the baby. Then he could have spared her the rigors of a life to which she was unsuited. He could have spared her . . . this. Perhaps then the baby might have survived.

The baby. There would be no child now, and that would hurt her most of all if—*when*, he corrected forcefully—she recovered. He thought about the grief it would bring her and he groaned. He looked at her slender body, lying so still now in the bed, and the pressure of seeing her near death for such a long time finally broke his strong spirit. He felt the heat and wetness in his eyes and, for an instant, gave in to it. He laid his cheek gently against her soft breast, over the damp cloth of her gown, and gave way to the pain at last.

Nora heard a deep, harsh sound. Her body ached, sore, as if it had been beaten. There was a pressure on her chest, a wetness that was warm, not like the chilled wetness elsewhere. Her blue eyes opened and she looked at the ceiling. It was dark just near the fireplace where smut had stained the thin white boards.

Her eyes lowered to a dark head lying on her chest. She frowned. Cal? Why was he here? Why, this wasn't her cabin. This was the big house, and she was soaked. Then she realized, all at once, what had happened. She remembered a terrible argument, hurtful words. She remembered feeling ill and then the fever . . . the fever. . . .

Her dry lips parted and she pushed at the head on her breasts. "My baby," she managed in a strained, hoarse, unfamiliar voice.

Cal stiffened. His head came up and his pale eyes glittered wildly for a moment. "Nora?"

She pushed at his shoulders. Her memory was coming back now in full force. She remembered every single, terrible detail of their last meeting, including the things he had said to her, the accusations he had made.

The weakness left by her ordeal made her misery even worse. Her arm went across her eyes to hide them. "Oh, why am I still alive?" she whispered brokenly. "Why didn't I die!"

He was shattered when the words reached him. "Nora, please," he said hesitantly.

"I've lost my baby, haven't I?" she whispered, and then waited, stiffly, dreading the answer, although she knew it. She knew, deep in her heart, that she was as empty as her life would be from now on.

"Yes," Cal said reluctantly.

The tears washed past her closed eyelids in a veritable flood. The sobs were silent at first, and more painful to Cal because of their silence.

He touched her coarse hair tenderly, but she jerked her head away, as if she found his nearness actually distasteful.

With a long sigh, he unfolded his length and stood up, lost. She wouldn't even look at him. He felt a sense of loss more sweeping than anything he had ever known. His pale eyes glittered over her frail body with painful wonder. How incredible that he hadn't known until now that he was in love with her.

While he was still absorbing the shock, the door opened and the doctor came in. He saw Nora's eyes open to seek the identity of the newcomer, and his whole face brightened.

"You've come through it!" he said with delight. He had had little part in her recovery—it had been more a matter of keeping the fever at bay and keeping her quiet—but he felt satisfaction just the same. "Thank God."

"I have lost my child," she whispered piteously, and began to weep.

The doctor grimaced. He glanced at Cal, whose tormented face told its own story. "Go and have something to eat, my boy," he said gently. "She needs a sedative and plenty of rest now. She will recover."

Recover and leave him, Cal was thinking as he gave her one last longing glance, which she refused to return or even acknowledge. She would go home now for certain. He doubted if any confessions of love or promises of happier times would console her. She would blame him for it all, for the loss of her child, for the bout of fever, for so much. . . . And she would be right to blame him. It was his fault.

He went into the hall and pulled the door closed behind him. Helen came out to join him. She was asking something about food, if he wanted to eat. He walked past her without really hearing her. Nora was alive. She would live. He had to be content with that. He kept walking, a man in a nightmare, oblivious to the whole world.

Helen, fearing the worst, quickly opened the door and walked in.

"Has she died . . . ?" she asked, because that was how Cal had looked; like a man who had lost everything.

But Nora was awake and aware. She looked at her

aunt and managed a weak smile. "I am alive," she whispered huskily. "Just."

"And she will be very well in no time at all," the doctor assured them. He held a glass of water in which a sedative had been dissolved and coaxed it past Nora's dry lips.

"Oh, thank God," Helen whispered fervently, coming to the bedside. "When I saw Cal's face, I thought—" She bit down on the words when she saw the closed look they prompted. "I'm so glad that you have recovered. We have all watched and waited together."

"When did *he* return?" Nora asked.

Helen knew who was being discussed. "Last evening," she said. "He sat beside you all the long night, and all of today. He was distraught. . . ."

"Has any reply come from the cable you sent to my parents?" Nora asked.

Helen flushed. "Oh, Nora, I am sorry," she whispered. "I meant only to show Cal that you need not stay here if you only approached your parents. I meant well."

"Of course you did," Nora said wearily. "You did cable them, however, didn't you?"

Helen winced. "Yes."

"And there was a reply?"

She hesitated. One had come, but she hadn't opened it. She didn't want to give it to the girl now, in case it served to worsen her drooping spirits.

"Please read it," Nora said gently, although she knew what it would contain. She knew her father very well.

She couldn't know how she looked to the two people at her bedside, pale and delicate and drained almost of life, but still brimming with spirit and inner strength despite it.

Helen wondered if Nora even realized what a change she had made, from the rather introverted would-be adventuress who had first come to Tyler Junction in August to this strong, fearless woman who no longer backed away from unpleasantness.

The doctor nodded, and Helen went to fetch the telegram.

Nora took it in unsteady hands, propped against the white linen of the pillowcases as she struggled with the yellow paper.

When she finally had it open, she knew that she had been wise not to get her hopes too high. The telegram was brutal. "We have no daughter," it read. It was signed with her father's initials.

Nora let it fall from her fingers with a long, weary sigh, like a dead leaf from a winter limb. She was truly alone now, although it was no less than she had expected. Had her aunt not interfered, she would never have lowered her pride so much as to beg forgiveness of her father. It was he who should have asked her pardon, not the reverse.

She sighed heavily. She would live. But her life would never be the same.

Chapter Fourteen

CAL BARTON SAT QUIETLY IN THE SMALL COUNTRY SAloon a few miles from Tyler Junction. The one saloon in town had closed down. Probably the proprietor had been afraid of that ax-woman coming to call, he thought with bitter humor. Whatever the reason, most men came out here to get a drink when they wanted one. Alcohol was explicitly not allowed on the ranch, although Saturday nights brought their share of inebriated ranch hands.

After the second whiskey, he began to feel a little better. He had tried to see Nora, but she had sent word by her aunt that she refused to let him back into her room now that she was conscious again. She added that she considered their marriage at an end, that she was going home to Virginia, and that she did not want to see him again as long as she lived.

He had been expecting it, but the terse message hurt just the same. How tragic to know that his misery had come from his own actions. If he had been more patient, and less judgmental, Nora might have settled quite happily even in such a dismal place. And if he had taken her to El Paso in the first place, she might still have their child in her body.

But looking back would not help now. He knew that his marriage was over. He didn't blame Nora for not wanting to see him. He blamed himself as much as she did for the way things had turned out. He had seduced her, not the reverse.

Everything that had happened was his fault. The baby was his fault most of all. He wondered now whether it would have been a boy or a girl, and mourned it. His mother would mourn for him, when she knew. He grimaced. His mother didn't know he was married. None of his people did. And before they knew it, he would be a divorced man. Nora's parents would surely forgive her now, and she would go home to Virginia and find a man who would treat her as she deserved. He decided that playing God wasn't very profitable after all, and he was never going to do it again.

He never got rowdy when he drank. He simply dulled his senses, paid his bar bill, got up, and left. Once, when he was much younger, he'd passed out, when he and King were drinking one weekend in Kansas City. King could always hold his liquor. It was he who'd carted Cal into the hotel in a fireman's lift and right up the steps to his room. King was married now, he remembered, apparently to a woman who was his equal in temperament. He hoped his brother was happier than he was at the moment. He dreaded telling his family what a fool he'd been, but one day soon, he would have to go home.

He tottered out to his horse and managed to get into the saddle. Good thing the animal knew the way back home, he thought dimly, or he'd never make it there. He closed his eyes with the reins tight in one hand.

"Easy, there, fellow!" A sympathetic voice woke him.

He sat up, blinking his eyes. This didn't look like the ranch. He frowned. "Where am I?"

"Dalton's Stable. You're in Tyler Junction." The old man grinned. "Tied one on, did you?"

"Looks like it." Cal got down out of the saddle, groaning.

"You'd better go over to the hotel and get yourself a room, young fellow. You're in no condition to make that ride home now. I'll take care of your horse for you."

"Thanks. Name's Cul ... Barton," he amended firmly, barely able to remember that he was using his middle name for his last one. He left the horse with the man and started toward the hotel, but the depot seemed closer. Much closer.

He walked inside to the window. "Beaumont," he said flatly. "One way."

"Why, you're just in luck," the agent said, glancing toward a loud hissing noise outside. "The last train is just pulling out. No luggage?"

"No luggage. No wife. No nothing," Cal murmured unsteadily. He paid for his ticket and went out the door. The agent stared after him, shaking his head.

Cal woke up in Beaumont with a splitting head. He got a ride out to the rig where Pike was just unfastening the last screw in a part that had unexpectedly given way.

"Damn, this had to happen now," Pike muttered. "We've got no spare, and the supplier doesn't have the part in stock. He says it'll be January before we can get one!"

"January?!"

Pike threw up his hands. "There's no help for it."

"Send to St. Louis, or New York, or Pittsburgh."

"No help there. You may not have noticed, but there are several people setting up rigs around here," Pike reminded him, and indicated the flat, sparse landscape dotted with tall derricks outside little Beaumont.

"I noticed, all right. Maybe we're all crazy," Cal said heavily. "It looks like the only thing we're going to find is water."

"Maybe that geologist was right after all," Pike replied. He had small eyes, beady eyes, and they fixed on the other man. "What if we bring her in?"

"We'll be rich," Cal said.

"We could split up the stock," the man ventured. "You know, to help defray the cost so we could get some more money to work with. Sell shares."

"We're not that desperate yet," Cal reminded him. Pike didn't know anything about Cal's background, much less that he was rich. He'd been careful not to talk about himself. Pike was a good drill rigger, but he had a shifty look that Cal liked less the more he was around the man. He would have replaced him, but he'd been too involved with Nora.

Nora. He groaned inwardly. He hadn't even said good-bye or tried to talk to her before he jumped on the train. She'd probably think he'd deserted her, which was not the truth. He'd only been hurting and drinking, and he'd done an impulsive thing. But did it really matter? She was probably on her way home even now, and wanting nothing else to do with the man who'd ruined her life. He would never forget the way she'd flinched away from him when he'd touched her hair. Her expression would haunt him forever.

She'd been so fragile, suffering from a recurring illness, and he hadn't even known about it. She'd told him nothing. He turned away from Pike, hardly hearing the other man as he talked. Perhaps if Nora had been completely honest with him from the start, and he with her, things would have been very different. And if he hadn't tried to play judge and jury, he might not be alone now.

"Where are you going?" Pike asked.

Cal hesitated. He thought about it for only an instant before he knew. His head lifted. "I'm going home," he said suddenly. "Send to Corsicana for that part we need," he added on a sudden inspiration. He gave Pike the name of the man he'd worked for after he left the army, a man who'd made a pile in oil. He ran several rigs, and if there was a spare part available anywhere, he'd know about it. Furthermore, he'd send it right on, out of loyalty to Cal.

Nora stayed in bed for several days, just long enough to get her strength back. Then she sat in the parlor with her aunt and cousin and forced herself to face the facts squarely. She had no parents to take care of her. Her husband had apparently written her off, vanishing without a word or a trace. She had no money and no means of earning any. But at least she was through this latest bout of fever, and despite her sadness at losing the baby, she was getting stronger by the day.

"I must find work," Nora told the other two women.

Melly, who was still struggling with her own personal problem of confronting her parents with an increasingly impatient Jacob, leaned forward. "There's a teaching position available at the school," she began.

"Melly, I cannot become a teacher," Nora said dully. "The thought of being around children makes me sad, just now."

"Forgive me," Melly said quickly. "I didn't think."

Nora waved her apology away. "In time, I might consider it. For the moment, I have no idea what I shall do."

"You know that you are welcome to stay with us," Helen said.

But Nora shook her head. "Not as a guest," she said firmly. "If I stay here, it must be as a working woman." It was hard to get the words out, a terrible blow to her pride. "If you will bear with me, while I learn the rudiments of housework—" her lower lip trembled, but she sat straighter and looked her aunt right in the eye "—I think I shall cope quite well."

Helen's eyes crinkled with sorrow. "Oh, Nora," she said miserably.

"It is not so terrible!" Nora assured her. "In fact, I can iron, you know," she said with a smile. "I learned while I . . . before I was ill," she corrected. "I am quite proficient with an iron. And if you will teach me how to get the pans the proper temperature, I think I may master cooking one day."

"Certainly I shall," Helen said eagerly. "You will be an excellent pupil. But, Nora, it is such a drastic change for you, for a woman of your station and breeding. Oh, how can Cynthia allow your father to be so rigid?!"

Because her father knew a truth that Helen didn't, Nora thought grimly. He knew that Nora had been pregnant and unmarried before Cal came to her rescue. She fought Cal out of her mind. If she thought about him, she would go mad.

"It doesn't matter. I would not go back to my parents now." She felt a new maturity, a new confidence. Her ordeal had tempered her, like steel in fire. "It won't hurt me to learn how to do things. I must start tomorrow."

"Are you well enough?" Helen asked gently.

"I must be. Now, as to where I shall stay." She hesitated. "The foreman's cabin . . . ?"

Helen and Melly exchanged miserable glances.

"What is it?" Nora asked. "Please. Don't try to protect me. I have learned that I'm strong when I must be. What is it?"

"Cal Barton has resigned," Helen said dully. "He sent a cable to Chester. It arrived this morning, from Beaumont."

"Beaumont? Is that where he is?" Nora asked with helpless interest.

"That's where he was when he sent it," Helen said. "He said that he would not be there past today. We don't know where he is going. He wouldn't say."

"Obviously he has left me," Nora said without inflection. "Well, it is just as well that I didn't have to send him packing myself."

"He never left you when you were so ill," Melly said in a subdued tone. "It was his baby, too, Nora."

"Melly!" Helen chided.

Nora bit down hard on her lower lip. She looked away while she fought down the pain. She could not bear to think about it, about any of it. "I know you mean well, Melly," she managed tightly, "but please, no more."

"Forgive me," Melly said guiltily.

Nora shrugged. She twisted her skirt in her hands. "I must lie down for a little bit. Tomorrow morning I will begin my duties." She held up her hand at her aunt's protest, looking at the older woman with tired eyes. "I don't want to embarrass you by looking for work in the town. You must appease me. I cannot stay here and eat your food and not work for my keep. It is unthinkable. Despite my father's claim, I am still a Marlowe. I will not accept charity, however well meant."

Helen got up and hugged her warmly. "You are still our niece, and it would not be charity," she reminded her. "But I will do as you ask."

Nora nodded. Impulsively she hugged Melly, too, who still looked guilty. "Someday I will be able to talk about it without becoming upset," she explained a little shakily.

She left the room, and Melly sat back down with her mother. "She is suffering. But I fear that Mr. Barton is, also."

"Chester will be lost without him," Helen said sadly. "What a terrible turn of events. So much sorrow."

"Didn't you often tell me that a sorrow is always rewarded by a joy?" Melly teased.

Helen smiled. "So I did."

Melly studied the print of her skirt quietly while her mother watched her.

"You know," she told the girl, "I have noticed that Mr. Langhorn is joining civic clubs lately. And he and Bruce were at services this Sunday."

Melly flushed. She wondered if her mother had noticed the brief minute she and Jacob had spent together while she explained what had been going on at the ranch.

Helen picked up her embroidery with a quick glance at her daughter. "I had thought we might invite him, and his son, to Sunday dinner next week. Your father agrees with me that he is not the roué we first thought him. In fact, your father is feeling very kindly toward Mr. Langhorn since he has offered him one of his fine breeding bulls at a very good price."

Melly was astonished and couldn't hide it. Her face lit up, and her brown eyes.

Helen laid the embroidery down. "Honestly, you are my child. Did you think I would not see the sparks when you and Mr. Langhorn were together? A blind woman could see that he adores you. And, I think, the reverse is also true. Why didn't you tell me?"

Melly ran to her mother and knelt at her side, hugging her with broken, incoherent words of explanation and joy.

"Jacob was afraid that you would not allow him to court me at all, that you and Father would be against such a match because of his reputation. But he is not a bad man, and his wife was a terrible woman."

"Yes, I know. Chester heard it from a relative of hers, not long ago," she said gently. "Your Mr. Langhorn is welcome here, Melly. Not for all the world would I put you in the position that Nora was placed in, having to run away in secret to marry. It has taught me a sad lesson."

"I, too, am sad about Nora. Her life has not been a happy one this past year."

Helen smoothed back her daughter's dark hair with a loving hand. "Nor has yours. But I see happier times ahead for us all, my dear. And Christmas is coming fast."

Melly grimaced. "It will not be a happy Christmas for our poor Nora. Or for Mr. Barton." She frowned. "I wonder where he has gone."

Cal Barton had gone to El Paso. More specifically, he had gone to Latigo.

A pretty young woman with golden hair and big brown eyes looked at him through the screen door when he came up onto the porch. She stepped outside, and that was when he saw the bundle she was carrying. He stopped dead, his lean, dark face briefly tormented as he realized that she had a baby in her arms.

Amelia Howard Culhane stared at the lithe, silver-eyed stranger curiously. Her father-in-law, Brant, mother-in-law, Enid, and brother-in-law Alan all had dark eyes and hair. But King's eyes were silvery gray, several shades lighter than this man's. And he had the same lithe, rodeo cowboy physique, with long legs and wide shoulders and narrow hips. He even had the faint arrogance she associated with her husband.

"Why, you must be Callaway!" she said suddenly as she remembered the description of him she had heard early in her marriage. "I'm Amelia, King's wife. And this is our son, Russell," she said proudly, smiling at the tiny thing in the blanket. "Do come in."

He took off his hat, belatedly, and ran a hand through his thick, dark hair as he followed her into the house. His bag was still in the carriage he'd hired. He'd turned that over to the stableboy, with instructions to bring the bag up to the house and leave it on the porch for him. It felt strange to be at home again after such a long absence.

"Enid!" Amelia called. "Look who's come to see you!"

A small, dark-eyed woman came out of the kitchen and stopped in her tracks as she saw the newcomer.

"Oh, my dear," she said softly, and opened her arms.

Cal lifted her bodily off the floor and hugged her warmly. His little mother. He'd missed his family so much. And now he needed them more than ever before.

"It's good to be home," he said, putting her down with a wan smile.

"You've been away for years, it seems," she chided, "and hardly ever a letter! Can you stay until after the New Year?"

He shrugged. "I might as well," he said. "We're waiting for a major part on the drill, and we can't get one until the first of the year."

"Why not use a part off another one?" she suggested sagely.

"Because this is a new type of drill. The old ones won't fit it, more's the pity. My partner is staying there to protect our interests until we can start again. Hopefully it will only be a delay of two or three weeks. I must learn to be patient."

"Brant and Alan and King will be glad to see you," she said. "They could never understand why you wouldn't settle here and be part of the ranch business."

He grinned. "Latigo is King's. We all know that." He glanced at the woman standing beside his mother and frowned slightly. "King, married and a father," he said, shaking his head. "I couldn't believe it when Alan told me he'd married."

"Neither could I," Amelia offered, tongue in cheek.

"We had a very rough beginning. But Russell has been our greatest joy. He is only two weeks old," she added.

Cal didn't touch the child. He tried to, but his face was rigid and he forced a smile. "I'm no good with children." He shrugged. "But he's sweet."

"He's the image of his father," Amelia said dreamily.

"King was never a baby," Cal corrected. "He was born throwing orders around and breaking horses."

"So I've heard," Amelia replied with twinkling eyes.

"Come and have some cake with us," Enid invited, pushing back her sweaty, gray-streaked hair. "I've just been cleaning the stove."

A reminder that she did her own housework, and it hurt. It brought back thoughts of Nora that were painful.

They talked a little until the coffee boiled and the cake was sliced onto a china plate. Then the baby cried, and Amelia announced that he needed changing and went down the hall with him.

Enid sat down with her son and the tray of coffee and cake that he'd carried into the parlor for her.

"Now," she said to Cal. "Tell me why you've come home, in mourning and wearing a wedding band."

He caught his breath audibly. He'd forgotten the band, which was one of a set he'd purchased in St. Louis when the train stopped there, figuring that a ring would make Nora less conscious of her condition.

He looked at the ring long and hard.

"You've married," Enid prompted.

He looked down, shamefaced. "Yes." He couldn't bring himself to tell her the whole sad tale. "She . . . lost our baby this week."

"And you left her alone?!"

"She didn't want me with her," he said. "It has been

difficult. She's an eastern woman, a socialite. She never wanted to marry me in the first place, but I . . . compromised her. I took her back to the ranch where I was working as foreman and installed her in the cabin. She had never cooked or cleaned."

Enid was getting a sad picture. "And . . . ?"

"The lifting was too much for her," he said coldly, not sparing himself. "Beyond that, she contracted a fever in Africa. It recurs. She became very ill and lost the baby."

"There is so much more," Enid said solemnly. "Isn't there?"

He smiled wanly. "I discovered too late that I love her."

"And she?"

"Oh, she hates me," he said pleasantly. "I cannot blame her. I dragged her into a life of drudgery to teach her humility. But it was I who learned the lesson."

"A socialite living in a foreman's cabin," Enid said heavily. "How could you not bring her here, properly, to your home?"

"I could not because she thinks she's married to a ranch foreman named Callaway Barton," he said with a mocking smile. "Because of the combine business, I couldn't tell her uncle who I was, much less could I tell her. She thought me a poor, dirty cowboy and bemoaned the fate that shackled her to me."

"Oh, Cal," his mother said, shaking her head. "You have made a mess of it."

"Indeed I have. She would not even speak to me. I had too much to drink and went to Beaumont. From there, I had nowhere else to go. Except here."

"Is there no chance for the two of you?" Enid asked.

His broad shoulders rose and fell. "She will have gone back to her parents in Virginia by now. Her father is the most appalling snob, and her mother does what she is told." He looked up with twinkling eyes. "Unlike the women in this family."

"Oh, I never did what your father told me to," Enid agreed. "Eventually he realized it and stopped trying to boss me. Amelia is just the same," she added with glee. "It's a treat to watch King try to get his way with her."

"She seems very gentle," he began.

"Looks," Enid said, "can be deceptive."

The sound of horses outside brought them both to the front porch, where a tall, lithe man with dark hair and silver-gray eyes dismounted beside a slighter, older one.

"King! Father!" Cal greeted, going forward to hug them.

King's eyes, so pale a gray that they seemed almost transparent, smiled into his brother's. "I'm glad you came home at last," he said. "How goes the oil business?"

"Slowly," Cal replied.

"Good. You can stay for Christmas," Brant Culhane chuckled, daring his son to refuse.

"I might as well," Cal said. "I have very little else to do. I've quit the Tremayne ranch."

"You accomplished the changes, then?" Brant asked solemnly.

"As many as possible. Now it's a matter of time. Chester seems to be on the right track. At least I think he is. It was a good idea, to let me go as a foreman and ease him into the changes, rather than send orders to that effect," Cal replied. "It also gave me the opportunity to be a short distance from Beaumont and the drilling rig. Pike can handle things until I return."

"Is he trustworthy?" King asked as they went into the house.

"That I don't know," Cal murmured. "There's something about him that makes my neck hair bristle. I'll watch him. But his character hardly matters if we're sitting on another dry hole."

"There you are!" Amelia laughed, coming forward with the baby to greet King.

The change in the older man was astonishing. The hard, ruthless look fell away from him. He smiled at Amelia, and there was such a radiance about him that Cal was shocked. In all their lives together, he'd never seen that sort of expression on his older brother's face.

"Hello, imp," King murmured, and bent to kiss Amelia with tender affection. His lean hand touched the tiny head in her arms. "How's my Rusty?"

"Don't call him that!" Amelia groaned.

"He's my son, I can call him Rusty if I like," he reminded her teasingly. "Besides, he's going to have red highlights in his hair, if it isn't red altogether. Your mother was a redhead, you once told me."

"Yes, she was," Amelia had to confess. She adored King with her eyes. "You look tired, my darling."

He smoothed back her hair. "So do you, little one," he said deeply. "You had no sleep last night at all. He was fussy."

"And you sat up with me," she reminded him warmly. "But I didn't have to go out and work all day. You did." She caught his hand with her free one. "Come along and I'll pour coffee and cake into you. It will refresh you no end. Enid's made a lemon cake . . . !"

"They go on like that all the time," Brant chuckled, watching them walk away. He shook his head. "Never saw anything like it."

Neither had Cal. He felt more empty than he ever had, because now he could see what it would have been like if he and Nora had been close, if they'd had their baby and were married because they loved each other. He loved her, but she'd never loved him. If she had, his supposed profession as a working man would not have mattered to her. It hurt him to know that.

Brant talked about the ranch as they joined the others.

"Alan went back to see that girl outside Baton Rouge," he said amusedly. "Looks like it may be serious this time."

"Yes, and he's talking about a career in banking, in Baton Rouge. I don't think he's going to settle here," Enid said over her shoulder as she poured coffee into more cups.

"I never thought he would," Cal remarked. He sat down again and sipped the rich black liquid. He glanced at his brother with warm eyes. "We've all known forever that Latigo would only belong to King. His heart lives here."

"In more ways than one," King replied quietly, with possessive eyes on his wife and child as he lifted his cup to his lips.

Enid picked up her own cup. "Cal is married."

"King!" Amelia exclaimed, grabbing at a napkin to mop up the scalding coffee that had landed on his jeans.

King was staring at his brother, oblivious to the coffee. "What the hell did you say!" he burst out. "Married, and you never brought your wife to us?!"

Cal glowered in his mother's direction. "I couldn't bring her here," he said before the question had completely escaped King's tight lips. "I was playing at being a ranch foreman, and she took it for the real thing. She's a rich easterner who had a problem with her attitude toward lesser beings." He shifted uncomfortably and averted his eyes.

"He was teaching her a lesson by letting her live as a ranch foreman's wife," Enid continued. "She taught him one instead and went home. He got drunk."

"Thank you, Mother," Cal muttered.

"You're welcome, my dear," she said sweetly.

King knew there was more than that, but Cal looked shattered enough. "Regardless of the circumstances, it's nice to have you home," he said firmly.

Enid knew she was being censured, without a word being spoken by her taciturn son. She grinned at him. "No need, King, dear, I'm finished."

He chuckled. "Harridan," he accused.

She nodded. "Living with your father caused it."

"That's right," Brant sighed, "blame it on me."

Cal felt secure again, welcome and safe. He sat back in his chair with a quiet sigh. But the smile on his face wasn't a real one.

══ Chapter Fifteen ══

B Y THE TIME CHRISTMAS DAY CAME AROUND, ON A
Tuesday this year, there was a big change at the
Tremayne ranch house. Nora had forsaken her stylish
eastern dresses for plainer clothing, and she was doing
most of the cooking and all the housework. Not that
Helen and Melly and Chester treated her like a domestic; she was still one of the family and joined them at
the table and in the parlor. But in all other respects, she
lived befitting her new status in life.

She had become adept at ironing. Her hands were
equally nimble at milking cows and churning the milk
to butter. She could kill a chicken, and clean it—that
had been a shattering experience, but with Helen's guid-
ance, she conquered her squeamishness and did what
she had to. She no longer had qualms about getting
dirty, something she had once had a horror of. She
helped plan a spring wedding for Jacob and Melly, and
she was slowly learning how to sew.

Acquiring these skills had worked another change in
her. She was less nervous and high-strung. She felt different, free of the shackles of her parents' attitudes and
rigid social class mentality. Helen had changed her attitude as well. She felt bad about her previous prejudice

against Jacob Langhorn, and he and his son were now welcome at the ranch.

Melly was giving Nora riding lessons. She still wasn't good at it, but she could stay on the animal's back. Often she thought of Cal and wondered where he was, how he was. He had not tried to contact her after she had sent him away. Of course, she had told him she was going back to Virginia so he would not know she was still with her aunt and uncle. She worried about where he was, and how he was making his living.

She felt some guilt over costing him a job he had enjoyed. She wondered if he blamed her because she hadn't told him the truth about her condition. Melly had remarked that Cal was shattered when her mother gave him her cold message. Her only thought had been for her own pain. She was sorry now that she'd refused to see him. As Melly had said, it was Cal's baby, too. He would have felt sad about that loss and probably guilty, coming home to find Nora in that terrible condition after their argument.

He was not a heartless man, as she knew so well. Possibly he had not meant many of the things he said. Her aunt had caught him on the raw with her comments about Nora's lack of help and with her well-meant interference in cabling Nora's parents. But Nora missed her husband more than she thought she ever might. Her life had never been so empty. All the wealth and status in the world meant nothing now. If her parents had still wanted her, she doubted she would have gone back to them. In her heart she couldn't stop hoping that Cal might come back one day.

Finally driven to desperation by the lack of news, she asked her aunt about him. "Have you heard from Cal?" Nora wondered as they laid out Christmas dinner.

The apparent nonchalance of that question didn't fool Helen. "Why, yes," she said.

Nora's hands shook. She put the plates down carefully. "How is he?"

"He's with his family," Helen told her quietly, pausing to set the dressing in its pretty china bowl on the table. "He said that he hoped you had recovered and that you were regaining your strength."

Nora's eyes brightened. For the first time since her ordeal, she looked alive. "Did he?"

"My dear," Helen said gently. "Do you miss him so much?"

Nora bit her lip and averted her eyes. "I was not fair to him. He knew nothing of my condition, and I had been too proud to tell him. We had a vicious quarrel before he left. I remembered too well some of the cruel things he said to me, and I refused to listen when he tried to speak to me. I was hurt."

"Of course you were."

She straightened the tablecloth. "There's something you don't know," she said. "The real reason we were married."

"Because of the baby?"

Nora's eyes came up, startled but resigned, a second later. "Yes."

"As I thought."

"He didn't love me," she said dully. "He told me so, before he left. He said that our marriage was a mistake. He was ashamed of me. So ashamed that he had not even told his family about me." Her eyes closed as she remembered how he had said it, the coldness of his deep voice outlining her faults for her. "Perhaps he was right. I felt very superior to other people." She smiled wanly as she looked up. "I have learned a painful lesson. Decency cannot be measured in dollars."

Helen's eyes sparkled. "I had to learn the same lesson when I came here to live with Chester. I, too, came from the stock of European royalty, and I behaved as if I had. It's only recently that I've learned to accept people without looking first at their clothing and social status."

"My father will always judge people that way," Nora said sadly. "And my mother will never question anything he does. I miss my parents. But I miss Cal, oh, so much more."

"It is sad that you could not write to him," Helen replied, trying not to remember her part in their problems. She had meant well, but her interference had been costly to her niece.

Nora looked at her, thinking. "But perhaps I could write to him. . . ."

"I meant that his letter had no return address at all," Helen replied with a sad smile. "And a postmark that was not even legible."

"Oh." Nora lifted a saucer and polished it with the clean cloth in her apron until it shone. Her heart felt heavy in her chest as she realized that she might never see Cal again. "Do you think he might write again?" she ventured.

"He did send the name of his attorney," Helen said reluctantly. "You see . . . he thought you might need it; to divorce him."

* * *

Nora didn't eat. She couldn't manage a single bite of the delicious turkey and dressing and cranberry sauce, with all the trimmings. She tried to smile and pretended to be gay, so that she wouldn't upset the huge family gathering that even included Jacob and Bruce Langhorn. But her heart wasn't in a festive mood. It was worse than she'd ever thought it could get. Cal wanted to get rid of her. He wanted her to divorce him. He had meant it when he said their marriage was a mistake. He had never loved her, and now there was no chance that he ever would.

She listened absently to the discussion of news after they ate, saddened by the reports out of Galveston that typhoid and malarial fevers were rampant there. The city still had not recovered from the devastating flood in September.

A more humorous note was struck by a news item out of Montana, about a dozen cowboys allegedly being chased for twenty miles by two outlaws. The incident was reported tongue in cheek, and the writer bewailed the passing of the brave "knights of the plain" of days past.

Chester had read the item to them out of an El Paso newspaper that had come for Cal Barton, who was no longer in residence.

"Interesting, this," he mused, having turned to the personal notes page. "The paper notes that all three sons of the Culhane family are together with their parents at Christmas for the first time in several years." He looked up. "That's the old West Texas ranching family I mentioned to you, the one that heads the combine that owns this ranch. The eldest son, King, and his wife had a boy of their own just recently."

"Why did Cal subscribe to an El Paso paper?" Nora asked with idle curiosity.

"Well, he and I did want to keep tabs on the Culhanes, if you must know," Chester said sheepishly. "It never hurts to know what they're up to, and whatever they do makes news in El Paso."

"There has been no further contact from them," Helen ventured. "They must be satisfied with the changes Mr. Barton helped you make."

"Apparently so," Chester said, smiling, "which makes this Christmas truly a blessed one for me." He glanced at Helen. "You haven't given Eleanor her letter."

Helen grimaced. "Chester . . ."

"Go on," he instructed firmly.

Nora's face brightened. Why, Cal had written to her! He must not have meant it after all, about the divorce.

Helen got up to produce a letter from a table in the parlor and came back with it, but she was slow in handing it to her niece.

Nora's face was full of hope until she saw the postmark. Her smile faded.

"Open it," Chester advised gently.

Nora looked at him fearfully.

"I had your aunt write again and tell them of your terrible illness," he said quietly. "They are not heartless, Nora."

Nora hesitated only for a moment before she opened the envelope. It was a Christmas card, gaily decorated, very expensive. She opened it and recognized her mother's handwriting immediately.

"We are sorry to hear that you have been so ill," her mother wrote. "If you would like to come home, your father is willing to accept your apology. Do write him, dear. Love from Mother and Father."

Nora breathed normally for a moment. Then she slowly got up and walked to the stove in the kitchen, opened the eye, and tossed the card in. She slammed the cover back on and put the lifter back on its peg.

"I . . . see," Chester murmured.

Nora rejoined the others, sitting down very primly in her chair. "My father wishes me to apologize," she explained. "I didn't mention before that he slapped me when we told him we were going to be married. He took exception to my choice of husbands."

Chester scowled. "My dear! I had no idea, or I would *never* have . . . !"

She held up her hand with a faint smile. "I have kept far too many secrets."

"To slap a woman in your condition!" Chester was outraged. "And what did Cal do?"

"He knocked my father onto the floor and dared him to touch me again," Nora recalled wistfully. "I was quite taken aback at first. So was my father."

"Good for Cal," Melly muttered, and her shocked mother nodded her own assent.

"My father had never been spoken to in such a way," Nora continued. "I expect it still festers inside him that he was bested by a man of such low social status." Nora's eyes twinkled. "If you could but have seen it! Cal was wearing a pistol at his side, and that fringed buckskin jacket with his boots and that tattered old black hat." She laughed softly, her eyes bright with love as she remembered how Cal had looked that day, so handsome that her heart ached with the memory. "My mother asked if he was a desperado!"

They all laughed at that, and Nora began to relax and throw off the pain the card had brought.

"Surely you won't apologize, will you?" Helen asked suddenly.

"Apologize! For what?" Nora asked. "For losing my child, and my husband, and almost my life?" She shook her head. "My father cannot change, but I have. I do not wish to apologize, nor do I wish to go back to Virginia. Why, I have a job, after all!"

They laughed even louder at the smug, mischievous look on her face. She didn't add that she had one other reason for not wanting to go back East. If Cal Barton ever came back this way, she was going to still be here, waiting for him. He was going to be a trial to her all her life if he did, but she loved him with all her heart, and it didn't matter if his boots were filthy and he had to work cattle forever. She only wished that he would come back, so that she could tell him so.

Cal mooned around at Latigo for two more days, wishing that he could have put a return address on the letter he wrote to the Tremaynes. His family attorney, old Walpole, hadn't heard a word from Nora or her parents. That might be good or bad. She could be ill again. The fever had a tendency to recur, the doctor said. It worried him that she might be sick even now, and he wouldn't know.

"It's time I left," he told his family at the midday meal the next day. There had been a quiet celebration, in which he hardly figured. He felt like an outsider, with his heart back in Tyler Junction.

"Back to the oil fields, I guess?" Alan asked with a grin. He'd come home from Baton Rouge very secretive and poised to return. "I'll go along with you and catch a train from Beaumont on to Baton Rouge."

"She must be some lady," King mused.

"She is," Alan said. "I'll bring her home with me in the spring."

That took everyone's mind off Cal's announcement and spared him the inevitable questions. But they came anyway, from King, later.

The older man propped his boot on the lower rung of the corral while they watched the wrangler break a new horse. He smoked his cigarette quietly for a minute before he spoke.

"You've hurt her, haven't you?" King asked.

Cal glanced at him, not surprised by his perception. He and King were much alike, not only in build, but in temperament. It had led to some terrible fistfights in their youth, but now created a special bond between them.

"Yes," he admitted. "I said some unforgivable things."

"And you're afraid to go back, because she might not want you."

Cal chuckled without humor. "I suppose I am."

King flicked an ash from his cigarette. "I know more than I'll ever tell you about being in the wrong with a woman. I've played hell myself and, fortunately, been forgiven. I almost lost Amelia. It changed me."

Cal rolled himself a cigarette while he chose his words. "This has changed me," he said finally when he'd finished and lit it. "I never thought I wanted marriage or children before. But I'd give anything to have a second chance."

"Go to her," King advised quietly. "Find out how she feels."

Cal smiled ruefully at his brother. "Her father will probably meet me at the door with the local constable. I hit him pretty hard."

"This time," King said, "dress like a gentleman. And act like one!"

"I thought that clothes and background wouldn't matter, if she loved me."

King scowled as he remembered the way it had been with Amelia, before they married. She had clung to him, adored him. It wouldn't have mattered to her if he'd been a sheepherder, she loved him so much. She still did.

His silence brought Cal's eyes to him, narrowed in thought. "It wouldn't have mattered. Would it?" he pressed.

King averted his eyes. "Go and see her before you make choices. It's always better to know for sure."

Cal finished his cigarette and dropped it to the ground. He pressed it into the dirt under the heel of his boot. "You got lucky," he said abruptly.

King's eyes were wistful. "Not at once," he said. "It was a rocky path, and for a while, she hated me. Those were hard days." He laughed softly. "But now . . . now I don't envy any man alive. God, how I love her!"

The emotion in that deep voice made Cal envious. A blind man could see that Amelia worshiped her husband equally. He hoped that they would have years and years together.

"I'll buy a ticket to Virginia," Cal said presently. He arched an eyebrow at his brother. "One way."

"I'd buy two, for the return trip," King murmured

dryly. "And carry her kicking and screaming to the train. So would you have, before this thing laid you low."

Cal burst out laughing. He and King were so much alike. The two of them swamped poor Alan. It was just as well that he had a totally different career in mind than throwing in with either of his brothers. Alone, he stood a better chance of being self-reliant.

King clapped his brother on the back and turned him toward the house. "I'll ride into town with you and bring your horse back."

"It sounds as if I'm leaving," he remarked.

King nodded. "Since you'll be going through Tyler Junction anyway, stop and see how Tremayne's doing. Tell him you heard we're pleased with his progress. That should reassure him."

"It's all vaguely deceitful, you know," Cal remarked.

King shrugged. "All for a good cause."

"I suppose so." Cal relented, but reluctantly. He wasn't best pleased with the idea of seeing the Tremaynes again after the way they'd parted company. And the memories of Nora in that house were going to tear him apart. For himself, he'd just as soon send them a telegram as go out there and deliver a message in person.

But in the end, he left Alan on the train as it pulled out of Tyler Junction en route to Louisiana, hired a horse, and rode out to the Tremayne ranch.

It was cold, as December often was, even in East Texas. He saw the fields spreading out bare and lifeless before him, but the cattle had feed, thanks to that new combine and the tractors Tremayne had bought at Cal's insistence. Everywhere he could see the benefits of the improvements, and he thought that his father and brothers were going to be pleased.

He'd cabled Pike in Beaumont and heard that the part had come in early. Pike already had the derrick put up and they were drilling. They had a problem with mud seeping into the shaft, but they'd been given some advice by another wildcatter and had solved it with a valve. Some oil and gas pockets had been found in Gladys City, but there was the possibility of a real strike on Spindletop Hill, where some serious drilling was being conducted despite the advice of one well-known geologist. Pike, like Cal, refused to listen to him. Cal had good friends at the large oil field in Corsicana, and they had invested in his several-hundred-acre tract of land. He refused to believe that they were going to find any more dry holes. This time, he told himself, they would find oil. He knew they would. He planned to swing by Beaumont on his way to Virginia and check that drill and the new valve before he left Texas. He'd worked with the men in Corsicana long enough to understand drilling, although he and Pike had a contractor who knew the business better than either of them.

The Tremayne house was quiet when he rode up and left his horse with the stableboy. He walked onto the porch and knocked.

To say that Chester was shocked to see him was an understatement. Cal looked different in his dark suit and string tie and dressy black Stetson and boots. He looked like a businessman more than the ranch foreman who'd left several weeks before. Cal's hand was shaken profusely and he was greeted like a long-lost son.

"We're just sitting down to dinner! Come in, come in, and join us. How have you been?" Chester enthused.

"I've been well. Things look good here," he added. "Very profitable."

"You'd think so if you saw the balance sheets. Sure you don't want your old job back?" the older man coaxed as they entered the living room, where Helen sat alone at the dinner table. "I haven't hired anyone else."

"No, I have other irons in the fire now," Cal said in a subdued tone. He swept off his hat and smiled at Helen as he greeted her.

She was staring as if she'd seen a ghost. She made a gesture to Chester, but he ignored it and told Cal to sit down.

A minute later, oblivious to their guest, a harried Nora, in a stained apron and a faded dress, swept in the door sideways with a huge platter of beef in one hand and a plate of biscuits in the other. She set the containers on the table with an apology when one almost spilled, and only then looked up and saw Cal across the table.

She went alternately white and red, and then began to tremble as her heart raced uncontrollably.

Cal's jaw clamped shut. He got slowly to his feet, made aware by the way she was dressed and what she was doing that she'd been reduced to the status of a servant here. He was all but trembling with rage as he looked at Chester.

"Would you care to explain this?" he asked curtly, with an arrogance and authority that made everyone suddenly nervous.

"Why don't you ask me?" Nora broke in, straightening as she struggled to regain her composure. She smoothed her stained apron and stared at him levelly. "I'm working to earn my keep. I didn't want to go home."

That bit of welcome news didn't stifle Cal's outrage at her changed status. "You're still my wife," Cal said furiously.

Her eyebrows arched. "I am? Imagine that, and here I thought you'd vanished off the face of the earth!"

"You had the address of my attorney," he said coldly.

"I've been too busy to use it," she lied. Her chin came up. "Why are you here?"

"Not to see you," he said with a cool smile. "I stopped to ask Chester about his progress. And to tell him that the combine thinks he's doing a fine job. I, uh, saw one of its representatives in my travels."

Chester beamed. "How fortuitous!"

Nora brushed off her apron. "If you'll sit down," she invited her erstwhile husband coolly, "I'll finish serving."

She went back into the kitchen. Cal got up and followed her, without a query or an apology.

She was putting biscuits into a big bowl, but she turned as he entered the room and closed the door behind him. "I'm busy," she said bluntly.

He leaned against the counter to study her. She was still thin, but she looked remarkably fit. She was just as pretty as she had been. His eyes fed on the sight of her, and he felt at peace for the first time since he'd walked out of this house the night she started to recover.

"Has the fever been kept at bay?" he asked.

She nodded curtly, and kept putting biscuits in the bowl. "I'm much better. I didn't want to go home and I didn't want to embarrass my people by getting a job with someone else. I do the housework and the cooking, and I stay in the house with them. Melly is getting married in the spring. She's gone to town with Mr. Langhorn and his son to shop."

"Good for Melly." He folded his arms across his chest. "I'm going to Beaumont," he said, neglecting to add that he'd planned to go on to Virginia in search of her. She wasn't very receptive. Not that he'd expected anything else. There were open wounds in her heart that he'd put there.

"Are you? Why?" she asked.

"I have some leases on a prospective oil field," he said honestly. "It's where I went on weekends. I have a partner. We're drilling our third hole. The first two were dry. We're hoping to hit oil this time."

She frowned. "The Beaumont paper has mentioned some minor successes there, but one of the better-known geologists says there is no major oil field there," she said.

"And I tell you there is," he said easily. "I worked in the oil fields in Corsicana before I started looking in Beaumont over a year ago. I have leases on several hundred acres of land, and a crew hard at work even now."

She was surprised. She had known less about him than she realized. She didn't want to ask how he was affording this expensive venture. Presumably his partner was rich.

She went to fetch the butter from the small icebox, where it was wrapped in a cloth next to the huge block of ice they had delivered from the plant in town.

"Are you staying to dinner?" she asked politely.

He nodded. "If it's convenient."

"You must ask my aunt, not me. I only work for her."

His cheekbones went ruddy. "You're my wife, by God," he said curtly. "I don't want you working as an unpaid domestic!"

She turned to him, her pretty face composed, her blue eyes eloquent. "I am not unpaid. I work for my keep. You walked out and left me," she reminded him calmly.

His jaw tautened. "I'm very well aware of the condition you were in when I left. And I will remind you that you told me to leave," he added curtly. "You gave me no opportunity to tell you anything."

"You didn't try!" she returned hotly.

He leaned back against the pantry door. "I was too upset. You had told me nothing about your health, except that you were carrying my child. I came back to find that you had miscarried and were at death's door. How do you think I felt?"

She grimaced. "I can imagine that you were shocked."

"Devastated," he corrected. "I knew that I had done you no service by bringing you here, to a life of drudgery and hard labor. You were too fragile for it. I was eaten up with guilt. Leaving seemed the kindest thing to do. I didn't blame you for not wanting to see me, Nora."

She saw the pain in his face, and her eyes softened. "You gave me the best life you could manage," she said gently, and wondered at the way he winced. "What made me angriest was my own inability to do the simplest things. I couldn't cook or clean." She laughed softly. "I find that I do both very well now. I'm no longer helpless. I've grown strong from my troubles."

"You should never have had to bear so many," he

said sadly. "After you refused to speak to me, I went out to a tavern and got royally drunk. On the way back, it occurred to me that there would be little purpose served in staying around the ranch. You would recover more rapidly without me, I imagined, so I got on the next train to Beaumont. I thought that you would immediately return to your family in Virginia and divorce me."

As she had guessed. No wonder he hadn't tried to contact her. She sighed. "My father would allow me to come home if I apologized," she told him ruefully. "Since I did not think that I had anything to apologize for, here I still am."

His face hardened. "Any apologies owed were on his side, not yours. Your father is a disgrace to his sex."

Her eyebrows lifted. "Indeed," she said. "And he works so hard at it."

It took him a minute to recognize the dry humor. When he did, a faint smile turned up the corners of his disciplined mouth. "So he does."

She covered the biscuits in their bowl so that they would stay warm. She felt equally warm, having Cal close again, being able to look at him. Life had become beautiful once more. "I should have told you about the fever," she said apologetically. Her eyes lifted to his. "If I had done so, if I had been honest from the start, you would have been spared so much sorrow."

"Neither of us has been particularly candid with the other, Nora," he said quietly.

She stared at his eyes and saw the new lines around them, and in his lean face. He was thinner. He had aged, somehow. Yes, he had suffered, too.

"Why did you hide the true state of your health?" he asked.

"At first because I didn't know you well enough to share such an intimate confidence. And afterward, because it seemed so harsh, to tell a new bridegroom with a pregnant wife that she had a disease which, if it did not kill her, would certainly plague her all her life." She lifted her face sadly. "You could barely keep us both on what you earned, and there was already the baby to provide for when it came," she said painfully. "I hoped to spare you . . . any more burdens."

His eyes closed. He turned away from her, to hide the anguish those words produced.

"Your parents . . . they knew you were ill and still would not relent after you lost the baby?" he asked with quiet guilt.

"They knew. I am an outcast." She smiled suddenly. "But I can iron a shirt!" she announced brightly. "And I can cook biscuits that do not bounce, and steak that melts in the mouth!"

Her radiance caught him unawares. He searched her bright blue eyes hungrily. "It was not the things you couldn't do that bothered me," he said huskily. "It was the fact that if you had truly cared for me, it would not have mattered to you how I made my living or what I had," he concluded. His eyes averted. "But you were contemptuous, of my station in life, of my work, even the way I dressed. I was cruel because it hurt me that you said you had married beneath you."

She didn't know what to say. He made accusations that were truthful. She had said those things, and felt them. But now . . . looking at him, her heart melted in her chest. She loved him, wanted him, needed him. She didn't care if he was a pauper, if she had to work as a laundress or a cook just to stay with him. The discovery was not even shocking. She loved him so much that nothing else seemed to matter. But the difficulty was in trying to express it, after all the painful things that had happened. She had no idea how to begin.

Chapter Sixteen

T HE OPENING OF THE DOOR CAPTURED THEIR ATTEN- tion. Helen walked into the kitchen, glancing from one to the other and not unaware of the silence and tension between them.

"The dinner?" she prompted gently.

Nora's blank eyes began to focus. "Dinner? Dinner!" she gasped. "Oh, Aunt Helen, I am sorry! We were talking and everything slipped my mind."

Helen only laughed. "I suppose I'm going to have to start cooking again pretty soon," she murmured. "Unless I miss my guess, you won't be here much longer?" She looked at Cal, who was frowning slightly. "Surely you plan to take Nora with you when you go?"

Cal hadn't, because he didn't think she would agree to go. But he looked at her, and his silver-gray eyes asked a question he didn't dare put into words.

"An oil camp is a rough place," he said slowly. "It's dirty and primitive, with few amenities and little privacy. You're fragile, and the weather is cold and unrelenting." He felt the truth of his logic acutely. He smiled sadly. "It wouldn't be wise to take you there."

Nora felt her last hope slipping away. "But I'm strong," she protested, shocking him. "The doctor says that even if the fever recurs, it won't kill me. And I can cook!"

He hesitated.

"Eat first, then you can talk about it," Helen said wisely.

They agreed. Nora put everything on the table, and they ate with only desultory conversation. Afterward, Nora cleared and washed the dishes, and then she and Cal sat down alone in the parlor to talk.

He rolled a cigarette and lit it. His dark suit jacket lay on the sofa beside him, leaving him clad only in dark pants, a white shirt, and a black and white floral print vest. He looked different in a suit to Nora, who had never seen him dressed in anything except denim and buckskin. It didn't occur to her to ask why he looked so prosperous when he had no job. Nora's eyes darted away from him, because she was remembering how it felt to lie against him and be held and wanted.

"It really is impractical to consider taking you with me," he said resignedly when he was smoking his cigarette. "You're better off here. In fact," he added with solemn reluctance, looking at her, "if you apologized to your father—"

"Never!" she said firmly. "It is he who should apologize, for insulting my husband!"

His eyebrows lifted. He smiled delightedly. "You have changed."

"I have had to," she said simply. "Shall I tell you the truth about myself? I was never an adventuress. I went to Africa and stayed in a magnificent home while my cousins went out to hunt. For one night I was allowed in camp, and during that night Edward Summerville became disgustingly amorous and tore my clothing. As a result, I was bitten severely by mosquitoes and I acquired the fever that will plague me for the rest of my life."

"A malarial fever," he said.

She nodded. "But not a fatal one, or so I am now told. I had thought it might be, which is why I did not tell you. I feared for our child." The memory made her sad. She averted her face.

"I am sorry about the baby," he said heavily. "I could have spared you the housework, Nora, simply by hiring a daily woman. . . ."

"How would you have afforded one?" she asked, missing the renewed flare of guilt in his face. "Cal, it does no good to look back. I have always felt that the Almighty decides matters of life and death. I, too, am sorry about my baby. But many people face such losses and go on. So must we."

He leaned back against the sofa and studied her with pale, quiet eyes. "There are still things about me that you do not know," he said, wondering how he was going to tell her his own secrets without making her hate him even more.

She straightened her skirt. "I would like to go with you to Beaumont."

"It's a small cabin, and my drilling crew lives in tents around it. We would not be alone out there, but there is also only one bed," he added stiffly.

She colored a little. "I see."

He stared down at his cigarette thoughtfully. "Of course, you could stay in Beaumont at a hotel."

She straightened her skirt again. "Yes."

His eyes lifted. "Even so, it would be harder for you than it is here," he said. "And I would be out at the rig with my crew. I don't like the idea of having you so far away from me, especially at night. Nora, it's a bad idea."

Her blue eyes clung to his. "Do you not want me to go with you?"

His face tautened. He took a draw from his cigarette and glowered. "If you want the truth, there is nothing I desire more."

The worry left her face. She looked amazed. "Truly?"

"What if you become ill?" he asked seriously.

"What if you do?" she countered. "You don't have fever, but you could go down with a cold or even pneumonia, and who would take care of you?"

His lips parted on a gush of breath. "You would . . . take care of me?"

"But of course," she said guilelessly. "And if I go, Cal, I will not stay in Beaumont," she added firmly. "Regardless of the hardships, I will go with you, to the drilling site. I don't wish us to be separated again. I am your wife."

His wife. His eyes slid over her body covetously and back up to her lovely face. His heart began to race. He should tell her the rest of it, about his family, his background. But if he did, she would hate him all over again. She would know that she had suffered unnecessarily and blame him.

But if he waited to tell her, just a little while, if he took her to Beaumont and he was kind to her, then she might begin to love him. And if she did, when he told her the truth . . .

He leaned forward, the smoking cigarette in his hand forgotten, and pinned her with narrowed pale eyes. "If I take you with me, you must tell me if it becomes too

much for you. Your health must come first. No shows
of pride, Nora. Never again."

"Very well," she said.

He watched her for a minute with growing need before he spoke. "And if you go with me—" he hesitated,
holding her eyes "—you sleep with me, Nora," he said
huskily.

Her cheeks colored prettily, but her eyes didn't fall.
They slid over his face, down to his mouth and lower,
to his chest. "Very well," she whispered shyly.

His high cheekbones flushed. His whole body went
rigid at the soft reply. He remembered, as she must, the
pleasure they could give to each other. She didn't even
pretend not to want him, thank God.

"Then pack your things, Nora," he said tightly. "I
want to leave before dark."

Her smile changed her face. "I'll go at once and tell
Aunt Helen!" she said, rising.

He rose, too, and stood towering over her with a solemn face and glittering eyes.

"It will not be easy," he said. "Even the cabin here
will look like a luxury in hindsight. There are rough
men and few women. In fact, before I left, a bordello
was trying to set up on the outskirts of the camp, where
the oil crews are working," he added frankly.

Her blue eyes widened. "Why, how exciting," she
said. "I have never seen one of those women."

"Nora!"

"You needn't look so outraged," she said pertly.
"Women are curious about such things, you know."

"No decent woman should be."

She lifted her chin and glared at him. "How superior

you sound, Mr. Barton," she taunted. She frowned as a thought occurred to her. "That bordello . . . ?"

"I have no need of bought women," he said shortly. "You insult me."

"You have done little else but insult me since we met," she pointed out. "And it is quite noticeable that you were not innocent when we married, or before!"

His chest shook with laughter he was trying to suppress. "You look like an angry little hen with ruffled feathers," he mused.

She pushed at the ruins of her high coiffure. "I am not a chicken," she informed him. Her brows lifted. "Did Aunt Helen mention that I can prepare a chicken? I am still a bit squeamish about it," she added conspiratorally, "but at least I no longer quail at the prospect."

The pronouncement didn't get the result she had expected. He looked as if each new mastered chore she recounted was painful to him. He moved forward and gently took her by the shoulders. His fingers lingered on the warm softness of the skin that he could feel through the cotton dress.

"That will no longer be necessary," he said quietly. "We will have to buy our meals—"

"We will not!" she assured him. "Not when I have spent an entire day having the bunkhouse cook show me how to prepare a meal over a campfire!"

His surprise was visible, and his breath caught.

"You see, you still think I am a dead loss," she fumed. "Well, let me tell you, I am no helpless Nellie! I can—"

Smiling, he bent and stopped the tirade with a warm,

hungry kiss in which tenderness and long weeks of abstinence were mingled.

The shock of pleasure sent Nora pressing close
against his long, powerful body, her arms meeting at his
back as she opened her mouth deliberately and pushed
upward.

He groaned, caught off guard. She felt his thighs
tremble against her as his arms contracted and his
mouth became bruising in its quest.

He moved her against him, loving the response she
gave him, loving the taste and touch and feel of her. Her
tongue shyly eased into his mouth, and at her belly she
felt, with something oddly like pride, the incredible
swiftness with which his body reacted.

He tore his mouth from hers and pushed her back,
holding her at arm's length with eyes so dilated, they
seemed black.

"We are married," she whispered, protesting breathlessly.

"Remember where we are, if you please," he said
angrily, although the dampness of his forehead and the
furious beat of his heart, visible under his shirt and
vest, belied his remoteness.

She smiled tenderly, her eyes drowsy with pleasure.
"I missed you," she said dreamily.

He drew in a long, steadying breath. "And I, you," he
said after a minute. "Are you sure, Nora?" he added. "I
could not bear to be the instrument of any further risk
to your health."

"My place is with you," she said simply.

He nodded. His eyes fell to her mouth and lingered
there. She thought absently that he looked like a different man in that suit. There was a new authority about

him, a sternness that was at variance with the easygoing man she had met when she first came here.

"You are like a stranger," she said, puzzled.

He traced her face with tender fingers. "I am a stranger," he said. "In more ways that you realize. You know me only as a lover."

Her cheeks became rosy as her gaze dropped to his firm mouth. "It is the only way in which you would permit me to know you," she ventured. Her hands toyed with a pearl button on his vest. "And I have been equally reticent in talking about myself. Shall we agree to talk to each other more in future?"

"Nights are long in the camp," he mused. "And we will have little privacy in which to do much else," he added with a rueful smile.

"But you said that I must sleep with you," she blurted out.

"And you must," he agreed. "But, sadly, that is all it may be between us. There are tents, very close to the cabin, where my crew stay." He pursed his lips, looking down at her with amusement and delight. "And you are very noisy when we make love," he whispered.

She hid her face against his vest. He held it there, chuckling tenderly above her disordered hair. "What a delight you are to me," he said huskily. His hand smoothed her nape. "Nora, there is something else to consider as well," he added. "Forgive me for being blunt, but I do not wish to make you pregnant again so soon. Your body will need time to recover from its ordeal." He felt her shiver, and his arm contracted around her shoulders. "When you consider that our child was conceived the first time we were ever together . . ."

"Yes, I know." She drew in a faint breath. "Do you

... want a child with me?" she asked hesitantly. "Someday?"

"What sort of a question is that?" He tilted her worried face up to his. There was censure in his pale eyes. "Why should I not want a child?"

Her lips curled inward. "You said that I was not the sort of woman you should have married," she began.

His thumb pressed softly over her mouth. "I said many cruel things. So did you. That is over. We are married, and I look forward to a long and happy life with you. Children will certainly be part of it, when you are healthy again."

"Oh. I see."

"Do not sound so dispirited," he coaxed. "It will not be forever."

She nodded, but she wouldn't meet his eyes.

He sensed disappointment and something beneath it. He bent and kissed her lightly, feeling her immediate response. Her caught breath went into his mouth and she shivered. And then he understood.

"I want you, too," he whispered softly.

She winced. "It will be so long," she said involuntarily, and flushed. "Forgive me. I sound wanton."

"You do not," he argued. "You sound like a very normal woman, newly married, who enjoys the embraces of her husband." He smiled. "Now, brace up. You look like the sinking of the *Maine*."

She peered up at him. "I feel it," she muttered.

"You have forgotten something I told you early in our marriage," he said.

"What?"

He drew his lips lightly over her ear. "That there are ways to pleasure each other that do not involve the possibility of creating a child," he whispered. "At the risk of darkening my reputation even more, I must tell you that I have considerable skill in that direction."

"Cal Barton!" she ground out, shocked.

He laughed, letting her twist out of his arms with a face that looked sunburned.

"Roué!" she accused, straightening her apron.

He lifted an amused eyebrow. "And worse," he confessed. "You will get used to it."

"I suppose I must, but I hope that you are reformed. Now that you are a respectable married man," she emphasized.

"We must both hope so. Now, will you get your things together, please, and I will ask Chester if he can take us to the depot. I hired a horse to come out here, and he will have to be returned as well. I think it a bit premature to expect you to ride double with me."

"I wish that I could ride," she confessed. "Melanie started to give me lessons, but I'm afraid I didn't get very far."

His face changed. "Riding will be something of a requirement for you," he said enigmatically. "It is one thing you will have to know."

"Why? We can hire a carriage in Beaumont, can we not?" she asked with some confusion.

He was thinking about Latigo and any time they spent there. Summers and holidays with his family would be expected, and she would love it there. He knew it. But first he had to find some way to tell her.

"Never mind that for now," he said.

"You ride very well indeed," she said. "It was one of the first things I noticed about you."

His pale eyes narrowed as they slid over her. "I noticed everything about you the first time I saw you," he said. "You were exquisite, standing there in your fashionable suit and that silly little French hat."

She was very still. "How did you know that the hat was French?"

His mother had one similar to it. He was hardly likely to admit it. He pursed his lips. "Perhaps you told me."

Her eyes darkened. "Perhaps another woman did."

His eyebrows shot up and he grinned. "Jealous?"

She whirled, her skirts flying, and went to open the door.

"Nora?"

Her head turned. "What?" she demanded.

He loved that temper. It was going to be a source of delight to him all their lives. It made her blue eyes sparkle like sapphires, and made her face radiant with color. "I haven't looked at another woman, in even the most innocent way, since the first time my eyes touched you."

The way he said it made her toes curl in her shoes. He had a deep, slow way of speaking to her that was exquisitely tender.

"But it pleases me that you would mind if I had," he added.

The doorknob was cold under her fingers. She caressed it slowly. "I would not have blamed you," she confessed tightly.

"I would have blamed myself, though." He joined her at the door. His big, lean hand covered hers warmly. "That will never become an option to me," he said. "If we argue, and we will from time to time, I will never consider shaming you in such a way. I am that much like my married older brother, who dotes on his wife and son. I think you will like them, and the rest of my family, when I take you home to them."

She shifted her eyes to his handsome face and caressed it with a gaze that made his knees feel weak.

"You are not . . . ashamed of me anymore?"

"Oh, my God, forgive me," he whispered with raw pain. His arms swallowed her up, crushed her, riveted her to him. He bent over her with such a wave of love that it almost buckled his knees.

She clung to him, a faint sob escaping her lips. "I was so wrong," she choked. "Wrong about you, about so many things! My father was such a snob, and I never realized how much I was like him until I came here. Now I cannot bear to go back and watch him denigrate people because they have less than he does."

He bent and kissed her hungrily, moaning softly as she answered his kiss and held on tight.

"This is so sweet," she whispered when they were both breathless and her cheek was resting on his chest. "We must kiss each other very often from now on."

"Not in public," he groaned.

She laughed, because she could feel why. It no longer embarrassed her. Well . . . not as much as it had. Her hips tugged back from him just enough for decorum.

"Coward," he said silkily, laughing down at her flaming face.

"Oh, on the contrary, I have become very brave," she teased. "Even my father would be amazed at the change in me, because I would not let him order me around now. He was good to me when I was younger, you know, even if he was very stern." She pursed her lips, and her eyes twinkled. "All the same, I am very glad that you hit him."

"At least you didn't ask me to shoot him," he said, and burst out laughing when he remembered the incident. "I thought Summerville was going to croak right on the spot!"

"He would have looked rather nice stuffed and mounted like one of the poor animals he shot in Africa," she recalled. She became solemn. "He was not even sorry. He wanted to marry me for my father's fortune, and he stooped to low means. It was terrible when he came to England and pestered me. I was mourning you and I wanted no part of him."

"We have spent an inordinate amount of time mourning each other," he observed, watching her. "In future, I do not plan to spend even a day separated from you."

She smiled tenderly. "What a lovely thought," she said as she stared at him possessively.

"Mmmmm," he murmured, equally fascinated with looking at her.

There was a knock at the door. They moved back and opened it, and Chester stood there.

"I wondered if you would like Helen and me to drive you to the station," he asked with a grin.

"How kind of you to offer," Cal said, smiling. "Nora is on her way to pack."

"It's the least I can do, my boy. Would you like to see the new hay baler while she's packing?" he added.

"Indeed I would!"

He bade Nora a fond farewell for the moment and went out with Chester.

"I don't suppose you might be persuaded to return?" Chester asked as they neared the barn.

"No. I'm sorry. I enjoyed my time here, but I've tied up too much money in Beaumont to divide my loyalties now. I'm prospecting for oil," he confessed ruefully. "This is the third well I've sunk and I'm hoping it will change my luck."

"Isn't oil prospecting a gamble?" Chester asked seriously, although the younger man's resourcefulness impressed him.

"Yes," Cal replied flatly. "But if I've learned nothing else in my life, it's that few fortunes are gained without some risk. I want to make my own way in the world and not be dependent on anyone else for my keep."

Chester misinterpreted that. "Well, you know, you were pretty independent here, and I'd try not to interfere. . . ."

He chuckled and clapped the older man on the back affectionately. "I know that. It wasn't what I meant. You know, you really should consider an investment in that field while there's still time."

"I've read about it in the Beaumont paper," Chester confessed. "And if there really is a strike, the price on that land will go sky-high overnight. But it's such a risk."

"Life is a risk," Cal told him. "I'm going to give you two percent of my stock." He held up his hand when Chester protested. He looked at him fully. "If I hit, that will amount to a hell of a lot of money. You can buy this place back from the combine and run it the way you want to. Now that you're on the right track with some modernization, you should have no trouble keeping it solvent."

Chester was flabbergasted. "But why would you do that for me?"

He couldn't tell the truth, that it was for Nora's sake, because they'd been so kind to her. Not only that, he'd nourished a real affection for the family since he'd been working for them.

He put an arm around Chester. "Listen. Wouldn't it just make you feel like a king to own part of a huge oil operation and tell your brother-in-law in Virginia how you got it?"

Chester whistled. "Tut, tut, I'd rub it in until he was chafed!"

Cal grinned at him. "So would Nora," he added.

"I see!" He burst out laughing. "All right, then, I'll accept your kind offer. But if you do hit it big, my boy, you really must take Nora back to Virginia to visit her family. Preferably in a golden coach."

"I have something a bit more grand in mind than that alone," Cal replied. His pale eyes were glittering, and Chester thought, not for the first time, that he was glad he had never made an enemy of the man. Cal had cold steel just under that characteristically warm good nature of his. He felt a bit sorry for his brother-in-law. And he sincerely hoped that Cal was going to bring in that well.

He would love getting richer. But what he would enjoy most would be seeing his brother-in-law bluster when the man he'd always looked down on turned up prosperous, with an elegantly dressed Helen on his arm. He didn't think Helen would mind if her sister saw her that way, either. The one time the two of them had visited the Marlowes, it had been very uncomfortable. Nora's father had considered himself so far above the Tremaynes that he spoke to them like servants during their brief stay. Cynthia hadn't said a word about the treatment her sister received, although her face was sad.

Chester had come home furious, and Helen hadn't smiled for a week. The two sisters had come from the same wealthy background, but like poor Nora, Helen had been disinherited when her parents disapproved of her marriage to Chester.

Chester had secretly felt inferior ever since he'd married Helen. Perhaps Cal understood that feeling, and it was why he'd made his shocking offer. Whatever his reason, the offer delighted Chester. He only wished he had something to offer Cal in return for that stock. He'd have to see if he couldn't manage a good thoroughbred horse for the boy. He knew a breeder who owed him a favor, and Cal had something of a mania about good horses.

Chapter Seventeen

Beaumont was a growing town with a few thousand inhabitants. A quarter of the population was made up of black people, and there were several Jewish businesses there. There were also Italian and Dutch immigrants and even a few cowboys. It was a friendly city, but it lacked many of the modern industrial assets that would be required if a big oil field did lie near its borders, something that worried Cal and other investors.

The huge Gladys City development had at first been the object of scorn, and still was not considered a serious proposition by some people. Cal had been scoffed at by local businessmen for sinking money into such a pipe dream, and even while they worked to build his derricks, local contractors laughed at him behind his back. But like the other oil seekers, he believed in the development and had great respect for it, and its founder.

It had been to Cal's advantage that no one locally knew of his background. It prevented anyone taking advantage of the fact that he had money.

His wasn't the only outfit working at dragging oil out of the ground here. Captain Lucas, a brilliant gentleman with a Slavic background, had a rig nearby and had come up with some amazing techniques to combat the drilling problems that were peculiar to this coastal area of Texas. He, like Cal, had contacts in Corsicana to whom he could turn for drilling equipment and advice. The innovations that he and his men used in penetrating the pressurized salt dome, which also contained quicksand and large rock, were to revolutionize the oil business. There was even a rumor that J. D. Rockefeller and his people at giant Standard Oil had their eyes on Beaumont. Everyone was waiting. Waiting.

Meanwhile, there were dry holes and premature reports of failure and wild stories of outlandish strikes put about by out-of-town reporters.

Cal related this to Nora, who listened with fascination while they spent their first night in Beaumont in a hotel. He had gone out to the rig to check on the progress of Pike and the crew and had come back dispirited and tired.

"What's wrong?" she asked when he took off his muddy boots and his jacket.

"Another snag," he said wearily. "Captain Lucas has overcome his quicksand problem, but ours plagues us still. We had to send for yet another fish-bait bit from Corsicana." He lay back in the chair with a groan. "I have so many people waiting, hoping, for success." His eyes slid over her body. "I'm impatient. Captain Lucas has been drilling since October. He hit a gas pocket, but no oil. Not yet, at least. You're so thin Nora," he added unexpectedly. "You must try to eat more, to regain your strength."

"I have had very little appetite," she told him. She smiled. "But now that you're back, I am hungrier."

He chuckled. "In a moment we must go downstairs

for the evening meal." He held out his hand. "But not yet."

She gave him her slender fingers and was pulled down onto his lap. He bent and kissed her, and for a long time, not a word was spoken.

His hand smoothed over her bodice possessively, while she curled up in his arms and lay waiting for his mouth to return to hers.

"I don't like to divert you," she whispered, smiling, "but supper will become cold downstairs, and there is an apple duff, which our landlady remarked that she made from apples she had hoarded in the fruit cellar."

He smiled back. "And you like apple duff?"

"I adore it. I adore you, too, but apple duff is irresistible at the moment."

"In that case, let me change my boots for a pair of clean shoes and we will go down."

He let her go while he went in his stocking feet to his suitcase and a minute later donned a pair of very expensive looking leather shoes. She didn't comment while she fetched her pretty black shawl to drape over her nice black dress, but she wondered about those shoes. Cal was still much like a stranger to her.

All the talk downstairs was of the Spindletop Hill, where Captain Lucas was drilling.

"Did you see the sky?" one boarder asked excitedly. "Lit up like a funeral pyre, it was, over that way." He pointed, as if his audience could see through the wall.

"Yes, we did," an elderly woman agreed. "It is Saint Elmo's fire," she added. "Sailors believe that when they see it, their ships will come safely into the harbor."

"This is not Saint Elmo's fire," the boarder said indignantly. "It comes from where Captain Lucas is drilling."

"He's hit another gas pocket, likely," another commented. "One day he'll blow himself right off that hill. Or catch the whole thing afire."

"They say there's oil out there," the boarder said.

"I'll believe it when I see it. Pass the potatoes, please," the elderly woman returned.

Nora and Cal exchanged complicated glances. He didn't mention that he had an investment in the oil field. Neither did he take the elderly lady's word for the lack of oil there. He needed an optimistic outlook.

Later, while Nora got ready for bed, he went down to the nearest saloon to meet his drill crew, as he'd arranged earlier in the day.

"Oh, it's been a slow process, trying to sink a shaft in that unholy spot," Mick Wheeler, the engineer from Corsicana, said, rubbing his bald head. The other four men, and Pike, who had joined them, nodded their agreement. "Like the other group that's drilling near us, we had a problem getting the pipe out to the site right off. Then we had to borrow a rig to unload it from the train. Once we got the pipe in, we hit quicksand and it piled in and collapsed the sidewalls of the well."

"Just like the first two wells," Pike commented, "but they were in other areas, not on the hill. The problem of the quicksand and gravel took two weeks, and once we got past that, we had a blowout from a gas pocket."

"Aye," Mick agreed. "We've had to keep those circulating pumps going around the clock, which has meant trying to find more men for the crew. We have plenty who stand around and watch, but nobody will hire on."

"They're probably afraid of being laughed at," Cal

said heavily, fingering his beer. "Oil prospecting seems to be the favorite joke in this town."

"They won't laugh long once we strike oil," Mick said curtly.

Pike looked not only worried, but nervous. He seemed uncomfortable, watching the door every time a new customer entered. "We should get back out to the site," he said. "I don't like leaving it unattended."

"There's a sentiment with which I agree." Mick nodded. "Even though all we've got right now is a gas pocket, who knows what we may hit when we get down further. Lucas hit rock when he was at eight hundred and eighty feet. We're at eight hundred feet now."

"We'll hit rock, too," one of the crew muttered, "and be right back where we started."

"No, we won't," Cal said shortly. "If we hit rock, we're damned well going through it! Lucas did, which means it has to be possible."

"But how, man?" Pike exclaimed. "Short of begging the captain for his secret, which I won't for one minute consider . . ."

"Cable Sam Drago out in Corsicana," Cal told Pike. "I don't care what it costs," he added when the other man protested. He handed him a twenty-dollar gold piece. "Use it all if you have to. Tell him what problems we may run into and ask him for advice. Tell him to come out here if he has to. I'm not stopping for rock. Lucas got through it somehow. I want to know how."

"You could ask him." Mick grinned.

"I could. But fair is fair. I don't expect him to help me beat him to the prize," Cal said. "It's a question of ethics. Besides, he's already helped us with the valve. That's enough to ask."

"You're right, of course," Mick agreed.

Pike didn't add his agreement. He still looked worried and out of sorts. "I'll wire Drago in the morning. Come on, men."

He was in an unholy rush to get going. Mick swallowed his beer with a wink at Cal and a whispered "Maybe it's a woman," before he joined the older man.

Watching them leave, Cal puzzled about Pike's unease. No, Pike wasn't the sort to like women. He was a loner by nature, and there was something shifty about him. He'd better keep an eye on the man. If there was anything going on, he'd put Mick in charge and take his chances. If Pike hadn't already found oil twice in other areas of the country, including Corsicana, he might have been less willing to take the risk.

When he got back upstairs, Nora was tucked up in bed asleep. He stood beside the bed, staring down at her beautiful thick hair spread all over the pillow and her long lashes pressed against the pale skin of her cheeks. She looked thin and not at all healthy. He wondered if he'd done the right thing, bringing her here. Only time would tell. Tomorrow they'd go out to the site, and she'd have to manage. He dreaded subjecting her to those conditions, but he liked even less leaving her in town alone. Any city was a dangerous place for a woman on her own. Even with the primitive surroundings, she'd be better off where he could look after her, and make sure she was taking care of herself as well.

He smiled as he watched her sleep. She was his. He'd never felt the kind of possessiveness he did right now. He thanked God for her father's inflexibility. Because of it, he had a second chance. He wasn't going to waste it.

They hired a buggy and rode out to the rig the next morning with their cases tied on the back.

The country four miles south of Beaumont was flat except for the hill where the drilling was going on.

"Patillo Higgins is the force behind this whole thing," Cal explained as they drove toward one of the derricks in the distance. "He'd almost given up, though, when Captain Lucas took him up on the lease. Now everything is riding on that well coming in." He shook his head. "For his sake, and ours, I hope it does."

Nora watched him from under her lashes, more curious about him every day. She had overslept this morning, and when she opened her eyes, it was to find him dressed and on his way down to see the livery man about hiring a buggy. She dressed in his absence and packed, and was ready to go right after they had breakfast with the other boarders.

Secretly she had hoped that he might wake her very early and teach her some of those secrets he'd hinted at. But his mind seemed very much on his oil well. She resigned herself to playing second fiddle until he either found oil or gave up looking. She had a hunch that he would never give up. It seemed to be in his blood. She wondered if his people were involved in the oil business. She'd have to ask him, when there was time.

She was introduced to Pike, and she disliked him on sight. He wasn't familiar or rude, but she sensed a lack of honesty about him. It was in the way he shifted his gaze when he spoke to her, even in the way he spoke to Cal.

Cal led her into the small, rude cabin and showed her around. There wasn't much to show; only one room, a few old cane-back chairs, an iron bedstead with a saggy mattress and worn sheets, and a fireplace with a Dutch oven hanging in it. On a rickety stand were a chipped blue-patterned ceramic basin and pitcher, and underneath, what must have passed for a towel. Nora thought immediately that she would not get a bath short of town.

"I know, it isn't much," he said through his teeth. It was freezing cold, to boot. He went to get an armload of wood from the porch to stack beside the fireplace. A small bottle of kerosene stood at the hearth where the poker rested. He arranged the wood and picked up the bottle.

"No!" she exclaimed. "Cal, you'll set the place ablaze!"

He turned, chuckling. "I don't like taking ten minutes to get a fire started. If you're shaky, go stand outside."

"Oh, Cal," she groaned.

He arranged the few knotted sticks of fat pine, doused them with kerosene, stood back, struck a match, and tossed it in. The wood blazed up explosively, but after a minute, the fat pine knots were burning. It wouldn't take long for them to catch the seasoned oak logs, and they would burn for a long, long time.

"Greenhorn," he accused affectionately. "Don't they have fireplaces back East, then?"

She glowered at him. "Yes, and we have paper with which to start fires!"

"You'll find that we have quite another use for our mail-order catalogs out West," he said, tongue in cheek. "Along with our corncobs. The, uh, privy is out that way." He opened the back door of the cabin and nodded toward a small wood structure that stood with a bag of quick lime beside it.

She lifted her chin and managed not to blush. "And chamber pots?"

"Chamber pot," he said sheepishly. "For a man, I'm afraid. We don't have a tall one for you."

That would mean the long walk to the outhouse at night with a lamp. Her next purchase, she decided would be a chamber pot for herself.

"I can see your mind working," Cal said with resignation. "I have to send one of the men in to get the food. I ordered supplies yesterday and forgot to stop for them on the way out of town. You'll have nothing to cook if I don't. I'll have him pick up the necessary item."

"That's very thoughtful of you."

"Very selfish," he chuckled. "I don't want to have to get up and light you out the back."

"You would do that?"

He moved forward and took both her hands in his. "These are good men, but there are few women to be seen. I would not have any unpleasantness, if it can be avoided."

"I do not like Mr. Pike," she said at once.

"I noticed that." His eyes narrowed. "Why?"

He wasn't belittling her remark. She wondered if he had reservations of his own. "It's nothing particular. Just intuition."

"You won't have that much contact with him," he said gently.

She turned and looked around. "Can we afford some

new ticking for the mattress?" she asked plaintively. "It looks as if a muddy army has slept on it."

"I ordered a new mattress," he said, to her delight, "and new sheets."

"That is an extravagance," she said guiltily. "I could have washed—"

"With what?" he asked politely. "We have no pot to boil clothes in, no tubs to rinse them in, no lines to hang them on—for there are no trees here."

She was horrified. He soothed her. "There is a laundry in town," he assured her. "You will not have to wear soiled clothing."

She looked worried just the same. "It will be expensive," she said slowly, hesitant to offend him.

"Your concern for my pocket does you credit," he said with a smile. "But we can manage. I have credit in town, you know."

"Oh!" She brightened. "That makes it better."

What she probably meant was that it made it understandable that he was able to afford things. She hadn't asked him about his source of income, but he knew she wondered just the same. Soon he was going to have to tell her the truth.

They settled in on the site. After the first few days, Nora felt more comfortable cooking on an open fire. She was good with stews, and even with biscuits once she mastered the art of cooking them on the fire. A cake was impossible, so she had Cal buy one at the bakery in town. They shared some of it with the men, whose own cooking seemed to leave much to be desired, considering their thinness.

The conditions were rough, and Nora had all she

could do to keep warm at first. But the cabin was fairly tight, and she was careful to spend most of her time inside. She mended the curtains and did what she could to keep the living area spotless. He surprised her with little things for the cabin, like a new decorated glass kerosene lamp and a chair with a crocheted cushion. His thoughtfulness delighted her.

At night she curled close to Cal and slept comfortably and secure in his arms. He held her, but he never encouraged her further than that. He didn't kiss her these days, and when her hand strayed to his bare chest under the covers, he moved it away. She knew what he was trying to do. He didn't want to risk getting her pregnant. Unfortunately, he didn't seem to want to do anything short of it, either.

"You said that we would explore other ways of pleasing each other," she whispered daringly one night.

"And we will," he said gently, kissing her eyes closed. "But not with my men camping on the porch," he chuckled. "The rains came unexpectedly and soaked the ground. They would never be able to sleep in the mud, Nora, and without them, there will be no oil."

"I know," she groaned. "It is just . . ."

"Go to sleep. Try not to dwell on it. I know that you are bored here. Perhaps we might get some magazines. Would you like that?"

She smiled. "Yes. But I would like some colored thread and some crocheting hooks, please. And some yarn and knitting needles. I can do handiwork, if I have the materials. I might make you a sweater."

"I never wear them," he murmured.

"Then I shall knit you some socks," she said, not to be outdone.

He wrapped her up against him. "Socks would be fine. Go to sleep."

She closed her eyes. But, as usual, sleep was a long time coming.

The next day, all hell broke loose on the hill. Captain Lucas's well exploded into the sky late in the morning of January 10, 1901, and all the doomsayers shut up for good.

"He did it!" Cal cried from the porch, because he could see the plume of oil rising majestically into the sky. "By God, he did it, Nora; come and look! He did it! There's oil there! Acres and acres and acres of oil!"

She came and stood beside him, watching the huge black gusher against the gray sky, with her arm around his lean waist.

"And we're right next door," he said, waving to his crew. They were jumping up and down and dancing on their own rig. It was only a matter of time now, and they all knew it. If oil could be struck one place on the hill, it could be struck all around. The land Cal owned was money in the bank.

Pike's small eyes gleamed now with excitement. He got his reply back from Corsicana, and the men followed the instructions Drago had sent. As time passed, they went down and down and down.

Then, the first week of March, there was a sudden explosion inside the derrick. Nora had been washing out her smalls inside the house. She came onto the porch and stood watching, her hand shading her eyes from the sun.

Cal yelled something at Pike, who started backing away. All at once, mud began to spurt up the derrick. Pike slid down the ladder, followed at once by Cal, who was yelling at Mick and the others to get out of the way.

The men fell back, covered with mud, and still the sticky brown muck flew up and up. Then, all at once, what seemed tons of four-inch pipe joined the mud and started up through the derrick. The crown block went, and the pipe started shooting up and landing stuck in the ground.

"Oh, no!" Nora whispered in anguish. She knew that Cal had invested heavily in this venture, and now it seemed that he was going to lose everything. Weeks of watching with him, hoping with him, were crumbling, just as the pipe and derrick that had been so expensive were now falling like tenpins. At least, thank God, Cal had gotten out of the way in time. If he'd been closer . . . It didn't bear thinking about! That falling pipe, in such huge amounts, would surely have killed him!

When it stopped, finally, Cal began cursing. He was so eloquent that Nora covered her ears, and he wasn't the only man on the place expressing his feelings about mud, derricks, pipe, and prospective oil in graphic terms.

The men stomped back up to the derrick, seeing impossible figures to replace it. Captain Lucas's strike had boosted prices beyond belief, for everything from land to lumber.

Cal squatted down to look at a piece of pipe with furious silver eyes.

"My God," he said heavily. "It will take thousands to replace all this. And then we'll have to start again, from scratch!"

"Hell of a shame, boss," Pike said. He looked nervous. Really nervous. "What a hell of a shame!"

Mick was more vocal as he swung toward the remains of the derrick. He muttered all the way up to it and turned to call his crew to start picking up the strewn materials.

He'd just opened his mouth when there was an ominous rumble.

"Get the hell out of there, Mick!" Cal shouted.

The Irishman made it in the nick of time, as more mud came spewing out in a flood. But this time it didn't end with mud. The mud was followed by a column of gas. And that was followed within seconds . . . by a thick, green, solid flow . . . of *oil*!

"Oil!" Mick screamed. His voice didn't even sound human. He held out his arms, and it covered him, oozed down his clothing into his shoes. "Oil, oil . . . !"

Cal had been holding his breath. Now he threw down his hat and ran into the flow with Mick. The two of them grabbed each other in bear hugs and then began to dance like two crazy people. Even reserved Pike joined in, along with the other men. Nora laughed and cried all at once as she realized what had happened. Cal's gamble had paid off. They were going to be very, very rich.

Cal saw her standing on the porch and ran up to grab her in a greasy bear hug, lifting her clear of the wooden flooring.

"We've done it," he laughed. "We've done it, we've done it, Nora; we're set for life!"

"Yes, I know," she laughed. She rubbed at the thick oil on his face, but he pulled her close and kissed her. She didn't seem to mind the taste of it, or the grime of his body, so he kissed her again. And for a few glorious seconds, they were alone in a world of their own.

Then the landscape exploded with people, in buggies,

on horseback, on foot from the camp around them. People came to exclaim over the well, to congratulate them, to offer suggestions.

While Cal and Nora answered the greetings, Pike was talking to a stranger in a suit and looking nervously toward the porch, where Cal was standing. Nora's eyes narrowed. Something very suspicious was going on. She hoped that Pike hadn't done anything in Cal's absence that would put a damper on this glorious triumph. She was going to have to talk to him about Pike.

She tried, when the bulk of the well-wishers had gone home, among them Captain Lucas himself.

"Listen, Cal," she began while he was trying to wash some of the oil from his face. "About Pike . . ."

"What about Pike, dearest?" he murmured into his towel. "He's as delirious as the rest of us."

"Did you see him talking to that man in the suit?"

"Hmmm," he agreed, wiping at his eyes. "That was one of the new lawyers in town. I met him earlier. He and Pike are friends, that's all."

Nora had an unpleasant feeling that friendship was not what had drawn those two men together. But not for all the world could she do anything to dampen Cal's spirits.

"This won't do at all," he muttered when he saw the residue of oil that covered him. "Not that I'm complaining," he chuckled when he saw the smudges he'd left all over her. "But we'll never get clean in a basin. Come on. We'll check into a hotel and have proper baths in town. And then you and I and this crew are going to celebrate. In fact," he added, swinging her gently around, "we're going to buy all the champagne in the saloon and drink ourselves right to heaven."

"I don't drink," she faltered.

"You will tonight," he assured her, with a grin that made her head whirl. "Because we have just hit one of the biggest oil strikes in history. And there is no way I'm going to celebrate *that* without my wife!"

Chapter Eighteen

THE CELEBRATION WAS LOUD, BUT NOBODY IN THE SA-
loon seemed to mind, even when glasses were broken. Cal poured champagne and urged it on Nora, who
felt conspicuous as the only woman in the place. Well,
except for two women who had come in with the men.
They were dressed in low-cut muslin dresses, and they
had eyes as hard as their hands looked soft. They
grinned at Nora, who grinned back even through her
blushes.

"You wanted to know what they looked like," Cal
whispered in her ear. "Now you do."

She hit at him.

"Drink up," he challenged. He was relaxed and getting more so by the minute, his eyes glittery with pleasure as he watched his shy wife. Over two months of
holding her without anything more ardent had taken its
toll on him. If he hadn't had the arduous quest for oil to
occupy him, he thought, he might have been climbing
walls or treeing the town by now. He wanted Nora desperately, but despite the gains in health she had made,
he didn't want to put her at risk just yet. He'd made
sure that she didn't have to do laundry or haul water
from the well on the property or do anything except the

very lightest of chores. She'd spent most of her time knitting and trying new recipes. He was truly astounded at the difference between the woman he'd married and the Nora who lived with him now. But there were things that hadn't changed, like her impish sense of humor and gallant spirit. He found himself more in love with her every day. He often wondered about her own feelings, but she'd become adept at hiding them most of the time. He'd been unkind to her. He didn't like to think that he might have killed any deeper feelings that she'd harbored before she lost the baby.

When he wasn't working, they'd spent time talking about general subjects, like the continuously changing situation in South Africa with the Boer War, and the death of Queen Victoria and the coronation of King Edward. She mentioned that she had been introduced to the monarch, and that she thought Victoria's death had a lot to do with the worry that stemmed from the Boxer Rebellion in China and the Boer uprising. Once he would have bristled at the reference to her superior social status. Now he only smiled indulgently.

It had amazed her how much time Cal had to spend on that rig. Someone had to watch it all the time, night and day, and he took not only his own shift, but sometimes stayed even longer to help the men. There were times, Nora told him, when she thought she had married a ghost. That amused him, but she knew that what he was doing was for their future and she never complained. He found her quite complex, now that she was relaxed with him, and he enjoyed their talks and debates. She was equally comfortable discussing the political situation with McKinley's reelection and the price of eggs in town.

When he was free, on Sundays, they went to a Methodist church in Beaumont and had the midday meal in the boardinghouse where they stayed infrequently to have a bath and rest.

She had asked if his family was Methodist, and he assured her that they were. But she noticed that he did not like to speak of his family and that he became irritated if she asked questions about them. He hated being that way. It was just that his guilt was ever-present. Even though they had grown closer together, he worried about her eventual reaction, because one day she would have to know who he was and who his people were.

Meanwhile, he discovered that she had suffered frequent mishaps as a child, and that despite being pampered, she had an adventurous spirit. He spoke little of his own childhood, except to recall that it had been boisterous and he and his brothers had been happy. He wanted to tell her everything, including how close he and King had been and the misadventures they had shared. One day, he promised himself, he would.

"You are very deep in thought," she said.

Drawn out of his contemplation, he smiled at her across the table. "And you are very pretty," he said, watching her brighten at the compliment. "And uncomfortable?" he probed delicately.

She was sitting stiffly, glancing around as if she were afraid someone might see her here, in a saloon.

"Cal, I have lived such a stuffy life," she confessed, laughing. "You must make a few allowances for me."

"You're doing fine," he said enthusiastically. "Except that you aren't drinking that champagne. It's the best they had. French, and of an excellent vintage."

Often he came out with remarks like that. He knew

things that should have been Greek to a working cowboy, like the fact that her hats came from Paris and
what vintage a good wine, or champagne, was. He
spoke quite intelligently about politics in the States and
even overseas, and he was perfectly at home in the best
restaurant in Beaumont, with table manners and charm
that would have befitted royalty. He amazed Nora with
his gifts. She had had no opportunity before to see how
versatile he was, or how educated.

"I shouldn't know that, should I?" he murmured, a
little less reserved than usual. He laughed at her expression. "Well, I wasn't always a cowboy," he told her.
"I've worked in oil fields and I've spent time in New
York. I've even been overseas, over most of Europe, in
fact, and not just when I was an army officer in Cuba."

An officer! She hadn't known that.

"An officer?" she ventured, hoping to draw him out.

"I thought I was going to be a career man. I enlisted
ten years before the Spanish-American War, two years
after I went off to college, when I was young and full
of vinegar. I rose to the rank of colonel and mustered
out after the war was over."

She was too impressed to be able to hide it. The rev-
elation was shocking to a woman who'd accepted that
her husband was an uneducated cowboy.

He smiled at her lazily. "Would you have liked being
the wife of a career officer, I wonder? It would have
suited you, giving afternoon teas and entertaining digni-
taries from Washington."

She flushed. "I like the oil business just as much,"
she said stoutly. "And I even enjoyed ranching, just at
the last."

"You lie beautifully," he accused softly.

Her hand lifted the glass to her lips and she sipped it. It had been a long time since she'd tasted champagne. She'd forgotten how smooth and fragrant a good vintage was. Her eyes closed and she murmured with delight.

"An excellent bouquet, is it not?" he asked as he finished his glassful. "I have not had better since Paris."

She was learning a lot about her mysterious husband. He was traveled and he had been an officer, so perhaps he was in long enough to have been given a pension. That would explain where he got the money to finance his oil well. But if he had gone to college, where had that money come from?

She looked around, frowning when she saw his crew. "Where is Mr. Pike?" she asked curiously, because she didn't see him with the celebrants.

"God knows. He's probably passed out and gone to his room," he chuckled. "He'd better get back on his feet quick. It will take all of us to cap the damned thing."

"I had forgotten that it would be necessary."

"Yes, well, you can't pipe oil that's shooting up into the sky," he mused.

"I did realize that," she laughed. She let him fill her glass again, and she began to be more and more relaxed as she drank it.

Cal got quieter by the minute. He didn't seem to be a violent man in his cups, but he looked at her in a dark, brooding way that was very exciting. After her second glass and his third, he stood up suddenly and took her by the hand.

"Time we left," he said, sweeping up his hat. "Say good night."

She called her good-byes to the men, who were a little too happy to notice, and followed Cal out into the night air.

He took her back to the boardinghouse, up the stairs, and into the room they'd rented. But for once, he didn't leave her to get ready for bed and then come in after she was asleep. He locked the door and proceeded to undress her, with all the lights on.

"You mustn't!" she gasped, because it had been a long time indeed since he'd looked at her, and she was shy.

He laughed deep in his throat. "Do you want the lights out?" he chided.

"Well . . . yes!"

"All right, chicken."

He turned out the gas lamps and then stumbled back to her in the darkness, laughing a little unsteadily.

"Cal, you said that we wouldn't," she began.

He pulled her to him and his mouth found hers. Even in his less than sober condition, he was tender and expert. She leaned into his tall body and felt his hands slide up to cup and caress her full breasts. She, too, was less than sober. He eased her down onto the bed and, between kisses, removed every stitch of clothing, first from her body, and then from his own. Then he proceeded to make her mindless with an uninhibited ardor that he'd never shown her before.

By the time he moved over her, she was totally receptive to him, her legs parted eagerly, her body lifting to accept the deep, slow, aching penetration of his.

He murmured something sharply and drew in his breath as he felt her absorb him in her warmth. He felt for her mouth in the darkness, and his breath jerked into her lips as he levered up and began to move on her taut body.

All at once, the abstinence and his need broke through the reserve he'd always shown her. He groaned harshly and his hands gripped her hips. He whispered things that brought the blood to his face, and suddenly there was a violence of passion in him that would have frightened her only months before. Now it kindled a heat that was startling in its suddenness and intensity.

He drove into her like a wild man, his hands touching her in ways he'd never touched her, his mouth on her breasts, on her lips, as he rolled over and back again with her body joined to his, pulling and pushing and dragging her against him until she was mindless with desire.

She pleaded with him for some relief from the agony of hunger he made her feel, her voice high-pitched and sobbing at the last.

He stopped, poised just above her, his breath coming quick and ragged while he waited.

"Please," she sobbed, shivering as she tried to lift, to bring him back. "Oh . . . please . . . I can't . . . live . . . if you stop!" she wailed.

He whispered to her, his voice a deep drawl in the silence of the room as he told her graphically what he meant to do. She whispered back, shocking things, provocative things. Her body arched slowly until her spine was strained, and she shivered as she felt him begin to lever down over her. She wished that she hadn't wanted the lamps out, because she wanted to see his face. She wanted to see his eyes.

"No!" he said jerkily when she tried to engulf him.

His hand caught her hip and stayed its movement. "No. Lie still."

"I can't!" she whispered desperately, gritting her teeth as the tension grew beyond bearing.

"You can," he said into her mouth as he lifted again. "I'm going to take you breath by aching breath. Just . . . like . . . this."

"Oh, I want you," she sobbed, clinging.

"Arch your hips to mine, very, very slowly," he bit off. He eased down, stopped, listened to her sobbing breaths. He moved again. It was killing him, too, but he knew, as she didn't yet, the violence of completion it was going to give them both.

"Cal," she wept.

"Lift up," he whispered. "Just a little, sweetheart, just a little. Wait, now. Don't move."

"Please," she whimpered, shivering. "Oh, please!"

He felt her fingernails biting helplessly into his shoulders. He knew to the second when she was going to go over the edge, and when he felt her control go completely, he pushed down, as hard as he could.

There were no words for what she felt then. She cried out hoarsely, stiffened, and abruptly lost consciousness in a burst of hot pleasure that surpassed anything she'd ever experienced in her entire life.

Poised on the edge, Cal went over with her, his body clenching with anguished pleasure. He laughed harshly and groaned, his voice loud in her ears as he convulsed over her. It never seemed to end, the wash of helpless ecstasy that tensed and released, tensed and released, until he was one long throb of satiation.

Nora was gasping for breath when the spinning stopped and he could make his lungs work. Under him, her body was trembling and damp with sweat. He could feel the heat of it like a brand, and he smiled, exhausted. He couldn't even move off her, for the exquisite fatigue he felt.

"Like dying," he whispered drowsily. "Too much pleasure for even a saint to bear. So good, Nora, my darling. The sweetest sensation I've ever felt in my life!"

She clung to him, her face buried in his hot throat as she came back to awareness. He slumped, and she felt his breathing grow deep and steady. He had fallen asleep, but his weight was precious, delightful. She held him to her, her body still locked to his intimately, and after a minute, she, too, fell asleep.

Sometime during the night, they had separated and gotten under the covers. Cal woke up first when the light came in the window, groaning as he felt the size of his head. Only three glasses of champagne, but they had been big glasses and on an empty stomach. He tried to sit up and took two tries managing it.

He moved, aware of a faint soreness that carried more than a trace of remembered pleasure. His eyes turned to the other side of the bed and he went very still.

Nora was lying beside him, totally naked, with the sheet thrown off and her body open to his eyes. He had had her in the night. It took no second guessing to know it. She was smiling in her sleep, and when he moved, her body writhed sensuously, as if in memory of the explosive culmination he'd given them both.

His first, terrifying thought was that there could be a child. He was obviously fertile, and what they had shared, even with the alcohol to enhance it, had been unique in his experience. He could not remember one single encounter that had dealt him such a devastating climax.

She stirred again, and her eyes opened slowly. They met his and she went scarlet.

"You should blush," he said in a stern tone. Then he smiled wickedly. "My God!"

Her hand grabbed for the sheet and dragged it up to her chin. Over it, her horrified wide blue eyes met his.

"You did it!" she accused. "You got me drunk and seduced me! It wasn't my fault!"

"I didn't really mean to, you know," he defended himself weakly. "But all that champagne . . ."

She clutched the sheet tighter. "I shall follow that woman's footsteps and take an ax to the saloon today without fail," she assured him. "Now that I have truly experienced the evils of drink."

He quirked an eyebrow in her direction. "Did you say 'evils'? You didn't seem to think so last night," he pointed out.

She went absolutely scarlet and her eyes fell. "I have never had more than a *small* glass of wine in my life until last night," she began in self-defense.

"Oh, I have no quarrel with your behavior, Nora. In fact, it tempts me to send out for several cases of champagne," he mused as he watched her.

"You roué!" she gasped.

He tugged the sheet out of her hands and rolled her into his arms. "Admittedly," he murmured as he eased her down on the bed and his mouth found hers. In no time at all, her weak struggles ceased and she clung to his strength.

He lifted his head and searched her soft eyes. "I tried to spare you the hardship of another pregnancy," he began.

She put her fingers over his mouth. "I am strong now," she assured him, her eyes bright and happy. "And I would very much like to . . . feel again the way you made me feel in the darkness of the night," she whispered.

"So would I," he said hungrily. He threw off the sheet and bent again to her mouth. "If a child comes of it, God knows, I shall not mind," he whispered ardently. And then he said nothing more for a long, long time.

The well was capped without Pike, who had apparently vanished into thin air. Cal, sensing trouble, went to see the local constable in Beaumont and explained the situation. The other officers were alerted to watch out for the man, but he did not appear. On a hunch, Cal went to the office of the new lawyer in town who had been friendly with Pike, but the office was closed, and no definite time stated for the return of its occupant.

"I can't find Pike," Cal told Nora when he returned to the cabin later. He scowled. "I don't like the look of things. He was good at his job and came highly recommended. Now I feel much less confident about him." He stared at her across the table. They were eating a light supper. "You never liked him. I should have trusted your instincts."

"I'm not so trustworthy," she said with a smile. "I didn't like you at first."

His eyes softened on her pretty face. "I found you enchanting," he said. "Pretty and spirited, and very much on your dignity. After a while, I could think of nothing except you."

She reached out and traced her fingers over the back of his hand. "You're not sorry that you were forced into marriage?" she asked.

His hand turned and captured hers. "I love you," he said gently, and his eyes looked straight into hers. "Of course I'm not sorry."

She flushed. It felt as if a bolt of lightning had entered her body. "What did you say?"

"That I love you," he replied simply. He lifted her palm to his lips and kissed it hungrily. "How can you not know, after what we shared in our room the night of the celebration?"

"I know so little of men," she admitted.

"Then let me reassure you that it is not quite a normal occurrence for a woman to faint and a man to sob like a child in the throes of ecstasy. Our experience was somewhat out of the ordinary."

"I . . . thought so, but I had no way of knowing. Even in the past, when we were together, I had not felt quite so . . . so . . . complete," she said finally.

He sighed, watching her lovingly. "And you, Nora?" he asked. "Is there some small part of you that still loves me, even after the pain I gave you?"

She looked shocked, and for a minute, he held his breath, waiting for her to speak. "Why, I have never stopped loving you," she faltered. "I never shall."

He held her hand to his cheek and closed his eyes in a surge of overwhelming joy. "Thank God," he whispered.

"You silly man," she laughed gently. "As if love can wear out on a man's bad temper! As much as you growl when you are working, mine should have fled for the hills months ago!"

"I'm so glad that it didn't," he whispered. "Come here, darling."

She got up, and he pulled her down onto his lap, kissing her until her head swam and his body made emphatic statements about its immediate needs.

"Yes," she murmured against his mouth, and curled closer.

He stood up, with Nora in his arms, dazed enough to start toward the bed even though it was still light.

The sound of footsteps on the porch halted him. His head lifted toward the door and he stood there with his burden, disoriented.

The knock was hard. "Mr. Barton? There's a man out here with some sort of legal paper. He wants to talk to you!"

"I'll be right out!" Cal called back.

He eased Nora onto her feet and they exchanged worried glances.

"I bet this has something to do with Pike," he said through his teeth.

He opened the door and stepped onto the porch, with a flushed Nora at his side.

The sheriff stood there, his badge bright against his suit coat, a folded paper in one hand. "Mr. Barton?" he asked, pausing just long enough to sweep off his hat and nod respectfully at Nora.

"Yes," Cal confirmed.

"I'm Sheriff Culpepper." They shook hands. "I have to serve you with this paper. It's an enjoinment against your oil well there and prevents you from making any legal decisions until ownership of it is established in court."

"I have no need to look at the signature to decide whose handiwork this is," Cal said heavily. "Pike."

"Mr. Pike and his attorney, Mr. Bean, met with the judge this morning to have the paper drawn up," Sheriff Culpepper said. "Now, most of us in town know that you were the boss of the outfit and Pike was just an employee. But that lawyer has a way with words, and he's about the nearest thing to a silver-tongued orator that anybody in these parts has ever seen. You want some advice, Mr. Barton? Get yourself the most expensive city lawyer you can afford. You're going to need him. Good day, ma'am," he added to Nora.

They watched him go out to his horse, mount it, and ride away.

"Damn Pike!" Cal said angrily.

She took the paper from him and read it over. "Cal, what shall we do? With the well enjoined, we have no money, have we?"

He glanced down at her and smiled gently. "Don't worry. I won't let you starve."

"It isn't that, not at all, and you know it," she said firmly. Her brow furrowed. "If I were to apologize to my father," she added tightly, "perhaps he would be willing to send his own attorney out here—"

"You are not apologizing," he said quietly. "Not ever. You did nothing to apologize for."

"But what shall we do?" she asked miserably. "We cannot just let Pike come in and take our oil well!"

He ran a gentle hand over her chestnut hair, loving its silkiness. It distracted him. "We are not totally without options," he said.

Mick came running up with the men as the sheriff went out of sight "What is it?" Mick asked. "It's an injunction, isn't it?" he demanded, reddening. "That Pike fellow! I saw him meeting with that city lawyer several times and would have mentioned it, but I figured it was your own business he was conducting, so I kept my mouth shut. More fool, me!"

Cal grinned at him. "Not your fault, Mick. And don't look as if the world has ended. We haven't even fired the first salvo yet!"

"That lawyer is smart. He's from Chicago, you know," he said. "I heard talk of him in town. They say he has no peer in a court of law."

"Oh, I think he may have one or two," Cal replied. There was a twinkle in his eyes that escaped description. Nora wondered what it meant, but he clammed up and said no more about it just then.

The next morning he went to town and sent a wire through the local Western Union office to Latigo.

Chapter Nineteen

CAL TOOK NORA INTO TOWN TWO DAYS LATER TO MEET the train. He asked her to dress nicely, in one of her neat blue suits with a lacy blouse and her Paris hat. He didn't tell her why, and all her urgings wouldn't produce one single statement as to what his plans were. He was the most secretive and exasperating man she had ever known. She told him so, frequently, to no effect.

Three men got off the train, to be warmly greeted by Cal. He tugged Nora up to meet them, his eyes beaming with pride as he introduced her.

The eldest had dark eyes and silver hair. Brant Culhane shook her hand warmly and he expressed his regrets that his wife, Enid, hadn't been able to make the trip with him. Perhaps Cal would bring Nora to meet her, he added with a pointed look at his son.

The oldest son looked so much like Cal that Nora was taken aback.

"Why, you look just like Cal!" she exclaimed when they shook hands.

He shook his head. "He looks like *me*," he corrected, and his silver-gray eyes, lighter than Cal's, danced as they met his brother's.

"We used to play king of the mountain as boys," Cal

drawled. "He usually won. That's how he got the nick-name. King," he added when she looked puzzled.

"Why, you named your horse—" she began.

"And this is Alan," he interrupted her, although King had already caught on and was chuckling silently.

Alan stepped forward and brought her hand to his lips, kissing it with exquisite courtesy. "It is a pleasure to meet my lovely sister-in-law at last," he said, with a glare at Cal. "One would have thought that the intro-ductions would take place before the wedding, wouldn't one?"

Nora recalled why Cal hadn't wanted her to meet his family, and she looked wounded.

He pulled her close. "It's a long story," he told the others. "I'll tell you all about it when I get the chance. Right now, my plate is full."

"Not for long." Brant turned and motioned to two well-dressed, dignified men carrying valises. "Mr. Brooks and Mr. Dunn," he introduced. "They're from New York. They handle all our family business," he added when Nora looked puzzled.

Cal shook hands with them. Mr. Brooks was short and dark and had an intelligent face. Mr. Dunn was a startling contrast; he was tall and elegant-looking, with pale blue eyes and wavy dark hair. When he looked at Nora, she felt a chill right down to her toes. He was po-lite enough as he tipped his hat, but he had a look that she hoped never to have to sustain across a courtroom. She'd never seen a man who looked less like an attor-ney, and when he spoke, his cultured voice had a few lingering traces of a Texas drawl.

Watching the men talk as she stood on the sidelines, Nora began to feel undercurrents. What family business? Why would Cal's father need a firm of New York attorneys? For the first time, she noticed the way his father and brothers were dressed, and it dawned on her that they were no rustic hayseeds. These were powerful, wealthy men. Was Cal some sort of black sheep, was he an outcast, forced to work for wages on a ranch? She must get the truth out of him. There had been one too many secrets between them already.

"There's an excellent hotel in town," Cal was telling the men. "And it serves meals that rival Mother's."

"Nobody cooks like your mother," Brant said with a wistful smile.

"Nora's on her way to such proficiency in the kitchen," Cal remarked as he drew his wife close against his side.

She smiled at the other men. "What he means is that my biscuits no longer bounce when they're dropped," she said.

They laughed, but without malice. "When you meet Enid, get her to tell you about the first turkey she prepared for me when we were newly married," Brant suggested to Nora. "It'll make you feel less self-conscious about your early days in the kitchen."

Nora smiled. "That would be nice," she said, but inside she was wondering and worrying if Cal still was ashamed of her. He wanted her and he professed to love her, but there was still the fact that he had never suggested taking her home to his family—especially to meet his mother. It was the one thing that kept her happiness with him from being complete.

There were meetings with his family and the lawyers for the rest of the week. The court case was set for the following Monday, and Cal spent most of the weekend at the hotel. Nora cooked meals that were ignored or forgotten. She felt neglected herself, although she knew it was for the sake of their future. She couldn't help but wonder if it was all business, or if Cal was keeping her away from his family for some reason of his own.

Actually, he was. He didn't want them to let anything slip about his life before he met her. He still had that obstacle to clear once the threat of Pike was out of the way.

"She's very pretty," Brant remarked over a drink in the saloon. "And obviously she adores you."

"And vice versa," King murmured with twinkling eyes. "Caught at last, aren't you, old son?"

"Caught and tied," Cal agreed. He fingered his whiskey absently. "She doesn't know anything about us. I didn't want to tell her at first. Now I do, but I can't decide how. She's going to hate me when she knows all of it. If I'd taken her home in the first place, instead of dumping her into a cabin at the Tremayne ranch without even a decent stove . . ." He groaned and threw down the rest of his whiskey. "If I'd been halfway human about it, she'd never have lost the baby or so nearly have died from fever."

"We've both seen fever before," King reminded him. "It's treatable. As long as she isn't overtired, she shouldn't have too many bouts of it."

"I've looked after her this time," Cal replied. "She's been remarkably healthy since we've been in Beaumont." He smiled, thinking of that long, exquisite night they'd spent together and those that had followed. He was still concerned about a child so soon after her illness, but she wasn't. In fact, she was knitting little bootees now, in anticipation of a child that would surely eventuate from the fullness of their inexhaustible passion for each other.

"You have to tell her," King said. "It isn't fair to let her go on believing that you're a poor cowboy or a penniless oil prospector."

"I might have been," he pointed out. "I still may. Brooks and Dunn may not be able to stand up to this man of Pike's in court."

"My boy," Brant said gently, "you have not seen Dunn before the bar yet. Reserve judgment until you do."

"Brooks is the research man," King explained. "He does the legwork. But Dunn . . ." He paused to smile secretively. "Well, wait and see."

Cal was unconvinced. Dunn looked formidable, of course, but there was more than looks involved in winning a trial. He brooded about the court case, cursed Pike for all he was worth, cursed himself for being so stupid as to leave the man to his own devices.

King walked with him back to the hotel. The night was quiet except for the noise of a hurdy-gurdy coming from a saloon nearby. Even that was a pleasant sound in the darkness, broken only by voices and the sound of horses' hooves as buggies passed by.

"We shouldn't have asked you to take that job with Tremayne," King said abruptly. "If you'd been here, on the spot, maybe Pike wouldn't have gotten so greedy."

Cal shook his head. "If I hadn't taken the job, I'd never have met Nora. She was worth losing the damned thing, if it comes down to it. I have no regrets."

"When are you going to tell her the truth?" he asked.

Cal stuck his hands deep in his pockets. "When I can't avoid it for one minute longer," he said doggedly.

King grinned. "You sound just like me."

Cal glanced at his brother. "I am just like you," he reminded the older man. "That's why it's just as well that you're inheriting Latigo, and I have an oil business to build here in East Texas. We'd end up squaring off in the corral twice a day over nothing."

King chuckled. "Probably," he had to admit. "All the same, you're the only man I know that I can bare my soul to."

"That might flatter me if I didn't know that you think of it as talking to yourself."

"You're that much like me," King admitted, "that it's the same thing." He stopped in front of the hotel, his face solemn. "What will you do if things go against you Monday?"

He shrugged. "I'll probably shoot Pike."

"That's what I thought. Listen, Latigo is big enough for all of us. There's no need—"

Cal clapped his brother affectionately on the shoulder. "I was joking," he said roughly. "For God's sake, I wouldn't leave Nora in the lurch by getting myself thrown into jail! And I'm not giving up. Pike's the one who should worry, if Brooks and Dunn are as good as you say."

"You haven't had any need of them over the years. We have," King said quietly. "You'll see what I mean."

Cal sighed. "I hope so."

He didn't tell Nora how worried he really was. It would mean starting over, borrowing more capital, and taking another huge gamble if Pike walked off with his oil well. He didn't know exactly what Pike was planning to do, and everything depended on documentation and the proficiency of the family attorneys. He tried to remember every step he'd taken since he'd bought the property and leased the mineral rights on land that adjoined it. But despite his best efforts to comb through the paperwork, he couldn't find a loophole that Pike could use to take over the site. On the other hand, Pike might have an attorney dishonest enough to make one that would stand up in court.

He wouldn't really shoot the man, but it was tempting. Pike would have gotten a share, just as all the men who worked on the well were going to. Cal had decided that from the outset. But Pike was greedy. He wanted it all. Now, if Cal had his way, Pike was going to end up with nothing at all, not one drop of the crude oil that had poured out of that well.

There was a rumor that one of J. D. Rockefeller's people had stopped by to ask questions about the new strike that Cal and his people had made. The man hadn't yet approached him, but that would be the next step. In order for the oil to mean any profit, it would have to be piped out and stored and refined. Cal needed someone to perform that chore for him. But he couldn't make one legal move until the ownership of the well was assigned.

Monday morning came, and Nora sat stiffly in the courtroom with Brant and King and Alan. She was dressed in a very becoming dark brown suit with white piping and a matching hat with a pretty bird perched jauntily on the crown. She watched the proceedings with worried eyes, glancing from the attorney, Dunn, to her own Cal sitting so quietly beside him at the defense table. The men beside her didn't seem to be worried at all. King, in fact, was smiling.

The judge spoke to both attorneys before the case began, and Nora noticed that he seemed to know Dunn. He was much more respectful to him than he was to Bean, Pike's attorney.

Pike was in court. He wouldn't look at the other side of the courtroom, although his beady little eyes kept darting around restlessly.

His attorney was good; very good. He stated the distorted facts of the case, twisted to make his client's case look stronger. Pike had filed a prior claim on the oil well site, he told the court, and he had the documents to prove it. Cal, already aware of the attempt Pike was going to make because of Brooks's legwork, glared furiously at the averted face of Pike. It amazed him that the man was willing to tell an out-and-out lie in court and perjure himself for the sake of money. He wondered if Pike's attorney knew it was a lie, and that any documents he produced would have to be forged.

Pike's attorney presented those documents, along with eyewitness accounts of Cal's long absences from the drill site and the hard work Pike had done to bring in the well. When he was finished, it looked as though Pike had done all the work, and Cal had done nothing and was now trying to jump Pike's claim.

Pike's attorney, Mr. Bean, sat down with a reassuring smile in his client's direction.

Then Mr. Dunn got to his feet. He was a tall, slender figure as he moved lazily around the courtroom, looking at the jury with eyes the pure pale blue of a winter sky. He wore glasses, but they only emphasized the strong lines of his face. He held a sheaf of papers in one hand as he approached the bench.

"Mr. Bean's arguments are quite interesting," he remarked absently. "He states that his client did most of the work bringing in the well and thus deserves the bulk of the profit from it. This assertion is ridiculous, so I will not dignify the claim by arguing it." He placed a sheaf of documents at the judge's fingertips. "However, the prosecution's claim that his client has a prior claim on—" he gave the lot number and location of Cal's oil well "—is invalid. These are the titles and deeds to the land, which is owned by my client," he said. "They have been duly notarized and their accuracy can be vouched for by witnesses which the defense is prepared to introduce."

He picked up the prosecution's evidence, a sheaf of documents with dates one day prior to Cal's filing on the claim.

"Now, to the matter of Mr. Pike's alleged prior claim." He looked at Pike with a faint smile that was chilling. "According to information provided by Mr. Pike's former landlady in New Orleans, along with affidavits from the owner of a saloon called 'The Gator' and an, ahem, employee known as 'Rose Lee' as well as the local constable, all of whom witnessed the incident, on the date of the aforesaid documents, Mr. Pike was as drunk as a skunk and sleeping off his excesses in an upstairs bedroom of the saloon. It would have been physically impossible for him to sign a deed on the date in question." He looked straight at Pike, who was jumping up to protest, while his attorney tried to restrain him.

"That's a lie!" Pike shouted. "I was here, right here, in Beaumont!"

"You were not," Dunn replied calmly. He stuck his hands in his pockets, and his deep, measured voice filled the courtroom as he turned to stare at Pike. "And even if you had been, your finances were not such as to permit the expenditure of so much money for the tract."

"It was cheap, I tell you!" Pike burst out.

"It was beyond your pocket," Dunn countered. "Nor is it logical that you would have risked such an amount of money on what was, at that time, a very slim chance of success."

"Sir, you accuse my client without proof!" Bean managed, taken aback by the revelations and searching desperately for a legal foothold.

"Do you think so?" he asked. "I apologize for wasting the court's time on such a trivial and unsubstantial bit of nonsense," he added, and his steely eyes made Pike fidget. "For nowhere in my experience has an employee been given such trust by an employer and yet abused it so completely. Mr. Pike was paid a weekly salary, an exorbitant one, for his efforts in behalf of my client. But the thought of so much money turned Mr. Pike into a greedy man who was more than willing to break the law in order to further his own financial ambitions. And yes, Mr. Bean," he told the prosecuting attorney, "I can certainly prove that the signature on these documents is forged. I have a full confession from the perpetrator, whom my colleague, Mr. Brooks, flushed out only this morning."

Mr. Bean said down, looking sick. He stared at Pike, who finally gave up the uneven struggle and hung his head. Having anticipated a long argument, flowery words, and a battle of wits between the attorneys, Nora sat nonplussed.

The judge pursed his lips and looked over the documents Dunn had given him. "The deeds do seem to be in order," he murmured.

Mr. Bean was fuming. He glared at Dunn and suddenly got up, demanding to be allowed access to the documents.

The judge agreed, handing them over.

"Aha!" Bean shouted as he read the name on the deeds. "Here is further proof of my client's claim. This is fraud on the part of the defendant! This is not the name of the man sitting at the defense table! He has misrepresented his identity, which negates the whole matter of his ownership!"

Nora's jaw fell. Beside her, Brant took her hand and patted it reassuringly, his eyes urging patience.

The judge looked at Mr. Bean over his glasses. "You have not lived long in Texas, have you, young man?"

"With all due respect, your honor, what has that to do with the documents in this case?" Bean asked.

The judge smiled at Cal and the people sitting just behind him. "Well, son, if you were a native, you'd recognize that name pretty quickly. The family is not exactly unknown, even here in East Texas. In West Texas, they're something of an empire."

Bean was looking less confident by the minute. "Sir?"

"Let me put it this way," the judge continued, pushing the documents aside. "You know how the name Rockefeller just shouts oil?"

Bean nodded.

"Well, in Texas, the name Culhane does the same thing with cattle."

Bean turned and stared at Cal with eyes that were suddenly frightened. Cal was leaning back, with his legs crossed. He glanced from Bean to Pike, who looked like a man who'd just tried to swallow a watermelon whole. Pike's distress was so obvious that Cal almost felt sorry for him. He knew without a doubt that if Pike had had any idea of his identity, he'd never have attempted this.

He didn't want to turn around and look at Nora, which was just as well. Her expression had run the range from shock to dismay to raging fury. Brant grimaced at King as he indicated the woman whose hand he held tightly in his. He felt a little sorry for his oil-hunting son.

"West Texas?" Bean exclaimed, with no thought of courtroom decorum. "Those Culhanes?!" He whirled and walked back to Pike, packed up his valise, and slammed it shut with a speaking glance at the skinny, beady-eyed man sitting beside him. "I withdraw from the case, Your Honor," he told the judge respectfully. He picked up his case and glared at Pike. "You damned fool!" He walked out of the courtroom without a backward glance.

"You are within your rights to appeal my decision, Mr. Pike," the judge told the man curtly. "But I find against you, and I assure you that, considering the legality of these deeds, so will any other court of law. Mr. Dunn is quite correct in his assessment; this case is an unforgivable waste of the court's time. Case dismissed!" His gavel sounded and he left the bench.

Pike hovered around the defense table. "Mr. Culhane, I didn't know," he said hurriedly. "I never would have . . .

That lawyer, he made me do it!" he said, inspired. "That's right, it was his idea, he made me . . . !"

Dunn turned those piercing blue eyes on him. "Mr. Bean has integrity," he said. "And you are asking for a civil suit for public embarrassment and desecration of character if you persist."

Pike swallowed. He backed away. For a lawyer, that fellow was physically intimidating. "About the well, Mr. Barto . . . I mean, Mr. Culhane," he continued doggedly.

"You were paid a salary," Cal said, rising from the chair. He looked more threatening than the lawyer had. "If you run, not walk, to the door, you may just make it out of town before I beat the living hell out of you!" He made a quick movement, and Pike took off like a scalded dog out the courtroom door.

King chuckled as he got to his feet with the rest of his family. "So much for that."

Cal shook hands with Dunn. "You're amazing. How did Mr. Brooks get the evidence so quickly?"

Dunn smiled secretively. "He didn't. I did. I know my way around the back streets, even in a small town like this," he said surprisingly. "I knew the documents had to be forged, so I went looking for the man best suited to do the forging at a price Pike could afford. I called in a favor and found him. It's all in a day's work." He nodded toward the Culhanes. "You'll have my bill in the mail. I'll collect Brooks and we'll be on the next train to New York."

"See what I told you?" Brant asked Cal, after he'd added his thanks to Cal's and Dunn had left. He gave his son a fatherly pat on the back. "This case was a piece of cake to Dunn. He's much more at home in criminal cases. I've seen him send witnesses to the nearest bar."

"That doesn't surprise me at all," Cal agreed. "But somehow, Dunn doesn't look like a lawyer," he added thoughtfully.

"Well, he didn't start out that way," King said as he joined them, with Nora lagging behind. "He was a gun-fighter in Dodge. His mother begged him to go away and get an education before he was killed in the streets, and by some miracle, he listened. He went to New York, read law at Harvard, and became a practicing at-torney." He chuckled at Cal's expression. "He can still handle a Colt, you know. Shot a man in Denver just last year for pulling a gun on him in court." He shook his head. "I'm not surprised that the judge recognized him. Most judges know him, even out here."

Cal whistled through pursed lips. "Well!" He turned to face his wife, reluctantly. She was staring at him with eyes that were demanding explanations and blood all at the same time.

"Oh, Nora," he said heavily. "At first I didn't want to tell you, and then I didn't know how to tell you."

She turned to Brant with the shreds of her dignity. "Thank you for coming to his aid," she said. "At least he will have an oil well to keep him company for the rest of his life."

"Now, now," Brant said gently. "I know it's a shock, but he had his reasons. It was my fault, really. I wanted him to help your uncle get that ranch back on its feet, but he wouldn't take advice from any of us. Cal was the only way left to keep him from losing it all over again." He shrugged. "I hate to see a good rancher go down.

His is one of several ranches we own, but I had a soft spot for him. So blame me, not Cal, for the deception."

Nora's eyes were pained. "He let me think he was a working cowboy," she said. "He took me to a cabin that would be too spartan for a convict. I lost my baby because of it . . . !"

She turned, weeping, and ran out of the building.

"Go after her!" King said harshly.

Cal did, without further urging. He'd never felt quite so terrible in his life. The day of reckoning had come at last, and he didn't know how to justify what he'd done. He couldn't. She was right about the cost of his deception. It didn't matter whose fault it was, he was the man she was going to blame.

He found her packing. It wasn't even surprising. He took off his hat and sat down heavily in an armchair to watch her with dull, lifeless eyes.

She glanced toward him. Her eyes were red, like her face. She turned back to her chore, and slammed clothes into the trunk with no thought of the wrinkles she was creating in them. They had moved into the hotel in town. All her things were here now.

"Do you have no excuse for me?" she demanded breathlessly. "No justification, no glib explanation for concealing your identity so completely from me over the months we have spent together?"

"I have no defense whatsoever," he agreed heavily. "At first I hid it because Chester was not to know that I was there on my family's business. Then, when you seemed so arrogant about my lack of social status, I kept up the deception in a halfhearted effort to make you accept me as I was." He stared at his dusty boot. "When I accomplished that, I was too ashamed to tell you the truth. You would not have lost the baby if I had not played the fool."

She paused to look at him. He looked shattered, and her soft heart overcame her burst of bad temper. "Forgive me. I should not have said so terrible a thing to you. It was the shock of learning that my husband is not who I thought he was. I was a terrible snob, was I not, Cal?" she added sadly. "Perhaps I needed a lesson in humility. And it was the fever as much as the work that cost us our child. I don't blame you. It was God's will. I know it in my heart as much as you do."

He averted his face. "Perhaps. That doesn't assuage my guilt. I did want to tell you the truth, Nora. It's just that I knew that you would leave me if I did, and I couldn't bear to lose you."

She turned back to him, her eyes wide, astonished at the expression on his face. "Leave you?!" she exclaimed.

His breath caught with exquisite joy. She looked shocked. "You're not leaving me?" he exclaimed. "But you're packing!"

"Of course I'm packing," she muttered as she stuffed one last suit into the case.

"Why?"

She looked at him as if he were hopelessly backward. "How can I travel without my clothes? I am going to meet your mother, after all."

He smiled. "You are?!"

"It no longer matters if you're ashamed of me," she said angrily. "I wish to know where you live and everything else there is to know about you."

He was out of his chair in a flash. He had her off the ground in his arms and he was kissing her. She clung, moaning softly, as he sat back down in the chair and turned her in to his chest.

"Of course I'm not ashamed of you! I never was. I lied to save my pride." He buried his face in her neck. "I wanted you to love me as I was, regardless of what you thought me."

"And I did. You are a silly man," she said against his devouring mouth, "if you think I would leave you now. I love you far too much, and my monthly is over a week late, and I lost my breakfast this morning! Why, Cal!" she exclaimed.

He averted his face, but not before she had seen the faint glitter in his eyes that denoted a shockingly sudden lack of control.

"Oh, my darling," she whispered tenderly, pressing close. She turned his face to hers and kissed his wet eyes with lips that were breathlessly tender.

"It's my fault. It was too soon," he began, fearful for her health.

"Bosh! I'm as strong as a horse, and I want this baby so much. I shall be fine." She kissed him again, coaxing until he kissed her back and some of the tension left his body. "Stop worrying, can't you? It was not anyone's fault that I became pregnant, it is an occasion for joy! I love you!" she whispered. "I love you, I love you. . . ."

He stopped the words hungrily with his mouth, overcome by joy and fear and, finally, unbearable pleasure. For a long time, she couldn't manage to get any more words out.

A loud knock on the door finally broke them apart. Cal took a minute to get his breath before he stood up slowly, still holding Nora possessively in his arms, and went to answer it.

"Open the door," he whispered, brushing her mouth with his.

"Put me down."

He shook his head, smiling.

Laughing delightedly, she reached down and turned the doorknob. He moved back to let his brother open it.

King's eyebrows shot up. He looked from one of them to the other. "I thought you might need some help convincing her not to leave," he remarked. He grinned. "Stupid idea, really. You and I think alike."

"What a handy thing to know," Nora mused. "I shall have to speak to your wife and we can correspond when one of you becomes hopelessly stubborn."

King's eyes widened.

Cal shook his head. "You may know me, but you do not know her," he said. "I fear that we have stormy seas ahead of us."

"Indeed."

"Please go away," Nora said politely. "My husband is groveling. I quite enjoy watching him grovel, and I am selfish enough to want to prolong it. When he has groveled to my complete satisfaction, I should love to come downstairs so that all of us can have a meal to celebrate our victory and discuss our forthcoming journey to . . ." she looked from King's amused face to a beaming Cal. "Where are we going, dear?"

"El Paso," he said.

"El Paso? The desert!"

He glowered at her. "I told you, the desert is beautiful when you get to know it."

"Yes, it is," King agreed. He pulled his hat back over

his eyes and stuck his hands in his pockets. "I'll, uh, tell Dad you'll be along. Meanwhile, I think the three of us will wander down to your drilling site with your foreman and take a look at the operation. If you think we have time," he added, tongue in cheek.

Cal could be just as deadpan as his brother when he wished. He nodded solemnly. "We'll wait for you in the restaurant, if you're not back," he said.

King nodded.

"Mr. Culhane," Nora called worriedly when he started to leave.

He turned. "King," he corrected with a smile.

"His real name is Jeremiah Pearson Culhane," Cal offered. "But only Amelia gets to call him that. I heard she usually does it when he's made her mad. She throws things, so don't ever get between them when they fight."

King looked indignant. "I'll do you an equal favor one day."

"I expect you will," Cal said irrepressibly.

"King, then," Nora continued. "Do you think Pike will really leave, that he won't try to blow up the well or set it ablaze or anything?"

"Mr. Pike has boarded the train for Kansas City," King informed her pleasantly. "In fact, he boarded it just minutes ago with several escorts, one of whom was wearing a badge. It seems that Mr. Pike has a case pending against him in Texas that he neglected to mention; something involving an assault charge in a dispute over a silver mine along the border. The sheriff kindly agreed to look the other way as long as Pike removed himself from Texas immediately."

"Why, how fortuitous!" Nora exclaimed. "And this charge simply walked up and presented itself?"

"Not exactly. Mr. Dunn cabled a gentleman he knows. Only minutes later, the sheriff received the wire about Pike." He pursed his lips. "Oddly, Pike seemed to know nothing of the incident in question."

"Oh, my goodness!" Nora burst out.

"Mr. Dunn makes a particularly bad enemy," King replied, turning. "I'll, uh, see you both for dinner in the hotel restaurant."

Cal lowered her so that she could close the door and lock it. She looked up at him curiously.

"Your family has some of the oddest sorts of acquaintances. . . ."

"Wait until you meet your in-laws," Cal said, his hands going to the buttons on her suit. "I have a brother-in-law who was a Texas Ranger. He is now a deputy sheriff in El Paso. Amelia's sister-in-law is the daughter of one of the most notorious bandits ever to come out of Mexico. I could go on," he added with a grin. "One of our wranglers used to rob banks. . . ."

Her hands lifted to guide his to the next button while her eyes gleamed with excitement. "You can tell me later," she whispered. "Right now I have expectations of something far more exciting than tall tales."

Tall tales indeed, he thought several hours later, sitting with her in the restaurant while she charmed his father and brothers and they discussed going to El Paso a day or so later. First Cal had put Mick in charge of the well and told him, and the other men, about the share he was giving them in the venture. They were ecstatic, and Cal knew that he had no more worries about the safety of his operation. He had also been contacted by the Rockefeller representative, with whom he was to meet the next morning.

"Cal has been telling me lies," she mentioned suddenly. "About bank robbers and desperadoes and Texas Rangers, all in your family."

The men looked at one another, and Brant smiled warmly. "Well, Nora, I guess you'll just have to come out to West Texas with us and see for yourself what's true and what's not."

"Why, that is exactly what I had in mind," she replied with a smile.

Chapter Twenty

THE TRIP TO EL PASO WAS LONG, BUT NORA HADN'T A single complaint. She'd never been so happy, upset stomach and all, and Cal was beaming at the prospect of fatherhood.

Amelia and Enid were waiting for them at the depot, and after the introductions and the ride to the ranch, Nora found herself firm friends with the women long before the men came back in from their wanderings around the ranch to eat the evening meal.

"You'll meet Maria tomorrow," Enid assured her. "She and Quinn have been in Mexico, where their daughter was baptized by a priest in the village where she used to live. We wanted to go, but we felt it would be an intrusion. They keep to themselves. Maria isn't really Mexican, but she was raised to be, and she's still a little shy with us because her adoptive father was an outlaw." She grinned. "She's coming around, day by day."

Nora had learned that Cal's tall tales weren't so tall. It was fascinating meeting so many people whose real lives were more interesting than her dime novels. She'd learned things about her husband and his childhood that still made her feel faint. It was a miracle, in fact, that he'd lived to reach his present age! Nora felt like the tenderfoot he'd once called her, but as she learned more about the ranch and his people, the more secure she felt.

She liked these people. Enid did her own cooking and cleaning, although she had plenty of help from the cowboys' wives on offer. The ranch was huge, much bigger and more efficient than her uncle's, and it took no time at all to see, from the contents of the house and the way Enid and Amelia dressed, that money was no rare commodity here. The warm reception she was given made her feel right at home, and the last of her doubts vanished.

She adored Amelia's baby boy. She spent long hours holding him and dreaming of the birth of her own child. Her one sorrow was that her father and mother would probably never see it. They had not tried to contact her again, nor had she appealed a third time to them. It was just as well, she thought, that she and Cal would be living away from Uncle Chester and Aunt Helen. It was unavoidable that Helen would correspond with her only sister, Nora's mother. The wound would never heal if it was constantly reopened.

Cal noticed her preoccupation and asked her about it that evening when they were alone in their room. She confessed reluctantly that she was still sad about the rift between her parents and herself.

"Your people will come around," he promised her. He grinned. "Meanwhile, I expect your uncle and aunt are on the verge of paying them a visit to do a little chafing."

She asked what he meant, but he waved her away with a laugh and refused to talk about it.

A letter came for her two weeks later, from her aunt

Helen. "We have been east to see your mother and father," she wrote. "They are much changed, Nora, and I think you will find them chastened and eager for you to visit. Do think about it." There was a postscript to the effect that no apologies would be expected, either. "And Chester said to tell your husband that he said nothing to your father about who your husband was."

That tickled Nora, who had sweet dreams imagining a meeting between her husband and her parents now, with Cal's revealed social status. "Imagine Aunt Helen going to visit Mother," Nora mused curiously. "Why, after her last trip to Virginia, she told me that she would never have the nerve to go back. They were, uh, rather haughty toward her and Uncle Chester," she added sheepishly.

"That will no longer be the case, of course," Cal returned.

"I don't understand."

He put a loving arm around her. "I gave him two percent of the well," he told her. He grinned wickedly. "I expect your father got both barrels, including the news that you've married a millionaire."

Her eyes widened. "A millionaire?"

"You knew I was rich, didn't you?" he asked easily. "Well, I'm richer now. Your father was never in our league, sweetheart, even when I was working as a poor, itinerate cowboy. It was one of the reasons I hated having you look down your nose at me. You see," he added gently, "from my point of view, you were the one staring poverty in the face."

She blushed. "I was silly."

"Oh, no," he said at once. "After all, you had the good sense to fall in love with me!"

She picked up a broom, and King happened to walk into the room just as she raised it. He turned right on his heel and went out again. Later he told Amelia that she'd better start writing her name on things she intended to throw at him, because Nora was starting her own collection.

Two months later, settled in Beaumont in a beautiful home with maids to look after the housework, Cal announced that they were going to visit her people.

She argued, but it did no good. He was adamant. So she put on her fashionable new suit, one that helped to disguise her blossoming body, and they took the long trip back East.

Her parents were both at home when they arrived, having been cabled by Cal before he and Nora left Texas. She glanced up at him with quiet pride. He was wearing a three-piece pin-striped suit, with an expensive wide-brimmed Stetson and handmade leather boots. He looked as prosperous as she did.

Her father opened the door. He was hesitant and a little uncomfortable. He shook hands with Cal and nodded at Nora, although his eyes were apologetic and he looked very different from the blustering man she'd walked away from so many months before.

Cynthia was less reserved. She cuddled her only child close, with tears in her eyes, and rocked her gently.

"I have missed you so much," she said.

Nora knew that she had, but that she would always defer to Nora's father, regardless of his right or wrong. She understood that tendency a little better now, knowing that she would stand by Cal if he did murder.

She drew back, and Cynthia dabbed at her wet eyes, carefully studying her daughter. When she saw the faint bulge at Nora's waist, she smiled.

"I am glad," she said gently. "Very glad. It hurt me deeply that I could not come to you when you were so ill."

"Aunt Helen took very good care of me," Nora said. She knew that she sounded a little stilted, but she couldn't help it. They had not parted as good friends.

"You both look well," her father said. "Well, and prosperous. Chester told us of your good fortune in the oil fields, my boy," he added to Cal. "I expect you feel different, now that you have some money of your own."

Cal lifted an expressive eyebrow. "I have never been without it," he replied with faint hauteur. "My people own a considerable amount of land in West Texas," he said, adding deliberately, "including the ranch your brother-in-law manages for us."

The looks on her parents' faces were just short of comical.

"You are part of the Culhane family?" Mr. Marlowe asked.

Cal nodded. "The middle son. I used my grandmother's maiden name while I worked for Chester. We wanted to make sure that he implemented our changes," he added by way of explanation. "My father liked him enough to ensure that he succeeded by sending me along to help."

"I . . . see," Mr. Marlowe faltered. "But the clothes, and the gun, and living like a cowboy . . ."

"Part of the facade," Cal explained.

"Nora, you never told us!" her mother chided gently, flushing.

"Nora didn't know," Cal replied tightly. "Not until our well came in, at least." He held out his arm and Nora slid under it, smiling at her father from its protection. "We can't stay," he said, surprising Nora. "I'm taking her to New York for a brief honeymoon before we go home to Beaumont. We expect to make you grandparents in a few months. By Christmas, perhaps."

Cynthia smiled. "I hope it's a happier Christmas for you this year," she said sincerely.

"It will be," Nora said dreamily.

Cal continued to stare at Mr. Marlowe, who found those silver eyes dangerously insistent. He cleared his throat. "Eleanor, I am sorry for what happened at our last unfortunate meeting. I want you to know that you are welcome here whenever you, and your husband, like to visit. And I hope that you will feel comfortable enough to bring our grandchild to see us when it is convenient."

Nora smiled at him, old wounds healing in the passing of time. "I think we might manage that," she said.

"You are sure that you will not stay?" Mr. Marlowe asked. "We have a spare room. A nice one."

"Another time, perhaps, thank you," Cal replied. "We must go."

They walked the younger people to the door. As Nora bid them good-bye, she hoped that her relationship with her own children would be warmer and less constrained.

She mentioned it to Cal when they were back at the depot, waiting for the train that would take them north.

He held her hand tightly in his. "Nora," he said softly, "can you imagine our children shaking hands when we tell them good-bye?"

She thought back to the reception Cal himself had gotten not only from his two brothers, and his mother, but from his father. She thought of the open affection between all of them, and the last doubt left her eyes.

"I think that we will share enough love with our children that there will be no secrets and no distance between us," she told him. Her fingers tangled in his. "I am very lucky."

He shook his head. "*We* are very lucky," he corrected gently.

It was a statement with which she had no argument whatsoever. Her hand lay gently on the warm mound of their firstborn, and her eyes were bright with excitement as the train pulled noisily into the station, puffing steam around like fluffy clouds in the faint chill of the early autumn air.

About the Author

DIANA PALMER lives in the north Georgia mountains with her husband, James, and their son, Blayne Edward. She spent sixteen years as a newspaper reporter and columnist before "retiring" to write novels full-time. Since 1979 she has written over forty books and won numerous awards, including four national Waldenbooks Bestseller Awards, two Reviewer's Choice Awards from *Romantic Times*, and a regional "Maggie" RWA Award. In 1985, 1988, and 1989 she was named one of the top ten romance writers in America by the *Affaire de Coeur* readers' poll.

Diana Palmer is also known to romance fans as Diana Blayne and Susan Kyle.